The Weight

A Novel

by

Todd Stackhouse

Cover Illustration

Patrick Phillips

The Weight is a work of fiction. Names, characters, places and incidents are the products of the author's imagination or are used fictitiously. Any resemblance to actual events, locales or persons, living or dead, is entirely coincidental.

PART I

A Break. An unforeseen opportunity created by luck, fate, coincidence or God. If we take advantage of it, we earn the right to claim its source.

The Squeaky Wheel Gets the Grease

GAROL OPENED HIS EYES to pitch black. He strained his muscles to move, but was met with a heavy resistance.

Oh, God! I've been buried alive!

His mouth opened wide to scream, but not even breath pushed forth. He sealed his eyes and rang an internal alarm.

Help! God! I'm sorry! Hellllppp...!

"Good morning," a voice said.

"Help!"

Garol opened his eyes again and saw smiling down at him a chubby-faced, curly-haired blonde wearing a heavy dose of blue eye shadow.

"You're fine, silly," the nurse insisted, peeking at him through what seemed to Garol to be eyeholes just above his face.

"I can't move!"

"You're in a full body cast."

"I'm...what? What happened?"

"A break."

"What kind?"

"An unbelievable one."

"How?"

"I don't know. I'm not a nurse. Well, I'm a volunteer nurse. I'm the third assistant to the head assistant volunteer's assistant. Although I'd really love to operate. It's funny, I've never even asked if I could operate. I think it's all about the squeaky wheel. You just have to go for things, don't you think?"

Dipping below his field of vision, the nurse shook Garol's cast covered foot and said, "I'd like to operate on toes. I just have a thing for toes." She popped back into sight, smiled broadly, crossed her eyes at him and asked, "Are you bored?"

"Bored? I thought I was dead."

"Well, you—"

"Get me out of this," Garol interrupted.

"Why didn't you read the note I put on your belly?"

"I can't move."

"I'm not dumb. Take that back, I am not dumb."

"What?"

"Actually..." she said, sniffing back tears and dodging out of his sight line again.

"Don't cry." Garol heard nothing in response and panicked. "Don't leave."

She sprang up again. "Actually...If I treat you as if you have a disability, you'll believe you do. Then what?" She bent her elbows and marched in place. "It's essential to strive."

"True," he struggled to say. "Will you read the note for me?"

"I don't care if you can't read. The note says, 'Don't panic. You're in a body cast. If you get bored flip yourself around and look at the picture on the wall.'"

"How?"

"You don't have to move yourself, silly, just swing the bed around. It's on wheels. See? Smart!" She hovered above his eyeholes, pursed her lips, moved them as far as she could to the left side of her face, and pointed her eyes up to her right temple, where she tapped her index and middle finger.

As sweetly as he could, Garol said, "Smart. Could you roll the bed for me?"

"Alone?"

2

"I'll help," he assured her, grunting.

"Okay."

The nurse rolled the bed around, then propped three pillows behind his back.

The painting was an aerial view of a quaint town, taken at its proudest moment. Every piece popped and posed confidently with the self-assurance of beauty. Trees covered the little hamlet, rolling like small mountains, only exposing the elements that accentuated the town's style and charm: red cobblestone roads, multi-colored Painted Lady Victorian homes, ornate street lamps, and colorful signs labeling the store fronts along Main Street. As a whole, the town represented the complete autumn color deck with red, green, brown and yellow hues.

At least a hundred years old, the town practiced a useful sort of senility that allowed it to forget what it did not wish to remember. It never occurred to the paint to peel or to the absent-minded wood to rot, and the multi-hued, daydreaming leaves disregarded the changing seasons. The lush greenery seemed unconcerned that it lay surrounded by miles of lifeless, barren sand.

A subtle swaying of the trees suggested the welcoming wave of an arm, and Garol sensed an invitation to join.

Soft music entered the room. Staring at the picture, the music entered Garol's soul, hypnotized him, and eventually whisked him away. Unburdened and weightless, he entered the picture. As he hovered above the tree line, people appeared. They walked along Main Street and ventured in and out of shops. A man fished at the edge of a pond. A family at the desert outskirts of town sat around a picnic table.

As he glided free among the trees, Garol sensed that the town was a whole, that each member was married to the next. He had a strange impression that everything was waiting for him, that he was the final piece of this perfect little puzzle and all he needed to do was accept and trust.

The obligation to believe struck an anxious chord in Garol, and an immediate sense of self-doubt overcame him. Instantly he cast himself out of the town and back to his bed, where he lay motionless under the constraint of the man-made plaster shell.

Two men walked into his room and removed the picture from the wall.

"What are you doing?" Garol murmured.

"We have a picture that will make you feel…more at home," one of the men said.

"I liked that one."

"That's surprising. This picture is more…'your style.' As the saying goes, you've made your bed and it looks like you'll be lying in it."

The other man gestured at Garol by raising the left side of his lip.

The new picture was a noir bar room setting with *The Hot Spot* written boldly at the top of the painting. Hand-crafted mahogany woodwork wove itself throughout the bar. Sculpted trim lined the entryway, bar front, and elaborately designed back, which housed a mirror between its wooden pillars, each topped with a carved gargoyle. Shelves of figurines, tiny statues, and shrunken heads lined the room just below the ceiling. Clocks, banners, paintings, photographs and signs covered the walls.

The bar's dark style reminded Garol of home, of safety, of relief.

He snickered at himself for becoming so involved with the first picture, for feeling a place like that could offer anything, solve anything, forget anything.

Through the window that faced the front of the bar, he saw a line of fresh-faced, eager young adults bustling through the doors. The procession of people stretched out endlessly, meandering through the streets and around buildings, eventually snaking between the mountains and finally seeming to disappear into eternity.

I guess it is *a hot spot.*

In the rear of the painting, near the bar entryway, high-spirited patrons enjoyed themselves as if they were experiencing their first taste. The painting projected a gradual decline from the youthful group in the rear, with a sloping floor that matched increasingly slumping shoulders, buckling knees, and shrinking spines as the regulars found themselves fixed farther from the entrance and closer to the mainstay of the painting— the bar's well. As the floor tilted, postures and expressions sagged and aged. The exuberance of innocence eroded, dipping with the floor towards middle aged men and women whose smiles cracked and fought to let laughter into mouths that opened only to judge.

Folks with buckled stances braced themselves against the tipping floor as they scowled at those seated in the bar stools they coveted. Stools tilted forward with the back legs off the floor, pressed along with their occupants against the bar. Finally the floor dropped off into the pit of the well, where drinks were served diligently at a steady pace by a small but affable-looking, round-faced man who lost very few customers to the uphill journey to the exit.

There was an empty seat at the corner of the bar. It looked a lot like Garol's regular seat, and a "Reserved" sign there seemed to beckon to him. He noticed the eyes of the people in the painting as they stared at him. He sensed the action halting at his presence.

A clock high atop the central mirror read "4? o'clock." Four PM was the witching hour for Garol. In Garol's life before the hospital, four in the afternoon had meant one thing: freedom. Almost. It meant that in one hour, the quitting-time pardon would release him from the confines of his office cell.

The period between four and five was a great one. Choices were acknowledged and decisions made. It was an anxious time when only fumes of the previous night's alcohol remained, and the day's cups and cups of coffee and mounds of sugar-filled snacks had crashed his adrenals.

Most significantly, the hour between four and five was when the internal hearing took place—the time for Garol to play judge and jury, medical and psychological experts, prosecutor and defendant and decide his fate for the evening. The trial

5

often lasted the entire hour, but when five o'clock smiled, the jury was always ready with a decision.

The prosecution was weak and desperately lacked conviction, a low paid civil servant with personal problems wishing he'd chosen a career in something that didn't involve people or conflict. The daily four o'clock trials and years of losing had left very little in him that believed in his case— he was a man who could easily have saddled up to Garol at the bar the previous night and every night before, complaining that he had some shmuck to defend in court at four the following afternoon. Then he'd raise his glass and say, "Fuck it! Better him than me." This was a lawyer who dropped papers and always brought the wrong folder before sputtering out words he struggled to recall, such as *love, rebuilding, faith,* and *belief.* Softly he charged that Garol was guilty of giving up, throwing in the towel, not fully living his life. He spouted frightened warnings about building a future and regaining the glory of the past. He mumbled the words *commitment, honor* and *pride.* He made barely audible accusations that Garol was stuck in the past and unable to acknowledge a future certain to leave him jobless and homeless. Then came his own advice for sentencing: "Go home, get some rest, put yourself back together. Get your strength back. Take baby steps. One day at a time."

The defense, on the other hand, was blindingly brilliant, a well-dressed team of experts who came to battle prepared, strong and determined. With every passing minute, their confidence doubled. They laughed and snickered throughout the trial with little concern for the prosecution, only amusement at the prosecutor's inadequacies and ridiculous mutterings of pathetic words and phrases.

The defense team stuck to the here and now. They argued, "Who the hell knows what the future holds…if it comes at all?" They reminded the judge and jurors, "There was a time when our client was on top of the world, but your 'future' and its unpredictable ways (Mr. Prosecutor), crumbled that mountain. That future has become the very past you claim our client is stuck in."

The defense's psychological staff and medical experts then came up and pronounced their prognosis and advice: "You're a victim. Get drunk. Self-medicate."

The prosecutor faced the jury for his closing statement with a desperate plea. "There was a time when life worked... when there was love...when there was a reason to get up in the morning. These pleasures can return. We just have to believe. It just takes time." Then he muttered other well-worn phrases about forks in the road and boot straps. Finally, he wrapped up his case by tossing God into the mix, and the courtroom thundered with laughter, forcing the prosecution to rest.

The defense attorney swaggered to the jury box, singing, "*Yesterday, all my troubles seemed so far away...*," then chuckled and surveyed the courtroom, bathing in the gazes of the impressed observers.

"My client is a victim of the invisible claims this blundering prosecutor alleges can save him: God! Love! Passion! Taking chances! There was a time when we did believe, and yet my client is here today. Haven't we learned from the silly assertions the prosecutor speaks of? We know that passion is fool-hardy. We know too well what happens when we take chances. And love? Love always goes away, and when it does, it takes everything. We aren't stuck in the past— my client is doing all he can to forget the past! Do we sacrifice a tiny slice of the future to forget the past? Maybe, but I call that a pretty good deal. My advice: I say we worry about this evening. I say we go to the bar and get drunk."

Before the judge could slam his gavel and announce, "Case dismissed. This man is finally free to get some relief," the cowardly prosecutor had exited the courtroom.

Inside the cast, Garol quickly ran through the trial. There was no need for the prosecution's arguments. The case was clear-cut, as was the ruling: "Victim, and obviously in need of relief."

Garol willed himself out of the cast and into the picture. Once inside, Garol sat on the empty seat at the corner of the turbulent bar, and noises sprang instantly from all directions:

ticking clocks, clanging glasses, jangling chains, and blasting buzzers. Humming drones echoed like a distant choir. A player piano aching for lessons beat the keys in the far corner. Loud, incessant talk came from throngs of men and women, each spouting diatribes of self-evasion, confessions of innocence, complaints, and loudly professed guilt and faults of others. Cries of, "Who cares?" and "We'll worry about it when we're old!" were repeated by bright-eyed newcomers near the entrance.

Garol searched his surroundings. Details began to change. A sign that announced, *It's Always Happy Hour*, now included the additional words...*or at Least 'til the Place Freezes Over*. A sign on the entrance that used to simply read, *Come in*, now had the message added...*and forget about all you could've been if you'd never*....then immediately began again, *come in*...

The wall clocks offered abstract interpretations of time. One clock exposed black space as its face. Another's 12, 3, 6, and 9 spots read *Eternal, Infinite, Endless,* and *Unceasing*. A third clock's hands switched maniacally back and forth between *Sloth* and *Gluttony*.

Garol thought about looking behind him, but noticed shackles and chains coming from his wrists, leading to the bar's well. Searching, he spotted the tiny, round-faced bartender. His head reached just shy of the bar, and, like an iceberg, one only saw the tip of the man. He wore a name-tag that read "Lu" on a fiery red vest with large gold buttons and a bow tie the color of money. The roundness of his face was perfect, the shape of a manhole. Lu glowed. He was genuine, the only face in the bar to be believed. He was the only one who knew why he was there. Diligently, Lu siphoned his liquid solution and made sure no glass ever ran dry. His mouth smiled continuously, always welcoming and drawing Garol comfortably in. His enormous eyes were the portal to his power, the pupils nickel-sized kaleidoscopes shaped somewhere between a square and a circle, like diamonds with the tips sanded. The eyes' colors moved, drifted like Mother Nature's elements trapped in a lava lamp. Speckles of gold surrounded the iris and flowed in a dashed circle. They hypnotized by filling Garol with Novocain in the areas of himself that he wished didn't exist. Once hooked, those big eyes turned to mirrors, leaving Garol surrounded with only an unquenchable thirst to regain the initial glory of his first meeting. Lou was a man you had to please. Around his wrist dangled a chain with twelve keys.

Garol noticed the eleven other people at the bar each wore a set of shackles and chains. He glanced in the mirror. Facing back at him was a man who shared many traits; each had straight, perfectly proportioned noses, identical mouths, and exactly colored brown hair and eyes. They even shared duplicate cheek scars given by a cleat during a high school football game. But the reflected presence displayed more height, strength, joy, boldness, and determination. The face looking back was leaner and the cheekbones popped, whereas Garol's hid. Like Garol, sitting behind the bar, his distorted doppelganger was visible only from the middle of the ribcage upward, but he sat at a table covered with white linen and flowers in the middle. Garol felt he was a poser, devoid of substance. As much as Garol despised his altered reflection, he couldn't glance away. A look in his eyes reminded him of his younger, college quarterbacking days, when his fiancé Beth was alive. What took Garol's breath was the skin that surrounded the eyes. The tiny talon tracks of age that indented the corners. The image was not a flashback to better days. The eyes that stared back at him had weathered the storm. They were those of battle-tested victory. Older, better, wiser. They'd found their way out of the woods. The eyes in Garol's image were a pair, if possible, he would trade his in for, but now if he could move, he would claw out his own to avoid their message. He sealed his eyes and screamed.

"Oh God. God," Garol cried out in horror. He wanted to run. He wanted a drink so desperately. He would pay any price for a smoke. The pain and the pictures had to go. He couldn't handle the weight.

"NURSE. SOMEONE. PLEASE. SOMEONE. HELP." Garol yelled for what felt like eternity.

"Is there a problem?" a tall, slender, short haired nurse demanded, while waving her crossword puzzle in the air.

"What's wrong with me? When do I leave?" he demanded.

"You want solutions? I could barely hear myself think with all of the commotion."

"Is this a hospital or a prison?"

"You won't be happy until you make all the nurses cry," she said and walked out of the room.

"Where are you going?" Garol shouted, "Get back here now."

The nurse entered the room with a black marker in her hand and sat on the edge of the bed. The cast's designer shaped its midsection to over-exaggerate Garol's growing beer belly.

The nurse wrote on Garol's stomach, "I'm fat."

"What are you doing?" Garol's eye holes didn't allow him room to see.

"Just signing my name," she said, and wrote, "And obnoxious."

"Are you still writing?"

"Last name," the nurse said and dotted the 'I' with a circle.

"I want to see the doctor," Garol demanded.

"You can't," the nurse said and drew a tiny grumpy face in the circled "I" dot. She then pressed her lips together to keep from laughing and looked at Garol.

"What? Yes I can."

"He doesn't make house calls."

"I demand an explanation."

"That's easy, you had an unbelievable break."

"I want specifics."

"How are you going to get to his office? You can't move."

"A stretcher. Anything. Carry me there."

The nurse smiled and leaned over and wrote on Garol's side, "Trip me." Then she said, "I have an idea," and walked out of the room.

Shortly, the two men from earlier plucked Garol from bed, propped him up, and began moving him in the same way they'd move a heavy refrigerator: swinging one leg forward, then the other. They rocked and pivoted him out of the bedroom, down the hallway of the old Victorian house he'd lain in, and then followed Main Street until it reached the doctor's office in town, and finally parked him at the receptionist's desk.

"I need to see the doctor," Garol said.

"Do you have an appointment?" the receptionist asked and blew on her wet fingernails.

"No."

"What's it regarding?" she asked, glaring at Garol.

"My full body cast," Garol said and rolled his eyes.

"Please fill this out," the receptionist stuck out a clipboard with a sheet of paper attached.

"I think that's going to be a little difficult."

"Can't read?" she asked raising her brow and lowering her bottom lip.

"Can't move. Do you see what I'm wearing?"

"I heard you like to make the nurses cry," she sneered. "Sir, it's just procedure. We aren't allowed to discriminate against anyone. Would you like me to treat you differently because of your handicap? Think about it. Do you want me to lose my job?"

"Honestly?" Garol questioned then paused. "How about if you ask me the questions and write down my answers?"

The receptionist dipped her fingernail polish brush into the bottle. "Ok," she pulled it out and dabbed a little on her index finger. "Have a seat; I'll be with you in a minute."

"Uh, God, I just want a sane response. Trust me, I'm doing everything I can to be civil, but this cast won't bend. I can either stand here or lie down. Those are my choices. Do you understand that?"

"You need to loosen up. So rigid," she said, putting the little brush in the polish, then grabbed the clipboard and began rattling through a series of questions, "Age? Height? Width? Which medicine tastes the best to you? TooMayTow or TwoMaToe? Do you like or dislike pain? Where does your source of pain reside? Rock, Paper, or Scissors? Any allergies? Prior surgeries? Do you ever want to get married? Are you ticklish? If so where? Normal reaction: Peeing, laughing or both? Do you have any idea how turned on I get by the strong silent type? Oh, and do you think I'm pretty?" She smiled, pushed her cheeks into dimples, and asked, "Or adorable?"

She looked at the two men in white suits next to Garol and said, "Would you bring him to room number1224--"

The two men rocked and pivoted Garol to the first door they came to in the four-door hallway. They propped him up against the examination table and exited.

The doctor walked in moments later.

"Hi. Dr. Jergens," he said, extending his hand.

Garol stared at his hand.

The doctor bobbed his eyes from Garol's eyes to his hand, "Awkward." He smiled nervously and put his hand down to his side. "So, what seems to be the problem?"

"I'm in a full body cast and I have no idea why. There's more— like how I've woken up in an insane asylum— but we can save that for later."

"No idea?"

"No."

"My guess is an accident. Probably...of some kind... maybe?"

"Obviously it was an accident. What happened to my body?"

"Can you remember falling off any buildings? Stepping in front of any busses? Can you picture yourself in the middle of a herd of bison?" The doctor asked very seriously.

"You didn't put me in this thing?" Garol asked.

"Could've been. You aren't going to want to hear this, but we just switched everything over to a computer, so all of my notes for the last, 'who knows how long,'" the doctor made quotation marks with his fingers, then motioned his right hand to the trash can and continued, "Were pitched. The kicker: computer's down. So I have no way of knowing... When we get the computer going again I can look it up. But...oh, darn it."

"When will that be?"

"I don't know. Are you going somewhere?"

"Not like this. So what am I supposed to do?"

"Let me check something," the doctor said, pulling a stethoscope from his pocket and placing it against the chest region of Garol's cast. A quizzical look crossed the doctors' face and he pulled the instrument away, shook it, and put it back against Garol's cast. "That doesn't seem good," he brought the apparatus down to his neck.

"What?" Garol asked.

"Oh, nothing," the doctor said and grabbed his reflex hammer, leaned down and gave Garol a soft tap on his cast just below where his kneecap should rest. There was no movement, "Puzzling."

"What?"

"Nothing."

He rolled his chair over to his desk and pulled down a thick book, opened to a section headed "Testing Reflexes," and skimmed down, whispering, "Uh-huh, did that." The doctor flipped a few pages and stopped on one with bold writing at the top, **"When the patient has no heartbeat or reflexes."** Below that was a drawing of a funeral, "Oh brother," the doctor slammed the book shut.

"Nothing? What are you saying? Are you a real doctor?" Garol asked.

"I'm a bit perplexed," the doctor said. "Without those notes, I can't really treat you like you're in a cast. I might miss something. Let me ask...how long do you want to be in that cast?"

"I don't want to be in this cast."

"So you look at it as a bad thing?"

"What's going on?"

"Here are my worries. You don't have a heartbeat, nor do you show any sign of a reflex. You could be dead. I know that's hard to hear, but I'm a doctor and I can't keep information from you. For now, we need to focus on the bright side. Broken bones are nothing compared to death. The cast is the least of your worries."

"Dead? You can't talk and breathe when you're dead, right?"

"I never should've said anything. Let's just wait until we get the notes back. So what is it you want to do?"

"Walk. Move around."

"Hmmmmmmmmmm," the doctor said, rolled his chair over to the desk and opened the book again. He opened to a section titled, "Walking with a Full Body Cast," perused through the pages softly saying, "Hmmm, I see, ok, that'll work, ok, interesting," then turned back to Garol.

"So?"

"Seems we can disconnect the cast at each section. For example, I can cut the legs around each ankle, knee, top of the thigh and then all the way around the waist. Same with the arms and neck. This will give you some mobility."

"You can do that? Sounds like a suit of armor."

"That's ridiculous, suits of armor are silver. I was thinking 'snowman.'"

"I thought the point of a cast was to keep the bones from moving, so they can reattach, or re-grow."

"I've got it: polar bear. No, because they don't walk upright. Snowman, definitely. I was right initially. What's that saying about doctors? Whatever they say is right? Trust your doctor, he's right? He never takes lefts? He's right handed? Oh, I can't remember. My memory sucks. I know, we could get you a corn-cob pipe," the doctor said and slapped his knee and laughed.

"Do I seem like I'm in a good mood?"

The doctor paused and grew serious, "You have a good point. If we knew your bones were broken, the cast would be needed for the bones to mend. But because we have absolutely no idea of what's wrong, then, as simple physics would dictate, there's no bad way to treat you. I'm reminded of the saying, 'ignorance is bliss,' and frankly," the doctor pumped his fists, "I concur."

"Am I some kind of guinea pig?"

"No," the doctor said raising his voice in frustration, "You're large, white, and don't have a trace of fur. Stay focused on the situation."

"You're a doctor, right?"

"See that certificate?" the doctor pointed to a white sheet of 8.5" x 11" printing paper on the wall with bold writing that said, "**DOCTOR**." Underneath was the printed name Dr. Hyde Jergens, and below that was his signature.

"Oh God...So if you make slits in my cast and I'm able to walk, then we'll know if any of my bones are broken, correct?"

"Yes."

"So why don't we make the slits and if there's no pain, we can remove the cast completely?"

"I can't without looking at those notes. There is a reason you have that cast on. We know the moon isn't made of cheese, but we still want to go there. You see? Once we perform the 'Bodycastslitinsertion'-operation, if there are no broken bones, you'll be able to get around. Soon the computer will be up and running. Patience is a virtue, Frosty."

"Why don't you remove the cast and, if we need it, put it back on?"

"Sir, when I accepted this position," the doctor pointed to his signed certificate on the wall, "I took an oath to perform this job to the best of my abilities. If there are no broken bones, then there must be some other reason," the doctor said, and smiled.

"Can you make an educated guess?"

"Well, we can eliminate fashion. So if not broken bones then possibly a severe body bruise, or maybe a body skin quarantine."

"Body skin quarantine? Are you making that up?"

"Sir, if you can't remember, how would I know? You haven't been any help in determining what the cause of all of this could've been."

Garol sat silent for a long moment, "So that's my only option?"

"Sorry."

"Ok, I guess. I mean it's bullshit, but do it."

15

The doctor took his electric cast removal saw and cut half-inch slits to dislocate all of the sections of Garol's body cast. Then the doctor made two little bathroom doors on the front and back pelvis sections.

"How am I going to open my little bathroom doors?" Garol said shyly.

"See here?" The doctor pushed the left side of the front one, swinging it open.

"Hey, man!"

"Oops, sorry. Don't be alarmed, I'm a doctor. Anyway, just push on the left side and the right side will swing open. We have fuzzy, disposable mitts you can put around your mitts when it's, you know, necessary. They're very soft. I almost prefer them to two-ply. We'll send a care package to wherever you're staying."

"Staying?"

"STOP BY THE RECEPTIONIST'S desk before you leave, she'll tell you what you need to do next."

"Just like that?" Garol slid off the table.

"Sure," the doctor said and began walking toward the door. Then he flipped around. "I don't get the impression we're dealing with broken bones, but just to be on the safe side, I need you to refrain from jogging or cycling until we're sure what the problem is."

Garol opened his mouth to answer, but nothing came out. He pushed himself from the table and then wrapped his mitts around the walls of the room entryway. The balls of his cast feet were round and he realized the need to summon the coordination and balance of his younger quarterbacking days. He slowly made his way into the hallway, then steadied himself with his arms against each wall and inched his way to the lobby.

Oh my God! Garol braced himself as his eyes met those of a woman sitting in the lobby. The woman smiled at Garol and her eyes sparkled. He stopped moving and took her in. Her features were light-blue eyes and blonde hair. *She's beautiful.* He smiled and remembered the plaster covering his mouth made that pointless, then released his right arm to wave, lost his balance, and slammed his shoulder in the wall. Embarrassed he looked away and continued his trek toward the front desk.

The receptionist was reclined with her feet on the desk holding an issue of the magazine, *Bored Office Workers' World*, in front of her face. The woman on the cover was napping, leaning forward from her office chair to her desk with her face embedded in a pile of paper airplanes, foam stress balls and wadded stationary. She wore a sleeveless green army shirt, a polka dot skirt, and torn pink fishnet stockings. Her left arm hung to the floor and revealed two tattoos: "Ask Someone Else," and "I Hate Authority."

Without lowering the magazine, the receptionist said, "Go see The Man. He's to the right, five doors down."

Garol started to ask the receptionist a question, but decided not to when he looked down and saw the sheet of questions she had rattled off to him earlier, now answered. Garol perused the answers as quickly as he could.

Age? 33
Height? 6'2" ish
Width? Fat
Favorite type of medicine? Dry Martini on the rocks with a twist.
Too May Tow or Two Ma Toe? Avoids fruits and vegetables.
Do you like or dislike pain? Avoids it like the plague. Can't handle the truth.
Where does your source of pain reside? In the head.
Rock, Paper, or Scissors? Rock definitely. Strong, silent type. Not sharp enough to be scissors, or educated like paper.
Allergies? Living life. Positive thought. Taking chances. Love. Healthy lifestyle.

Stuffed animals? No attachments should be frowned upon at this point.
Prior surgeries? Zest for life removed.
Do you ever want to get married? A long way from that being a possibility.

"Anything else?" the receptionist leaned around her magazine and asked snottily.

Garol remembered the beautiful girl sitting behind him in the lobby and decided now was a bad time to be confrontational. Balancing himself on the desk, Garol spun around so he could calculate his exit strategy: *Slow and steady or quick? The walls are too far apart to help me.* The beautiful girl was reading. He looked back at the receptionist who was still peering around her magazine. *Get out of here quick. Go.* He pushed off the desk and lunged his right foot forward, which landed on the inside ball of the round bottom, tilting him to the left. His left foot stubbed early off the mark. He manufactured one more stride from determination, natural balance and a strong desire to go unnoticed. Soon, though, Garol was sliding face first into the wall. From his belly, he rolled himself around to his back and used a chair to push himself to a standing position. *Don't look at her. Maybe she didn't notice.* Garol knew his knees might collapse from under him if he felt the girl in the lobby had witnessed the event.

The doctor, nurse and receptionist had assembled in a small huddle to witness the commotion. Garol looked at their unemotional gazes. *Calm down. This is a doctor's office. They see this all the time.* Normally, the anxiety from a situation like this would have left Garol catatonic, but his body's hospital detox from alcohol, caffeine, and sugar, combined with the anonymity of the cast helped Garol face his embarrassment and move forward, with only weak knees.

The challenges loomed: his audience and the distance to the door. The only thing that seemed to be going down was the odds of success at leaving the office. He looked at the three faces that stared at him. *Fast or slow?* The faces were making it difficult to concentrate. *Run. If I go too far I'll hit the wall, then I can ride the wall to the door, or crawl out. Run.*

He took off and this time hit the balls of the cast and made his strides perfectly. Learning to stop would have to come later. Garol slammed into the wall in an upright position. He stood still for a moment and then began inching his way, using the wall for balance, to the corner and rode with the 90 degree angle to the left. When he made it to the door, he was relieved to see he could push it open.

As he moved through the swinging exterior door, Garol heard voices behind him.

"Thanks for coming. Have a great day."

"Come back and see us again," the doctor said cheerfully.

"Thanks," Garol yelled.

"Move it or lose it, you son of a bitch," were the words Garol heard just before a thunderous force connected with his upper torso.

Happy is a Country That Has No History

A SHOULDER SIDESWIPE ACCOMPANIED the phrase, "Move it or lose it, you son of a bitch." Garol toppled like a domino, then braced as a pair of feet hurried across his back. Garol raised his head high enough to see one red pump carrying a thin calf dart around a corner.

Garol remained face down on the walkway and inched along on his stomach in a breaststroke fashion. It felt like he was trying to maneuver on top of several large pillows, increasing the work involved in pushing with his legs and pulling himself along with his arms.

The post office door was open, and, like a fat lazy snake, he slithered in, pushing with only his feet to rest his worn out arms, then rolled over on his back, looked up into the face of the man working behind the counter and gasped, "Is The Man here?"

"That's me," said a thin balding man peering down through a pair of spectacles behind a counter. Garol assessed his age as fifty-eight by his lack of hair, wrinkles around his mouth and eyes, and his slight turkey neck. He looked like a high school principal; one that was a stickler for the rules, but rarely if ever lost his temper. He appeared very serious, an all-work-and-no-play kind of guy. Garol imagined he didn't smile much.

Garol waited for his breath to return. *The Man? This old balding guy? I guess in this town becoming "The Man" would be a breeze.*

"Are you coming up or should I go down there?" The Man asked.

"What if we meet in the middle?" Garol half joked.

"My knees couldn't take it, but I'll help you up if you need it. I'll even help you back down when we're through."

"I've mastered getting down…and if I have any problems, there's some neurotic woman in a hurry that can probably help me again. Nice town."

The Man walked out from behind the counter and offered his hand. Garol extended his right mitt and The Man pulled him to his feet and helped him over to the counter so he could lean.

"I get the feeling you're probably going to be in town a while."

"Sounds like you have less confidence in Dr. Dingbat than I do."

"I have all the confidence in the world in him. I was just going to say you probably don't need to go back to the hospital. You have mobility now. You seem fine."

"I seem fine?"

"Relatively speaking. You can be of use."

"Well, with all due respect, sir, I don't feel fine. I feel like a prisoner. The only thing I want to do more than get out of this town is yell at that doctor's Human Resources department for hiring all the nuts who work there. Now, if you could please tell me where I am and where I can catch the nearest train or bus, I'd like to get back to where I came from."

"Sure, I can tell you where you are. I'm sorry I can't make out your first name on the identification we found on you. It looks like G-A, or S-A. Your last name is Schand, is that right?"

"Yes," Garol said.

The Man reached into a desk drawer and pulled out a driver's license. He pointed to the first name and said, "See, it's impossible to read the name."

Garol looked at the lettering for the first name. Only the top part of the G was visible and it could be construed as an S. "S-A," Garol said.

"S-A, that's what I thought, but that's all I could make out," The Man said.

"Sam," Garol jumped at the chance to change his name. "Sam I am. Well, Sam you are," The Man said, smiling. "It looks like you're trying to get back to Eastdale, Pennsylvania?"

"Eastdale, Pennsylvania? No, Baltimore, Maryland."

"That's not what it says here." The Man had the license in his hand and he was looking at the back.

"It says Baltimore, Maryland right there," Garol said, looking at the front of the license.

The Man put the identification on the desk face down and said, "It looks like you updated that with Eastdale, Pennsylvania about six months ago. My guess is you wouldn't have done that unless you moved to Eastdale."

"That's impossible. I grew up in Eastdale but I left when I was 18. I couldn't wait to get out of there. There's no way I'd go back. No, no, I live in Baltimore. No, I buried everything about Eastdale years ago."

"I was afraid of this," The Man said.

"Afraid of what?"

"You may be experiencing temporary memory loss. It happens often when people suffer a harsh blow or tragedy of some kind. It's a way the mind helps itself cope."

"Wait, so you're saying my temporary memory loss only includes the town of Eastdale. Why wouldn't I forget living in Baltimore, too?"

"I'm not saying that. Do you remember leaving Baltimore?"

Garol tried to think, "No, I didn't leave Baltimore."

"Well obviously you did, unless you can explain this," The Man said motioning with his eyes to the license in his hand. "Look, you said you grew up in Eastdale? There's a good chance if that was the last place you lived before this happened, then your mind would have mixed up all those new memories with the old ones. Just give it some time; everything will come back to you. The mind is a funny thing; you never know how it's going to react to events."

"I don't get it. I can't even remember what I did to get in this thing," Garol shook his head. "No idea."

"It's my guess that while it was happening, your mind turned off to protect you from reliving the nightmare. Unfortunately, it had to shuffle things around to do that. When your mind feels it doesn't have to protect you anymore, it'll gradually give your memories back. You may never get the incident back, which I doubt you want anyway, but you'll be fine. Just give it time. Patience is a virtue, remember that."

"Oh God! Trust me, I'd remember and I'm not afraid of any accidents, especially after the fact."

"Don't discount the mind. It's absolutely fascinating. We constantly create a vision of who and what we are and therefore decide our own fate. Do we imprison ourselves, or free ourselves to be who we're supposed to be? I'm not saying it's easy or magical—it takes work. You don't wake up one morning and declare you are free or that you're the president, but you can wake up one morning, decide you want to be, and set out to achieve that goal. Some claim there have been more presidents than free people, but that's an exaggeration. Freedom has no limits or terms."

"Let's take a quick reality break. Where'd you find me? How'd I get here?"

"I didn't find you, but it was explained to me that you had a fall."

"I fell? From what?"

"From 'something' would be my guess. What that something was, nobody here knows. My assumption is great heights. We'll find out in time. You were out for quite a while."

"How far is this place to the nearest city?"

"Two hundred miles, approximately."

"Where's the bus station?"

"No bus. No train. There's a road, but there aren't any vehicles in this town. Sorry, the inhabitants of the town prefer privacy. That's why they're here. They choose to march to the beat of a different drum."

"There's a road?"

"Yeah, but I wouldn't recommend you walk two hundred miles through the desert in a full body cast. You'd never make it over the mountains."

"Through the desert? Are you messing with me? This place doesn't look like a desert. There are trees everywhere."

"I agree."

"How the hell does that happen?"

"Consider it an oasis."

"I wish I didn't have to consider it at all. This doesn't make any sense; you must have some way of getting out of here, some way to get supplies."

"We do. Generally we don't need to, but twice a year a helicopter shows up, or…"

"Or?"

"Or if we elect a new mayor, he has to take a helicopter to the capitol to be sworn in. Unfortunately for you, we already have a mayor and he left the day you dropped in."

"What if someone gets fatally sick?"

"We have a hospital here."

"Oh God! So I'm supposed to wait until someone gets elected mayor or the service helicopter shows up? Can't you call me a helicopter?"

"Sam, you're in a full body cast and you can't remember where you live. I can't allow you to leave. When you get rid of that thing and put the pieces of your life together, then absolutely, but now I just can't. Sorry."

"What the hell's going on? Baltimore. I live in Baltimore. Just send me back to Baltimore."

"I'm sorry Sam, I just can't. But hey, I've got good news for you. I could really use your help while you're in town."

"Yeah? You've been looking all over for a guy in a full body cast?"

"The cast won't be a problem. So what do you say? While you're getting rid of that thing," The Man said, pointing at Garol's cast, "do you want to help me out?"

"Doing what?"

"I have a place in town that needs to be looked after. It's easy; the tenants have all been there a while. Just make sure there are no problems. You won't be asked to do more than you can handle."

"What's in it for me?"

"Free room and board, three square meals a day at the cafeteria, and no charge for medical services."

"It's nice to know I won't be charged for malpractice. What about money?"

"I'll set up a bank account for you and put some money in there. When you're ready to leave, you'll have a little saved."

"You'll throw 'a little' in a savings account for me? I bet it'll be a little. Quite a racket you have going on here. No wonder they call you The Man. What's your real name? Forget I asked; I'm not going to be here long enough to send Christmas cards...But sure, I'll stay at your place 'til I'm gone. Why not?"

"Like I said: when you're able to, I'll personally make sure you get back to where you're supposed to be."

I am able to. "So what now?" Garol asked.

"You could either stop by the cafeteria or head home. Your apartment is in the fifth house on the right. The entrance is off the driveway." The Man said, pointing west down Main Street. "The cafeteria is the last building on the left. You'll love the menu. I get seconds sometimes," he said smiling for the first time.

"Ok," Garol said and looked away. Then turned back and asked, "Do I have any responsibilities?"

"Don't worry about that; I'll let you know. Just focus on getting rid of that thing," The Man said and pointed to the belly of Garol's cast.

Garol assumed he meant his cast and not his belly, but wondered a little.

"Is that it?"

"One last thing. You may get a lot of unwanted attention from the people in town. You're an oddity. No one has ever come in the way you did. You may find yourself in situations where you have to go against the grain. That's ok; it builds strength, character. Growth is never easy, but it is vital. Not everyone walks around in a body cast, but everyone gets put in unexpected situations out of their control. It seems unfair, but it's a matter of how you view opportunity. Often, the apparent obstacle is not the obstacle at all. Just something to think about."

"Did I hear you right? Are you saying my full body cast and the fact that I'm in a strange town in the desert 'is not the obstacle'?"

"Sounds funny when you say it like that. Nonetheless, that does seem to be what I said. I can't help but ask: they say live like it's your last day, and you must have thought you were on your deathbed when you awoke in the hospital. Are you feeling exceptionally motivated today?"

"I'm overflowing," Garol said in a bitter dry tone, and pivoted around on his left foot.

GAROL TEETERED, TRIPPED, SLITHERED, and rolled down Main Street, eventually reaching a large, Queen Anne-style Victorian house. The structure looked clean and fresh, as if the painters had packed up their brushes and rollers just moments ago. Taupe, dark-blue, green, cream, brick-red and bright white covered every part of the exterior: siding, trim, turret, banisters, spindles, window frames, and porch. Touches of color in lavender and rose adorned the spindles and sills. It seemed so alive it brought to mind a beautiful garden in full bloom, each separate section, puffed with pride, equally pleased with its polish. The whole ensemble worked together brilliantly. Reflexively, Garol exhaled deeply, in awe of the work of art.

The large porch began in the front of the house and wrapped around the side along the driveway. Garol followed the driveway slowly with his eyes, witnessing the enormity of his new residence.

"Sam?" asked a tiny, orange-haired man dressed in a tuxedo, sitting at a table on the porch.

"Sam?" Garol questioned.

"I was told a man named Sam would be moving in. I had a hunch it was you," the man said squinting his eyes and moving his head slightly back and to the left.

"Oh yeah, that's me," Garol said, shaking off his exhaustion to recall his most recent lie.

"If that's confusing, I'll just call you Shotgun. I'm Whirby. I live here."

Garol steadily scaled the three steps up to the porch and balanced himself on the railing. *Did he say Shotgun?* Whirby's tiny legs barely reached the floor from his seated position. Garol assessed him to be about four and a half feet tall.

Whirby's shiny black tuxedo was accentuated with a colorful, red and green polka-dot bow tie. His dull orange hair looked like it began fiery but ran out of fuel, cooling to a sun-scorched clay. Garol's snap impression of Whirby was a 4th of July firecracker which never reached its intended height, a fizzled dud that fell to earth. Whirby seemed to pose less of a threat, yet all the annoyance, of a tiny dog that nipped and yelped at boots.

"Have a seat, Shotgun," Whirby gestured to the chair at the opposite side of the table.

"You play chess?" Garol looked between a chessboard on the table and Whirby.

"Of course. As do you?"

"No. Chess is a game for arm chair quarterbacks who love war, but don't want to ruin their manicures. I prefer action."

"I love it. Bang, bang. What other response would I expect from Shotgun? By *action*, do you mean watching it from a bar stool?"

Smartass. Garol stared threateningly into Whirby's eyes.

"Have a seat," Whirby said.

"Can you tell me where my apartment is?"

"Judging by the sign that says, 'Welcome Sam' above that door," Whirby said, pointing to the sign above the door right next to them, "I'd say that's yours. You *are* Sam, aren't you? I didn't get a lot of confidence from your answer." Whirby peered deep into Garol's eyes.

"That's me," Garol snarled. "Where'd you get Shotgun from?"

"Have a seat and I'll explain the whole thing."

Garol paused.

"Come on. Come over and sit with me. What's your lucky number?"

Garol pushed down on the L-shaped knob to his apartment.

"You say you don't play chess, but you're wrong. Chess is unavoidable--it's life, everybody plays. We're always playing," Whirby said.

"I don't," Garol fumbled his mitts around the doorknob.

"Don't be in such a rush. Come on, sit down." Whirby prodded, and then added after a slight pause, "Eight. That's your lucky number."

"How'd you know that?" Garol turned his head sharply. *Who is this wise ass? What does he think he knows about me?*

"Good guess, maybe, but I don't believe in coincidences. The eighth square on the board harbors the castle or rook. They're the same piece. We'll use *castle*."

"So?"

"So? Bang, bang. Look at your defenses come out," Whirby raised an eyebrow.

Garol stared at the odd little man with contempt.

"Sit down. Come on, Shotgun," Whirby said.

"Where did you get Shotgun from?" Garol questioned.

"Because you are always blasting. Bang, bang— that's you. Bang, bang," Whirby said with a sly grin. "Have a seat. Come on, sit down."

Garol settled his hip on the wooden porch railing, looking down on the table with the chess game. "I'm sitting."

"In a way," Whirby said.

"Did you want to show me something?"

"You're in no frame of mind to listen. I'm wasting our time," Whirby said.

"I want to know what you think you know about me," Garol said.

"Bang, bang," Whirby said.

Garol stood up and faced the door.

"As I said, the eighth square on the chess board harbors the castle. I love the castle. I love all the pieces, but the castle is probably my favorite," Whirby picked up a castle from the board.

Garol turned around and faced Whirby.

"You know exactly what you've got with the castle. It displays no razzle-dazzle or flash. On the board, as in life, it can be rutted in position, but when it acts, it moves laterally, forward or backward. Sound familiar?" Whirby asked, looking into Garol's eyes.

"No," Garol quipped.

"The castle is unique. It doesn't resort to trickery or jump over any other piece like the horse. It doesn't come at an angle like the bishop. It isn't pampered like the queen, who can go anywhere she wants. It receives no protection like the king. It isn't slow and in the way like the pawns," Whirby said pointing at each piece he mentioned.

Garol grimaced, forgetting that Whirby could not see his face.

"You like football?"

"Of course," Garol said, nodding. "Football has nothing to do with chess."

"Chess invented football," Whirby said.

"That's insane."

"I'll prove it to you. Who's the best college quarterback of all time?"

Could have been me. Garol felt suddenly agitated.

"This guy," Whirby said picking up the castle from the board.

"Good God!" Garol said, but felt relief he could stop examining the question.

"Hear me out. The castle possesses the complete package—strength, speed, smarts, courage," Whirby released fingers with each descriptive word. "If I were a college football coach, I'd heavily recruit castles to quarterback my team. They can heave the ball down the field with strength. They can run the option with speed. Their blind passion makes them great motivators, unconcerned with getting dirty or taking a hit for the team. The warrior in them never quits until the whistle blows. You want a quarterback to bring your team from behind in the fourth quarter? Throw a castle in. He'll get the job done...or die trying."

"You don't think the bishop could do that?" Garol asked sarcastically, battling an emotional gut prick from the memory of the sack that permanently shattered his shoulder, bright football career and life. A seven-second play, to cap a celebrated span of quarterbacking begun at the age of seven and ended one crisp autumn day, only a month before his twenty-second birthday. A brief play in a college football contest that barely lasted longer than tossing a rock into a pond. Like the rock splashing into the water, his shoulder smashing against the turf rippled with consequences. Unlike the pond's waves heading away from the impact, dissipating at the shore, the swells from his injury turned inward and rose in undulating heaves of fear and self-loathing, crashing against his future, his purpose, and his self-definition. They grew to threatening rogue waves and created defensive, knee-jerk reactions with results beyond repair: dropping out of college, irrational arguments with Beth. Unforgiveable consequences, like the fight with Beth before she stormed out of the house to get in her car for the last time.

Whirby tapped his right hand on the table. "Great question. I thought you might ask that. Bishops are quick and smart, but they're a little too pleased with their looks to put themselves in harm's way and, with noses stuck up to the scoreboard, they are more interested in reaching the end zone than motivating teammates. Like any parent, I love all my pieces, but bishops are not innate leaders. They do well in politics—or at least in elections. They don't always do so well in office. Honestly, though, politics bores me."

"Parent?"

"I call it parenting because I have such a vested interest in their futures. The truth is I worry too much, but...I just want everything to be perfect. I never want to see anyone knocked off the board. It happens though. Every time, I think it's going to get easier, but it never does. What can you do, really? You can't make someone's decisions for them."

"I should probably get inside and take a look at my apartment," Garol said, standing.

"This won't take long," Whirby picked up the bishop from the board. "The bishop is a prince or princess…or that's what they think, and who could blame them, with so many adoring admirers? They are a finesse piece. They angle in with great speed, but you can spot a bishop a mile away. They are generally the best looking and always the best dressed. A castle that's gotten off course doesn't like the bishop. It says it's because the bishop hits when it isn't looking. The castle doesn't reveal much about itself, but I'd say the reason for the dislike is more personal. It envies the bishop. The castle fights as hard if not harder; even the king knows this. He never calls on a bishop or horse to stay and protect him. Only a castle. Still, it's the bishop that gets the glory, the storybook romance, wins the election. So it's easy to understand the envy when the castle loses sight of what really matters…but it's heartbreaking nonetheless, because it shows that the castle has drifted off course."

"I thought you had information about me," Garol said, shaking his head.

"Be patient and *listen*— don't just hear. This part is important. I'm amazed when the castle lets the bishop get to it because it's really the horse that offers it the most challenge. If the castle were a rock, then the horse would be its paper," Whirby used his right hand to envelope his left fist. "All's fair in love and war, but a word to the wise: don't trust the horse. As soon as it has your confidence, it pounces. Pop in and pop out— a surprise attack and then game over. Chess is a funny game. Much like life, there are long periods with no movement, or the action is going on somewhere else. But intangibles develop: work, friendships, and relationships. Countless affairs have developed when pieces sit next to each other on the board unable, for one reason or another, to do battle. I've witnessed relationships strike up between an opposing horse and castle in the middle of the board, next to each other, but at an angle, unable to fight. Twenty turns could go by with the two of them conversing. What the horse knows and the castle doesn't is that the castle is passing time 'til its next battle while the horse is plotting. The horse, though, is patient; it isn't its physical prowess that gets it ahead, but brains and timing. A horse will sit back and nod. It will charm. It will tell tall tales of life on the other side. Anything it can to get into the castle's head and throw it off its game— maybe even convince the castle to jump sides. I've seen it happen. The two may even get drunk together, or have a relationship. If a male castle shows no attraction to a female horse, he'd be wise to take cover. 'A woman scorned,' as they say."

"God—even female chess pieces are crazy?"

"Pawns are necessary and as in life, the most common piece on the board. They possess the least inheritance, whether it be money, talent, fortune, or education. Because they begin at the bottom, they can only move upward. Not to say they all do. Occasionally one will advance all the way to the other side and turn itself into a queen or some other enviable piece. It happens, and it is glorious when it does. But, as a rule, pawns are followers looking for a great leader to help their cause...to lighten their load. Fair warning: Don't tell pawns anything you don't want repeated because they can't keep a secret. You really have to know your pawns and use them wisely. This is easy if you pay attention, because they are an obvious read."

"I'm tuckered out," Garol said and brought his cast mitt in front of his mouth to block his yawn.

"The queen is interesting. The most talented piece on the board, she is both chased and pampered. She's the reason you fight, and much too important to lead from the front. The goal is to capture the opponent's king, but the queen is the motivation. As you know, when the queen is gone, so too is the foundation. The backbone. I've seen many wonderful castles crumble in the midst of a great game when they lose their queens. Such a tragedy," Whirby looked deeply into Garol's eyes. "They lose sight of the fact that not only can they get a new queen, but the goal is the king."

"What does that mean?" Garol asked feeling defensive, but unsure why.

"Relax, Shotgun. All I'm saying is that the king is really nothing more than a representative piece to define ourselves by. Aren't we all trying to capture the king? Because aren't we all kings? Only the size of our manors differ, and wouldn't you agree that we are ultimately defined by how we govern those manors?"

"I have no idea why you are telling me any of this."

"A lost castle won't be able to focus clearly on the game. It will spend its time filling its needs and plugging holes. A castle lost in fog could mistake the exterior beauty of a bishop for his queen. Maybe envy for its opposing bishop will foster brooding and the false belief its destiny's been robbed, instead of it creating its own. It may run in terror of the female horse's backlash, or— even worse— follow the opposing male horse and buy into its promises of the other side. Perhaps it will ignore its pawns' capacity to become queens. All these things are unknown. What is known is the lost castle will face hard, dangerous lessons that a castle with its head screwed on correctly already knows."

"I hate it when that happens," Garol said, yawning and stretching his arms.

"Me too," Whirby said enthusiastically, "But things happen. When a piece is carved, it possesses innate skills. Then other factors— consequence, timing, luck, choices, reactions, drive, and even diet— create its outcome. Ingredients dilute. The fastest, strongest castle will amount to very little if it rots in the corner of the board. Some castles run out of the gate conquering, only to find their talents wasted by congestion in the middle of the board. Others play it safe, keeping away from the battlefield to protect the king, and never realize their true potential. Some castles lose their queens early in the game and thus their motivation. Some get sidelined with injury and no longer understand their mission or themselves without the ability to fight. So many things can go wrong. The question is: what do they do?"

"You are talking about the little chess pieces, right?"

"They react in many ways. Unfortunately, when the castle can't find a way to battle outwardly, it will often direct that battle inward. Their need to battle and lead brings shame when they are side-lined. The castle's impenetrable fortress walls carry the burden of an inability to reach out. They suffer in solitude. Even its most trusted ally, its twin, is all the way on the other side of the board and likely living the life it isn't. The castle, like many other pieces, escapes its internal despair by hiding. Too often they drink."

"Little marble pieces?"

"All pieces are capable of escapism. Look at the pawns, on a constant cocktail of Zoloft, Paxil and anything else they can get their hands on to numb them to the fact that the word *retreat* is absent from their vocabulary. Rare is the pawn without post-traumatic stress disorder. Poor things. The castle's pain is different. It tells itself, 'Don't talk. Don't confess. Fight. Fight. Fight,' and never asks for help, only exhausts itself trying to dig out of the rut. A fearless, gallant, but misguided warrior blindly fighting his enemy to death—never realizing he is his own worst enemy.

"Here's something I bet you didn't know: other than the pawns, statistically, the castle is the most likely to have excessive vices. It has pain. If it doesn't figure out how to relieve its load, it carries an enormous weight. A massive internal growth, like a cancer."

"Fruitcake," Garol said, a little louder than he'd hoped.

"Good enough. You're tired. We can finish your orientation some other time. Speak of the devil— here are two pawns that'll never get in your way," Whirby said, greeting the two young men walking up the steps to the porch.

"Jimmy and Toby," Whirby said, pointing to the guys, "This guy calls himself Sam."

Jimmy and Garol shook hand to mitt and Garol extended his mitt to shake Toby's hand.

"Shotgun here is going to be taking care of things around the house," Whirby said to the boys.

"Sounds good," Jimmy said and Toby nodded.

Garol had a strong desire to get away. *Shotgun* was filling his mind with images.

Garol excused himself and immediately felt his knees beginning to buckle as he made his way around the front of the house and out of view and had a seat on the stoop.

"Shotgun," Garol said softly, "that's me."

The memory was so vivid Garol could hear Mike's voice in his ear as if it were happening right now.

"Is Shotgun there?" Garol could remember Mike's voice asking.

"Who?" Garol asked.

"You. Didn't you read the article?"

"No," Garol answered.

Mike read it aloud.

Shotgun Garol Blasts Through East Pittsburgh High's Defense

Garol "Shotgun" Schand took over the command of the Miners after senior quarterback, Jordan Grier, left the game with an ACL tear in the fourth quarter of Friday night's game. In a miraculous comeback, the team won their first game of the year. The quick glimpse of our newfound team leader has everyone begging the question: can this team rise to the heights they reached back in the glory days? The high school championship drought has been going on far too long. Maybe it's in the blood. Not since Garol's father, the onetime Pittsburgh Steeler lineman, has this team been blessed with the kind of talent it has now. Too early to tell? Definitely, but it's nice to see some renewed excitement among the fans. Come out and watch Shotgun, the sophomore phenom, who wears the number eight proudly and seems to be loaded at all ends, blast through the Trojans' defense next Friday with his legs, and use his golden arm to shoot bullets past the defense for touchdowns.

A man moving in the front lawn interrupted Garol's memory. He looked to see a man wearing water flippers and an old fashioned men's one-piece swimming suit that stretched from his shoulders to his knees. Around the land swimmer's waist there was an inner-tube with a duck's head in the front and a duck's tail in the back. The man in the suit and flippers appeared to be performing a concentrated exercise routine. He would walk sixty feet or so in one direction while moving his arms in a swimming motion, and then turn and come back. *Land laps?*

Garol watched the man go through his routine and noticed he had an uncanny resemblance to the doctor he had just seen. *They must be brothers. Possibly twins.*

Garol felt compelled to say something. "I think I may have had a doctor's appointment with your brother, earlier."

He received no reaction.

"Nice day for a swim."

The man continued to swim, giving no sign that he'd heard.

"How does the water feel?" Garol asked.

Still the man continued to swim through the air without acknowledging Garol.

WHERE THE HELL AM I?

An Apple a Day Keeps the Doctor Away

A VOICE SINGING THROUGH the wall speakers ushered in Garol's first morning out of the hospital:

It's time to gett-getty up, getty up.
It's time to gett-getty up, getty up.
So let's go out and get the day.
Just do it in your own special way!

Startled, Garol shot up and rolled himself off the bed. With his face against the floor he couldn't hear where the loud singing was coming from. Frantically, he used the bedpost to help him get to his feet then lost his balance and fell to his knees. He sprang up and yelled, "Who's there?" Then heard the singing once again shoot out from the wall.

The ultimate victim. The biggest victim in the world. No one in the world is or has ever been a bigger victim than I am.

Garol walked onto the porch and saw Whirby studying the chess board.

"Morning, Sam," Whirby said.

"Whatever. Nice sound system. Who's the singing

baffoon?" Garol asked.

"Barney Beaver. He gives the public announcements. That was the wake up call. Maybe I should have warned you? How'd you sleep?"

"Like a baby. I woke up every two hours crying. This cast isn't as comfortable as it looks."

"I didn't see you after our talk. Did you make it down to the cafeteria yesterday?"

"I poked my head in. I was trying to avoid everyone."

"Did you?"

"No," Garol said and turned himself around to display the writing on his back. "Half the idiots in town wrote on my back. I was too annoyed to enter the Nerdshack Café, so I left."

"Well, writing on your back is better than riding your back," Whirby said, smiling.

"Give 'em time," Garol said and thrust his right leg forward revealing the word "Asshole." "Some sweet little old woman wrote that. Classy. It doesn't matter where you go, people never change. I'm not sure I want to see what the rest of it says. Of course, I can't, because my apartment doesn't have a mirror for some reason."

"No mirrors in town. We don't put much emphasis on externals here."

"You found the perfect place for you."

"You have to see who you are in the faces of those around you. If you're paying attention, you'll know who you are and how you appear."

"Who's the weirdo swimming on the lawn? The one that looks like that doctor goofball?"

"That's Split. He's fascinated by water and the motion of swimming. Do you want to join us for breakfast?"

"What is this—a town for nuts? What the hell am I doing here? I don't want to join you for breakfast, but I will 'cause I'm starving. Then I go see Dr. No Notes. Moron. This cast comes off today. Then I go home. Enough of this asylum."

"It always feels better with someone to blame," Whirby said very seriously.

"No shortage of people to blame in this town. This is one hell of a town. You can take all the lunacy and incompetence. You can take this cast; you can take the fact that I can't remember anything. Well, I remember certain things, but nothing since December…December 21st, I think it was," Garol gave it some thought. "You can take all that, and the worst part: the boredom. I'm so bored that, if I could, I might actually read a book. Of course, that would mean my hands were free and I'd be doing something else."

"Like drinking?"

"You got that right. And smoking."

"I've got a copy of the local paper if you'd like to take a look."

"No thanks. I can't hold it."

"Would you like me to read it to you?"

"No. I'm trying to forget about this town, not learn about it. You ready to go eat?"

"One second. You ran off before I got to explain that I always have a chess game going on with myself. I'm just about to make a move. I can feel the Castle wanting to move. He's just itching to battle, but I'm afraid there are a few pawns in his way today."

"Boy, did I miss any other treats?"

"Sam!"

"What?" Garol said.

"Your front door is open."

"I hate this cast," Garol looked down at his midsection and slammed the door shut.

Whirby moved a White pawn one step closer to the other side. "All set."

Garol, Toby, Jimmy, and Whirby walked to the cafeteria. Inside, they entered the buffet line. Jimmy and Whirby grabbed trays, and Jimmy put a tray for Garol in the line so he could slide it along the shelf to pick up his food. Garol watched as they placed a glass of orange juice and an egg-white omelet full of vegetables on their trays. Disgusted by the thought of eating such a healthy, tasteless meal, he said, "Where do we put our order in?"

"We don't have to. Everyone gets to eat the same thing," Jimmy said.

Garol pushed his tray forward and a woman behind the counter said, "Welcome to town," and placed a 24-ounce mug on Garol's tray with a large straw in the middle.

"What's this?" Garol asked.

"It's a blended egg-white-and-vegetable omelet shake," she said and smiled, then placed a glass of orange juice on his tray.

The three of them sat down at a cafeteria table and Garol stared at his shake.

Garol's agitation grew as he felt the full cafeteria staring at the new mystery man in town.

"You should probably get out and explore the town today. This town has a lot to offer. I think you're really going to like it," Whirby said.

"I'm leaving," Garol said staring at his omelet shake.

"You should dig in, it's wonderful," Jimmy said.

"Wonderful? Egg whites and vegetables? The chef's a real gourmet. You couldn't make me eat what you're eating. I'd rather be dead then drink it. No thanks," Garol said and pushed his mug to the side.

"You have to eat," Jimmy said.

"I'll pick up an apple or something," Garol said.

"How?" Whirby asked.

"Son of a bitch! These mitts are coming off," he said and stood up slowly from the table and teetered and balanced his way out of the cafeteria in a slow motion huff. He followed the walkway three doors down to the right and entered the doctor's office.

Garol leaned against the receptionist's desk and said very sternly, "I need to see the doctor, now."

"Please fill this out, sir," the receptionist said and placed a clipboard with a blank sheet of paper in front of Garol.

"No, no, not this shit again. Just get the doctor."

"Sir, calm down. Which doctor are you referring to?"

"Which doctor? Dr. Dingbat? Dr. Lunatic? I don't know.

The tall guy with dark hair who can't remember anything."

"How's your memory, sir?"

"I'm a patient."

"It's amazing how much of a difference there can be between the meanings of patient and patience," the nurse said.

"I'm supposed to have problems, I wouldn't be here otherwise," Garol said through clenched teeth.

"Admitting it is the first step. Good work," the nurse said and smiled cheerfully.

"Where's the doctor?" Garol said and slammed his right cast mitt on the desk.

"He's away for a while, the parent said to the child," the nurse said and stuck her tongue out at Garol.

"What? How? Where?" Garol demanded.

"I don't know," she said tossing her arms in the air.

"You don't know? Aren't you his secretary? Is it a vacation? Do you know what he's doing? Maybe he's getting the computer fixed— is that it?"

"Sure," she said.

"Sure? Is that a 'yes'? Garol asked.

"Yes, sure, that's it," she answered eagerly.

"Unbelievable! When's he coming back?"

"Later, not now. Sometime in the future. Yes, I believe that's what he said."

"So he did tell you?"

"No. Well, sort of. He said he would send me an email about leaving and coming back sometime. I can't remember. I know what I'll do: when he gets back and fixes the computer I can check my email and let you know. Would you like me to call you then?"

"Do you listen to yourself talk? How could he send you an email if the computer isn't working? I don't get it, is there something in the water around here? When he comes back you don't have to ask him when he's coming back."

"My apologies. Wait…I thought you wanted to know."

"I do. Never mind. You said there's another doctor?"

"I never said that."

"You asked me which doctor I was referring to."

"Right, that's one of our standard customer service questions. It makes the experience more enjoyable for our customers. Patients like to know they're being treated with kindness and respect, so it's important to put on fake smiles and ask sweet, caring questions. That's why I asked that question, sir."

"You're a real expert. Holy shit," Garol said and spun around. He thought about walking out of the office, but said, "I think I'll have a look for myself," and began walking down the hall to look in the rooms.

"Sir, sir," the receptionist said getting up from her chair.

The door was open in room #12,24-- and Garol peered in and saw no one. He looked in an open door across the hall with the same result.

The receptionist raced down the hall and he heard a door slam. Garol popped back into the hallway and headed toward her. He passed the operating room and saw no one.

The receptionist stood in front of the door she'd closed.

"Please get out of the way," Garol said sternly.

The receptionist moved in front of the door handle.

"Why are you blocking my way? What are you hiding?"

The receptionist pulled a nail file out of the pocket of her shirt smock and leaned a little to the side and began filing her nails. "Hiding? I'm not hiding anything. This is the employee break area. I'm just taking an employee break," she said and yawned.

Garol looked above her head and saw the room number was #12,21--.

"Please get out of the way," Garol demanded.

The receptionist moved reluctantly out of the way.

Garol put his cast mitts around the large, round, stainless-steel door handle. He was unable to get a grip on the doorknob. "Will you please open the door for me?"

"No one is allowed in there," she said, still filing her nails.

Garol tried the handle one more time and then threw his mitts in the air. "I'm tired of the crap going on around here.

Things are going to change."

"That's what needs to happen. Good idea. You're on the right track," she said, and walked back to her desk.

"Damn right," Garol said following her to the front.

When she reached the front desk she pulled out a clipboard with a sheet attached and asked, "Would you like to fill out a customer complaint form?"

"Oh you're funny. Disgusting. Shameful. You should be ashamed of yourself. Nobody holds me prisoner. I blame you for this," Garol said and stormed out the door.

"Have a wonderful day," the receptionist said cheerfully.

Garol left the office and heard the words, "Watch where the hell you're going, you dumb son of a bitch."

A blasting sideswipe spun his shoulders. Attempting to regain his balance, he reached for the guardrail that separated the walkway from the street. His aim was a little high and Garol toppled over the railing head first down to the cobblestone road. On his way down, he caught a glimpse of the same woman in pumps who'd toppled him previously. "Why?" he gasped, but it was drowned out by the thud of his landing.

Garol felt a hand on his back, "Leave me alone," he muffled.

"Just trying to help," The Man said.

"Some woman is trying to kill me," Garol said, rolling over.

"That's just Gladys. She's generally in a hurry. Maybe she has a deadline to meet. She works on the local paper. You know how newspaper people are." The Man extended his hand to help Garol to his feet.

"In a hurry? In this town? What the hell is there to get to? There can't possibly be any breaking news. I'm in a hurry to leave, but people keep knocking me over or getting in my way. People either run around like they're nuts or they get nothing done at all. You should name the town Senseless. Lunatics talking about chess pieces like they're alive, crazy women knocking me over, guys swimming on the lawn, deranged doctors, rude receptionists, nutty nurses, konked-out computers. This place sucks. Everybody just needs a stiff drink," Garol complained as The Man pulled him up.

"That's not the way we choose to deal with our problems here," The Man said, smiling.

"Deal with problems? They don't deal with their problems. A doctor sticks a guy in a body cast and then flies off to Tahiti. Where the hell did he go? You told me you can't get out of here, and now my doctor's gone. Who's gonna fix the computer? And honestly—he sticks a patient in a body cast and two days later can't even recall why? It's not like everyone in town is walking around in a body cast, it's kind of rare. Normally people remember things like that. I'm not a doctor and my memory isn't what it once was, but if I stuck someone in a body cast, even a month later I'd remember why."

"I'll admit it's odd, but he has an impeccable reputation. Granted, his approach is a little unorthodox, but he always gets the results he's looking for. He really is one of the best."

"What? What are you talking about? It's odd enough that no one can tell me why I'm in this body cast, but I'm walking around in it. I'm living a normal life: I've got an apartment, a job, I guess that's what it is. I go to the cafeteria. I mean, it's boring, but most people in body casts aren't healthy enough to do these things. You don't generally see them walking around."

"Sounds like you are struggling today. Don't worry, things will get better. The beginning is always the hardest. You have to let your mind adjust to the situation before it can process and move on."

"Once again, you've lost me. I know the situation, but nobody else does. Look at this," Garol thrust his right leg forward, "Can you believe that? People write on me all the time. Most of them I can't see. I don't even want to know what the stuff on my back says. Who does that? Who plows a guy over wearing a body cast?"

"Well I was hoping this wouldn't be such a bad time to ask."

"Ask? Ask what?"

"We're starting a remodeling project in the upstairs apartment of the house you're looking after. I really need you to be the project manager."

"Is this a joke? I can't even hold a pencil," Garol held up his mitts.

"You don't need to do any writing. You just need to make sure things are getting done."

"I don't know anything about the trade."

"Then you'll learn. You'll start tomorrow morning after breakfast."

"You know I'm trying to leave, right? That I don't plan on being here long?"

"In the meantime, think of it as building a track record. Do what you can. Move as slowly as you'd like. Doesn't matter. Just show up. That's all you have to do. Let it happen naturally and it will. It certainly will," The Man smiled a half smile and turned around.

Garol turned and walked back to the house swearing under his breath the whole way. When he reached the porch to his apartment he saw the local paper, 'The Gossip,' lying on the table next to Whirby's chess game. The top article was titled, "Marshmallow Comes to Town."

Marshmallow Comes to Town

Please take the time to welcome our newest community member. He goes by the name Sam and is as easily recognizable as a snowman at the pool or a polar bear catching some rays at the beach. In short, he looks like a giant, grumpy marshmallow. Be careful, and don't hang him over any fires; he's a little fat, and you may hurt yourself. Be friendly though, welcome him to town or say hello. The picture on the second page gives you an indication of what this oddly put together man looks like and the area on his cast he is unable to view. We strongly recommend all derogatory marks be written on these sections. Also, it should be noted that the cast protects him from any harm due to spills he may have, so tripping him is optional. If he gets in your way, hit him with your shoulder, he's top heavy.

— Gladys P. Calumny

The Way to a Man's Heart is Through His Stomach

GAROL HAD OFFICIALLY FINISHED his first full week as Project Coordinator in the remodel of the vacant apartment upstairs. When the week began, Garol had tentatively entered the upstairs construction site to find Toby surrounded by tools and wearing a hard hat. Garol's position as the boss put him in a pickle between complete confusion about what they were doing and having to give the orders.

Deciding it would be a mistake to let his subordinate, Toby, know about his lack of experience, Garol decided to act first and figure out what he was doing later. He directed in vague and subtle ways. The first thing he did was compliment Toby on his hard hat, acknowledging, "Safety first," then motion to his cast and add, "Completely protected. No need for useless injury. Just some things I've picked up through years of training."

"Very smart." Toby was kind enough to come across as sincere.

Garol found the style of leadership necessary to optimize their time. By saying, "Ok, so let's get together on what we're doing and what needs to be done," he found Toby would run through the list. Garol would pause and say, "Yeah, that sounds good, let's do that." The first week, he watched Toby and occasionally held the end of a board in the air, or handed him the wrong tool, after fumbling it around in his mitts. When he felt his superiority threatened, he asked Toby what he was doing, and then repeated back to him what he had just told him in the form of an order (or assignment, depending on how secure he felt about his leadership and life in the moment). Toby handled it all very good naturedly. All of the nailing, lifting, pounding, grunting and groaning Toby performed each day left Garol feeling absolutely exhausted by the end of his first week of work. Not to mention the toll of pretending to be the boss, covering up for his ineptness, avoiding old memories, creating excuses to keep from lending a hand, and fighting boredom.

The week's work done, Garol, Toby, Jimmy and Whirby walked to the cafeteria together. Whirby explained excitedly, "The Castle did indeed make a forward move and, with a stroke of luck, positioned itself nicely on the board. Although I think there's a good chance the opposing female Bishop will move close to him and cause quite a disturbance."

Garol did an excellent job of ignoring the chess conversation as Jimmy and Toby asked questions.

"Why do you think the Castle will get distracted?" Jimmy asked.

"Beauty, my friend. The Castle is a sucker for beauty," Whirby said.

"What if the Castle decides not to notice?" Toby asked.

"That would be nice. It would save him a lot of trouble, but some of the best lessons are the toughest ones to learn," Whirby said.

The four men entered the dining hall and got in line to get their food. Garol was trying to mentally prepare himself for a flank steak, broccoli and baked potato shake when he felt a tap on his shoulder.

Garol turned around to see the blonde girl with light blue eyes from the doctor's office. She smiled sweetly and said softly, "I see you aren't tripping anymore."

Garol's body grew tight and he had a hard time forming words. He eventually pushed out in a gasp, "Tripping?"

"You seem to be getting around much better," she said.

"Oh, yeah," Garol said, but couldn't think of anything else to say.

"That's great," she said and smiled. "The Man sent me down to see you. He said you might be tired of drinking your dinner. I'm here to feed you a normal meal. The Man wanted to congratulate you on your first week of work. He said you really enjoy your new assignment."

"I do," Garol said.

"I'm Sara."

"I'm Garol," Garol said without realizing.

"It's nice to meet you, Sam," Sara said quickly, then nervously smiled and grabbed a tray and some silverware.

Garol was excited about eating a regular meal, but he knew it wasn't the reason he was shaking. He was experiencing a feeling he hadn't felt in years. There was a chemistry he felt for Sara. He was enamored by her beauty. He loved her smile and was instantly taken in by her gentle tone of voice.

Garol followed Sara to the table and didn't take his eyes off her as she cut his food and brought it up to his mouth. He couldn't think of anything funny, interesting, entertaining, or witty to say, so he kept his mouth busy chewing.

Finally, fearing the meal was coming to an end, Garol said, "Would you mind cutting the food into smaller bites?"

A few times Sara broke up the silence by saying as she brought the fork to Garol's mouth, "Open the tunnel for the train, chugga, chugga, chugga, toot-toot!"

Garol laughed nervously, sounding like a toddler.

When the meal was finished Garol was stuffed, but asked Sara, "What's for dessert?"

Sara smiled beautifully, showing her perfect teeth, and said, "They have a wonderful flourless, sugar-free cake with an amazing healthy icing substitute."

Garol was able to suppress his gag reflex and said, "I love that."

"Isn't their menu amazing?" Sara said cheerfully and ran up to get their desserts.

After Garol had filled his body with the meal, three deserts and all the cherry, pomegranate juice and water he could take, he waved his cast mitts in the air to indicate, "No more."

Sara pulled out a pen and asked, "Do you mind if I sign your cast?"

"Please," Garol said.

Sara leaned over and wrote on Garol's cast just above his heart.

Garol closed his eyes and smelled her hair as she wrote. As he exhaled he gave out a soft, "Mmmmmmmmm."

"Are you ok?" Sara asked.

"Yes. Sorry, ummm, what?"

"It was very nice to meet you," Sara said before she left to take the tray, plates, and silverware into the kitchen.

Garol stopped by the Post Office.

"Thanks for the helper," Garol said to The Man standing behind the counter writing in a ledger.

"My pleasure. I'm glad you stopped by; I need to ask you something."

"Ok," Garol said.

"There is a town hall meeting coming up, and I hate to say it's mandatory, but I really feel it's important for all project leaders to attend."

Garol agreed to go.

"MORNING?" GAROL MUMBLED WITH foggy confusion through a clenched jaw in answer to Barney Beaver's cheerful rendition of the morning song. "I can't stand this cast. I now own the wake-up-in-the-middle-of-the-night record. That's my only accomplishment in life. The only reason I'll ever be remembered. My life truly sucks."

Garol decided to wait out the song and try to sleep, but it never stopped. Finally, he popped out of bed.

"Shut up you oaf," he yelled at the speakers. The motion sensor went off and the music stopped.

Garol jumped back in bed, which re-activated Barney's song. "Ugghh, you win. Are you trying to break me, is that it?" he yelled at the speaker.

Garol stormed out on the porch and met Toby on his way up to the upstairs apartment. "You going up now, boss?" Toby asked.

"Doctor's office, then home," Garol said without looking at Toby and huffed his way into town.

"You're getting around pretty good now," Toby yelled at his back.

When Garol entered the doctor's office, he saw the receptionist sitting behind her desk with her feet up polishing her toe nails. When Garol got to her desk, she shot him a look intended to be interpreted as, "No matter what this intrusion is for, the reason is not good enough."

Garol checked his temper and said very calmly, "I'd like to see the doctor please."

"Sir! Control yourself. This is a doctor's office, not a barn. Am I making myself clear? Now have a seat. I swear I don't get paid enough for this shit," she yelled and threw her arms in the air, and after a brief pause, smiled and stuck her tongue out at Garol.

Garol stared at the receptionist. He wanted to say something, but he was too wiped out to think of a rational response. Instead, he gritted his teeth and made a loud, long "UGGGGGGGGHHHHHHHH," noise.

"Clever. Now have a seat sir."

Garol continued staring. When the receptionist went back to polishing her nails, he felt foolish, pivoted on his right foot, and stepped toward the waiting room.

Once seated, he leaned forward and rested his arms on his legs and then his head on his cast mitts. He only saw a pair of calves in white stockings walk past him then sit down.

The nurse sat down, pulled out a sketch pad and began scribbling intently.

Garol eventually pulled his head out of his mitts and sat back in his chair. He didn't feel like noticing anyone who sat near him, so he looked around the office to avoid it. On the wall he saw a picture of three beings sitting around a bar, while a fourth served as a bartender. The layout of the painting was similar to a painting that hung on the wall of his apartment in Baltimore, but the characters in this picture were four alien-looking things with small bodies and disproportionately large heads. Each one a different color: pink, blue, green and violet. *What the*...Garol looked at the title and saw it was called, "Boulevard of Broken Extra Terrestrial Dreams." Garol stared at the painting. *Whatever it is, I hope it isn't here. Maybe that's the local bar? Oh, Christ! Of course, any bar would be nice.*

From the corner of his eye, he noticed the receptionist had not stopped painting her nails. On her desk there was no computer or telephone, just her feet, some paper wads, and a couple bottles of nail polish. *Is she even going to tell the doctor I'm here?*

Garol watched her going through her routine for the next ten minutes: paint, yawn, stretch…and repeat. He felt an uncontrollable desire to get up and start screaming. He began to leave when the nurse finally got up. He sat back down and watched her walk, notepad in hand, down the hallway. A moment later, the doctor walked in and said, "Come on back to the Limb Removal Room, I'm ready for you."

"Thanks Doc."

Garol was hesitant about entering the "Limb Removal Room" so he stood in the doorway, surveying. In the far corner an umbrella stand housed a chainsaw. "I just have a question."

"You can come in," the doctor said.

"Is that new?" Garol asked pointing at the 'Limb Removal' sign on the door.

"Depends on what you mean by new. Is that all you needed to know?"

"What's that?" Garol said pointing his mitt to the chainsaw.

"A chainsaw," The doctor answered smiling.

"I know. What's it here for?" Garol said.

"Questions are funny. They're like potato chips. They always lead to more questions. Chips, you see, lead to more chips. I mean eating them. Not that they multiply. That would be rabbits. That's a joke," the doctor said.

While the doctor talked Garol noticed there was a meat cleaver on the desk.

"Come on in. Don't stand in the doorway,"

"Is the computer fixed yet?"

"Are you the computer specialist?" The doctor asked.

"Do I look like it?"

"You guys all look the same to me."

"Must be the cast."

"Maybe. I never thought about it. I bet you're right," the doctor said, giving Garol's suggestion ample thought.

"I wanted to know if the computer is fixed so we can figure out what's wrong with me. Do you remember me?"

"I remember you. Breast cancer, right? We'll take care of that. It'll just take a minute."

"No, wrong guy. I'll give you a hint," Garol said and pointed his mitts to himself. "Full body cast."

"Hmmm. I'm confused, so that's not your uniform?"

"I was in a week and a half ago. You said you had to wait until the computer was fixed to find out what was wrong with me. Remember? We cut the cast in sections so I could walk around? Is this ringing a bell?"

"Let's go take a look. Maybe they've got it up and running," the doctor said, walking past Garol in the doorway and down the hall to Room 0.

Hesitantly, Garol dragged behind the doctor down the hall to Room 0, where he stood in the doorway surveying the new room for any sharp objects. When he saw none, he walked in and stood behind a man leaning over a desk.

The man in the room was in a white smock and looked down on a computer hard drive taped to at least twenty or so D batteries. He vigorously rubbed his hands through his hair and shot Garol a textbook perplexed look, with squinted eyes and squunched lips as his head scooted from side to side.

"How's it coming? I brought you a specialist," the doctor said and smiled to Garol.

The technician sized Garol up.

"I don't know anything about computers," Garol said raising his mitts.

"Not as well as I'd like," the tech replied, "I can't seem to get any juice to the hard drive."

"Where's the rest of the computer?" Garol asked.

"In that box over there," the tech answered.

"What are you doing? Why do you have batteries taped to the hard drive?" Garol asked.

"I'm trying to build a bridge, so to speak, for the energy to travel across to the hard drive. The way I figure it, there's a bunch of concealed energy in the batteries and if we can get it over in the hard drive, our problems are solved."

"That ain't gonna work. Do you have any experience with computers?"

"I'll be back in a minute," the doctor said and walked out of the room.

"Yeah, I was part of the 'Jock Squad' for a year. It's the tech support unit for the retail chain, Worst Bargain. You've probably heard our jingle," and the tech started singing out of tune, 'You'll pay a little more, cause you're our whore.' The tech shook his head and said, "Man I miss that job. We didn't have to do shit. We'd get an order and just go over to those nerds at the other place and make them do our work. Some things never change," the tech said with a loud, evil laugh. "It was awesome. Then one day the company went out of business. I couldn't believe it. They had the right idea; they knew profits were more important than the customer. I hit the bottle. Then I got this job. Who cares? The way I look at it, as long as this thing doesn't work, I've got job security. I'm the only guy in town with any computer experience. Come on, I'm a jock, I don't care about computers. Now if this were a women's body, I'd have this puppy up and running already. You know what I'm talking about," The tech laughed loudly again. "You a jock?"

"All American quarterback my junior year in college, listed as a hopeful my senior year for the Heisman trophy, and slated to be drafted in the first round to the pros."

"Wow! Mr. Big Shot. I could probably get you a gig working with me. It's totally cake."

"No. I need that thing fixed. I don't plan on spending any extra time in this town."

The doctor came back, followed by the nurse carrying the sketchpad.

"Dr. Jergens, the x-rays are finished." The nurse handed an envelope to the doctor and left.

"Very good. Thank you." The doctor grabbed the large sheet

she'd torn from the pad.

The doctor turned off the office lights and walked to the desk in the corner of the room. He pulled out the contents of the package, laid it on the desk, and flipped on a black light.

"Very interesting," the doctor said, "look at this."

Garol hesitated and then slowly walked over to the desk. The picture was a caricature of Garol. He was in his cast, but his face was uncovered. It reminded Garol of a picture he'd had done at the state fair with Beth. *How did the nurse know what my face looks like?* His head was enlarged, and his facial expressions lowered his IQ by about twenty points. She had also added a bib to the drawing and enlarged his already over-sized cast belly. His right hand swung a rattle.

Garol was too busy being offended to notice what the doctor was referring to.

"See here?" the doctor pointed to his head.

The head was a blown up skull similar to those in the picture of the aliens in the waiting room. In the black light, images appeared inside the skull: a sacked quarterback, a woman displaying her engagement ring, a person sitting with shrugged shoulders on a bar stool, a bottle of beer, cigarettes, two men in an argument, a poison symbol, two cars colliding, two graves, and an anvil.

"Well, there's your problem," the doctor said.

Garol studied the picture. *What the hell?* "That's not what an x-ray looks like," Garol said.

"This is a mental x-ray." The doctor looked very concerned. "NURSE! NURSE!"

"Yes, doctor?" The nurse peered into the room.

"Nurse, this is all wrong," the doctor said, annoyed.

"I'm sorry doctor, did I miss something?" She asked.

"Look at his cast mitts. How in the world can he hold a rattle?"

"I'm sorry. Would you like me to draw it again?"

"No, no, I'll work with this. I just would've expected more from a professional." The doctor shook his head.

"What problem? The graves?" Garol asked.

Garol turned to see the doctor walking towards him with a fork clasped in his palm, prongs thrusting forward.

"Hey!" Garol yelled and jumped back.

The doctor walked past Garol to the little fridge in the corner of the room. "I get so hungry at this time of the day." He pulled a salad out of the fridge, placed it on the table, and began eating.

"So what does this mean?" Garol asked.

"Don't know, never seen anything quite like that. A first for the anvil. Looks like one hell of a weight to carry around."

"What are you saying?"

"I can see why we're having such a hard time diagnosing this whole situation." The doctor then pushed a button on his phone which allowed him to speak to the receptionist at the front desk. "Could you make an appointment with our doctor in the woods? The sooner the better, we've got a real case." The doctor looked Garol up and down.

"Who's the doctor in the woods? Does he know what he's doing?" Garol asked.

"Oh, yes, he's remarkable. He works with cases like yours. He's a one of a kind. The receptionist will tell you where and when to meet him." The doctor pulled out a long tube with a half circle at the end from his desk drawer.

Garol started to leave, then turned around to see the doctor wearing a snorkel and goggles, glaring at the empty fish bowl in the corner of the room.

Garol walked up to the receptionist's desk.

"Wow!" She leaned forward towards Garol, "Things are far worse than we imagined, huh?"

"What does that mean?"

"Just messin' with ya," she said, waving a hand at him. "Actually, the situation is no worse than I thought. It's so hard to face your own problems, so it's nice when others look out for you. I'll make an appointment for you with Dr. Mitchell. He's the psychiatrist in town. He'll fix you up."

"I don't need to see a psychiatrist. Hello? I am in a body cast. My problems aren't mental, they're physical."

"Oh, I know," the nurse responded.

Garol leaned in, feeling he'd finally made a connection.

"Like I said, it's so hard to see our own problems. He will help, really. He did wonders for me. Believe it or not, I used to be really hard to deal with." The receptionist began singing, "Insane people who need people, are the luckiest nutjobs of them all, because when their loony they need thoughtful people…"

Garol turned around and began walking out the door.

"I'm just messin' with ya. You're so stiff! Lighten up, drop the weight, jeez."

It's Not Work that Kills You, but Worry

STAY CALM. EVERYTHING IS going to be ok, Garol told himself as he walked to the town hall meeting. Large social groups filled Garol's mind with anxiety, triggering both a need for several drinks and a lack of coordination that made it appear he'd drunk them. These panic attacks were the real reason he stopped selling. He never told Mike, his ex-boss and ex-best friend; he preferred Mike believe he didn't give a shit about anything anymore. He didn't need anyone else to know how far he'd fallen. The last thing he wanted was a second opinion on whether or not he'd lost his mind. He knew his self-diagnosis was the only one that mattered, and there was only one way to medicate that problem. The cost of his medicine was irrelevant— any price can be paid in the future when you can't imagine one.

A few folks dressed in hairy beaver outfits from head to toe mingled in the entryway. Stepping inside the auditorium, Garol was shocked to see identically disguised beavers everywhere. He instantly felt like a snowman at the river on a sunny day, and began to melt from the inside. His sweat trickled like a slow leak, but the strain of the situation offered the possibility of a pipe burst. For the first time since arriving in Nutville, he felt caged and exposed.

Head down, Garol started towards an open seat next to the exit in the far corner of the room, but an usher grabbed his mitt and led him past several empty chairs to the middle of a row on the left of the center aisle.

Fluid escaped his pores as if fleeing a disaster area. Once the usher was out of sight, he debated going to his intended seat by the exit.

In an instant, beavers clogged the row in both directions, cementing Garol's decision to have a seat.

"Let's give it up for the Beaver Bangers, those men and women who consistently bang out the most work," a voice called through the speakers.

Fourteen furry men and women sauntered onto the stage waiving to the audience with their upper teeth displayed over their bottom lips. Audience members sprang to their feet and clapped, hooted, and hollered. Garol followed suit, getting to his feet and pounding his cast mitts together.

"Please welcome the Head Beaver," the speakers roared.

Garol clapped his mitts together loudly several times before the faces of those around him turned on him with raised whiskers. Their faces remained locked on his while they made a beaver noise using their lower lip, tongue and upper teeth. Unable to mimic their gesture, he closed his eyes and hid inside the cast.

The Head Beaver, now positioned behind the podium, quieted the crowd by raising his paws and lowered them, and everyone sat down.

The Head Beaver stood at the podium in silence and began slowly piling twigs. The crowd breathlessly awaited the placement of each stick and pulled forward until their seats only held a fraction of their animal bottoms. They let out synchronized "oooooh's" when the Head Beaver pulled back his bushy paws from the pile in progress. During the placement of the fourteenth stick, the woolly man jostled his paw and the stack tumbled. The crowd met the defeat with a long "aaaaaaaaaaaaw" and looked around to one another, throwing fists in the air and gesturing with their paws to indicate, "Almost had it." The Head Beaver raised his paws to quiet the crowd and began again. During the next five attempts, the Head Beaver managed to get somewhere between twelve and fifteen sticks stacked— all accompanied by enthusiastic "ooooooooh's"— before clumsily knocking the pile over.

Garol eyed the exit signs like a lighthouse in a sea storm, considering his options. He could feel himself sweat and feared that others could hear his pores snapping open in the silence. He wanted to yell, "Take off the damn paws, you jackass!" He sat inside his suit twitching with hatred.

Finally, as Garol was on the verge of either yelling or running, the crowd stood and the Head Beaver said, beaming with pride, into the microphone, "The dam has been erected. The meeting will begin."

When the crowd stopped their beaver sounds and sat back down, the Head Beaver said, "The meeting will begin with progress reports. Let's begin with the construction of the airplane. Adam, please inform the crowd how the progress is coming."

Adam walked up to the podium and said, "Hello, Beavers." The crowd roared. Garol squeezed his eyes closed. "I think everyone will be pleased to know that we're making great strides in the direction of aeronautical flight. We gave up the idea of invisible stilts and are moving on to developing a craft powered by vacuums, which will pull us into the sky and then in all directions. Then, of course, the craft will be equipped with a reverse vacuum to bring us down. The vacuums will also be strong enough to get rid of any household mites residing in your sofa."

The crowd stood and cheered.

"We hope to finish it someday," Adam said and raised his arm in the air, which caused the crowd to go wild; both clapping and making beaver sounds. Garol followed suit.

Then came the progress report on the Pen-cil, which could be used as both a pen and a pencil. Then the Frisbee plate, intended to speed the distribution of full plates at picnics. Then, finally, a report on Medium Foot: normal sized footprints found in the desert, which struck fear in the hearts of the town's inhabitants. Adam flipped a page on his easel and circled two footprints. One was marked "Average-sized footprint;" the other "Medium Foot." The prints were identical. "We now have proof Medium Foot exists. You can see from these identical footprints that he has the same size foot as the average adult male." Adam then stepped in front of the podium and with a voice just shy of a yell demanded, "Stay out of the desert, everyone. It's for your own protection. You will not come back."

Throughout the meeting hall, beavers were horrified.

After all the projects were discussed, the Head Beaver walked to the podium and said, "At this time, I'd like Mary to go over any changes to the beaver schedule this week."

Mary spoke directly into the microphone and asked, "Is everybody excited?" The beavers roared. Garol felt dizzy from all the water leaving his body. "Everyone has been chipping in and doing their parts so selflessly. Not one complaint about anything from anyone," she stepped back from the microphone and clapped. The crowd joined her applause. "Yeah, you earned it," Mary yelled into the microphone.

"I know there has been some trouble with the computer, but it appears that will be finished in time for,"and she turned her head to the right, away from the microphone. Garol couldn't hear her. The crowd didn't seem to have any difficulty and clapped enthusiastically.

"Gladys, I'd like to thank you for the hard work you've been putting in on the *Gossip*. Thanks so much for keeping us informed of what's going on around the village. You always work so thoughtlessly," Mary said, and again the crowd cheered.

"Great piece this week," Mary said and surveyed the room. "So it sounds like we've got a new member to the community. Is he here tonight?"

Garol sat still.

"Apparently he's easily recognizable. I hear he looks like a," and again pulled away from the microphone leaving Garol to wonder what she heard he looked like.

The crowd laughed.

"I wonder, is he here tonight? I'd love it if he'd stand up so we could all get a view of our new friend," she raised her right paw to her brow and slowly swept her head across the room from left to right.

No. No. Garol slunk as far down in his chair as he possibly could. He closed his eyes and wished he were gone. He opened them to look at the exit signs again and immediately saw beavers staring directly at him. He raised himself slowly in his seat. The higher he crept, the more beaver faces appeared until he was seeing a mass of beavers large enough to erect the Hoover dam in a day. Finally, Garol's eyes met Mary's. *OH GOD!*

"That looks like our new guy," Mary said. "Welcome. Stand up so we can see you."

As Garol's heart raced, his movements slowed proportionately. He got to his feet in slow motion.

"Welcome, neighbor," Mary said cheerfully. "One of the things we like to do with newbies," Mary continued talking as she walked ten paces away from the stand toward Garol's side of the room, but again, Garol could hear nothing.

As Garol stood, Mary talked enthusiastically while her arms bopped around like a conductor wielding his stick. Garol felt she talked for hours. The crowd responded like a band to their maestro, tilting their heads to the left to listen, nodding in agreement, and laughing hysterically in sync and a bit too often for Garol's liking. What Garol could hear were exuberant cries of, "Oh, what a great idea," "You'd love that," "What fun," and "I wish I could go back and do that again."

Then suddenly Mary stopped completely and stared at Garol.

One of those seated within earshot howled, "Do it, you must do it," another whooped, "What a great opportunity," while another voice bellowed, "You'd have to be insane to turn an offer like that down."

Garol stared at Mary. Dizziness and nausea blocked thought and words. The only clear thing was that the crowd wanted him to do something. Arguing was pointless. If he somehow mustered the courage to oppose her and the crowd with a "no," he'd have to explain. *Nod yes. Nod yes— it's the only way to end this.*

Garol nodded. Cheers went up around the hall and Mary smiled, threw up her arms in celebration and walked back to the podium. "Well that settles that, now lets move on..."

That was the last thing Garol heard for the remaining twenty-five minutes of the meeting. He didn't care what job he signed up for. He didn't care about anything. He just hid in his cast, thankful for it for the first time since coming to this town, because no one could see the shades of red he was still turning or the perspiration that sopped his body.

Once the attention vanished, he sat feeling irritated and dizzy for the next ten minutes, wondering what the hell just happened and what the probability was of it happening again. The surging adrenaline had vanished with all the water in his body, and he was left devoid of energy and feeling.

I have to get out of this town. I have to find a way out of this nut house.

Every Man is the Architect of His Own Misfortune

A COPY OF HERMAN Melville's *Moby Dick* rested before the hump of the cast's beer belly as Garol lay in bed. Positioning the book and opening the hard cover to page one wasn't easy, and maneuvering through the rest of the novel had the potential of being more draining than reading the book. Garol had never read a novel, or any other book. *I was an athlete, not a nerd*, he defended himself against the side of his brain constantly reminding him what an intellectual zero he was.

Lying rigidly, careful not to disrupt his platform, Garol occasionally read a phrase that gained enough momentum to make it all the way to a period. Then he would exhale and let his mind wander. *What did I just read? Why am I so stupid? I hate reading. How long is this book?* He desperately wanted a total page count. See how much of the treacherous journey there was left, but knew if he tried he'd have to wrestle the book with his mitts back to page one.

He picked the book due to Whirby's suggestion that reading in bed could help him fall asleep. He needed that. Sleeping had been a huge problem since he showed up in Kookville. Whirby had asked him how he fell asleep before he came to town, but

Garol brushed off the question, declining to answer, "When I was drunk enough, I just passed out."

A few nights prior, at his wits' end, his insomnia forced him to search through the bookcase. Most of the titles made his eyes gloss over, but they lit up when he saw *Moby Dick*. He'd seen the movie stocked in the backroom of the local video store in Baltimore. He wasn't sure how good a pornographic book could be, but considering his options, it seemed like the best choice. When he grabbed the book, he had to laugh; he'd heard that a book is always better than the movie, but in this case they had to be wrong.

He re-read a note that had been posted to his apartment door while he was at the cafeteria for dinner. The note read, "Dr. Mitchell, Psychiatrist. Tomorrow after breakfast, tighten those noggin bolts. Follow the path at the end of Life Street through the woods. If you go over the cliff, you've gone too far—just kidding. Not really. Hope it works, hot stuff. Your loving receptionist."

This whole town is crazy. Why do I have to see a psychiatrist to tell me why I'm wearing a body cast? I've got nothing to say to this guy. I could help him fill journals with the kooks in this damn town. Stupid psychiatrist.

In frustration, Garol rolled over, knocking *Moby Dick* and the note to the floor.

"God, what a freak show," Garol said. He rested his head against the two pillows he had stacked behind him and closed his eyes.

Garol lay still for a few minutes, hoping the reading would tranquilize him enough to fall asleep, but the carousel of thoughts rolling around in his mind gradually increased speed until he couldn't stand it anymore. He popped open his eyes and sprang to a sitting position. "Ungh!" he yelled in frustration. "Uhhhhhh, I'm going nuts."

"Weird, weird," he played with the word. *Weird is a weird word. What is weird, anyway?* The question rolled around in Garol's mind. Any attempt to answer it would be too confusing. He felt like the answer somehow lay in the question, so he repeated, "What is weird?" Garol just wanted things to be straightforward, 2 + 2= 4. *You don't have to dwell on it after the fact. It is what it is. Nothing here seems to be what it is, or was, or whatever. But if I don't know what weird is, then what is normal?*

The riddle he'd created let his mind wander and soon Garol drifted off to sleep. When Barney began his cheerful morning song, Garol's eyes had already opened and cleared.

As breakfast was ending, Garol asked Jimmy, "Where's the Street of Life?"

"It's at the end of Happiness."

"How do I get to Happiness?"

"Happiness is the way," Jimmy answered.

"Just point."

Jimmy did, and Garol began his trek to the psychiatrist in the woods.

Life Street led Garol to a fence opening onto a path that travelled into dense thicket. His eyes followed the path as far as possible before it vanished behind some trees, offering no clue to what his immediate future held. He didn't like the idea of going to the psychiatrist, and stepping into the dark mystery of the forest made him second-guess the necessity. *Ludicrous to have to see a psychiatrist for a body cast.* Looking again into the forest, Garol saw a sign twenty feet up in a tree that read, "Can't see the forest for the trees." He took a deep breath and followed the path into the woods.

The path was slick, and although hiking boots weren't mandatory, casts with rounded bottoms and no traction weren't recommended. Garol spent his journey cursing the town, the psychiatrist, his horrendous luck, his horrible lot in life, and the fact that he was the biggest victim that ever lived. Finally, he made it through. He stood in front of a gate in a white picket fence across a red brick walkway, which carried him to the grey wooden steps, which lifted him to the wooden, grey porch of a large white Victorian home. Then he looked at the wooden sign that hung from a post. Its green letters read, "Dr. Mitchell, Psychiatrist for the Mentally Misaligned. Making marvelous miracles of the mind more than a maybe. Power-pushing past problems to potential. Breaking barriers and busting burdens of the brain."

Garol walked up to the door, raised his hand to knock, but paused when he saw a pair of feet resting on an antique desk through the front door window. Garol's curiosity drove him to move a few paces and observe. The view allowed him to see a man reclining at his desk and talking on the phone. Through the open window Garol heard the doctor saying, "That's interesting; well, why don't you make an appointment and we'll talk about it." Then the doctor removed his feet from the desk, opened a drawer, pulled out a small sheet of paper, and began scribbling. Then raised his pen, scowled and tossed the pen into the corner of the room, out of Garol's view. The doctor stood up to search for another pen and spun around, revealing the ear that was supposed to be covered by the phone, but it wasn't. Garol fixated on the doctor's left hand, clasped over his ear. *How small is that phone? How large are his hands?* Garol became so obsessed with prying to dispel the mystery of the object the doctor was talking into, he mindlessly moved further in the frame of the window.

The doctor grabbed a pen, sat back down, jotted a note, and said, "Sounds good, we'll see you then," and placed his left palm on the desk.

For the next few minutes, the doctor rapidly jotted notes, pulled ledgers from the desk mantle and searched through drawers, all while rotating around his left hand, which didn't appear to move from its position on the desktop. The psychiatrist then stopped, touched two fingers of his right hand to his temple, said, "Of course, that's what I'll do," and picked up his left hand from the desk and began pushing spots on the palm of that hand with his right index finger. Once the number appeared to be dialed he raised his left hand to his left ear and said, "Charles, I'm so sorry I missed you, I've been trying to find the Snooberman and Stratten Psychiatry Manual. I'm looking at x-rays for an appointment today and I'm trying to figure out what some of these symbols mean. I was hoping you could help me. If you get a moment in the next few minutes, please give me a call." He lowered the hand phone back down to the desk.

The doctor went back to his routine of scurrying around, leaving his left hand completely still. He picked up a device, pointed it to the corner of the room, and appeared to push something. The noise of a phone ringing happened immediately. The doctor raised his right arm to indicate to some higher power, "Please stop all the calls." The doctor then simultaneously pointed the device at the corner, picked up his left hand, flipped open his fingers, pushed something on his palm, and placed his left hand with the thumb reaching toward the ear and pinky to his mouth and said loudly, "Hello, Dr. Mitchell." Then after a brief pause, "Lawrence my good friend, how in the world are you?"

The doctor spun his chair around, facing Garol's full body cast in the window. Garol froze as their eyes locked. The psychiatrist smiled and motioned with his right hand for Garol to come inside.

Garol shuffled to the side of the window and paused for thought. *Leave. Run.* He made it down two stairs before his hurried motion caused his left leg to trip his right, which sent him toppling down the remaining three stairs.

The doctor burst through the screen door and threw his arms open wide. Garol, lying on the ground, looked up at the doctor. The two men stared at each other. The doctor smiled the widest smile Garol had ever seen. *He's going to eat me.*

"Sorry, I was on the phone. I didn't hear you knock," the doctor said, still smiling.

"I didn-," Garol decided to stop himself from finishing.

"Come on in," The doctor strained using both hands to simulate reeling in a big fish. "Wow, I got it now," he said, leaning back to emphasize the enormity of the catch.

"You're good with your hands," Garol said working himself to a kneeling position.

"Not a problem," the doctor answered.

The psychiatrist held the imaginary fishing rod with his left

71

hand and spun the reel with his right. "Come on boy, come on," then released a little line, "Give her some slack, don't let her go," and reeled in again shouting, "I got her…ease her in…here she comes," as Garol rose to his feet.

The doctor pulled back every step Garol ascended and leaned forward every time Garol stopped on a stair, using his facial expressions to emphasize the size of the catch. When Garol climbed to the porch, the psychiatrist hooked the end of the line to the imaginary reel and placed the pole inside the door. "Well, we won't be needing that anymore," he said smiling, and extending his arm to shake Garol's mitt. "Dr. Mitchell."

Dr. Mitchell was enormous, about seven feet tall and impressively wide. He was at least 100 pounds heavier than Garol, possibly 150. Garol hoped he was a nice guy; otherwise, he could spend eternity in different sections of the doctor's freezer. His hand engulfed Garol's mitt. The doctor was horseshoe bald, and the enormous size of his head made Garol wonder if his scalp had just kept growing, causing the hair follicles to split down the middle. The hair he did have was dark, peppered with grey, and so thick and full that the bald section looked like a valley, or a large ski slope where all the runs met in the middle.

Dr. Mitchell put a hand behind Garol's back and said, "Come on in."

"Did I come at a bad time?" Garol asked.

"No, just taking calls and doing some paperwork," the doctor said, still smiling widely.

"Great," Garol said, then paused when he saw the doctor's oversized pupils.

"Come on in," the doctor said very gently, "Yeah, that's right, swell. This is real swell. Uh-huh, we'll just go inside and talk about what's bothering you."

Garol followed Dr. Mitchell into his study.

The doctor sat in the reclining chair in front of his desk. "Sit anywhere."

"Anywhere?" Garol surveyed the small room, unable to find

a chair.

"Yeah, that'd be fine," the doctor said, looking at Garol. His hands were on his knees and he appeared eager to start counseling.

"Should I sit on the floor?"

"Oh jeez no, sit anywhere. The floor?" the doctor laughed, "How uncomfortable."

"There is nowhere else to sit," Garol shrugged his shoulders.

The doctor's expression grew serious as his eyes explored the room. "Well, that does pose a problem." The doctor grinned and he said, "Let's make lemonade."

"Lemonade?" Garol felt like a musical chair outcast.

"Yeah, like when you get a bunch of lemons and you have to do something with them. I love lemonade. What I really love is lemon sprinkled over fish: Halibut, Whitefish, Tilapia. Just incredible how lemon adds so much flavor. Oh my God, I love to fish. See what we've done, taken a negative and completely turned it around? Look at us. Session over. That'll be $250. Just kidding, there's no charge in this town." The doctor stood up.

Garol stepped forward, assuming the doctor was offering his seat. The doctor quickly brushed his seat and sat back down, then looked at Garol, now almost on top of him. "You trying to bum rush me?"

"No."

"Then do you mind stepping back? I'm always a little nervous around patients until I find out what kind of crazy they are, you know what I mean?"

"I'm the crazy one," Garol rolled his eyes and turned away.

"True enough. Let's see, you could sit on the desk, or the bookshelf. If the trashcan wasn't full I'd flip that over, unfortunately..." The doctor trailed off.

"Where do people usually sit?" Garol asked, looking at the eight-foot tall bookshelf. The tallest shelf was about two feet.

"Good thinking. I don't know where my head is today. Absolutely, sit in the usual spot. Great idea," the psychiatrist said, returning to his jovial self.

Garol saw a couch and chair in the parlor. "You know, I

could sit in here."

"Yes, yes, yes, of course, splendid idea. You see what happens when you search for results? You really seem in control now...Big change from when you were at the window and on the stairs, unsure of what you wanted to do."

Garol sat down on the couch and wondered if he should lie down, but decided to keep running an option. Garol surveyed his surroundings and noticed nothing that indicated the man in the other room was actually a psychiatrist. There were no plaques or diplomas on the wall, nor any psychiatric journals or books lying around. A book lying on the coffee table was called *Taking Control of Your Origami*. He'd heard of origami, but couldn't remember if it was a type of mental illness or a type of psychiatry. Either way, he felt it legitimized the psychiatrist.

Garol fidgeted impatiently waiting for Dr. Mitchell and finally asked, "So how long have you been a psychiatrist?"

"Interesting. Did you come here to discuss my career?" The doctor asked from the other room.

"No, but I thought it might be a good idea to know something about you," Garol answered.

"Ok, ask away," the doctor said.

"So, where did you study?" Garol asked.

"Psychiatry school," the doctor said condescendingly. "I think that's standard. If you want to be a psychiatrist, you go to psychiatry school. If you're interested in the Arts, you go to art school. Come on, give me a challenge. This is too easy."

"Were you thinking about coming in here?" Garol asked.

There was no answer.

"Hello?" Garol asked.

"Give me a challenging question," the doctor said.

"Don't you think it's better to see the patient's face when talking? You know, facial gestures, body language?"

"I can't see either one of yours, no matter where I sit. How's that for an answer?"

"Can I use your phone?"

After a long silence, the doctor asked, "Who are you going to call?"

"A friend."

"Where?"

"Baltimore."

"No."

"Why?"

"I don't have long distance service."

"I'll call someone local."

"Who?"

Garol couldn't think of anyone who had a phone. The two men sat in silence for a while. "I don't think this is going to work out," Garol said.

A telephone rang. Garol sat up to listen.

"Dr. Mitchell speaking," then a pause. "Thank you for calling back...Yes, he's here right now... One word: bonkers. It's worse than the x-rays. I caught him looking through my window. He watched me for fifteen minutes...Tried to sit in my bookshelf... He really needs some help...Oh, gotta go."

Garol grabbed the doctor's hand between his mitts and yelled, "Who's there?" But the doctor slipped from his grasp and slammed his hand down on the desk.

"What are you doing?" the doctor yelled, "You can't interrupt my phone calls. Are you insane? Well, obviously, you're *here*."

"I'm insane?" Garol yelled back, "Me? You're talking into your hand. This is not a phone," Garol pointed to the palm of his cast mitt. "There are no numbers, there's nothing to talk into. It's impossible to call someone from your hand. Impossible."

The doctor leaned back in his chair with a smirk, "I still don't know what all of the things in your x-ray mean, but some are becoming quite clear."

Garol didn't say anything.

"Let's start with control freak. You see things that aren't the way you'd like them and you have to change them. Destroy them. I would say by your little tirade that you obviously have some deep-seated anger issues. Ambivalence or a lack of power? You almost sat in my bookshelf. Who does that? Would

75

you like me to continue?" The doctor said.

"No, you don't need to say anything at all. I'm nuts? You know what, give me a call, freak," Garol said raising his left mitt to his ear. "This whole town is full of nuts and you might be the nuttiest. I hate to admit it, but with all I've got going on, part of me actually wanted to talk someone, but..."

"But what? Come on, have a seat. I know you're hurting inside. Let's get things out there. I was kidding about the bookshelf. You aren't nuts, no, just a loose screw. Let me get my mental tool set. Come on, it's what I do."

Garol stood and looked at the doctor, then conceded. "But I don't have a screw loose."

"No, of course you don't. Just sit down and we'll tighten it back up," the doctor said.

"Are you going to sit in the parlor?" Garol pointed.

"Yeah, of course, just tell me what's going on, I'm right here." The doctor added softly, "You're really hurting."

The doctor followed Garol into the parlor and sat in an antique chair. Garol sat on the couch and the two looked at each other.

"Come on buddy, open up to me, what's going on?"

"I'm so confused," Garol said then slumped back in the couch.

"Confused?" the doctor asked nodding his head. He was sitting with his legs crossed, a pad in his lap, and a pencil in his hand.

"I just don't get what's going on," then leaned forward and tilted his neck to face the ground. "This town," Garol added softly.

"I'm sorry?" The psychiatrist interjected.

"This town," Garol raised his voice's decibel level.

"Ok, what about this town?" the doctor was scribbling on his notepad.

"I don't get it. Why am I here? What happened to me? Where are the answers?"

"Sometimes the answers are within."

"Oh, man, you too," Garol raised his head to look at the

doctor. "I'm talking about this cast. There has to be a reason I'm wearing it, but either no one knows, or no one wants to tell me."

"Maybe they're hoping you'll figure it out."

"Why? You wouldn't stick someone in a sling and hope they figured out their arm was broken. That'd be ridiculous."

"But obviously you have no broken bones," the doctor shaded something in on his pad. "Would you mind turning just a bit to your right?"

"Exactly. Thank you," Garol said moving his torso slightly to the right. He now saw the doctor peripherally. "That is obvious, but only to us. You see my problem? Why did you want me to move?"

"So, why are you wearing that cast? Don't worry about what I'm doing. Remember: control issues. Let go," the doctor said, erasing.

"What do you mean? They put it on me."

"Why is it still on?"

"Because they don't know what's wrong," Garol held himself as steady as he could.

"They don't or you don't?"

"Neither. Can I move?"

"What do you think is wrong with you? Yes, move your arms into a running motion. Put your right arm out in front and your left arm behind. Please remain faced as far to the side as possible while still being able to look at me," the doctor said, picking up his pad and putting it at a few different angles in front of him, then placing it back on his lap.

"Like this?" Garol placed his arms in the position the doctor requested.

"Perfect."

"Nothing is wrong with me."

"Wow! So, your life is perfect?"

"No. I'm stuck in Moronville, USA, in a body cast."

"So, before you got here your life was perfect?"

Garol shrugged.

"Ah, now we're getting somewhere," the doctor said,

looking at his pad. "Ok, you can sit back."

"What? How are we getting anywhere?" Garol rested against the back of the couch.

"You said your only problems were your cast and this town, but your life was far from perfect before those two things entered the picture. Can you tell me what life was like before you got here?"

"As soon as someone takes this cast off."

"That's up to you," the doctor had his index finger between his lips and squinted at his pad. "Do exactly what you were doing before, but facing the opposite direction."

"No, it's up to the doctor and his computer," Garol said moving his torso to the left and placing his arms in a running position.

"So you have no control over your handicaps?"

"Not when I'm at the mercy of a doctor. Does anyone in this town ever listen? Everything is circular."

"So who is the man you were arguing with in your x-ray?"

"X-ray? That caricature of me?"

"Yes. Who is he? Someone close to you, I imagine?"

"Was I close to the little guy some nutty nurse drew in my head? Not that I recall."

"Why is there a beer bottle crossed out?" the doctor placed the pad face down on his lap. "You can sit anyway you'd like now, thank you."

"Beats me. I like beer," Garol said sitting back against the couch.

"Any problems with that?"

"Yeah, I can't get any."

"There are two graves in the drawing. What do they represent?"

Garol fidgeted. He leaned forward on the couch until he seemed to be only hanging on by the skin of his cast. He paused for a long moment and then said, "I thought you might be able to help me get this cast off. There is nothing written in the head of an over-sized carnival cartoon of me that gives you any right to barge into my life. You call yourself a psychiatrist? You're as nutty as the rest of them. I can't believe I'm baring my soul to some guy who thinks he's talking on a phone through his hand," Garol said flailing his arms.

"You aren't baring your soul. In fact, you haven't said anything," Dr. Mitchell said very calmly.

"And I'm not going to. What kind of information are you lunatics looking for? What could I possibly know that's so important? Why the torture? What do you want?"

"Let it out."

Garol stood up, "What's going on with my life? This is not what was supposed to happen. I was a college quarterback, All-American. I was going to play in the pros. I had respect. I was engaged." He stopped and looked away. "Now..."

"Keep going, don't bottle it up. Let's remove that cas—"

"Now, I can't even get a drink." Garol flopped back down on the couch and put his mitts over his face. "I just want a drink. I just want to forget and be left alone. In Baltimore, I finally had it, so people stopped bothering me. They stopped reaching out. They stopped annoying the shit out of me. Now I'm in a town full of crazy people who won't leave me alone. I can't sleep because I can't block thoughts about things I haven't thought about in years. Things that were gone, done, over. I don't want the thoughts back because I can't have the things back. I just want the thoughts to go away."

Just then a variation of a cuckoo clock announced the time. Instead of a cuckoo bird, a kookoo patient in a straightjacket trumpeted, "Session's over, take your problems elsewhere. Session's over, deal with it. Session's over, get a life."

Garol looked at the clock with disbelief, then at the doctor with wide eyes, "What does that mean?"

"Session's over," the doctor responded.

"So, what happens now?"

"You leave, hopefully."

"Do we meet again? Do I get some advice, or something?" Garol asked desperately. "How about some sleeping pills or pain meds?"

"Not now. If you would've stopped clamoring long enough

for me to say something during the session, then yes, but not now. You're on your own pal, lesson learned. Life sucks, then the vacuum cleaner breaks down, so you buy a new one," the doctor said.

"Huh?" Garol asked, confused.

"Look, we can meet again, but this session is over. Would you like to meet again? You just told me you wanted to be left alone."

"What do you think?"

"I think you get out of things what you put into them. If you want to be left alone, then soon enough you will be. It sounds like that plan worked successfully in Baltimore. People get what they feel they deserve. I think it's a shame when people punish themselves for no good reason. Not that they only punish themselves; everybody loses. But what do you care? You think it's you against the world."

"I don't know about that. I mean, we could meet again just to see what happens."

"Here," the doctor tore the top piece from his pad, handed it to Garol, and walked into his office. "We could meet in five minutes," the doctor said, looking over his appointment book.

"What? You want me to just sit here, take a little intermission or something?"

"No, go to the other side of the gate. Wait for a minute, then come back and knock on the door. Like a normal patient visit."

"Seriously?" Garol asked.

"Yeah, and don't be late."

"So what's this?" Garol said looking over several drawings the doctor had made on his sketch pad of a guy wearing a body cast doing an assortment of activities.

"I looked at your x-rays and your whole self-concept is bad. Not one positive thing. So I drew you some positive situations to make you think about all you are capable of. I call it visual focusing. It's no problem; I'm a bit of a novice cartoon artist." He beamed. "It's just something I do for my patients."

The doctor had created five sketches of what looked like a giant marshmallow playing softball, helping an elderly woman across the street, speaking to an audience, holding a woman in his arms, and laughing with a group of friends.

"This lumpy thing is supposed to be me? I don't get it— am I supposed to run out and do these things? What the hell is this?"

"I don't expect you to run out and do those things, but over time, yes. You have to see changes and want them before you can make them. Fill the negative with positive. We'll discuss it more at your next appointment." The doctor put a hand on Garol's back and led him to the door.

Garol walked down the steps and out the gate. He thought about leaving, but just stared into the woods for a moment before he turned around and headed back to the house. He was hoping the woods would give him some peace of mind, but he kept repeating, "This is ridiculous."

He walked through the gate head down, crossed the walkway and climbed to the door. He turned the handle, but it was locked. A sign read: THE DOCTOR'S OUT. GONE FISHING.

Garol tried the handle again, but it was still locked. The lights were off in the parlor window. There was no sign of the doctor. Garol continued to look, his face pressed against the glass. A few minutes later, he gave up and headed off. On the other side of the gate, he looked back once and noticed the curtains move slightly. He kept walking.

God Sends Meat, the Devil Sends Cooks

ON THE WAY HOME from dinner, Whirby explained to Toby, Jimmy and Garol the importance of a leader emerging to coach the softball team. Garol lagged behind, mulling over a much more important topic: the conversation he'd just shared with Sara. It cycled in his mind, a slice of time he didn't want to leave. Tonight was the fifteenth dinner since Sara first raised a utensil to his mouth, and, prior to this evening, all their talk pertained to food. The pressure to attract his beautiful helper grew as each meal came and went. The longer he waited for magical words, the less likely it seemed they would come.

Convinced the pressure of their first conversation was affecting his ability to perform his managerial duties at work, Garol had decided tonight had to be the night. He was out of practice. Clueless, he decided to break the barrier with the dream he'd had the night before.

"I had the weirdest dream last night," Garol had said, his tongue wrestling a piece of lettuce caught in his teeth.

"Do tell," Sara said.

"I was at a bar...Have you seen that picture in the doctor's office with the four aliens?"

"I don't remember it."

"No? It's on the wall," Garol said.

"Doesn't sound familiar."

"Oh," Garol decided to stop.

"So what happened?" Sara asked.

"I was sitting at the bar with three of them and the fourth was the bartender. Every time I'd ask for a drink, he'd pull out a little rubber mallet and bonk me on the forehead."

"On the cast?" Sara asked.

"No. I don't think I was wearing the cast. Was I? I couldn't see myself. I don't know."

"These are your friends?" Sara asked.

"No."

"Just drinking buddies?"

"No. No, I'd never met them. I don't think they're real. If so, they aren't from America. Geography isn't really my thing. Actually, the picture was the first time I'd ever seen them. It was like one of those paintings where the dogs are playing poker," Garol said.

"I like those. I like the one where the hippo, giraffe, raccoon, kangaroo and gerbil are swimming against each other in the Olympics," Sara said enthusiastically. "That one is crazy."

What the hell? "That's great," Garol laughed along with her, not wanting to spoil their first real conversation.

The build-up to this conversation had been so stressful that Garol felt he'd lost a hundred pounds of stress with the laughter.

Garol rode the wave of the good feeling and asked, "What do you think it means?"

"Maybe they were trying to tell you to stop doing something," Sara said softly.

"Oh," Garol shut the conversation down.

When the four of them reached their house, Garol noticed a large blue bag resting on the porch, directly in front of his door. Jimmy and Toby excused themselves and Garol and Whirby walked up to take a look.

"What the hell is this?" Garol asked.

"It's a mailbag."

"What's it doing here?"

An envelope taped to the top of the bag had the name Sam written on the front. Whirby leaned over and picked it up. He handed it to Garol, but Garol held up his cast mitts.

Whirby pulled the letter out of the envelope and asked, "Would you like me to read it?"

"Please," Garol answered.

> Sam,
> You are a real lifesaver. Everyone, including myself, was completely shocked when you volunteered to deliver the mail. This type of position is not so easy for someone so new in town. You'll do great.
> Thanks again,
> Mary

"No, I didn't. I'm not delivering this shit. Who's Mary?" Garol said loudly.

"Mary is the Work Schedule Coordinator. You must have told her you would deliver the mail at the town hall meeting."

"The woman who talked without a microphone? I remember her looking at me and moving her mouth. That was it," Garol said, annoyed.

"You must have given her some reason to believe you wanted to do the job."

"I agreed so she'd stop talking to me. So everyone would stop looking at me."

"Agreeing is agreeing," Whirby said very seriously.

"I'm not delivering this," Garol bent over to look in the bag. "There must be four hundred letters in here."

"You're still new in town. People get upset around here when you volunteer for something and back out," Whirby said. "You should think about that."

"I didn't volunteer, I was coerced." Garol clasped five letters between his mitts and dumped them on the porch. Garol didn't see any house numbers. "Do you recognize any of these addresses?"

Whirby picked up the letters from the porch and read,

> "Betty Bear,
> Blue house on the corner with the wonderful lilacs"

"What? Where's the address? How do I find that?"
Whirby read the second address.

> "Kim,
> The home of the best apple pie in town"

"Is this for real? How would I know who makes apple pie around here? I didn't think there was any. She should bring it to the cafeteria. That food sucks."

"Maybe she'll give you a piece," Whirby said.

"No. I'm not walking around asking people if they can tell me where the best apple pie in town is for a sugar free apple pie shake."

Whirby read another.

> "Pumpkin Patch Patty,
> With the chatty little catty"

"Chatty catty. This is too bizarre. Something's wrong with this," Garol said.
Whirby read the fourth.

> "Santa,
> The ice is cold, I've been told.
> To live without you, I would need to be so bold
> My wish list"

"Santa? Really?" Garol said, looking into Whirby's eyes. "These people are nuttier than I thought. Who used to deliver the mail? Why me?"

"He left a while ago, and you volunteered," Whirby said.

"He left? How?" Garol asked.

"Here's one I don't recognize," Whirby said then read the fifth envelope,

"Garol
Horoscope:
Venus has gotten to your head
But your head is in Uranus
Don't think with your heart"

"I'm not familiar with Garol," Whirby said

"Who cares? They're all crazy," Garol said, grabbing the letters from Whirby and tossing them back in the bag. "This is completely insane. How am I going to find these people? No one here needs mail. The whole town is only six square miles and everybody sees everyone, every day. There's no need for this shit."

"People around here love to get letters. Sleep on it," Whirby suggested. Then he motioned to the chess board, "Things are getting interesting; the Castle seems restless. Right now he's positioned next to the opposing female bishop, but I've got a bad feeling her beauty is flustering him. He could attack her, but I think he's blinded by love and a bit rusty, so I wouldn't expect that. He's too fidgety not to move; the problem is, his only safe move would pin him next to the opposing horse. He'd be at an angle, of course; no immediate threat, but the horse is smart. Something tells me if the horse hitches his reins to a saloon, the Castle will saddle up next to him. What could happen after that worries me."

"Good luck with that." Garol stared at the mailbag.

Garol felt he'd seen enough to confidently decide that he wasn't going to deliver the mail. He put the bag strap around his neck, picked it up and walked into his apartment, dropped the bag and sat on the couch to weigh his options. He thought about taking the bag down to The Man at the post office and explaining, but feared The Man would say something like, "Well, it's a tough situation, but why don't you just take one for the team and deliver the mail this time?" Garol knew he'd have to completely refuse in order to get out of the job. Once he'd done it, it would become permanent. *That's the way shit jobs work. Thus the expression "caught holding the bag."*

Garol decided the fewer people involved in the decision, the better. Then it occurred to him what he must do. *Throw the bag in the dumpster. Say I put it outside so it would be ready to go in the morning and it was gone. These people will believe that— they're all nuts. I'm sure one of these lunatics wants a big bag. Maybe the land swimmer could use it as a raft.*

After dark, Garol strapped the mailbag around his shoulder and headed up the long hill leading to the dumpster in the desert, placed on the outskirts of town. On his way to making his first and last delivery as a mailman, he heard a piano playing in the distance. Behind a dense set of trees, light shot through a large window. Inside, a man behind a bar counter polished glasses. *A bar?*

"Oh thank God," Garol hooted, waiving his mitts in the air. A rusty iron gate blocked the entry into the walkway leading to the bar so Garol opened it. A sign read,

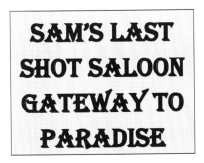

**SAM'S LAST
SHOT SALOON
GATEWAY TO
PARADISE**

Garol dropped the mailbag and made his way down the brick covered path to the door.

The bar was deserted, other than the bartender, who stood at

the other end of the bar, and an extremely large man who spilled over his bar stool and stared sullenly into the contents of his rocks glass. Neither gentleman made any sign that they noticed Garol.

Garol sat ten stools away from the large man at the bar. *How many drinks would it take a guy of that size to look that way? Sixty? Don't look at him. Don't bother him. Just get one drink and go.* A plan he'd never been able to fulfill in the past.

The bartender glanced at Garol but didn't stop polishing glasses.

Garol waited patiently, softly clearing his throat a few times, but couldn't get the bartender to ask him what he'd like. He moved three seats closer to the two men.

"What," Garol said softly and stopped himself, then, "What," a little louder and stopped himself. Then finally, "What," and, surprised how loud he'd said it, stopped and looked at the big man and then back at the bartender.

The bartender smirked and looked at the big man and said, "Looks like we've got the company of a stuttering snowman."

"I didn't know marshmallows could talk," the large man said, and the two men laughed like a couple of bullies.

"Do you have something to say, Stuttering Stanley?" the bartender said, replacing the smile with a sneer.

"What do you have on draft? I meant to say," Garol said nervously, regretting walking through those doors.

"Nothing on draft."

"Ok, a bottle of beer."

"No bottles,"

"A can?" Garol asked, confused.

"This guy wants a can," the bartender said to the large man. Then looked at Garol and said, "Tourists drive me crazy... No cans, Frosty."

"I'll just have what he's having," Garol said unable to think of anything else.

The bartender stared at Garol for a long awkward moment, then walked over to the man at the end of the bar, grabbed his drink, and walked it over to Garol.

"I didn't mean his drink," Garol said to the bartender in a panic. The large man stared at Garol, expressing that he didn't like to share, especially his alcohol.

"Hey, I'm not your damn errand boy. Give it back to him if you don't want it," the bartender looked at the large man and back to Garol and laughed, "I'd do it soon."

The man turned his entire body toward Garol, displaying his gigantic size. He looked like he'd be much more comfortable on two, maybe three barstools: one for each section of his body. Discomfort, though, looked more like the rule than the exception for him. He was the kind of big that inspired the same awe as an ocean, leaving those in his presence feeling small, insignificant and mortal.

Garol's mind emptied when the large man rose from his stool.

"I think Steve would like his drink back," the bartender guffawed.

Garol placed the drink between his cast mitts and slid it down the bar until it reached the man. "Sorry, there was some confusion. The bartender misunderstood 'what you were having' to actually mean your drink. I just wanted a drink…Of anything," Garol said quickly.

Steve stared at Garol. "You're new around here. Oh, what the hell, have a seat."

Garol put out his mitt. "Garol, I mean Sam." His heart was racing.

"You sure about that?"

"Oh, I don't know anymore," Garol said.

"Steve Atan," the large man began laughing hard. "You are new. At least you still have some idea of who you are, probably more than most of the freaks in that town. Watch out, it happens quickly. How long have you been there?"

"I don't know. I was in the hospital for a while. I've been out a month, give or take."

"I don't know. Give or take," Steve laughed hard. "I love it. I know exactly what you mean. Could be a month, a year, ten years. Who knows? Soon you won't, that's why everyone in that little town of yours is crackers."

"Crackers?"

"Yeah, nuts, bonkers, zany, out of their minds-crazy. If you don't think those people are crazy, I've got bad news for you," Steve stared at Garol.

"What?"

"Then you're crazy. As long as you can see crazy, you're sane. Once you don't realize those people are nuts, you're one of them. You do know those people are crazy, right?" Steve asked looking into what little he could see of Garol's eyes.

"I haven't met one normal one yet, other than Sara...and The Man is *kind of* normal," Garol paused for a second and added, "Annoying is different than crazy though."

"Those two are the scariest of them all. Sara? Don't let a pretty face fool you. And The Man runs the damn asylum. That guy wants your soul. I bet he's already got you lining his pockets, just like the rest. Sucker. Between the two, they'll take your heart and your soul," Steve shook his head. "You're right, annoying is different, but these people are annoying because they're crazy. You don't want to start making excuses for them. That's the first sign you're going to slip into their world."

"Slip into their world?"

"Become one of them," Steve said with raised voice.

"That's possible? I don't think I could."

"Do you think those people started out there?"

"I never thought about it. How would they get here?"

"How the hell did you get there?"

"I don't know."

"I love it," Steve laughed and pounded the bar with his right fist.

"How'd you get here?" Garol asked quietly, looking at the bar for a crack made by Steve's thunderous blow.

"It's a long story. Anyway, I'm not there anymore. You could say I was cast out...fell from the sky," Steve answered

"They told me I fell. Cast out? You mean body cast?"

"No, cast out, so to speak. You really think somebody could dress me up like a snowman and tell me they don't know what's wrong with me? Maybe you are insane!" Steve Atan pounded the bar so hard Garol almost fell off his stool. Steve then gathered himself and calmy said, "I used to be in that town, but things didn't work out. I pretty much ran the place while The Man rested on his throne. He preached about equality and virtue, but didn't follow through with me or my staff. All talk. You've probably had a bad boss before, you know what I mean. You do all the legwork and they reap all the profits. I got a little sick of it. So I took those faithful to me and started my own place out there in the desert. Since I left, that town has gone to hell. When I ran things, everyone was happy; now it's filled with nut-jobs and marshmallows like you."

"This cast is coming off soon."

"Really? Does that mean it's time to stop hiding? Will the world see you for who you really are?"

"No, that's got nothing to do with it," Garol said, still awed by the thunder bolts Steve slammed on the bar. "The computer will be up soon and we'll know what's wrong with me. Then we'll remove it, unless it needs to be on," Garol said looking straight ahead.

"It's your life, pal. You want to trust morons, feel free. Maybe that's not it, though. Something tells me you're the kind of guy that gets what he's given and sucks on it, too afraid to go against the grain. You'll fit in perfectly. I'm a pretty good judge of character and I'd be willing to bet you've been a model prisoner for a long time."

"I've never been to prison," Garol interjected.

"You don't need bars in front of you to be locked away. Many men surrounded by bars have freedom you could only dream of. Nah, you live the life of a perpetual victim. Once in a while, you get uppity and muster up enough courage to do something rebellious— which never amounts to anything more than you shooting yourself in the foot— but mostly you just sit in the corner and suck on it and blame somebody else. 'Look at me, whine, whine, life keeps kicking me in the ass, when do I get my fair shake?' Shit, the first thing you'd do with a leg up is trip yourself. You just add one more to the pile of losers in that damn town. Losers and victims to the point of insanity. What a shame."

"No, that's not me. I don't want to be here."

"Yeah, you gotta better place to go?"

"Home?"

"What happens at home? Is that where they only tar and feather you? Make you walk around in a mascot uniform? Home is where the heart is and I don't see a lot of heart coming from you. If somebody set me up in your position I'd have this town on its ear. That's heart!" Steve said and thrust his index finger into Garol's cast covered chest. "I got a feeling you were just as heartless before you got here—probably worse— but hey, what do I know? That's not my call anyway. And to be honest, I don't really give a shit."

Garol started to say something but stopped.

"Exactly what I thought. So you don't want to stay here, but you've got nowhere to go. Wow! You've got two choices: make a move or slowly lose yourself. Not that a pathetic move on your part will ensure that anything happens, but any stand is good."

"What about you? Why are you in town?"

"Well, right now I'm here to enjoy a drink."

"Can I get a drink?" Garol looked around for the bartender, but he was gone.

"Looks like he's stepped away."

"I don't understand why you stick around town."

"I'm a liberator and this place is my lighthouse. When I left town and started my own colony, I decided to keep an eye out for wayward souls. The Man has his little town, which I personally think is a prison camp. Think about it: you can't drink, smoke or do anything worth a damn. I stick around so I can get good people to safety. People that like to live life—I get them to a place where they can do that, hopefully before they're unable to make decisions."

"How?"

"I escort them to my village."

"Why don't you just go into town and get people?"

"I don't go into that town and The Man doesn't come in here. We have an agreement, but I leave my light on and trust that lost souls will find their way."

"What's the other place like?" Garol asked.

"There's people like yourself there. People that drink and smoke and know how to let loose. People don't get bogged down in stuff that doesn't matter. Everybody takes care of their wants and there's plenty to go around. Consumption. And if you want to check out, check out, nobody bothers anybody. Nobody cares about your business, nobody gives sermons or tries to change your ways. It's heaven, man, it's everything you could ask for to the power of ten."

"Wow!"

"It's unbelievable. In that little town you call home, the best you can hope for is to have your needs met. You get a roof over your head, which is nothing more than a stuffy little place with nothing to do but stare at the walls or, worse yet, read a book. A cafeteria that serves tasteless, sugar-free garbage. If you want to go somewhere, you have to walk. I meant *have* to, there's nothing in that town you *want* to do. You get what you need and that's it. And that's only sometimes. What about your medical care? You can't even get the answers you need. Awful shame!" Steve shook his head. "We take needs for granted. Wants! We focus on wants. Needs are for prisoners. Wants are for the free."

"Take me, I'll go now," Garol said beginning to stand up from his stool.

"Settle down. We'll go, but I need you to do me a favor."

"Sure, anything."

"I need you to go back into town and recruit some of those people."

"Why? We don't want any of these fools with us."

"The more the merrier. You get these people out of that town you're staying in and they'll return to normal, trust me. It's that town making them crazy and you're next, pal."

"Yeah, but these people don't listen to me. They're not going to follow me. They don't drink or smoke or know anything about fun."

"You just need to get involved and work on your leadership and people skills. But keep your wits about you and don't get sucked in. What do they have you doing?"

"I'm a project manager for a construction project and they just assigned me to deliver the mail, but I'm gonna throw the bag away. I'm not doing it."

"A project manager, boy is he lining his pockets off your back. That sucks, but deliver the mail. The walking will do you good, make you strong, slim you down. You'll look like a leader. Charisma makes people follow. People love the mailman, they love getting mail, and plus you'll be meeting everyone. You'll get popular quick. That's what we need. I got the last mailman out of there for good and he was able to coax ten people into joining us. They're happy as clams. I need you to do the same."

The bartender walked back in and said, "Ok guys, I have to close things up for the night."

"Can I get a drink?" Garol asked.

"It's a little late for that pal. You should've asked earlier."

I did.

Steve began to stand up and said, "One last thing: don't let anyone know you came by here. They try to paint me as a monster. I'm freedom, which is the scariest thing to an oppressed society run by a tyrannical dictator. Just keep things hush hush."

"How do I get them in here?"

"Earn their trust. Get them to me and I'll explain things. I can be quite persuasive. I don't lose too many once people see what I have to offer."

"When is this place open? When will I see you again?"

"I travel back and forth a lot and this place only opens for me. One of the perks of power. No need for you to worry, you'll see me again, that much I know. Once you're ready to come with me you'll have everything you could ever ask for." Steve stood up from the bar stool.

Garol got up and looked down at Steve's feet. He was amazed at how little they looked compared to the rest of his body.

Steve noticed Garol looking at his feet, "My feet? It's unusual to see a medium-sized foot on such a large man. Oh well, what are you gonna do?"

GAROL WOKE UP EXCITED and immediately joined in with Barney Beaver, "It's time to gett-getty, getty up. Go out and get the day. Just do it in your own special way."

He'd had his best night of sleep since he showed up in Silly Hollow. Life, for the first time in years, offered things worth having. Sara. A bar. Steve, a friend who offered a better place. The good feeling made him appreciate not waking up with a seemingly eternal hangover or the nagging pressure to make sales quotas and excuse why his life wasn't working. He enjoyed breathing more easily now that it had been a month since he'd smoked. Gone too was fighting the clock until he could have that first drink and forget.

With the mailbag strapped around his shoulder, Garol stepped onto the porch, where Whirby hovered over the chess board.

"Playing a game with all of your friends, I see," Garol joked.

"Friends are great, aren't they?" Whirby answered and smiled.

Oh shit! Don't encourage any weird stuff.

"Seems to be a strong buzz in the air today," Whirby said.

"Did one of the bishops tell you that?" Garol wished he'd just kept walking.

"No, not the Bishop," Whirby laughed.

"One of the other little marble guys?"

"Well, not in words, it's just that so much movement is going on, which is good, albeit potentially scary. But any action after such a long period of isolation is good. At the very least it demands outcome. Look at this," Whirby said pointing to the Castle, "Can you believe that?"

"I'm speechless," Garol said, without looking at the board, "I'm going to the front porch and get the mail ready to be delivered." Garol took a step and then, unable to resist, turned and said, "but I'd be happy to send a psychiatrist over. He'd be interested."

"Oh, just a quick look," Whirby said.

Get it over with. Garol walked to the chess table.

"Look at him," Whirby said pointing to the Castle. "See how excited he is? Almost antsy. He's charged. I've got a feeling the day will cause him to make an impulsive decision, which will get him away from the opposing female bishop. It may seem bad at first, but ultimately it will do him a lot of good. He's got a while to go before he removes the rust and cleans out the cobwebs. He hasn't even entered the attic yet, so to speak. My hunch is that the opposing horse gained his trust and got into his head. That part worries me. But this will make you laugh. Are you ready for a good laugh?"

"Should I sit down?" Garol quipped.

"The Castle's only safe move is right here," Whirby pointed to an empty square on the board. Hah! How do you like that?" Whirby put his hand over his mouth trying to suppress laughter.

"Amazing," Garol said without any inflection.

"You don't see it. I can almost guarantee you that if that happens," Whirby pointed to the black horse, "the female horse will move right next to him. See? It makes sense now, huh?"

"All cleared up, thanks…I should probably get to the mail," Garol said and pointed to the front of the house.

"Oh, I'm sorry, the anticipation of that move kills me. It seems rare, but it happens more than you'd think. Initially he'll be safe. He'll want to take her out, I can promise you that, but for reasons he won't be able to understand, she's protected, very protected. Taking her out would mean he'd be ushered off the board in an instant. Let's hope he realizes that. Even with his newfound bravery, he's still not equipped with the brawns-and-brain package he once possessed. Still too many demons." Whirby looked at Garol. "We're on the verge of something very pivotal. Play on, I say," Whirby announced, clapping his hands together.

Garol used this as his cue to leave. "Alright."

"I'm glad you decided to deliver the mail. What made you change your mind?"

"I ran into one of the pawns last night at dinner. We split a chicken and cauliflower shake. He has no arms you know. He talked me into it," Garol said, walking to the front porch.

Garol dumped the contents of the bag and sorted through the letters, hoping to organize them into different piles: one for places he recognized, another for places he wasn't sure about, and a third for the descriptions that left him clueless. Those he was able to scoot around with his mitts all ended up in the "no idea" pile. He then concluded he had no way of picking them up off the porch. He raised his arms in the air. "Why me? Why does this shit happen to me?"

Toby walked around the side of the house wearing a postal carrier's uniform.

"Toby! Hey. God am I glad to see you. Can you help me?"

"That's what I'm here for," Toby said.

Toby accounted for every letter then looked at Garol and said, "Hmmmmmmmmm."

"Hmmmmmmmm?" Garol answered back. "You might as well deliver the mail without me, I don't think I'll be of much help."

"Why would I do that?"

"It makes sense. You know where these freaks live."

"It would be quicker with two people."

"Not if one can't do anything. I wouldn't want to slow you down."

"I'll be right back," Toby said.

Toby came back with something in his hand.

"I'll put this on you," Toby said.

"What's that?" Garol asked.

"It's an apron with five slots. Each block has five houses. At the beginning of each block I will put a letter in each slot in the order that they need to be delivered. You'll take one side of the street and I'll take the other. Just clasp your mitts around the letter and drop it into each mail slot. It'll be easy."

Toby pulled out the apron. It was cream colored with flowers and hearts printed all over it, as well as the sayings, "Hugs and kisses are free," and "I feel adorable," stamped in a few places. It also had a large, red, lipstick kiss in the center.

"I'm not wearing that," Garol said with a sneer he wished Toby could see.

"It'll be good for you," Toby said.

"Good for me? I'll look like a gay snowman. Jesus!"

"It's the only way," Toby said.

"There is one other way," Garol said.

"I'm not doing your work," Toby said.

Toby tried tying the apron to Garol's waist, but Garol's belly was too large to reach around and grab the letters. Toby decided to tie it across his chest.

Garol complained as Toby tied the apron. "I look like a sissy. This is great. I'm gonna get my ass kicked. Unbelievable. I didn't even sign up for this shit. Now I'm gonna walk all over town looking like an effeminate polar bear. Unbelievable." Garol then moved on to bitching about, "Who are these weirdos? Who is Pumpkin Patch Patty? What is a chatty catty? Are there talking cats in this town? That's messed up. I'm not staying in a town where people think cats talk. No way."

Garol and Toby both cruised through the first couple of streets with no complications. Garol was able to pull each letter out of the pouch and slip them into the slots in each door.

Half way through their route Garol walked up to a porch and was startled by a voice coming from behind a screen door. "I love the mail."

Garol looked through the screen and saw an old woman smiling at him. "Oh yeah?"

"Oh yes," she went on gleefully, "I respect the mail. Very much so. I don't believe I could sit in a little envelope and be lugged around in that cramped bag all day. It would be very hot and uncomfortable. No, I would need my own personal bag, but no one would go through that kind of trouble for me. I'm just a little old lady. That's my two cents."

"It does seem uncomfortable," *you dingbat.*

"I've always thought it would be a lot of fun to walk around with all those letters. They must keep you in stitches. Well look at you, you're in a full body cast. That's much more than stitches! Anyway, that's my two cents. Look, now you've got four cents. Stick with me kid, you'll be loaded." She shot a couple of finger pistols at Garol, blew off the tips of her index fingers, and shoved them in her pockets.

"The letters would?" Garol wished he'd just said, "I have to be going."

"Yes. A letter is so full of life. Don't ya think? People write the funniest things."

"They're a lot of fun," Garol said awkwardly.

"You look so hungry. Look at all that fat on you, waiting to be fed," she said, looking directly at the mid-section of Garol's enlarged cast-belly.

"It's just the way they made the cast," Garol said defensively.

"You hardly notice it with your little sports bra."

"It's an apron ma'am. It's just to help because of these," Garol held up his cast mitts.

"Oh stop. You look adorable. You don't need an excuse to look the way you want to. Come in and let me feed you. I have the best looking chocolate chip cookies in town."

"I have to deliver the mail... I'd have to take them to go."

Garol waited while she ran into the kitchen and came back with a clear bag of cookies in her left hand and placed a cookie in his mouth with the other. Garol bit into the cookie, but not very far— it was hard rubber. He screamed, "What is that?" and spit the cookie onto the porch.

"Zero calories." The woman dropped the bag of cookies in his apron and waved goodbye. She stepped inside her house.

After delivering the letters to the last three houses on the street, he caught up to Toby, who was sitting on the curb, waiting patiently.

"I have cookies in my pouch if you want any," Garol said to Toby.

"No thanks," Toby answered.

"Oh shit," Garol grabbed Toby and pulled him down to the ground behind bushes. Garol held Toby firmly as he tried to wrestle his way free. "Take my bra off. Take my top off," Garol said over and over again.

Gladys P. Calumny ran out of her front door with a broom to see what was going on in her bushes.

"Get your hands off of him," she yelled, holding the broom high.

Garol stopped holding Toby down and Toby got to his feet.

"Now get off my property and leave that young man alone," she said swatting the broom in the air a few times.

"It's not what you think," Garol said, backing away. He was relieved to see Sara was no longer around to witness the event.

"I know your kind. Now get," she yelled.

The two of them didn't mention the incident and worked through the remainder of the late morning. Other than three hugs from strangers, accompanied by comments about his floral top, there were few interruptions until the end of the route. On the final street, Garol walked up to the driveway of a house with a large flower bed in the front lawn. From a garage behind the house, Garol heard someone call for his attention.

Garol was exhausted and his feet throbbed from the lack of cushioning within his cast, so he pretended he didn't hear the voice and continued walking up to the porch. After Garol dropped the letter in the mailbox, he hesitated, trying to think of an escape route out of view of the man in the backyard. He decided to walk across the flower bed in the front lawn. The flowers were placed tightly next to each other and Garol played a little game of Twister to keep from stepping on any of them. "Right foot next to purple plant, left foot forward by yellow flowers, right foot forward next to roses, left foot forward near other yellow flowers." Then, as if commanded by a person calling out the movements, it was, "Face first, fall forward, wiping out azaleas, roses, petunias and lilacs." He lay face down in the flowers.

"What are you doing?" yelled the man.

Garol sat up and rested his arms on his knees. Then he raised his arms a little to express he was both sorry and confused.

"You look like an idiot," the man said.

"Sorry. It was an accident."

"What are you doing in there?"

"I fell," Garol said, unsure of how to answer that.

"From the steps?"

"I think so. I can't remember," Garol said.

"Get out of there. Don't worry, I wouldn't hit a man with a floral top," the man said.

Garol got up, picked up his bag and began walking back to the walkway.

"Be careful," the man yelled. "Don't step on anything else."

Garol tried to leap from one opening to the next, cautiously, but his leaps were shorter than he intended. Each time his foot squashed a flower, the man yelled, "Watch it, you idiot."

"Look at that mess," the man said disapprovingly when Garol reached him.

Garol couldn't think of anything, so he just opened his eyes wide to say, "Shocking."

The man extended his hand to shake, "Jim Brown."

"Sam," Garol answered extending his mitt.

"Jim Brown isn't my name, it's a saying I like to use, like Jiminy Cricket, you know?"

"Sam isn't my name either."

"Bill Sniffly."

"Sam," Garol said.

"Ok?" Bill said and the two of them just looked at each other. "Come on back, I want to show you something," Bill said and started walking to the back of the house. Garol followed. In the garage Garol saw spoons of all different sizes hanging on the walls and strewn out on tables. There were spoons so large they looked like small shovels and spoons so small they looked like they were for mice.

"Pretty amazing, huh?"

"Spoons?" Garol was happy to see Bill smiling.

"Spoons," Bill said proudly. "The largest spoon collection in the world. The oldest spoon collection in the world."

"Wow!" Garol said. Worried the man might have picked up on his disinterest; he followed that up with, "That's really something. Wow!"

"Takes your breath away, doesn't it? Like falling face first in a garden," Bill laughed.

"Yeah," Garol answered.

"Can you tell me which spoon is the largest one in the world?"

Garol looked at the biggest spoon in the room and pointed.

"Yep. Smallest?" Bill asked.

Garol pointed at the smallest.

"Yes," Bill said with an impressed tone. "You know your spoons. Spoons are everything. Did you know you can trace the fall of mankind to the spoon?"

"No."

"Oh, yes. You see, it's when we got lazy. Way, way, way back, cavemen would use the smallest spoons. It kept them strong," Bill said and looked at Garol.

"It did?" Garol asked.

"Sure. It's common sense. Small spoon, you work your muscles. Big spoon, you cut out the work. Everything got too easy. People didn't work their muscles. They had too much time on their hands. They could get everything up with one spoonful, where it used to take hundreds. Double problem: muscles got weak, and too much time on their hands. People got lazy."

"Interesting." *Moron.*

"Fascinating. It gets worse. People got scared, they knew they weren't working their muscles so they got bigger bowls, and then filled those bowls. It worked for a while, until they made bigger spoons. Then bigger bowls, then bigger spoons. Now the bowls are huge and the spoons are made to keep up. Supply and demand. So now people are fat. I can tell you like a big bowl and a big spoon," Bill said looking at Garol's midsection.

"I don't like soup," Garol said, a little tired of all the fat comments.

GAROL'S FIRST DAY OF delivering the mail was over, but so too was the upbeat feeling he'd awoken with. From the beginning of the route to the end he'd been treated like an effeminate polar bear with a weight problem. Strangers accosted him, tossing their arms around him and kissing or pinching his cheeks because of the apron's statement, *Hugs and kisses are free.*

Garol lay in the tree-shaded bushes just before Main Street, unable to move his stiff muscles, waiting for Barney Beaver to announce, "It's time for a mouthwatering mid-day meal."

You have to have heart to do what I did this morning. He responded to the conversation he had with the Steve the night before.

Garol looked down and saw the apron that lay across his chest, "Toby," he said with raised voice. Toby was gone. *I can't go to the café with this thing on. I'll show him heart. I don't have heart? This whole cast comes off, now. No more aprons.* Garol stood up and began marching to the doctor's office.

"I need to see the doctor," Garol said sternly after stomping into the doctors office.

"Don't you look adorable?" the receptionist said.

"Just get the doctor."

"Sir, drop the attitude. Can you tell me what the visit is regarding?"

"I'll tell the doctor."

"Grumpiness," the receptionist pouted her lips mockingly.

"Get the doctor," Garol said.

"I still don't know what it's regarding."

"My body cast. I want it off immediately."

"Ok, I recognize you now. Do you know that the average customer complains about an incident 1.3 times? In customer service, we assume that people will go away if we don't give them what they want. But you, sir, keep coming back as if we owed you something. You act like you are entitled. Like you have rights. What is it with you? It's people like you that make people's jobs difficult. Is that your aim? To make people work? To keep people accountable? What is it with your obsessive compulsive need to make people accountable? You are like a talking parrot." The receptionist began bobbing her head up and down like a bird, "Are you accountable? Are you accountable? Be accountable. Garol wants a cracker," she opened her eyes wide and stopped speaking.

"What did you say?"

"Accountable," the receptionist said softly.

"No. Who wants a cracker?"

"I don't, if that's what you are inferring," the receptionist said, her attitude back.

"The name. What name did you say?" Garol said pointing his cast mitt at her.

"I didn't. I said carrot or a cracker. You know like the bird, carrot or a cracker, baaawwck, carrot or a cracker, baaawck? Polly wants a carrot or a cracker. Sorry, I just get so nervous when I flirt," the receptionist said, and smiled her cutest smile.

Garol decided the best he could do by questioning her about his name would be to prove himself a liar.

"You must have a thing for snowmen," Garol said.

"Well yeah, the really rugged ones. Who doesn't?"

"Good luck with that. I'll find the doctor myself," Garol walked past her.

Garol walked down the hallway as if he worked there. The doctor's office was open and Dr. Jergens sat at a desk with a tube next to his ear that extended four inches above his head.

"Doc," Garol said tapping on the door.

Startled, the doctor swung around in his chair and said something far too muffled for Garol to interpret.

Garol noticed the doctor was breathing into a snorkel and had been looking in an empty fish bowl. Garol stood silently, taking in the peculiar sight. He waited for the doctor to take the snorkel tip out of his mouth and repeat what he'd just said.

The doctor left the snorkel tip in his mouth and began speaking a muffled incoherent, gibberish.

"I can't understand you." Garol motioned to his own mouth.

The doctor repeated himself.

"Take the piece out of your mouth," Garol said annoyed.

"Sorry," the doctor said after pulling the snorkel tip out of his mouth. "I've actually never told anyone that before. I hope you can keep that between us."

"How's the computer coming along?"

"Honestly, I've been too busy to check. Let's go see."

The two of them walked into the computer room and saw it was empty. On a table in the center of the room, the hard drive had been opened up and was lying on the table in several pieces. Also, there were four magnifying lenses of various sizes stacked on top of each other.

Just then, the tech from the Jock Squad opened the door and walked in.

"We stopped by to see the progress. Looks like things are really coming along," the doctor said.

"I think I'm getting closer," the tech said enthusiastically. "Have a look through this," then held up a magnifying lens above the main part of the hard drive.

The doctor walked over and looked through the lens, "Wow! Amazing!" He then looked at Garol with wide eyes and shook his head up and down.

Garol looked away.

"Yeah, well just because we know the problem doesn't mean we're out of the woods yet. We still need to find them and communicate, but at least we're on the right path," the tech said.

"Find?" Garol interrupted, "Are you looking for a who or a what?"

"Excellent question," the doctor interjected.

"Huh?" the tech asked Garol.

"Another great question," the doctor remarked.

"Are you looking for a thing or a person?" Garol asked.

"Can't be sure they're a person, but definitely an intelligent life form of some kind. They may have human features, but are obviously very small and don't speak English. Which...well, a lot of humans don't, but...well they probably speak one of the many computer languages, but no one around here does. Without being able to let them know we're here as friends, we can't gain their trust to find out their problem. We need to let them know they have no reason to fear us. The concern is that until we make communication, they're going to stay hidden under any one of the many surfaces in the hard drive. So now we just need to find someone who speaks COBOL, Pawn, or Pascal, or whatever they speak, and make contact. Unfortunately, that's not the only problem. As you see, they're unwilling to come out. This leads to the possibility that they'll starve to death. So, we may be working with a very small window of time in which we can communicate. But we've been working hard. I have a partner who may have learned the universal language for the phrase, 'Come out— we mean you no harm.' We can only hope they trust us. I imagine they've been burned before."

"So you haven't seen them? I thought I saw one of them. I actually thought he was waving a white flag," the doctor said very seriously.

"That would be remarkable. Maybe. I just know they're scared to death. Poor little guys."

"Oh God!" Garol's body tightened up. "So let me get this straight. You aren't going to be able to fix the computer until you can get in touch with the little people hidden somewhere in the hard drive? Which you may never be able to do because they'll probably starve to death? If you make contact with them, what would you hope to achieve?"

The doctor picked up a magnifying lens and said very softly, "Come out little people, we mean you no harm." He waited a second for a reaction and then said, "Wump-wump-wump-wump-wump." He waited briefly again and quietly, placed the magnifying lens on the table, and whispered, "I hope I didn't offend them."

"Please, just to be on the safe side, let's not refer to them as little people," the tech said seriously. "We can't forget the possibility that they understand everything we say and would be very offended to be stereotyped as people. So let's refer to them for now as a height challenged life form. Or a super-special little life form. But yes, to answer your question, then we could ask them what was wrong with the computer. It's always best to go to the source," the tech said, smiling and winking at Garol. A wink, Garol noticed, the doctor saw as well.

Garol recognized the wink as a symbol that he and the tech were in on a secret together. "Oh no. No, no, no. Do you see what is going on here?" Garol said to the doctor.

"I do," the doctor said, looking at Garol's apron. "I'm going to leave you two alone. Take all the time you need. I don't need to know anything," he left the room, closing the door behind him.

"No, you've got it all wrong," Garol yelled to the doctor's back, then looked at the tech. "You need to figure out what the hell is wrong with that computer and fix it. I want some answers. I mean it. I'm not wearing this thing forever. Get that damn thing fixed or I'll stick you in there," Garol said waving his cast mitt in the air above the tech before heading to the door.

Garol tried to get his cast mitts around the door handle, but couldn't get a grasp and they repeatedly slipped off.

"You're no different than me," the tech said

"Huh?" Garol said, still trying to work the knob.

"You're no different than me. You know if you get that cast off you'll have to start working. You don't want that. Hell, you've got it made around here. You have a place to stay, food to eat, no pressure to work. You can do whatever the hell you want. You get that cast off and who knows? Maybe they send you back to your dead-end life. You go back home and go from dead end job to dead-end job, drink yourself away every day. You barely exist. Shit, you'd better hope I don't get this computer fixed. Think about it, sportsman. Quarterback. You get that thing off and you're back barely struggling to make sales quota. Not getting laid. Living in the past. If you really wanted it off, it'd be off. You know that as well as I do. Then again, I could be wrong…about you knowing it, that is. I doubt that truth is your forte."

"You're out of your mind," Garol said, still facing the door.

"Ok, jock buddy. That cast to you is this computer to me. We're on the same page. I got a degree in bullshit, too."

"I'm not your buddy. You don't know shit about me," Garol said, and gave up on trying to open the door and knocked loudly.

"Come in," he heard the doctor's voice say.

"Doc?"

"Yes. Come in."

"Doc? I can't. I am trying to come out."

"Oh! I'm sorry. Come out."

Just then the tech's hand reached around Garol and opened the door. Garol walked into the hallway and startled the doctor, who said, "Oh my God, you scared me."

"Look, you're gonna take this cast off me. I'm sick of it. Unless you can tell me what's wrong with me and why I need to wear it, you have to get it off me."

"Obviously, you need it. You wouldn't have it on if you didn't need it. No one just wears a cast. Casts are annoying."

"No shit! What's the worst that can happen if you take it off?"

"I don't know. Maybe you could disappear, or just crumble to the ground. You might be jello in there. I really can't say."

"I want a sane answer."

"Anything is possible. I mean, I can't see any part of you. Maybe you aren't really there. Or maybe you're there, but you're in a Jello form. Haven't you ever heard of a Jello mold?"

"I don't think that's gonna happen. I'm pretty sure I'm in here."

"Ok. What if we just chose one body part and took that off? A trial to see how things go."

"You mean to see if I'm jello?" Garol asked, but he was thinking about what the technician had said to him. *Maybe I don't want the cast off. Maybe I don't really want to leave, just yet. What if they just sent me away? I'd have to get a job. Doing what? The last I can remember, my net worth was only $600. That wouldn't last very long. I probably would start drinking again.* As much as Garol liked the idea of a smoke or a drink, he had to admit it was nice not being a slave to those demons. He had wanted to quit for quite some time, but could never take the first step. He felt healthier now, and as bad as the food was, he didn't have to prepare it or pay for it. Dinner used to be fast food burgers, a coke and fries. That only made him feel good while he ate it.

"Yes, but don't think that just because we successfully take off a piece today, you aren't Jello. We could take the mitts off and you could look fine. Possibly, the Jello hardened because you have been in a mold for so long. We'll just have to see how things go for a while."

"Have you ever seen anything like this before?"

"Well, not seen, but read about. It happens much more than you think. 'Bodycastjellomoldification' I believe is the clinical term. I have probably read about this condition thirty times," he said, gesturing to a much-bookmarked science fiction novel, *The Adventures of Jello Man.*

Garol had been extremely skeptical that he could either disappear or turn into Jello. But now, as they considered removing a part of the cast, he became nervous. Something had to change, though. He was tired of being in the cast. Walking wasn't that bad; he was getting good at it. He could pivot like

111

no one else. In fact, he believed that with the cast, he might very well be the best true pivoter on the planet. Hands down, he was the best pivoter in town. His balance had gotten to the point that he could pull one leg up around the other knee and spin like a figure skater.

Garol gave special consideration to which body cast part to remove. There were really only three choices: the feet, head or hands. The feet weren't really that bad, now that he had gotten pretty good at maneuvering with them. *I might trip and fall in a watered garden, but who's to say I wouldn't trip with shoes on? Maybe I can just get some traction added to the bottoms. Not on the balls, just the tips. A little brake. I'll have to check into that while we wait to see if whatever body part I choose turns into jello.*

The second option, the head, Garol wasn't quite ready to remove. *First of all, why take a chance that my whole face disappears, or, worse, turns into jello? Either way, game over. I don't think I could do much without a head.* On top of the slight possibility that his face might just be gone, Garol wasn't sure he was ready to reveal his face to the town. *What if someone recognizes me? After all, I have been in the paper several times, albeit a long time ago, for football. I was even in three seasons of college football programs. You never know.* Plus there was an advantage of being hidden behind the mask. It gave him a feeling of comfort. No one could completely tell his reactions. He was somehow able to fit in better. For a second, Garol wondered if the head part of his cast were removed, would everyone see just how crazy he thought these people were. *Maybe I should hold off on the face?*

Garol considered other sections. The chest area wasn't a hindrance and removing only that portion would do no good. There would be no reason to remove the legs or arms if his feet or hands weren't free. It would be a little like removing his pants first in a game of strip poker. He wondered about removing his pelvis section, but he was getting pretty used to not using that region. Plus, it could be really frustrating to have that section available while his mitts still shackled him.

112

Garol thought about the mitts. *What would be my excuse not to work? Maybe I could wear a splint or something during the day. Possibly we could put hinges on the cast so I could put it on and take it off? Just to keep the jello at bay? Not because I'm lazy. No more sucking my food through a straw.* Garol decided the hands were the best choice, but then he remembered Sara. *Will she still feed me? Probably not...I'll just have to ask her out...Can I do that?...Of course, but maybe she isn't going to date a marshmallow.* Garol thought about the apron he was forced to wear while delivering the mail. *Oh, God!* Not to mention relying on Toby to fill his apron pockets at the end of each block made him feel like an invalid. *The mitts have to go.*

"So how long do you think it will take before we know if there's a problem?" Garol asked the doctor.

"Well if you're not in there, we'll know right away. If you're Jello, it may take time before it seeps through your pores. This is a very *rare* condition. I would say you should probably stay away from Jello or pudding until we at least know for certain what the problem is."

Garol felt nervous about the possibility of finding out he either didn't exist or was a big ball of Jello. *Pudding?...* he hadn't even considered pudding. He took a deep breath and said, "Remove the hand mitts. We'll just do one at a time."

Dr. Jergen's took out his cast removal kit and cut off Garol's left hand cast mitt. He cut the mitt perfectly down the center all the way around. Garol was relieved to see his hand was still there. He held it up and the doctor felt it all over to see if there were any traces of Jello. There wasn't, and they both gave a huge sigh of relief. Dr. Jergens took off the other cast mitt.

December 21st
A Bridge to the Past

AGAIN GAROL RECONSTRUCTED HIS memory trying desperately to build a bridge between Baltimore and Castland. The last day he could remember was December 21st, and it started off when he pulled into the parking lot across the street from his office building. Just before the street, he looked down at the old man and his dog resting against the chain link fence.

Garol handed the man a zip-lock bag with a cream cheese-topped bagel, then pulled out a piece of cheese from his pocket, bent over and held it out for the dog. The dog snatched the large chunk and bobbed its head, chewing and working the clump down its throat. Garol interpreted the head bouncing as a gesture of appreciation.

"Enjoy it, buddy," Garol said, feeling a tinge of sorrow because in merely a few seconds he'd checked off his whole Christmas list.

Wanting the festivities to continue a little longer, he dipped in his wallet and put his fingers around a dollar bill, but paused and looked at the twenty dollar bill behind it. Garol knew his boss and one time best friend, Mike, had left him a note stating he wanted to meet with him today. Garol had a strong suspicion he might never be back this way again. He pulled out the twenty dollar bill and handed it to the man.

The man said in a raspy voice, "Bless you. Oh, bless you."

"Merry Christmas," Garol said and pet the dog's head.

Garol's brief reprieve from life disappeared when he turned his attention across the street and read the sign above his office building with the printed company name. Garol's eyes usually avoided the sign. There was too much shame in his association. It was too eye opening. Too long of a measurement to show the depths he'd fallen.

As Garol crossed the street he examined the dismal condition of the sign, alarmed to see how much it had eroded since he'd last looked. It was supposed to read, "Bentro Office Furniture," but there were too many letters missing for anyone to know exactly what the hell happened inside those walls. The sign now read, "entro O fice urnitu e," on top of a fire red background, that had large chunks stripped by weather to reveal a charcoal backdrop. The sign now seemed to jump and dip like flames. Garol then looked down to the dirty tinted black windows of the office building entryway. *"entro O fice urnitu e"* he said aloud several times on his way to the front door, as if he was deciphering a bumper sticker of a Greek slogan, and answered, "Entering the fires underneath," as he opened the door and walked in the building.

Garol closed the door to his office, leaned against it and let out a few anxious breaths until his heart slowed down. His rapidly increasing anxious demeanor was heightened by the upcoming confrontation with Mike and he was relieved to reach his office unseen. He hung up his coat and looked out the window at the man and his dog.

Garol glanced at the clock. The hands of the clock lay flat at the 9:15 position, perfectly reflecting Garol's disinterest in the hours ahead. A day of waiting. Waiting for Mike. Waiting for five o'clock. If he were still an employee at five he would be an employee at Bentro at least until the new year as operations shut down for the holidays. But Mike wanted to meet. And it had been a long time since the two spoke. Spoke as anything other than boss-employee, that is. It had been at least a year since the awkward interrogation at Mike's house during supper. A snooze fest with no booze in the house and a lot of uncomfortable conversation and long silent moments.

"So what are you doing with yourself these days Garol, we never see you," Mike's wife Jan asked, while Mike waited breathlessly as if the two were writers acting in their own poorly written caper movie. Garol assumed while they were hiding the alcohol on his drive over that they ran through their lines together, "You ask him what he's been up to honey. He'll see it coming a mile away if I ask." Jan answering, "Ok honey, but make sure you act natural when I say it." Then embracing and saying, "Together we'll get to the bottom of this."

Garol answered by spilling his milk, literally, all over the table. A nervous response that turned out to be the best answer he could've ever given. A sudden commotion that led to them rushing to clean up the mess and he himself. The perfect distraction to ease an uncomfortable situation, induce genuine laughter and buy time.

"So how do you spend your time these days?" one more attempt by Jan during dessert, but this time Mike glancing away. Too obvious.

"I go around ruining dinners."

And once again later while looking through photo albums.

"I've already spilled the milk, don't make me spill the beans?" Too much time to prepare. Too easy. And by that time he'd won them over anyway. Allowed them to believe what they wanted to believe. He's here. He's loose. He's sober. He's looking at pictures and laughing about the old times. And then a picture of Beth appeared, and it was them that were on the hot seat; nervous and apologetic.

A great time to leave. "Well, thank you for a wonderful evening. So much fun. We have to do this again, soon."

"Our home is your home, Garol."

Garol standing at the door underneath a sign that read, "If you have a heart, you always have a home."

On this Friday before Christmas, Garol waited like a prisoner in his cell for the jury's decision. There was no question he was guilty.

The questions now were: What does the prosecution know? And what will the sentence be? A reprimand? Possibly. Firing? Likely. It all depended on the evidence.

His production had trailed off significantly in the last year. Part of it was the economy leading to company cutbacks. Part of it was competition, old customers going to the box stores. Part of it was how tired he'd become. And all the "No's." "No's" that became the only answer he heard, the only answer he told himself, the only answer he believed. No's shot in from the outside, like arrows, or tiny pin holes in a boat that eventually become the whole because the vessel no longer sustains the ability to stay above water, choose its direction, outcome, destiny. No's that evolved into dont's and cant's. "You can't do this anymore. You don't have what it takes." Each one affirming he's a puppet in a tragedy play.

The fall took time, but the crash came quickly. He could remember when his crime started. A week into his new territory. A new area assigned to him due to his complaining about the stagnant sales region he'd been floundering in. Complaints he'd made to excuse his lack of sales and buy himself time until his mind was right again.

He'd planned to begin the day by visiting Paladium Office Park. Walk in to each of the twelve businesses inside, acquaint himself, gather information and leave his card. Hung over and tired, though he sat in the parking lot, and pulled the mirror down to practice, "Hi, I'm Garol Schand with Bentro Office Furniture and I just wanted to stop by and introduce myself. I was wondering where you get your office furniture? And who makes those decisions?" He spoke in an auto pilot monotone while examining his stressed complexion and fat cheeks. Then pinched his expanding belly, feeling ashamed of the fat furniture salesman he barely recognized.

"Office furniture. Who gives a shit?"

"Hi, I'm Garol Schand, a fat, pathetic slob with my whole life behind me and I'm going door to door to let people know that I have the worst job in the world. And I was wondering why life turns out like it does? And who makes those decisions?"

Garol sat in the parking lot for an hour looking at the building. The night before at Sam's Bar he'd convinced himself that sales was a numbers game, that no's weren't personal, and his routine was rehearsed to the point he could do it in his sleep, so he didn't have to stop drinking at ten, eleven or twelve. But as he looked at his reflection everything seemed personal and that big office building was a 'no' factory waiting for him to go down its production line, each office a station to stamp rejection on his forehead.

Garol wrote the names of each company down on his cold call sheet and wrote under the first entry, 'Talked to Stacy. Told her about Bentro Office Furniture. She told me Alice Martin is the office manager and makes those decisions. Said Thursday mornings are the best time to reach her.' There was no rejection in filling in false names. He filled in the rest and pulled out of the parking lot.

At the same pace Garol's professional career took a nose dive his expertise at hiding soared. He dragged himself out of bed every morning and stuck to the same routine of going in for a few hours as though he were still organizing his day. Then left the office to work his territory, where he parked on some side street and slept, if he could. Always he headed back to the office around three thirty to wait out the remainder of the day and be available, to show he had nothing to hide.

A surge of nervous adrenaline raised Garol in his chair and he dug into his suit pocket for his cigarettes and lighter. He plucked one from the pack, lit it, and picked himself up and walked to the window, popped it open, took a drag and stuck his hand outside. It wasn't raining at the moment, but it had the feel of a rainy day and it was cold. He looked at the old man and his dog huddled together with their backs against the chain link fence, facing him. The rising cigarette smoke, mixed with the bleak weather and vacant building behind the parking lot made Garol think of Eastdale, where he grew up and the constant rising factory smoke. Garol raised his hand and positioned it as far as he could to the right and out of his sight, to block the vision.

The man waved a hand.

Garol smiled because it was the same hand move to block thoughts of Eastdale, in early October, that made Garol realize the man could see. For the first month the man and his dog came around, Garol thought he was blind. He wore sunglasses and always had a hand on his dog. Due to his assumed blindness, Garol felt free to study him, like a mysterious work of art. On his way into the office he slowed his walk and sometimes stopped and stared directly at the man.

The man's physical appearance was full of contradictions. He was the kind of old that made you wonder if he were a hundred, or a terribly worn fifty. The type of physical decay the factories and coal mines of his hometown produced. But unlike the men he'd grown up with there was no edginess or hardness about this man. No visible anger or tightening or clenching. Instead, a constant trace of a smile and look of contentment. He had deep lines running throughout his face, like he'd spent his life under the sun, but skin that looked almost baby soft. His hair was dark and his cheek bones were high and to Garol he looked like a mix of nationalities with a strong influence of Native American Indian. 'Sitting Dog' Garol nicknamed him and thought of him at times like he were an Indian chief because it seemed he had a message. A message Garol often tried to decipher, with his cigarette held out the window, waiting for the final hour of his confinement to tick away. He wondered if he was a man that had lost everything, but Garol wasn't convinced he was a bum because his face resonated with tranquility and peace as if he'd always walked the streets without a thing to lose and he never asked for anything.

If he'd ever asked for anything, Garol never would've dipped into his wallet. Garol despised bums and it had nothing to do with the holes in their clothes or any stench they emitted;

he feared bums like zombies. The walking dead. Their presence was a frightening reminder of the course he was on, and the sight of one felt like a warning, but a cruel and pointless one, because the power to change course never equaled the fear. For a while he'd felt insulated by the thought that he drank at night, had a lease and a job to show up to, but those things only lasted because of effort, and he was aware he'd been running his life on fumes for far too long, but saw nothing to fill up with. Only alcohol to slow it down, which he used as if he were a shocked, clueless captain plugging a leak in a boat while trying to steer it upstream, to a previous port. Every morning, though, the leak returned, a little wider, and the current moved a little faster.

Too, there was envy. It aggravated Garol that essentially they were in the same profession, but bums didn't have bosses, bills, quotas, or expectations, and their product was superior. With a new set of clothes and a little training, they could do his job. But he could never sell what they sacrificed. Bums offered two dollar interactions with the divinity, laying at one's feet a karmic insurance in the form of well-being. He still had too much pride to be God's medium. It was a calling he never received, like a priest being shoved into the field without faith. Garol could only sell office furniture. And Garol reaped no benefit from a bum's commodity. He didn't want the eyes of God looking down at him. It was the reason he'd stopped going to AA. It was the third step, in which you are asked to turn your will and life over to the care of God as you understand him. The God Garol understood couldn't be trusted. He didn't have what it took to carry out a plan correctly.

Garol wondered why the man chose this spot to sit. It wasn't for the foot traffic. The building was near the end of an industrial drive and the two buildings beyond were vacant. Garol assumed he lived in one of the buildings.

Over the course of Garol studying these two he felt like the pair was something of a bridge because they offered a different way of looking at things, a calming presence that stepped over fear and allowed for the peaceful entry of tiny bits of perspective. That they had the answer, while the rest of the world was running around like rats, scared, desperately trying to feed, earn, and spoil themselves, but always missing the point, if there was one. But these two crossed over all that, disregarding the rules and the order of things. Instead they cut to the head of the line, or better yet formed their own line. As if they set up a booth at a trade show that offered the answer. Individual booths advertising how to, "Win more love," "Make more money," "Get more," "Make others envy you," with long lines of desperate people hoping to gain the knowledge to pick them up from their dismal lives. The man and his dog sitting at a booth with no sign, only a suggestion of contentment and satisfaction, offering no instruction because there was nothing to do, and it would never be something you could earn.

Garol thought the man and his dog were perfect for each other. One of those couples who stay together so long that they begin to look alike. Both of them had stringy, greasy dark and grey hair, long pointy noses and soft beaten-down brown eyes that conveyed gratitude and struggle. The dog was a German Shepherd mixed with something like a wolf, and you knew the two took care of each other. The man had a hand to receive, and the dog suggested you keep a certain distance. Their devotion to each other was unquestionable. They were bound to each other in an enviable marriage. For better or worse, in sickness and in health. And they looked like they could tell stories. Inspiring stories with meaning like the destiny that brought them together and little gestures of love along the way that made them appear as one, or two halves of the same coin.

And it was their devotion that led Garol to bring in a cream cheese covered bagel for the man and a piece of cheese for the dog. Because he wanted the two to continue. To be all right. Because there was something about the sight of the two in front of his office that made him think of Beth and himself. And although he'd come to convince himself that love was something that was given only to be taken away, these two suggested that sometimes things do work out. Garol wanted to support that, but not because he wanted God to look down and see the wonderful thing he was doing, but so he could look up in spite and say, "You didn't know what you were doing. You don't know how it works, but I do."

It was four thirty. Other than going through the drive-thru for some fast food, Garol sat in his office the whole day. He was agitated and no longer cared about anything other than a drink. He knew Mike was going to barge through his door any second. Knock and open it at the same time because he owns the place and everything in it.

Garol sat hating everything about Mike. That he'd become a family man, a company man, a man. That he no longer admired Garol for what he could do on the football field. That he looked at Garol with concern and sorrow for the losses he couldn't get past. That he acted toward Garol like he was always trying to help. That he commented on Garol's choice for dealing with his problems. That he believed Garol to be something he wasn't, anymore. Every time he saw Mike he saw the disappointment Mike couldn't conceal. The sight of Mike forced Garol's mind to bring back the good old days, but then erased them and redrew them in a way that made Garol wish they'd never happened. He hated Mike for suggesting the idea that you're too good for the way you're living your life, buddy. You're stronger than that, buddy. He hated Mike for threatening his new friend, numbness, alcohol. No future, no past. An even trade. Mike could only offer memories, expectations and a supportive hand. And Garol hated the way he did it, naively, unwittingly cruel, like offering a walking stick to a legless man, with good intention.

A knock came on the door, and before Garol could answer it, his door swung open and Mike walked in and tossed three months of cold call sheets on Garol's desk.

He glared at Garol sitting on the ledge with a cigarette dangling out the window and said, angrily, "Sorry! Is this a bad time?"

PART II
It's Easier to Break a Man than Build Him Up

REMOVING THE CAST MITTS ushered in a feeling of freedom Garol hadn't experienced since he handed over his life to alcoholism. He used his hands continuously, as if he were testing out a new pair, picking up items and moving them around with his fingers or clamping them in his palms. Occasionally, he grabbed an object and dropped back a few steps, bringing the item to his ear and springing his arm forward to feign a pass to some imaginary receiver down a football field. For the first time since his injury, he thought of the exhilaration of throwing passes, quarterbacking and all sports. He excitedly told Whirby he wanted to coach the softball team. He picked up books and flipped through their pages, even stopped to read three quarters of a page in *The Weight* before getting bored and marking his place with a bookmark. He began actually working alongside Toby in the upstairs apartment remodel, learning what the tools were for, when they were needed, and how to use them. He was friendly with people on his mail route and in the cafeteria. No longer did people jot derogatory remarks on his cast. Now they smiled and wrote messages of hope and kindness such as, "Freedom," "You're doing great," and "Keep it up." They showered him with compliments and remarked how handsome he was.

He kept his comments to himself and actively faked listening when Whirby discussed the most recent chess moves, which was relatively easy because Whirby had little to report since Garol's mitts were removed, saying only, "Very little activity lately. There seems to be a truce. The Castle almost seems reborn, extremely curious and protected in this stage, almost like an infant. It will be fascinating to witness the remaking of the man. This is just the beginning."

Garol's new attitude extended to the community. A sign-up sheet hung in the post office for village members in need of a handyman. Toby had been the only handyman in town and was falling desperately behind in his load. The Man raised the idea of helping to Garol. Garol balked at first, claiming he still didn't feel confident, but The Man assured him that he would only have to tackle the minor problems. He also explained that increasing his skill set could allow Garol to start his own company or work for someone else in the trades while he figured out what he wanted to do with his life. Garol eventually agreed to help.

Most people signed up had household issues that were out of Garol's troubleshooting range and therefore assigned to Toby. There was one name written on Garol's sheet: Gladys P. Calumny.

Garol moaned when he saw Gladys's name, accompanied by the problem of a clogged kitchen drain. "Have to give that one to Toby, I don't know anything about plumbing."

"You've just gotten off on the wrong foot with Gladys. She's really a wonderful person. Everyone in town is crazy about her."

"Wrong foot? Not me. She, on the other hand, used both to walk across my back after she tackled me."

"It's a quick repair, just pour that down the drain," The Man handed Garol a bottle of chemical drain unclogger.

"She doesn't belong in this town. She's not the same kind of nuts. These people swim on land and talk to chess pieces, she topples and slanders cripples. She should be moved to a different wing, don't you think? Or maybe a town where it rains all the time," Garol said, looking over his shoulder.

"She's an integral part of this town; you'll see that. Do you know where you're going?"

"I'll just look for a gathering of vultures. Yes, I've delivered mail there." Garol walked onto Main Street.

Garol was surprised when Gladys greeted him peacefully at the door, then brought him into the kitchen and quickly explained the problem before excusing herself. Garol was left in peace as he poured the Drano— which fixed the problem— and tested the sink. As Garol was ready to announce "Problem solved," Gladys emerged, wearing a bright, many-colored silk Oriental robe. She saw him to the door and stood on the porch waving, and repeating, "Thank you so much, sweetie." A small gathering of people stood in the street.

Gladys's name became a nightly fixture on the schedule. The kitchen and bathroom drains of the first two nights were the most challenging. The descriptions after her name explained "outlet cover fallen off," or "drawer knob fallen off," or, "light bulb replacement." The skill set needed to tackle her new annoyances involved the ability to pick up a screwdriver and turn it...or merely turn his hand to the right while holding a knob or a light bulb.

The routine over the next few weeks remained steady. Gladys greeted Garol, showed him the problem, excused herself, and reemerged wearing the robe. Then she walked him outside, thanking him endlessly and calling him "sweetie" as he walked away. The only thing that changed was a slightly growing gathering just outside Gladys's property.

Garol felt a sense of pride as questions began trickling in as he walked about town, as if he were the owner of a small, but busy business, such as "Going over to Gladys's tonight?" from someone that happened to see him pass by, or the occasional praise from an elderly home owner on his mail route, "You're the nice looking young man spending all that time at Gladys's. Oh, I wish I were young again."

The time he spent at Gladys's house in the evening was short, but enough to see the softer side of Gladys, and he liked it. He felt a little sorry for her having to ask for help with such easy tasks, and wondered if she wasn't just lonely. He never complained about having to walk out there every night.

He bumped into the receptionist from the doctor's office, once again, on his way to Gladys's.

"Hey good looking. You off to Gladys's?"

"Yes," Garol said.

"She told a bunch of us you've been over there screwing every night."

"I think she's lonely," Garol said empathetically.

"That's nice of you."

"I thought about teaching her how to take care of it herself, but I think she likes having someone else to do it. I don't mind."

"Maybe I'll put myself on the list," she said and winked.

"If you do I'd like a little something more than what I'm doing over there. There's not much to it."

"Are you sure you're ready for something deeper?"

"I don't know," Garol said and walked out to Gladys's.

On the way, Chuck Atwatter was out pruning his hedges as Garol walked by, and said, "Off to screw at Gladys's, I see."

"She's on my list. Apparently she liked what I did with her knobs and the way I slipped in those covers so quickly," Garol said, holding up a light bulb.

"You've got a list? Better protect yourself."

Garol thought it was nice he was concerned about using a screwdriver to put in outlet covers and said, "The trick is to go slow, no quick movements, stay in control. Then just pull your tool away when you're done. The chances of anything going wrong are slim, but thanks."

"Ok, Casa Nova," the man said

Garol walked for a moment. *Casa Nova?* Then turned around, but Chuck was out of sight. *Casa Nova? What did he mean by Casa Nova?*

The Casa Nova remark hung on Garol's mind, so the following day when he was standing in line to get his lunch and

Norman Peters said loudly from one of the cafeteria tables, "Going over to screw at Gladys's place tonight? She was telling all of us that you went over to unclog her drains over two weeks ago and have been back screwing every night. I can't help but assume you'll screw tonight. Are you?" He decided to take action and address the baby elephant in the room, before it was full grown. Garol announced loudly, with force, to everyone that heard the question, "Screwing is exactly what I'm doing over there, but that's all it's been, just screwing, and that's all it's gonna be, do you understand that?"

After lunch he stomped to the post office to check the board. When he saw Gladys's name with, "light bulb replacement," he told The Man, "This is the last imbecilic job for Gladys."

"I agree. I was going to have a talk with her. Just this one last job," The Man answered and handed Garol a light bulb.

On the walk to Gladys's house, Garol replayed the bulk of the comments he'd heard the last few days. *They couldn't be thinking me and her. No. Me and her?* A sudden feeling of nausea stopped his walking and he bent over and felt a sudden tickle from his gag reflex. *I don't think it's possible with this cast. No, they're just concerned about me and they're all odd, that's all.*

When he reached her house, he knocked once, and she yelled for him to enter. Garol opened the door and saw that she was sitting on the couch in that silk robe, applying body lotion to her leg. Garol was about to say, "Bad timing," when she said, "Perfect timing."

"This should only take a minute," Garol said.

"This feels so good," Gladys said, rubbing the lotion into her skin.

"Let me show you how to do this," Garol said, doing his best to ignore her.

"I'm so relaxed," Gladys answered, smudging her makeup with her long nails.

"Gladys, look at me."

"Anything you say. Anything at all."

"This will take care of that list. This bottom end of the bulb screws into this piece of the lamp." He screwed the bulb into the lamp and then unscrewed it. "See?" Garol screwed and unscrewed the bulb again.

"I don't get it," Gladys said through pouted lips.

"Screw. Unscrew. Screw. Unscrew," Garol said demonstrating the procedure. "Pretty simple stuff, really. Not exactly brain surgery. Do you want to try it?"

"No, I'm nervous," she said putting her fingers to her cheeks to imitate dimples.

"It's really, really easy. You can do it," Garol didn't know whether to laugh or scream.

"Too heavy. I'm a lady. Ladies don't mess with heavy construction stuff. We're interested in other things." She leaned back and winked at Garol.

"Ladies don't change light bulbs? It's really pretty light."

"Thank you, that was very sweet. I knew you thought I was pretty, but that is the first time you ever said so. Am I blushing?" Gladys asked, smiling.

"The LIGHT BULB is pretty light WEIGHT," Garol said, correcting whatever she might have heard.

"I look pretty in the light, silly. You're nervous. Well then, aren't you glad you screwed the bulb in? I actually have something else I want you to insert. I need to use your snake."

"It's impossible! I'm wearing a cast," Garol blurted.

"There is something stuck in the drain. Could you stick your snake in and get it out?"

Garol looked in the drain and saw nothing.

"Oh, never mind, I'll stick something in there and put you back on the list."

GAROL CHECKED HIS TWENTY-SEVENTH tally since his cast mitts were unshackled. The initial invigoration of freedom had faded; doorknobs were once again just doorknobs—maybe a little better, but nothing to get excited about. The thrill of learning new trades now mixed with the fact that it was still work. In the last twenty-seven days, he hadn't given any thought to checking on the computer's progress or seeing if the bar's light was on. He didn't feel any hurry to be anywhere else. The last thing he could remember about Baltimore was losing his job and then getting drunk at Sam's bar. He couldn't remember one thing about returning to Eastdale. *Why would I move back? Maybe after I got fired? It doesn't make sense. Maybe?*

Garol sorted mail on the front porch with Toby while Whirby looked over his chessboard, periodically shaking his head or commenting, "I think the truce is coming to an end. This move is a telltale sign. Sure enough, when the Castle's Bishop comes out to give him a message, it definitely means something is under way. The question now is what the Castle does with the message, if he even hears it at all."

Garol watched Toby listen intently to Whirby. The sight made Garol want to laugh, but he tensed his muscles to suppress it.

Whirby excused himself and headed inside the front door of the house.

"Never thought I'd be delivering the mail," Garol said to Toby.

"No?"

"No, thought I'd be launching touchdown passes," Garol leaned back to take a break and sip his green tea.

"Yeah?" Toby looked at him quizzically.

"I used to play football. Quarterback. It looked like I was going to get drafted in the first round," Garol said with an air of confidence.

"You didn't?"

"Not unless they forgot to tell me."

"Something happen?"

"Forget I brought it up, we got a lot to do."

"Oh," Toby had stopped sorting mail and was watching Garol.

Toby's eyes went wide and Garol turned around to see Split walking briskly around the corner of the house, wearing a charcoal pinstriped three-piece suit and carrying a briefcase. Garol wondered if there was a third brother he didn't know about, but assumed Split had just put on a suit.

"What do you say, fellas?" Split said quickly and aggressively as he walked up the porch stairs. "What do you say boss, gonna be a nice one?" Split looked at Garol.

"They all are," Garol said, referring to the constant 75-degree sunny weather.

"Not too bad, huh?" Split said, smiling.

Garol was a little worried that if he answered, the question might continue recycling, so he decided to get to the point. "What brings you out so early this morning, Split?"

"Split? No, Mr. Hill," Split grinned at Toby and Garol, then straightened his expression. "Gentlemen, I've got an idea. Yes, that's right, I've got an idea to run by you."

"Ok," Garol said.

"You see," Split rushed forward with his proposal, "I haven't had the chance to talk with you earlier, but my company has done some testing and we have been able to figure out that this here property is perfect for a pool. Yep, that's right. The test results are in. You could say the back yard perks for a pool. It sure does."

"That is great news." Garol went back to sorting the mail.

"My friends," Split paused until they looked up so he could make eye contact, "have you ever had a vision turn into a dream?"

"No," Garol said.

"Me too," Split rushed forward, "So you know the feeling of exhilaration when it comes to fruition. Trust me," Split held his briefcase in the air, "your dreams are about to be realized."

"You're gonna get me out of here," Garol said.

"If all goes right, you'll be escaping," Split said, surprising Garol that he'd paid attention. "In this briefcase, I have the plans for a place where people or humans can escape into a world of wetness and relaxation. Why and how, you ask?" Split opened his arms wide. "Same answer. I want to do dig a hole and put water in it, for swimming, see."

"Great," Garol said without emotion.

"In my possession, boys, are the plans for something I like to call a pool," Split put the briefcase on the porch and snapped it open. Then he stared into Toby's eyes, then Garol's. "Boys, have you ever been so hot you just wanted to cool down?"

Neither one of them answered, but Split wouldn't stop staring at them, so Garol finally said, "Yeah."

"Well then, boys, this may be your lucky day," Split said.

"Not so far," Garol said.

"I can feel the water. Feel the water with me. I can see you diving in, Toby. You are having fun," Split smiled and shook his head, then pointed at Toby and said, "You really love it."

Toby smiled and put his head down.

"Sounds nice, but it costs a lot of money. Not gonna happen," Garol said.

"I got a way to come up with the dough," Split said.

"Oh, yeah?" Garol wished Split could see his smirk.

"What I'm gonna do is," Split lowered his voice, looked over his shoulder, and leaned in towards Garol and Toby. "With my checking account, ya see, what I'm gonna do is write myself checks."

"Checks for what?" Garol said.

"Well, let's just say I got $400 in my account," Split leaned in farther, "Now let's just say I write a check for $400. Wow! Bam!" Split smacked his hands together. "All of a sudden I've got $800. Then the next day I write a check for $800. Can somebody give me a $1,600, thank ya lord," Split raised his hands like two birds flying away from each other, then brought his right hand down to close his nose, "Going under baby, I'm swimming."

"It won't work," Garol said.

"How can it fail?" Split asked. Toby looked at Garol disapprovingly.

"Because they take the money out of your account to give it to you," Garol said.

"I don't care where it comes from," Split laughed. Toby nodded and laughed too.

"They can only give you what you have," Garol said annoyed.

"That's all I'm asking for," Split said.

"You can't just walk into a bank and say 'double my money,'" Garol said.

"I won't say that," Split said.

"It won't work." Garol shook his head deciding to drop the conversation.

"Look, let's see if I can explain it to you in a way you will understand," Split said.

"I'm not the one that can't understand," Garol said.

"If I wrote you a check for $400, who gets the money?" Split asked.

"I do, but—" Garol answered.

"Which makes you $400 richer?" Split interrupted.

"Yeah, but.—"

"So if I write me a check for $400," Split seemed to insinuate Garol wasn't quite smart enough to figure out this very easy concept, and slowed down his speech, "it makes me $400 richer, see? Same, simple concept. Fairly basic stuff, my man." Split rolled his eyes.

"No," Garol said shaking his head in disgust, "you're way off."

"Ok, shall I explain it again?" Split said.

"They take the money out of your account. God, this is stupid," Garol said loudly, leaning against the back of the swinging bench he sat on.

"If I wrote you a check, they'd take the money out of your account? Who are you banking with?" Split began laughing and Toby joined in.

Garol gave Toby a stern look. "That's the dumbest argument I ever heard. There are no limits to stupidity around here. It's amazing. It blows my mind." Garol took his eyes off Split and tried to get back to sorting the mail, but his mind was racing and he couldn't help himself from uttering, "What a jackass. Go swim in the backyard, you freak."

"Gotta go boys, mull it over. If you want something bad enough, there's always a way. Toby, explain it to him. Take some risks buddy, you need to," Split said.

"If you want to do it, do it, but I'm not. It has nothing to do with risks," Garol stood up and looked over at Split.

Split backed down the stoops, pointed his finger at Toby, then at Garol, and said, "Let's talk later, boys...Yilmono," he said and winked at Toby, "It's a foreign sounding way of saying tomorrow." Then looked Garol in the eyes and said, "The best things in life are free, just sometimes you have to use your imagination to get them— remember that."

Toby's eyes grew wide. Garol remembered Toby saying he liked foreign languages.

"They're not free to me," Garol yelled at Split's backside.

The two of them went back to sorting mail. It took longer than normal, as Garol couldn't get focused and mumbled off and on throughout the next hour, "See ya tomorrow? As who? Backyard swimmer? Whoever this guy was? Mr. Hill? Psycho! Probably can't even swim. That stupid inner tube. Ridiculous. That guy makes his doctor brother look smart."

Every time Garol started rambling, Toby took his eyes off his work and looked at Garol, who pretended to be sorting. But if the mail can be delivered through all weather conditions, it can make it through any annoyance.

It's Too Late to Shut the Stable Door
Once the Horse has Bolted

GAROL LAY IN BED, bracing himself for Barney Beaver's song, but it never came. *Did I sleep through it? I didn't think you could.* Well rested, he decided to get out of bed anyway.

Garol poked his head onto the porch, where Whirby sat staring at the chessboard, "I think I overslept."

"It's a day off. No work today," Whirby answered.

Garol ducked inside before Whirby could comment on his chess game. *A day off? That's cool. What the hell am I gonna do?* Garol ran through his options: *Go back to bed, sit on the couch...* He couldn't think of anything else. *Why the day off? What's the occasion?* This was the first day off since his hands were free and he'd actually begun working. He hadn't given it much thought. He just woke up every day, went to the café for breakfast and either went to the upstairs apartment or delivered the mail if the bag was on the porch. Garol had spent so little time in the previous years celebrating, he'd forgotten there were holidays. Garol felt a little tense; he'd associated the word "holiday" with lonliness.

Garol was clueless to fill his time, so he sat himself in the vacant seat next to Whirby at the chess table. Garol watched Whirby study the board. For lack of anything to do, he asked, "How is the game coming?"

"You don't want to know," Whirby said, but a large smile slowly swept across his face.

Garol interpreted the smile as Whirby saying, "I knew you were interested." So he replied, "Truer words have never been spoken."

"Hell hath no fury like a woman scorned," Whirby said, and smiled again.

"That's true too," Garol threw back.

"You can reset clocks, but you can't undo events in the past."

"Amen," Garol said.

"You see where the castle is?" Whirby pointed to the white castle.

"I do."

"With his position on the board, he can be taken out by the female horse. She could easily wipe him off the board, and something tells me there's nothing she'd like to do more. She won't, because she too would be wiped out, but I think she's got a plan to make the Castle crazy enough to do something really stupid. If she's planning what I think she's planning, it just might work. If she can get him to move out of her range, well, the opposing male horse is right there. Move over here, then there's the opposing male bishop. She wouldn't have to do a thing. She stays in the game and...I hope he keeps his head. It's not going to be easy, but boy, will he come out stronger. Other than that, the castle has no moves. He can't move back because his pawns are in the way. He can't take his eyes or mind off the opposing Bishop and she seems to have her attention on her counterpart. It's a hot mess."

"Alright, well, it sounds like you've got it under control." Garol felt confident he'd feigned sufficient interest. He switched the subject, "So what do we do around here on a day off? Why is today a day off?"

"It's Mark Clark Day," Whirby said

"Mark Clark? Was he a president?" Garol asked, confused.

"No," Whirby answered.

"What did he do?"

"He was a great guy. The kind of guy who would give you the shirt off his back if you asked."

"You wouldn't even have to ask. Just a great guy," Jimmy had just walked up on the porch.

"That's true," Whirby said.

"Other than being shirtless, what did he do?"

"He was just himself. He was very comfortable in his own skin, so to speak," Whirby said.

"I guess he didn't need any of the shirts he gave away, then," Garol said, but neither of them seemed to appreciate his attempt at sarcasm, so he asked, "Really, what did he do?"

"He was just an incredible guy," Whirby said.

"Incredible. Very relaxed," Jimmy followed.

"Whatever. I don't really care anyway. I'm going to get breakfast." Garol walked down the steps and towards town.

Garol mulled over Mark Clark Day on his walk to the café. *Liars. How stupid. Who knows what they celebrate in this town, though? But nice guys don't get holidays. They should call it sap day if he's such a nice guy. Shit, I could have a holiday. I'm a nice guy. Relaxed? I am the king of relaxed. Morons. I was nice enough to listen to that imbecilic chess crap. I should have a holiday.*

After breakfast, Garol walked through town and saw that all the shops were closed. The post office door was open so he decided to say hello to The Man.

"Hey," Garol said when he saw The Man standing behind the counter, "I thought today was a holiday. Why are you working?"

"I always work. At my age, there's nothing else to do."

"You look pretty young."

The Man smiled and said, "So what brings you down here?"

"Just walking around. So what's the occasion for the day off?"

"Mark Clark Day," The Man said.

"What did he do again?"

"He was a great guy," The Man said.

"Was he a president?"

"No, but really good with people. He knew what mattered," The Man said.

"Great," Garol said, trying to sound sincere. He knew The Man wasn't playing a game with him. *Only these people would celebrate a day for someone who did nothing.*

"Any closer to getting the cast off?" The Man asked with concern.

"Who knows? The Doc is afraid it's Bodycastjellomoldification. That can be pretty serious, I guess. We don't really want to rush anything. Once you turn jello, there's no cure," Garol said, shaking his head and looking at the ground.

"I see. Other than that, things are good?"

"Yeah, everything is fine."

"The calm before the storm," The Man said and chuckled.

"What does that mean?"

"Oh nothing. Just a figure of speech."

The two men stood in a long, awkward silent moment until finally The Man said, "Whirby told me today that he has quite a chess game going on. He said the female horse will move into position against the castle today and the opposing male bishop will show the castle its face for the first time. Whirby plays some really fascinating games," The Man glanced down at his paperwork.

Garol silently watched the top of The Man's head as he filled out paperwork behind the counter. The chess comment pushed a button with him and he decided to ask a question that had been on his mind, "So when do we get paid? Should I set up a bank account? Do you give me cash or a check? Cash is fine. I'll work under the table. I don't have a problem with that."

"No need to get a bank account. I set one up for you. You'll get paid when you're ready to leave."

"Is this a prison camp?"

"No. Everyone who is here wants to be here."

"The Man? The Man? Manson. Charles Manson. Every one of his followers wanted to be there. They were in some weird little desert commune too."

"Our styles are a little different. There is no need for money. Everything in this town is free. Well, unless you want to build something. In this town we believe if you want something badly enough you'll find a way to get it done, whether it is to draw from within yourself or to motivate others with your passion. Exchanging currency erases the passion. But construction projects need to be paid for. We have to have the supplies brought in."

"Shouldn't I be able to see what you're putting in my account? Isn't that a legal right?"

"You can get free legal representation in this town."

"Oh God! No thanks. They'd probably sue me."

"Sam, you have to trust me on this one. I'm certain you'll think it is more than fair trade for your services when you leave."

"No. Sounds like you're hiding something."

"Sam, you have a place to stay, free meals, free medical care, and access to anything you want in town. The reason I hold the money in an account is because I don't want money to be the motivating force for achievement. Work's true reward is the knowledge one obtains and the happiness one feels from helping and achieving."

"Oh God, you're good. I was a salesman. I know bullshit. Money may not be the only thing, but it gets you the good stuff. The spice of life."

"Such as?" The Man asked.

"Rent, food."

"Ok, ok."

"Transportation."

"Don't need that here," The Man answered.

"A nice car. A sweet ride."

"So you can impress on the outside enough to ignore what's really going on inside."

"No. You clean the inside when girls get in the car."

"You are gallant. What else?"

"Pizza, beer, cigarettes."

"Healthy, life-enhancing choices. Unfortunately, you can't get those here. Although the café serves an amazing cheeseless vegetable pizza on whole wheat crust."

"Let me guess: that's free?"

"For community members, sure," The Man said smiling.

"A jet ski," Garol blurted out, although he had a terrible fear of water. "Braces."

"I think you have nice teeth."

"I didn't mean for me. I meant for kids. If they needed them they would need money."

"It's nice to see you are so concerned about the children of the world. If a child in town needs braces, the medical team puts them on for free."

"They'd probably put the kid in body braces, or just wrap him in barbed wire, or..." Garol was interrupted by the thought of Gladys P. Calumny. Like thunder before rain, Gladys always seemed to arrive well before he could see her, if he saw her at all. He faced the door as Gladys stormed through the entrance.

Gladys marched in and slammed a box on the counter, "It's imperative that this box goes out today. I'm not at liberty to explain the contents, but everything inside is of the utmost importance. Normally, I'm an open book, but not today. This is top secret." Gladys took her index finger and thumb and zipped her lips. "Sorry, not telling."

"That's fine, it's your business," The Man said, "but unfortunately nothing goes out today. It's Mark Clark Day. And you know that the helicopter for outside mail doesn't come in again for another five months or so."

Gladys jumped up and down and clenched her fists, "All the more reason it be processed today— it has to be on the very top of the pile when it's time. It simply must be first."

"I'll make sure it is processed tomorrow," The Man said.

"Why are we celebrating that idiot again? That incompetent boob doesn't even have to be here to ruin my day," Gladys turned toward Garol and shot him a nasty look. She folded her arms across her chest and pouted at The Man.

"I apologize Gladys, but you know the rules," The Man looked at her empathetically and said, "I'll have to have you fill out a 'send to' address slip. Excuse me," he said and walked into the back room.

Garol, who had moved up to the side of the counter to get a front row seat for Gladys's frustration, had not taken his eyes off Gladys since she burst into the room. When The Man left, she turned to Garol with a disgusted look and said in her nastiest tone, "Small world."

"Just a small town," Garol said now taking his eyes off her.

"So where is this going?" The Man asked Gladys when he returned with a "send to" slip.

Gladys handed The Man a slip of paper with three squiggly lines.

"How is your sister?"

Garol couldn't understand how The Man could tell anything from her writing.

Gladys threw her arms up in the air and didn't say a word.

The Man laughed heartily, interpreting the gesture as something funny about her sister. Garol interpreted it as "Gladys is bonkers."

"Is there some way to ensure that nothing happens to this box?" Gladys asked sweetly. Then she turned to Garol with a cold stare and said, "The light went out."

"Sounds like a mechanical problem. That's something I know nothing about."

"I don't think so. I think it is something you can fix and had probably better. Soon."

"Maybe it's time to bring in a professional. I can change light bulbs, not rewire lamps."

"Why don't you come over and change it again? Maybe the bulb was bad."

"All the bulbs have been new. It's a wiring problem. I can't help you."

"So that's final?" Gladys said out of the corner of her

mouth.

"No, you could change it," Garol said.

"You aren't coming over?" Gladys asked again, still talking out of the side of her mouth and facing The Man. "It is extremely important we make sure nothing happens to this box. Could we send a group of men to oversee it? What is your suggestion?" Gladys locked a wide smile in place and positioned her hands underneath her face to frame it.

Oh, God. Garol closed his eyes tightly to block out the sight.

"We don't have a group of men to travel with boxes. What is inside? Is it fragile?" The Man asked.

"A letter. A very important letter," Gladys answered.

Garol rolled his eyes and looked away.

"The letter explains," she stopped speaking and rubbed her hands together, "well," she turned to Garol with a look of hatred, "that," she looked at The Man with wide eyes and her cutest smile, "I'm going to be a mother soon," then fanned herself with her hand. She leaned towards Garol and buckled her left knee to show him she was fainting. Garol moved to get out of her way. She stopped and started the same motion backwards. Garol moved back to her left. She regained her balance and shot an evil look at Garol.

"That is amazing news. Isn't that wonderful news, Sam? It's been a long time since we've had a newborn around here."

Garol didn't say a word. He didn't look at either one of them. *How could that be? Who could be the father? Oh, gross. Good, he can change her light bulbs.*

Neither of them appeared to notice Garol scoot out of the post office, and he quickly cleared two shops before Gladys yelled, "Goodbye, Sam."

Garol gave a slight look over his shoulder to see if Gladys might be coming from behind for an open field tackle. She wasn't, but out of the corner of his eye he thought he saw a man standing in the clothing store window. The person looked familiar, and Garol felt compelled to stop and get a better look. It wasn't a man, but a mannequin. This made sense because it was a clothing store, but he'd never noticed it before. The

145

mannequin was tall and lean, with brown hair and brown eyes. The mannequin was professionally dressed in a black business suit, and, as mannequins tend to be, it was very nice looking. *Weird. Very weird. The hair. The dimples. The cheekbones. The shape of the eyes. Not the nose though, that's a ski slope nose, mine is broader, pointier. Looks almost exactly like me. At least when I was twenty. Could pass as my kid. Very odd.* Garol studied the mannequin a little longer and noticed its eyebrows didn't match. One of the eyebrows was large and furry like a caterpillar while the other was pencil thin. *I thought mannequins were supposed to be perfect? I guess that's why they shipped it here.*

Garol's attention snapped back to the post office when Gladys yelled, "You've made your bed, Sam, it's time to lie in it. People do what I say. You didn't. It's too late now. You're cornered. The horse got you; here comes the bishop! You're done, smartass. You should have done what I wanted. Good luck, Daddio, you'll need it."

He walked quickly back to the house.

When One Door Shuts, Another Opens

"PERFECT. ONE DOWN, NINE to go," Toby said as the two of them bolted an upper kitchen cabinet to the wall.

Garol looked at his wrist for a watch that wasn't there, then feebly attempted to wipe a brow covered with cast.

Toby noticed the odd nervous behavior and smiled.

"You never know what time it is in this town," Garol groused.

"Everything happens for a reason; what better timing could there be than that?"

"I don't agree with that. If there aren't any clocks, how come events have times attached? So everyone can be late?"

"So everyone can be on time— their time." Toby reviewed the kitchen blueprint.

"Their time? What does that mean? Time is time. You show up on time or you don't."

"Have you ever heard the saying, 'When the student is ready, the teacher shows up?'"

"Yes."

"It's the same thing."

Garol looked out the window. "I don't see what you mean," he said in frustration.

"You're always where you're supposed to be. Time has to do with choices and signs. See the signs, make the right choices, and you'll end up at your desired destination."

"Oh, God!" Garol grumbled.

"Is there somewhere that you have to be?"

"I'm supposed to be downtown at eleven thirty," Garol said hoping the conversation would drop.

Toby snickered.

"What?"

"Are you going into town for the yoga class?"

"I signed up for it," Garol avoided the question.

"Sara's teaching that class," Toby said.

"Is she? I didn't know that," Garol lied.

"Yeah, she's good. I took her beginner class, but I don't know the poses well enough for this one. You do?"

"Yeah, yeah. Oh yeah," Garol said confidently. "I was an athlete. It's all self-explanatory. Just stretching. I'm limber."

"That's good, I don't think she gives any explanation in that class. Expects everyone in it knows what they're doing."

"I don't really need anyone to teach me how to touch my toes."

The two looked at each other. Toby seemed dumbfounded.

"NO, NO, NO, THAT'S NOT THE WAY TO DO IT," a voice from the backyard shot through the window.

"Did you hear that?" Garol asked Toby.

"How do you know how it's supposed to be done? You don't do any work," another voice fired back.

"I don't do any work? I don't work? Is that what you think?" The first voice yelled.

"Well, what do you do?" The second voice shouted.

"I planned this whole thing," the first voice retorted. "Without me, this wouldn't be happening. I'm the brains. THE BRAINS. Which you wouldn't know anything about, because you're the brawn. You need both and I'm the brains, so you can't be. Do you know why?" the first voice argued.

"Oh please tell me, your majesty. But while you do, please be reminded that I'm the one holding the shovel," the second voice threatened.

Garol and Toby had been staring at each other quizzically during the exchange. Now Garol was concerned, anticipating a loud thud from the end of a shovel.

A third voice called from the backyard, "Come on, guys, knock it off. We've got work to do...You guys are friends...So what if you have different strengths? Let's work together."

"He thinks I'm stupid," the shovel carrier shouted.

"No, he doesn't," the soothing third voice answered.

"That's true," the first voice shouted.

"That's it," the shovel wielder yelled.

Garol ran over to the window and saw Split on the ground. Assuming Split had been struck by the end of a shovel, Garol moved as quickly as his cast would allow. When he reached the backyard, Split was rolling around with his arms locked together by clasped fingers.

"Say uncle!" Split groaned.

"I won't quit," the shovel holder's voice answered angrily back from Split's mouth.

"Break it up you two, stop it," the third calming voice pleaded, also from Split's mouth.

Garol jumped back as if he'd witnessed a three-car pile-up involving only one car. *Holy shit!*

The wrestling continued until Split called, "Truce!"

Garol decided to head downtown for his yoga class, walking cautiously around Split.

As Garol approached the town center, it was apparent that some type of tragedy had occurred. Something had gone wrong for these perfect little odd people. He felt a little good, because they never seemed to fret about anything, and a little relieved that not one person paid any attention to him. People stood in the middle of the street reading copies of the *Gossip* and others spoke in loud incredulous tones, "How could he have done this?" Answers would then fly back, "There must be some mistake, he wouldn't do this," or, "I bet that was his plan all along."

Garol gave some consideration to what he might have done lately that would've had people up in arms, but he couldn't think of anything. So he smiled that some other fool was on the hot seat. *About time.* He walked into the studio.

Garol saw Sara. She wore a form fitting black yoga outfit and Garol felt a jolt as the blood surged through his body. He felt completely alive everywhere except his brain, which seemed temporarily numb, null, and void.

"Here's my student," Sara greeted.

Garol offered her his hand, but no words came forth.

"So glad you could make it, Sam. I haven't seen you in so long. I heard you had your mitts removed," she said grabbing Garol's hand with hers.

"Bodycastjellomoldification," Garol said wrapped in an exhale.

Sara looked down at their clenched hands.

"It's not contagious. I really don't even think I have it, anyway. Just precaution. The cast," Garol said nervously still holding tightly to Sara's now limp hand.

Sara's eyes widened as she raised them from their hands to his eyes.

Garol released his grip.

"Ok," she said pulling her hand back, "It looks like it's just the two of us."

"Oh! Great!" Garol paused, "More for me."

"Well...you know this isn't an instructive class? This class is for those that have been doing yoga for years and don't need any instruction. I like to use this time to incorporate my own flair and style. My students find this a great atmosphere to experiment and find their freedom. Is that what you're looking for?"

Holy shit. "I just want to be free. Let it all hang out," Garol perfectly mimicked her enthusiasm.

"That's great," Sara said so peacefully that Garol wished he wasn't scared to death.

Sara led Garol into a large room. Garol stood next to her and she looked forward, addressing an empty classroom, and stated, "Let's make a row in front of me."

Garol moved in front of her.

"Ok, let's get everyone to back up a few feet so you've got some room to work."

Garol backed up a few feet.

"Lets start off with a downward facing dog," she said cheerfully.

They stared at each other.

"Ok, why don't we get into the downward facing dog position?"

Garol nodded his head and slowly dropped to one knee and then the other. He looked at Sara to follow her lead, but she hadn't moved. He leaned forward on his hands and, firmly planted on all fours, hung his head to the ground. He looked exactly like a dog facing downward. He heard Sara shuffling around.

"Feel the stretch," Sara said.

"Oh yeah," Garol grunted, facing the ground.

After a few moments, Sara instructed a Mountain Pose. Garol got up slowly, once again hoping to follow her lead. She repeated her instruction. He did his best impression of a mountain by spreading his legs wide and extending his arms out and putting them in V's to show the peaks and valleys of the mountain range.

He watched Sara as she began rocking in all directions and then started lifting her kneecaps. Sara had her eyes closed the whole time. She then announced the One Legged King Pigeon pose. Garol hopped up on one leg, thrust his chest forward and bobbed his head back and forth. Sara proclaimed, "Feel the freedom," and Garol began squawking. As she called different poses, Garol followed with his best interpretations. Finally she called out the Hero's Pose and Garol held up both hands as if he had an invisible trophy and did a victory dance. When he came to a halt, he faced Sara. Sara looked at his midsection and her eyes grew wide. A huge smile spread across her face. Garol wished she could see his smile. Almost immediately, she declared, "Ok, well that's probably good enough for the first class. Thanks to everyone for coming." She hurriedly left through a back door and closed it behind her.

Outside the studio Whirby stood in the walkway, leaning against the railway, reading a copy of 'The Gossip.'

Garol looked down and saw his orange hair. "I can barely see you behind that paper."

"This is not good." Whirby dropped the paper. "I can see much more of you than I care to-- your front door is open."

Garol looked down and slammed the door shut. "Sara!"

"She couldn't have seen much," Whirby said and folded the paper under his arm and walked in the cafeteria.

Garol followed behind at a distance feeling exposed and disoriented. As he stood in the food line and sat down to eat he agonized over when his front door must have flipped open. During the political discussion that followed between Jimmy, Toby and Whirby the only thing Garol added were sudden exasperated cringes as his mind ran through the possibilities in his yoga session and he recalled each of Sara's facial expressions.

"Don't blame yourself; I voted for him too. I think everyone did. He was so smooth."

"What happened?" Garol asked finally regaining himself.

"The mayor we just elected went to the capital to get sworn in and sent a telegram yesterday to say he's not coming back. It's all in the *Gossip*." Whirby handed Garol a copy.

"Never coming back? He can do that?"

"It's happened before, but no one thought he would do it. It leaves us in a bad position," Whirby expressed.

"Yeah?"

"Yeah, we've got no government," Jimmy threw in.

"Do we need it?"

"Yeah, hello, anarchy," Jimmy said.

"Ok. So appoint someone else."

"No one wants the job. That was what was so great about the last guy."

"He didn't run for office? He just said he wanted to do it and then he was the mayor?"

"For the most part."

"I thought you said you voted. Someone must have run against him."

"No, the election is more to ease people's minds."

Garol read the article.

Stood Up

It appears our newly appointed mayor has found better things to do with his time. The man we elected in a landslide decision, the one that created a vision for a new tomorrow, has vanished into the outside world. Leaving, of course, our hearts behind. Only mayor for a short period, he, in fact, only spent twelve hours here between being elected and boarding the chopper to the capital. So now we are left alone, but hopefully a little wiser. I think it is just hard for us to get our minds around the idea that someone would lie to us, in the form of offering heartfelt promises, to get out of our town.

–Gladys P. Calumny

A WEEK, MAYBE TWO? Garol was trying to determine the amount of time it had been since the day Gladys stormed into the post office. *It couldn't have been much longer than that.*

"Are you sure?" Garol questioned Jimmy after hearing the news that Gladys had just given birth to a boy.

"Positive," Jimmy answered.

"Doesn't make any sense. I saw her about a week ago in the post office; she was trying to get a letter to her sister to say she was pregnant. I got the impression she just found out. Her stomach was flat. Seems odd. Not that I'm an expert. I have a little experience with pregnancy, but none with babies," Garol's voice trailed off and he looked away. Then he came back with a question he was certain he knew the answer to, "She isn't married?"

"No."

"Was she?"

"Not that I've ever known."

"When did she have the baby?"

"Last night. Dr. Jergens delivered the baby just past midnight," Jimmy answered.

"Oh, God!" Garol said as disastrous visions filled his head. "This whole thing is really weird. You can't be eight months pregnant and just find out, can you? Aren't there cycles? Like menstrual, or Lamaze and stuff? Hold on, I get it: doesn't pregnancy mess with your hormones? Now I see why she was always knocking me over and acting so strange. That's why. A pregnant woman probably shouldn't be tackling people, though. I'm no doctor, but..." Garol shrugged his shoulders.

"I guess as long as she isn't getting tackled, it's ok." Jimmy shook his head and put his arms in the air to reveal he had no idea.

"Does anybody know details, like who the father is? Possibly someone that lived here well before I moved to town? I got it," Garol snapped his fingers, "It's that disappeared mayor. The guy ran. I bet it's him. Can you believe that? That's awful. Poor kid is going to grow up without a dad. What a low-life," Garol envisioned being married to Gladys and his body tightened up. "He wouldn't have to live with Gladys, but he could play a part in the kid's upbringing."

"I haven't heard who the father is," Jimmy answered.

"Does anyone know?"

"I think she does."

"Thanks. I mean, anybody else?"

"I haven't heard."

"A scandal. I wonder if she'll write about it." Garol began laughing, "Probably not. She only writes about grumpy marshmallows," Garol shook his head. "The fire starter. Hey, takes the pressure off me. I guess the polar bear outsider isn't so strange after all. Huh, huh, huh, ha," Garol forced out a maniacal laugh.

"What about the kid?" Jimmy said.

"You're right," Garol calmed down. "Can you imagine having her as a mother? Of all the places to come into. If the kid grows up to be normal, it'll be a miracle."

"I like Gladys," Jimmy said. "Anyway, the baby will be the responsibility of the town. It'll be fine."

"Have fun changing diapers. Babies aren't really my

thing— everyone else can raise the kid, it'll be fine without my influence. Probably better off, actually. I'm not much of a role model."

"I'm going over to see the baby. Do you want to come?" Jimmy asked.

Garol thought for a second and decided, *I've got to see this thing.* "Yeah, I'll go."

As they walked to Gladys's house, Jimmy said, "You could be a good role model."

"Coulda, woulda, shoulda. Life doesn't always turn out the way you think it will."

"You should be grateful for what you do have."

"I'm starting to feel grateful Gladys wasn't my mother," Garol answered and laughed.

"This is kind of ironic," Jimmy said.

"How so?" Garol asked.

"Well, Whirby was telling me earlier that the relationship between the white castle and the opposing black bishop is just being born and there is a baby born today. It just seems ironic."

Garol sighed loudly.

A large crowd at Gladys's flowed from inside the house to the porch, down the steps, and onto the lawn, pooling as a serene basin of people in the street. The whole town wanted to see their newest member. The crowd made Garol wished he'd stayed at home, but he took satisfaction in realizing that the anxiety which used to fill him in crowds didn't show up.

He couldn't fight the feeling that something strange was in the making. The crowd stopped speaking as he neared. Their bodies moved aside to allow him entrance. As he moved through the openings, he felt pats on the back and tugs at his arm, while congratulations came from several directions.

Just outside the front door, a woman Garol had spoken with several times on his mail route grabbed his arm, looked him in the eye sockets, and declared emphatically, "He's absolutely beautiful."

Alarmed and back on his heels, Garol swung his head in a rounded motion, to muddle through the confusion and responded, "That's great."

"Really, just a dream," she said again.

"I believe you," Garol answered.

Garol felt several taps on his back and slipped through the door. The crowd in the parlor stepped out of his way. Someone yelled, "Make room!" and a wave of people parted in the living room. A voice bellowed, "He's coming!" and Garol followed the path the crowd dictated. Dr. Jergens stood at the end of the hallway, facing Garol.

Dr. Jergens was dressed in a white smock and wore a stethoscope around his neck. His arms were folded in a look of professional concern, like a doctor on *General Hospital.*

"She's doing swimmingly," Dr. Jergens said, and threw his arms out in a breaststroke. "There was no treading water. She dove right in and paddled through the whole delivery. Not a splash of a bad word. Amazing. I've never seen anything like it," he said, looking deeply into Garol's eyes. "She's upstairs resting. It took a lot out of her. You can talk to her later. Go in and see the baby, he's a great looking kid. Looks like you've got a real swimmer on your hands." Dr. Jergens squeezed Garol's arm around the bicep of the cast.

Garol looked down and saw the doctor was wearing flippers. *Split?* Jimmy grabbed Garol's arm and pulled him into the room.

He turned to walk out the door, but received a pat on the back from Whirby who said, "Congratulations, buddy. Go have a look."

Congratulations? Whirby pushed him towards the cradle. A couple moved out of the way. At the cradle Garol began to feel very dizzy. He saw the baby's brown eyes, cute pink cheeks and placid smile. *THIS SUCKS. What do I do? Do I just walk out? Do I say something nice? Why are they congratulating me? I am not the father. Do they think I'm the father? My cast. I can't be the father. Oh, thank God for this cast.* Garol faced the baby with his eyes closed for a minute or two, being patted, tapped and squeezed on his arms and shoulders. He gave no reaction to the "Isn't he adorable," and, "You must be so proud," comments. The baby didn't flinch either.

Garol studied the baby, waiting for the expression to change. It didn't look real. Curiously he reached in and touched the baby's cheek, softly. *Too hard.* He kept his finger there and still there was no reaction from the baby. Garol brushed his hand in front of the baby's eyes. *No blink, nothing.* He extended his middle finger and thumb and gently put them over the baby's face, across his mouth. It was so hard. He squeezed softly. There was no movement. He squeezed a little harder, but still no movement. Garol pulled his hand away and looked around a little, then leaned in as if to smother the baby with kisses. He heard a woman say, "Oooooh, isn't that sweet?" When he felt he couldn't be seen, he knocked on its forehead. He heard two hollow thuds and tried it again with the same result. The baby was plastic. A doll. Gladys had given birth to a doll baby. *AND EVERYONE THINKS I'M THE FATHER.*

"It's a doll," Garol gasped backing away from the cradle.

"He loves it," someone called.

"It *is* a doll. A beautiful little doll. A real doll baby," someone else yelled.

Garol backed away from the cradle. He made his way out of the house, trying to ignore the, "Congratulations," and, "Here comes Daddy," comments. Once outside, Garol quickstepped back to his house.

GAROL'S MIND WAS SCATTERED. Some of it hid deep within him, while what could travelled to Baltimore and Eastdale. He hardly touched his food. Things had been going fine since he'd freed his hands; he'd come to like the town. There was a safety here he hadn't known in years. He liked freedom from alcohol, and the strength of body and mind he could feel evolving. He'd grown used to the cast and felt proud of how easily he maneuvered himself. The cast was like an extra finger or hand; although it made him stick out, it did offer advantages. It had been so long since Garol had been comfortable in his own skin, but here he never felt judged. Garol hadn't been able to view himself as handsome since Beth's passing, and any admiring gazes brought shame and guilt. Initially, others' attention to the cast was difficult to deal with, but now it seemed the attention to a monkey strapped onto his back. He kept really intrusive attention away with his victim shield, the cast armor.

But the birth of "Doll Baby" and presumption that he was the father changed that into an unexpected blitz. Even in a small town in the middle of the desert, where he had no link to any reality he'd known, the rain clouds had found him again. He sat inside his cast and wondered if there was any place left for him to hide. He'd believed he could fade into the background in this tiny village. Now that idea seemed not only threatened but gone. To fit in completely would involve admitting he was the father of a newborn plastic doll. *And then what? Raise the plastic thing with Gladys? Go insane? Was there a difference?* He was torn. What had become of his old life? From what he could remember, there wasn't one person left that cared about him. Not one.

Garol wished he could laugh. Expect the unexpected—hadn't he learned that from Beth? She'd mumbled that in the car after the doctor told them he'd never play football again. At the time, the ironic words made him smile: expect the unexpected. They took a brief intermission from despair to wonder, "How do you do that? How do you expect the unexpected?" A riddle they couldn't answer. They were kids that essentially everything had gone right for. They determined that you couldn't expect the unexpected, because once you did, it was no longer unexpected.

The riddle stuck with Garol for the next eleven months, but any amusing part of it vanished. Six months later came Beth's pregnancy, the second unexpected strike. He finally answered the puzzle when Beth pulled out of the driveway in a huff after another stress-related argument. Garol watched her chuck items into the car and storm away to stay with her parents, expecting her to call after she'd cooled down. Never expecting the phone call to come from the police. With the third strike he'd finally solved the riddle: expect the unexpected and only the unexpected. *I could've handled never playing football again. I would've been fine with Beth. I definitely never would have been here.*

So why was this unexpected news so upsetting? There had been a time when he and Beth would've laughed themselves blue about it. It wasn't funny now. He felt alone, outcast by fate's plot to dismantle anything positive. One more outcome to make him shake his fist in the air and curse God for sticking it to him, AGAIN.

Whirby pushed Garol's shoulder, "You okay in there? I've been trying to get your attention. I thought you slipped into another world. We have to get out of here; they have to set things up for the holiday. It's Babar Day."

The next day, Garol stepped out on to the porch. Jimmy leaning against the railing, and Whirby sat opposite Toby, playing chess. Garol was surprised to see that Toby appeared to be in command of the game. He had most of his pieces, but Whirby was left with only a bishop, a pawn and his king.

"What's going on?" Garol asked sarcastically, "I thought you were Mr. Chess."

Neither one of them acknowledged Garol's comment, so he leaned against the railing next to Jimmy. They stood silently for a minute, watching the board. Then Jimmy turned his body to look away from the table. Garol did the same.

"Have a good time last night?" Jimmy asked Garol.

"Yeah," Garol said with a smile, "you?"

"Yeah," Jimmy said, "those suits get kind of hot."

"It's alright, kind of like a sauna," Garol said.

"It's my least favorite of the holidays. The big heavy head makes my neck hurt. All that padding in the suit gets hot," Jimmy said.

"It's only once a...whatever," Garol said. It was the first Babar Day he'd witnessed. Garol had a lot on his mind when Babar Day was first introduced to him. The name didn't register with Garol until all the suits were doled out and he peered into the faces of hundreds of identical elephants.

Garol had seen a photo— or maybe a drawing, he couldn't remember clearly— of Babar. He asked the man fitting him for his suit who Babar was. The man hurriedly answered, "An elephant man," before zipping Garol up and ushering him along. When Garol saw hundreds of identical elephants standing around, it became clear: Babar was the Elephant Man. He'd passed the movie in video stores and come across the title channel surfing, but never felt any need to investigate. Garol had fallen for Bigfoot and the Loch Ness Monster when he was young, and he didn't want his intelligence ridiculed by people claiming to see some high-powered elephant walking around Wall Street. He figured it was only an urban legend.

"The conversation was good," Garol said.

Jimmy just looked at him.

Garol really hadn't noticed the heat or the heavy elephant head all evening.

Babar Day was an anonymous holiday. All body parts were covered and height was hidden by padding shoes and slightly elongating the heads when needed. All elephants at the party were within two inches of each other. A muffler in the mouth transmitted voices and deepened them to elephantine levels.

The transformation was so quick and complete that by the time the absurdity annoyed Garol, he saw himself as one of a herd of elephants and no longer felt the agitation. Instead he felt comfort and fascination: amongst people he'd stood out from the past four months, he was as invisible as a clone. On top of that, he had no preconceived notions and made no judgements about himself or anyone he spoke with. He recognized a few people from their conversation. Someone carried on about the need for a pool, which he felt was Split. Another person complained about the lack of sleep that accompanies colicky babies and single motherhood, but explained that that's what you do when you're a martyr and a saint. Other than that, he had no clue who anyone was. Once he turned his back to them, they disappeared into the sea of elephants. Throughout the evening, he felt relaxed, going from one conversation to the next, speaking freely. He surprised himself by being witty. He walked and talked with an air of confidence that comes from being completely protected.

In the middle of the evening, Garol found himself on the dance floor, all alone, dancing and singing along with the ABBA song "Dancing Queen." He wished he didn't have the Babar shoes on so he could pivot quickly and really showcase his skills. After a while, the rest of the town joined in and Garol found himself leading the "YMCA" dance. He raised his hands high and yelled, "Y," put them down for the, "M," arched his body and yelled, "C," then spread his legs wide and yelled, "A." He led all four hundred townspeople in The Hustle, a dance Beth had urged him to learn in preparation for their wedding.

Garol eventually left the floor, giving high fives to everyone. After hearing several, "You rock," statements tossed his way, Garol got to the edge of the dance floor and did one quick spin for everyone to enjoy.

Garol moved over to the punch table and grabbed a beverage.

"I like the way you move," Garol heard a voice say.

"I can't take the credit. The real credit goes out to ABBA," Garol answered.

"ABBA rocks," the elephant said, shaking its head and moving its hips.

Garol was curious to know more about this person. It was definitely the first time an elephant had aroused him that he could remember.

"What's your name?" Garol asked.

"You're a sly one. You know the rules. No names," they said.

"I'll tell you mine if you tell me yours," Garol said.

"Oh yeah. How do I know if you are going to tell me your real name?" It made the little dance move again.

Garol was unsure what name he would give. "You move pretty well yourself."

"I know," it said, and turned to walk away.

Garol was afraid that if whoever it was got out of his sight, he'd lose her in the sea of elephants. His eyes followed as it walked to the other side of the dance floor. When it stopped and turned to look back at Garol, he saluted as coolly as he could. The elephant with the nice dance move waved cutely back. Garol headed back to the dance floor and motioned for it to come out too. It did. The two of them danced together for the remainder of the evening.As the night ended, the two held hands and walked off the dance floor.

163

"How will I know you?" Garol asked.

"You'll know me. We'll see each other again. That much I know." It turned to leave.

Garol grabbed the elephant and swung her around, then smushed his Babar mask against hers. They held each other for a long while. "I had to do that," he said when he pulled away.

Garol felt a little in love, but was embarrassed when he realized there was really no way of telling whether he was talking to a man or a woman. Whoever it was, it seemed like a woman. *She moved like a woman, didn't she?* He really wanted to know who it was. Babar Day meant complete anonymity, but he decided to try and find out anyway.

"That party sure was weird," Garol said again to Jimmy, not wanting to let the conversation drop.

"Huh?"

"Weird party. Fun though," Garol said.

"My neck hurts," Jimmy said rolling his neck.

"It's kind of weird that you don't know who you're talking to," Garol said.

"I don't like it. I like to know who I am talking to," Jimmy said.

"Yeah, I hear that. I wonder if we could find out. That would be interesting, huh?"

"No, can't. Completely anonymous. Can't find out,"

"Is there a list of who was at the party?" Garol asked.

"Everyone was at the party," Jimmy said. Then he asked Whirby, "You can't find out who you were talking to last night, can you?"

"No, that defeats the purpose of the evening," Whirby said.

"There was a purpose?" Garol asked.

"Yeah," Whirby said, annoyed. "To speak to people anonymously."

"Oh yeah, of course," Garol said sarcastically.

"Why?" Whirby sat back and smiled at Garol.

Garol felt he was caught and thought about his response, "Just curious."

"Uh-huh," Whirby said and Toby grinned.

Garol looked at the board again. The situation had completely reversed: Whirby had most of his pieces and Toby was left with only three.

"Anyway, why would someone reveal themself to you if you can't reveal yourself to someone else?" Whirby said.

"Huh? What do you mean by that?" Garol questioned.

"Oh nothing, Sam," Whirby said, looking at the chessboard.

Garol said to Toby, "Don't let him cheat you."

"Things aren't always as they appear," Whirby said.

Garol turned away from the board. *That must have been Sara I was dancing with. It must have been her. Who else? It had to be her.*

The Tongue Always Returns to the Sore Tooth

GAROL RECEIVED A LETTER in the mail.

Hey Sport,
Sorry about our second visit. I had forgotten
that I made plans for a fishing trip. It wasn't
anything I wanted to get out of. You know
what they say: "A bad day fishing is better than
a good day working." Not a more accurate
saying in the human language. Think about it;
who wants to listen to people ramble on, blah,
blah, whine, whine, when you could be out on
the lake catching fish? Not this guy. Anynuts,
I'm ready for you. Come on in and we'll clean
out that demon closet.
Dr. Mitchell, Psychiatrist
Graduate from Psychiatry School, College
P.S.—Is your phone working? I tried to call,
but I couldn't get through.

Garol read the letter five times. The only thought he could form was *Really?* Garol wadded the letter up, but then smoothed it and laughed. *I have to show this to Mike.* Wanting to share something with Mike caught Garol by surprise. It had been at least two years since he'd had a friendly thought about Mike. The final blowout put the nail in the coffin, but that had been building for a long time.

Garol wadded the letter back up and threw it in the trash.

The loss of Mike was like the long, painful extraction of a rotten tooth. The final tooth. The other teeth of his once beautiful smile had been ripped out suddenly. Their pain was leg curling, but swift and soon covered by shock and numbness. But the final tooth hung around as a reminder of the smile. It offered the memories of the smile crowding the mind with pain as it endlessly jabbed the nerve. Pain doubled by the mind's obsessive ordering of the tongue to steadily and firmly root out the tooth. Get rid of it. Drive it away. An order of compulsive attention that increased the striking of the nerve and disallowed any thought other than those of the once beautiful smile. Then when it's uprooted, the tongue searches fervently for a trace of the past, the mind realizes it can move on, but mostly wonders, "What have I done?"

Garol decided to ignore the appointment, or whatever it was that Dr. Mitchell offered. He had several mean replies he felt might hit the target, but he couldn't see the doctor understanding the intended message. Too, he knew he would have to deliver the letter. *Hey, here's your mail. It's a letter from me, and it says you're a jackass.*

Three days went by before Garol delivered the mail again. Once again, there was a letter from Dr. Mitchell.

> Current Resident,
> Excuse me. I hate to bother you, but this is the address of a former patient of mine. I'm hoping you can possibly give me some information as to his whereabouts. He recently did not show up for a scheduled appointment, and given his history

of running...which is meant to be taken figuratively because in the literal sense he hasn't done much running in a long time, if you get my meaning. A tiny weight issue. Oxymoron. No, no, I meant running from problems. He's more of a hider and isolator. Who knows? Maybe he's still living at your new address. Check inside the heating vents and under furniture. Don't be alarmed: he's touched by demons, but not crazy. Nothing violent, I assure you. No, for the most part he avoids conflict, emotions, and people, like a rat does light. Fortunately, he's easily recognizable and generally dons a white hard shell that covers his entire body. Not the world's most creative dresser. Although there's a lot of black marker etching over his shell. In fact, if you look hard enough, you'll even see a small advertisement for my practice. What else? Oh, he's an alcoholic in denial. He's been sober for a little while, but is still blind to the fact that sobriety is the key to his success. Given the opportunity, he'd go right back to drinking. Dry drunk. He's had some real serious trauma in the past that he's unable to move beyond and onto a happy and productive life. He has very little faith in God and humanity due to the events of the last ten to twelve years. And, just between you and me, he walks a little funny. You didn't hear it here.

Dr. Mitchell, Psychiatrist

Graduate from Psychiatry School, College

PS—Any information would help. I tried to call him several times. The phone number I have for him is middle palm, middle palm, index finger, thumb. Any idea if that's changed?

The first time Garol read the letter, he expected to laugh at the loony doctor again. He chuckled at the letter's opening. His smile disappeared when he reached the part about his weight issue. When he read the comparison of him to a rat, his temperature rose. The letter's declaration that he was an alcoholic in denial boiled his blood. He was enraged. He wanted to smash something. *Who the hell does this son of a bitch think he is?*

Initially, he wanted to march out and smash the doctor. *Who cares how big he is? The bigger they are, the harder they fall.* Garol paced his apartment trying to calm down and get a clear thought. Soon memories of Mike clouded his anger toward Dr. Mitchell. Mike had challenged him the same way. Too many times to count, Mike and Garol had stood together at the end of work, Mike going home to his family, Garol heading off to the bar. Usually they avoided direct conversation about the elephant in the room, but Garol always sensed it. He knew what the look away meant when he told Mike he was heading to the bar.

Then there were the less subtle approaches. Garol had less contempt for them, but even more resentment. "You've been going to the bar every night. Maybe you should slow down a bit. Get some rest. You seem tired." *Mind your own damn business.*

Garol paced his apartment. He still wanted to clomp out to the doctor and set the lunatic straight. Shove his phone up his ass. *No. No, he wants me to lose control. He wants me to get emotional. Then he can pick apart my defenses. "Why would you care if I called you an alcoholic if you aren't one? What difference would it make if I said you can't move on from your past events if you have moved on?" He wouldn't understand why none of it's true. He doesn't get things.*

Garol remained in his apartment into the evening, ignoring knocks on the door and skipping dinner. He didn't want anyone to see him in his state. He paced continuously and blamed any person or situation he could think of. Angry thoughts about the lunatic doctor and Mike shared time with God, his parents, football, and the cruel nature of life. He even cursed Beth for getting pregnant. He paced and paced and paced. Occasionally he needed to punch something or throw something, but he always stopped himself. *Don't lose control. You don't know where it will stop.*

Garol sat sullenly through his overly-nutritious breakfast. The expression-shielding cast mask was a great advantage during times of sullen quandary. He could quietly face conversation and everyone would assume he was happily paying attention. He was dizzy from being up all night, but enough adrenaline coursed through his body to keep a normal state. After breakfast, Garol stormed out of the cafeteria and began to stomp down Main Street to the psychiatrist in the woods who, "puts people's minds back together," *just after he drives them crazy.*

Garol ground to a halt at Life St. Covered with water and mud, the troubled terrain was baffling because there had been no rain. Not even a cloud. *Must have been a pipe burst.*

Ditches filled with water lined both sides of the street, leaving Garol the choice of chancing his tractionless cast feet against the mud or turning back. Garol decided it was important to speak to the doctor and cautiously balanced his way until he felt comfortable enough maneuvering to pick up the pace a bit. Soon he was swiftly sloshing with swagger.

Roughly a quarter of the way down Life, feeling confident of his footing and looking well ahead, Garol took an unexpected step into a waist-high ravine. The sudden fall and the trickle of water creeping inside his cracks brought a sudden sense of shock. His cast shoes unable to form a bond with the wet soil, he lay with the top half of his body in the mud covered road. He dug his hands in to the dirt and dragged himself forward, squirming like a seal. Garol twisted in the mud, reservoirs trickling through the slits of his cast. Once he'd worked most of it out, he stood up, covered from head to toe in mud, took four steps…into a ravine a foot deeper than the last.

Garol wanted a redo. He knew there was a reason to go forward, but mostly he just wanted to go back, get dry, and remove the mud. Mope in his apartment. If he turned back now, he knew where the trouble was— but if he kept moving, how many more ravines lay in hiding? Garol lay in the mud, feeling paralyzed. There was still much of Life St. to traverse. He didn't want to fume in his apartment. He was tired of that. A drink would solve everything, but that wasn't an option. He was already muddy and miserable, and moving forward could inflict no more damage. Other than landing in a hole too big to get out of, nothing.

Garol dropped the swagger and travelled with more caution for the rest of his trip. He looked down instead of forward for gullies of water and steered clear of imminent danger. Finally, he reached Happiness Way, which had large enough patches of dry dirt to avoid the mud, and smiled.

Garol turned to the opening to Dr. Mitchell's porch looking like Frosty the Snowman's distant cousin, Goopy the Mudman. From the top down, he was different shades of brown depending upon how dry those areas were.

Garol spotted the doctor standing in his doorway and he charged forward like a play's lead rushing on stage to deliver his lines. The doctor, struggling with something on the inside of the door, met Garol's charge with a look of annoyance. As their eyes met, suddenly Garol felt unprepared and unrehearsed, as if he'd completely forgotten his lines and character. He slowed his charge to an uneasy saunter and wished a curtain would fall.

The doctor remained in the doorway, struggling. He held his right arm out toward Garol. He clenched his right fist and backed through the doorway, onto the porch, with both arms held out and both hands clenched. He spun and looked at Garol like he was holding an invisible bucket in each hand.

"Mind getting the door?" the doctor said with a puzzled look, moving his head back and forth from Garol to the door.

Garol slowly walked up the porch steps, grabbed the door handle, and pulled it closed.

"Thanks." The doctor nodded to the porch floor just below the window and said, "Will you grab the backup bait? My hands are full."

Garol scooped up an invisible handle.

"On second thought, bring the box next to it with the larger bait. Sorry, I should've mentioned we're going to lure the beast today— the Great White."

Garol grimaced and placed the imaginary box in his hands on the porch floor, then scooped his hand upward and looked at the doctor before he stood up. The doctor nodded approval and Garol stood with clenched fist hanging at his side.

"Very good," Dr. Mitchell said. "I got a good feeling today. Something seems right. I can't explain it, but something is dead on. A truth has been revealed. And because of that everything from here on out will be different. Once you know, you can never go back and I know now." The doctor walked swiftly in front of Garol to the side of the house.

"What truth?" Garol rushed to keep pace with the doctor. "Where are you going?"

"To fish. Why else would we be carrying all this gear?" Dr. Mitchell stopped and turned toward Garol. His eyes opened wide, "What did you do with the bait?"

Garol saw his hands were not in any position that could be considered carrying something.

"Oh, there it is," he said, pointing ten paces back, near the bottom of the porch. He shook his head and looked at Garol with judgement.

Garol sighed loudly then said, "This isn't the reason I came."

"Explain once you've picked up the bait," the doctor scolded, extending his long finger to the porch base.

Confusion crept through Garol as the doctor marched around the corner of the house.

"I don't have enough bait on me to last very long," the distant voice of the doctor called.

Garol dropped his shoulders, and turned to face the porch, cursing. He moaned loudly, leaned, clasped air in his right hand, stood erect, and double-checked his right fist to ensure it remained clenched before venturing into the backyard. There was no trace of Dr. Mitchell. The open grassland on the side of the house declined to a valley before rising to form a ridge. Bait in hand, Garol traversed the valley and climbed the ridge to get a better view.

From atop the hill, Garol could see the doctor, thirty feet away, on the outskirts of a pond. The doctor dipped backwards and quickly shot his arms toward the center of the pond, then swooped his left hand toward his navel. He positioned the right only inches off his belly, reeling it in small, steady circles. Silently the precise motions repeated: lean back, extend arms to the pond, reel in and repeat. *Casting.* Garol counted the seconds between line casts, but that proved very little to discount the accuracy of the doctor's actions because he varied the thrust and direction. He was fishing; sometimes he reeled in quickly and other times he let the bait dip and drag seductively through the water. The original cast and speed of his right hand reeling always matched perfectly.

The doctor's mimed fishing unsealed visions of childhood expeditions with Mike, adventuring through the bear- and Indian-inhabited woods behind Mike's neighborhood to the underwater world in its pond. The quack maneuvering an imaginary rod returned Garol to the child's stage and unlocked memories from a savings account, returned with accumulated interest. It transposed Garol to a time long before the lessons of doubt and disappointment, when there were always enough rocket ships to carry grown boys to the moon and NFL teams to quarterback— when the king and his queen lived together happily ever after. It was no more real than an imaginary beast reeled in without a pole in a tiny pond; just dreams, visions, child's play, yet it was the only truth, the driving force. A perfect playhouse with a foundation of concrete, supported by steel beams, until doubt rained through cracks and rust appeared. Until guilt chipped into time spent on childish activities and the grownup world shut down the playhouse, condemned it due to bills.

A loud grunt erupted from the doctor. He was anchored in a running stance: left leg forward and knees bent, his weight leaned back and his hands tensely clenching and reeling. Even dug in the sand, the struggle slowly dragged this enormous man to the water. Anxiously, Garol searched the pond for a glimpse of an enormous fin and re-clenched the bucket.

Violently, the doctor plunged backwards, ending the tug-o-war, then abruptly sturdied himself by digging his heels in the sand in front of him and leaning back, still holding his left hand around his naval and the right hand tightening the reel. The underwater beast appeared to come to the front of the pond with the intention of gathering all its momentum and dragging the doctor into the water. Garol tensed as he first noticed the doctors face contort and then his heels began inching a path toward the pond and then slowly his back was dragged upward to a standing position. The doctors grip on the pole dug his fingers into his palm, while his right arm could no longer budge the reel. It had to be the Great White the doctor had spoken of. Garol half expected to see the fin surface.

"The net," the doctor grunted.

Garol tensed as if he'd received an emergency call in a foreign language.

"The net!" The doctor yelled, leaning much farther forward.

Garol took a step, lost his traction, and slid on his backside until he reached the shore.

"Where?" Garol clutched both fists and lined them up to hand off the net directly.

"There," the doctor said and motioned to the area Garol was.

"Got it," Garol said stepping to the doctor.

"Go in," the doctor yelled, using both arms and every bit of strength to hold the line.

Garol jumped up and down twice and then darted into the pond. Moving the net in coordinated finger-to-thumb circles, he attempted to raise his knees high enough to run through the water, but quickly tripped and fell face first.

The doctor crumbled forward, knees in the dirt, ribs pulled down on top of his knees, and arms extended straight ahead. His hands and fingers worked fervishly. Then his body crashed and he lay in the fetal position. Garol stood in the waist-high water, motionless, dripping wet, but still gripping the net with both hands, waiting for the doctor. The doctor moaned softly. Garol exhaled. The doctor moaned louder several times and then went quiet. Garol remained still, clutching the net, forgetting the water he stood in as the doctor very slowly, one vertebrae at a time, arched to a sitting position, staring at the pond.

"Do you know how long I've been trying to catch that beast?" the doctor said.

Garol started to answer, but no words came forth.

"I'm embarrassed to tell you. I have to get a new fishing pole," the doctor hung his head as Garol watched him intently. The doctor turned toward Garol, "You know what I really love?"

Garol shrugged his shoulders.

"The chance to try. Who knows what you're gonna get? Some days I feel like no matter what's on my line, it's mine. For some reason, this monster hasn't bit my line those days. Maybe she's smarter than me. Sometimes I wonder if it's me," he said and looked at Garol. "What are you holding?"

"The net," Garol looked at his clasped hands.

The doctor raised his right hand, now shaped in an O, and said, "This net?"

Garol relaxed his arms and they dipped in the water. He began walking back to land. Feeling suddenly self-conscious, he asked the doctor, "Why do you wonder if it's you?"

"Part of me wonders if fear holds me back from catching the Great White."

"That was the Great White?" Garol asked, still sloshing through the water.

"Did you think you were just chasing an enormous fin?" The doctor shook his head. "I wonder if I'm afraid to catch her because I'll have to move on to the Killer Whale, and I don't think I'd have a chance with the Killer. Too big, too powerful.

Maybe I sabotage myself so I don't have to move on. It's hard to move into a future you can't imagine."

"Looked like you were trying pretty hard to me." Now out of the water, Garol shook himself.

"Maybe. Too often, we fool ourselves. What's the difference between a ninety percent effort and a hundred percent? The difference could be your world. It's ok, though, because we make sufficient excuses for our lack of effort. And they work on the surface, but deep down we always know. We act like we don't, but we do. I wasn't feeling good, my pole sucks, my net guy can't find the net," the doctor glanced at Garol. "More often than not, we just keep ourselves comfortable. There was a moment just before she got away that I felt I could reel her in. I hesitated. Why? That's what I need to figure out. I believe I'm just afraid of what's next. The unknown. I may never have an equal challenge again. I might either easily win, or easily lose, and that scares me."

The doctor walked up to Garol and held his hands out.

"Do you mind carrying this?"

Garol held out his arms like he were ready to be stacked with firewood.

"Just grab it by the handle," the doctor laughed.

"Tackle box?" Garol said and held his hand out.

"Yeah," the doctor answered, handing Garol the box and gathering the rest of his invisible equipment. "You've got a lot going for you. You should get into politics."

"Yeah?"

"You're a natural: handsome, coordinated, well-spoken, always looking for a way to help, a nice guy. Brave! Holy Moly, you ran into the water after that monster without a net! Were you planning on dragging the beast to shore? Crazy man. You earned my respect."

"I don't think I'm cut out for politics."

"You know why I believe no two snowflakes look alike?"

"No."

"To remind us that no two realities are alike. What you see is different than what I see."

"That much is true," Garol couldn't help laughing.

"Reality is nothing more than interpretation. I think you'd be a great politician, but you don't see it. Why? We're looking at the same person."

"I know me a little better than you do."

"You think so?"

"I've spent a lot more time with me than you have."

"That's a bit harsh. It's interesting that people base their realities on what they think they see. Too frequently, we never step back and assess our situation accurately. Each day is new, but unfortunately we bring all of our old baggage. I came out here and once again failed to pull in the coveted Great White. The question is, how do I react? Convince myself I'll never catch her? Stop fishing entirely, something I love to do? Or do I up the level of my game? Maybe get a new pole, try a new type of bait?" the doctor laughed and slugged Garol softly on the shoulder.

"What?"

"You dropped the bucket when you fell down the hill. No problem, you were excited." The doctor stared at Garol for an uncomfortably long period.

"So you think you need a new pole?" Garol asked, glad the doctor couldn't see his face.

"That's it," the doctor said, impressed.

"The pole?" Garol asked.

"No. I just figured out who you remind me of. A patient of mine. I knew when I saw you earlier you looked like someone, but I couldn't put my finger on it."

"I do?"

"Don't be offended. You aren't him, thank God…he's a mess. In fact, I'm expecting him to show up today, any minute potentially," the doctor grimaced.

"Who is it?" Garol asked.

"Well I can't give out names, but like you he's covered in a hard surfaced shell. Yeah, I know," the doctor laughed. "Yours looks good; you've done a lot with it. You've got the black and all the other colors on top—real nice. He's not too creative. Too busy wallowing in the mud...Oh well, here we are." They reached the porch steps in the front of the house.

The Worth of a Thing is What It Will Bring

AFTER THE FISHING EXPEDITION with Dr. Mitchell activity raced at a glacier's pace for weeks. The mail sack appeared at Garol's door only once and the upstairs remodel stood at a stalemate because the supply helicopter showed up in the middle of one night, mistakenly loaded with fixtures for a kitchen remodel in Milwaukee.

"Milwaukee? Milwaukee? What the hell does Milwaukee have to do with anything?" Garol charged to The Man like a foreman with a deadline. Garol's kneejerk reaction had more to do with the threat he felt from an intruding helicopter than keeping up appearances as an uptight, in-charge leader. All prior incoming helicopters carried a past or future tense: nothing current, and besides, this present outside crew of idiots were incapable of telling the difference between this place and Milwaukee. It pricked a patch of sensitive nerves. Garol spent the rest of the day and most of the next explaining to everyone within earshot what had happened, "Can't work because the morons, 'the powers that be,'" he emphasized with finger quotation marks, "can't tell the difference from a small town in the desert and Milwaukee." Several times he said, "Milwaukee?

I've never even been to Milwaukee." He also said more than five times, "Why would I? Why would anyone ever go to Milwaukee?" certain there was a correlation between his lack of travel and a shipping mishap. He spouted complaints until the thought of the intruding helicopter faded and took with it the question, *If it showed up and I saw it, would I climb aboard?* Finally, he convinced himself, *Of course, if I were absolutely certain I no longer had Bodycastjellomoldification.*

The lack of activity made it feel like the town waited with baited breath for Dr. Mitchell to replace his fishing pole. Garol milled around and occasionally spouted, "Milwaukee," to fill his lackluster days. He sat for long periods listening to Whirby commentate on every chess character like a stock analyst feeding steady streams of knowledge, spelling out the pros and cons of their options. Garol blocked the information and watched Split land-swim in the backyard, snuggly wrapped around the waist by a soft, dry, feathered duck's-head flotation device and wearing a one piece old fashioned swimming suit. Using the breaststroke, he flip-flopped across the lawn, until he reached the picket fence and raised his head for air. Then he plugged his nostrils between thumb and index finger, lowered his head and swam to the arbor on the other side and began the process anew. Eventually, Whirby's constant noise and Split's motions put him in a trance, where thoughts waded in a molasses pool and he would feel one hundred percent convinced, *No helicopter showed up here. No one knows about this place. It is on no map. The land of the misfit toys would be condemned if anyone knew it was here. Milwaukee!*

After roughly four days of no routine, Garol made a spontaneous choice to window-shop. An odd decision, due to Garol's past— he'd moved from home to the dorms to off-campus living with Beth. Until Beth's passing, Garol was convinced that items needed just appeared. Beth rationed their modest finances and made sure pantries and closets stayed stocked with necessities and fashionable items. It was not that Garol believed in a shopping fairy, but the casual distain he felt about shopping was the only reason he and Beth ever fought.

Beth deemed his behavior childish; whenever she asked him to stop by the store to pick up milk or eggs and Garol moaned, believing it would just be easier to let it take care of itself as it always had. Since Beth's death, Garol did just enough shopping to keep him clothed and alive. He purchased toothbrushes, toothpaste, and soap in bulk. He bought clothes one to two sizes too large to allow for growth. The only shopping he really enjoyed was perusing the menu in the drive thru line at a fast-food restaurant, but even there he always knew what he wanted.

Only three shops into his browsing, Garol heard a familiar tromp and saw Gladys galloping, head down, chest thrust forward in a sturdy, body-cast-toppling motion. He quickly ducked into the clothing store. Gladys steam rolled past the window and Garol pivoted to see if anyone had witnessed his cowering. The mannequin he'd previously seen in the shop window posed with a cheerful smile and friendly waving hand. He walked toward the plastic version of himself, examining a smile he couldn't recall from their first quick meeting through glass. Other than the ski slope nose, large eyebrow and the pencil thin one, it looked identical to when he quarterbacked at State. *But how? Why?* He surveyed the room, expecting to see a plastic recreation of Beth. What he saw were several other versions of him.

"Would you like to try this on?" a woman asked, referring to the black pin stripe suit the mannequin wore.

"The suit?" Garol was too enthralled in the surreal to be surprised by the real.

"You seem to be admiring it. It is a very nice suit." She ran her hand up the plastic model's sleeve.

Garol almost explained his confusion about the mannequin's appearance, but silently looked at the female associate.

Another pair of hands wrapped a measuring tape around his waist while the woman in front measured his arms and inseam and placed his feet in a large silver tray to measure shoe size. The two women dragged him from aisle to aisle within the men's department. A lifelike plastic Garol donned whatever type of dress that section offered. The Garols came in many poses. A solemn Garol stood with one leg on a chair, chin in his hand, smoking a pipe and sportily clad like a hip Harvard professor in corduroy slacks, an argyle sweater vest and tweed sport jacket. There was a contented Garol lounging in cashmere pajamas, robe and slippers, sitting in a chair with a copy of the *Gossip*'s the article "Marshmallow Comes to Town." A politician dressed in a navy blue suit, smiling widely and raising the victory sign, a V created between his index and middle fingers. A baseball player clenched his hands to bat and drive the ball over the fence. There were nine in all. They all had a ski slope nose, one large furry caterpillar sized eyebrow and the other pencil-lead thin. Garol wondered at each one, going through the gamut of expressions on their faces and wanting desperately to look in a mirror, if not only to see if his eyebrows matched, while the sales associates filled bags and bags with stylish clothes.

Garol had a new activity to help fill his days: dressing. He began the day reclining on the porch wrapped in cashmere robe and pajamas, watching Split pace his morning swim and listening to Whirby recall chess activity from the sleeping hours. He strolled to breakfast in a leisure or exercise suit with sneakers. Afternoons, he threw on jeans, overalls or carpenter pants with a sweat- or t-shirt and a pair of boots. Formal attire struck his fancy in the evening, but whether he'd dress in one of the many colored suits or settle for slacks, a buttoned polo shirt with a cardigan sweater wrapped around the neck depended on the amount of breeze he felt when he stuck his finger out the window.

Dressed to the nines, Garol attended dinner and the nightly movie they'd begun airing in the Town Hall Center. He knew Sara would be there, and anything to break the monotony was welcome. The videos they played in the evening were titled, *Happiness is Within, It's All in the Mind, Removing Addictions, Dealing with Alcohol, The Diet to Decrease Anxiety, Eliminating Negative Thoughts, The Gift of Gratitude and Appreciation, You Can Do Anything You Want*, and a few other self-improvement types of movies. Compliments flowed from all directions on his flair for style, how dashing and handsome he looked. Several comments came directly, but mostly they were overheard: his good looks and polished appearance were fit for politics, acting, or modeling. An abundance of talk that the town focused on the desperate need to replace the mayor, conveying a fear rising in the town. Suggestions such as, "Garol should run for mayor because we need a strong, handsome leader to pull us out of the current crisis," sank in. Garol never asked what the crisis was. He never felt there was a crisis other than his own.

Initially, Garol brushed off the compliments, but the honeyed words kept coming every evening. The townspeople's praises tiptoed through condemned spaces of his mind evacuated from lack of hope's required funding. He dabbled in thoughts of winning an Oscar or posing with beautiful models, but taking steps in those directions was daunting and deflating. Something about becoming Mayor slithered past his internal defenses: no one else wanted the job, which meant no chance of a painful, humiliating public loss. Moreover, no need for canvassing or kissing babies, shaking hands, giving speeches, or making promises.

The waterfall of compliments and exciting possibilities illuminated the blue skies in Garol's world. For years, a bleak, grey, ominous cloud dominated his sky, interrupting action and suspending plans by continuously forecasting rain. It barked menacingly, "Any picnic will be rained out," then patronized by failing to drizzle. The intimidating skies suggested he seek shelter, but brought no tornadoes, typhoons, or any satisfying reason to hide. Cowering from a bully with no fight, it shamed Garol.

Therefore, when Garol glanced into bright skies, skepticism cast a long shadow. The potential glory of the day conjured Beth cheering him on in the stands, but also old reminders: "Things can go painfully wrong...The best laid plans...Life is random...To put oneself out there is to take chances."

He loved being in the spotlight again, but it scared him to death, but being on stage might get Sara's attention.

Garol searched his horizon for the first time in years. The bubbling surge of adrenaline both excited and frightened him, and he split his vision between the bright skies and a storm search. The more his excitement grew the harder he looked for a flood to drown his enthusiasm.

Eventually he spotted a large, lumpy black storm cloud in the distance: Gladys. She entered the scene as an unexpected blitz from the side, and grew with an article written in the *Gossip*. A cloud he didn't see expanding as he walked into her house, night after night, to fix imbecilic problems. Then darkened and became lumpy with the birth of a plastic baby and the ridiculous insinuation he was the father. *Was I in any way to blame? What could I have done differently? No. Nothing. A set-up. Just like everything else.* Until it finally splintered into several menacing clouds when he witnessed her stroll the baby in town and heard community members tell her how beautiful the baby was. Now Gladys sat between the backdrop of his blue sky, a threat to the sparkling new roof of his world, like insidious polka dots of lumpy black storm clouds and the constant reminder—Life is a setup.

Garol was nervous about greeting Steve Atan as he huffed to Sam's Last Saloon. He hadn't been to the bar in a while and sensed Steve would feel betrayed. Garol wasn't exactly sure why he hadn't been to the bar recently. He'd seen the light on a few times but declined to visit. *Maybe because I'm supposed to be recruiting people and I haven't even brought the idea up to anyone?* Garol didn't think that was the whole reason. Something about the colony in the desert didn't make sense. *If it sounds too good to be true, it probably is. An occasional drink sounds good, but can I only drink once in a while?* At times he enjoyed himself, and didn't really want to leave the odd little town. Meeting with Steve brought on guilt, as if he were backstabbing the community members. Too, he was a little embarrassed knowing he would have to stifle his excitement about some of the things going on in his life because Steve would think them ludicrous. Yet those feelings were uncomfortable and Garol couldn't help but wonder if now might be the best time to exit stage left. *Get while the getting is good, before the storm hits.* Either way, he wanted to leave his options open, hear Steve's argument again, and buy himself a little more time.

The tavern light was on. He peered in the window. The bartender was polishing glasses as a player piano played a mournful tune. Steve rested his elbows on the bar in an inverted V, holding his head and staring into his rocks glass.

Garol opened the right saloon door and entered slowly, quietly. Instantly, the player piano amped up the volume and started an upbeat version of, "How I Love Ya."

Steve and the bartender looked at Garol.

"Look who decided to grace us with his presence!" Steve looked at the bartender.

Garol awkwardly waddled toward Steve.

"Where's the rest?" the bartender sneered at Steve.

"Just me," Garol sat next to Steve.

"That's a little disappointing. You never stop by and you don't recruit. What am I supposed to make of this?" Steve frowned sternly at Garol.

"I just need more time. I'm trying to make sense of a few things."

"Exactly what I feared. It's impossible to make sense of anything in that town. That you try is particularly frightening. Do you understand what I'm saying?"

"No."

"The only sense you can make is their kind of sense. Making sense?"

"No."

"What the hell are you trying to make sense of?"

"There's a woman named Gladys," Garol said softly.

"I know the hurried dingbat."

"She ever try to knock you over?"

185

"Is that a joke?"

"Oh, yeah. She had a baby and claimed it was mine."

"You dog. Was it?" Steve punched Garol's shoulder. He grew serious. "Don't waste your time. Where we're going there are more women than you could ever want. I told you, everything you want is there, everything, and you're knocking up Gladys. Come on."

"I didn't. They set it up. They had me going over there to screw every night and then the next thing you know she's claiming she's pregnant."

"Sounds like you set yourself up."

"No, I mean they had me screwing stuff, not screwing. Anyway, the kid was a doll, plastic, but it seems everyone thinks I'm the father. As if I'm abandoning the two of them."

"They're trying to make you crazy. I warned you. They'll throw things at you that push your buttons. Things that you'll know are wrong. They'll test your will. They're beating you down. I can see it and I don't like what I see. Eventually, you'll give in. I don't think it'll be long before you're changing the plastic little thing's diapers."

"No, you've got it all wrong."

"No, *you've* got it all wrong. Sad. So what the hell are we going to do?"

"I don't know. Can I get a drink?" The bartender was gone.

"A drink? You want to drink at my bar, but what have you done for me? You haven't even attempted to recruit. When you came in, what did you want to happen?"

"I was hoping to get a drink and let you know what's been going on."

"Nothing, that's what. I offer to get you out of that hellhole and you do nothing for me. Now you want my alcohol for free? What is it with you? You really disappoint me."

"Sorry," Garol said looking at the bar.

"Sorry. The thing is, I believed in you. I was excited. I thought I had my guy with you. I really didn't think they'd get you this easy, but now I'm seeing a weak waffle. Am I wrong?"

"No," Garol said softly.

"No. So you are a coward?"

"No, I meant yes, you've got it wrong. No, they aren't getting to me. I don't want to be there. I'm just a little out of practice at persuading people."

"Come on, I can tell you're a manipulator. A liar? Hell yeah! I still don't know if your name is Sam or Garol. The question is, do you? You believe your lies, which is good. You have what it takes to be something in my town. You're a spokesman, and that's why I'm asking you to be my representative. Dig deep, do what's right and use your powers to get people in here. So what's the hold up?"

"Everyone says I should get into politics," Garol said.

"You should get into politics. You'd be perfect for it, and then…"

"Then?"

"Become mayor of Looneyland make it a law that people come here. You earn your wings in my town by the number of recruits. The more you get me, the more you get what you want. Bring me the whole town and I'll stock this bar every night with the finest Scotch. What do you drink?"

"Beer."

"Shit, that's easy, but you've got to help me. I want you to dig. I'll give you it back tenfold. A thousand fold."

"I heard the mayor left. Apparently, they are just looking for someone to step in and take over. I could, but I don't really want to run this town."

"Run the town? Run it into the ground for all I care. I just want you to become mayor so you can understand your influence. You have influence and you could use it for me, for good. I want you to sign up for mayor."

"Ok,"

"Now get the hell out of here and don't come back until you've got good news."

"I'VE GOT GREAT NEWS," Garol bursted with pride and a mouthful of egg-white-and-vegetable omelet at breakfast. "I'll be mayor."

Whirby, Jimmy, and Toby simultaneously saluted, then converged for a group bear hug.

When they relinquished their grips, Garol assumed the worst was over. He started to ask Whirby, "When do I start making laws?"

Whirby, though, dashed to the front of the cafeteria, his head only a foot higher than the tables. He raised his arms in the air and shouted, "Important announcement."

Everyone stopped eating and faced the front.

"Our political problems are over – almost." He pointed his finger toward Garol, "Sam has volunteered to become our savior. He's decided to lead us out of the fog."

The cafeteria exploded in cheers.

"Get up here, Sam," Whirby shouted and flailed his arm toward himself.

Hands pushed Garol to the front of the cafeteria.

"Speech!" the crowded cafeteria chanted.

Garol felt as if he'd been driving down a long boring highway and suddenly run over a patch of black ice, flinging him over a cliff.

Saucer-eyed faces with frozen toothy smiles waited for their new leader's message.

"I'll be mayor," Garol said with a quiet, high crackle.

The crowd continued to stare. Garol tried to say something else, but got stuck on the idea that he could see their eyes growing.

Whirby moved in front of Garol. "Thanks for that, Sam. Well, there's our first candidate. It's time to get the political process started; this is going to be an exciting race. The first debate will be this evening in the Town Hall Center after dinner."

A woman stepped between Garol and Whirby and asked, "What's your plan?" before he could ask Whirby what "debate" meant.

"Plan?" Garol asked watching Whirby move away.

"What will you do once elected? If you are elected," she said through squinted eyes.

"Make laws," Garol said as his eyes went back and forth between the growing number of people encircling him...and Whirby's backside, now exiting the cafeteria.

"What is your timeline for space flight?" A man asked, scribbling in a pad.

"Everyone knows you guys at the top are just puppets. What's your staff like?" Questions poured in. "What are your thoughts on clocks?" "What about Medium Foot?" "Where do you stand on the issues?" "What are your thoughts on healthcare?"

Garol began to answer the question on healthcare with a knee jerk response, but lost his train of thought when someone asked, "Are we going to go to multiple deliveries a day for the mail?" He spent the rest of the morning doing his best to act dumb and deflect any questions until finally he was the last person in the cafeteria. He went to find Whirby.

When Garol reached the house, Whirby was gleefully studying the chessboard, rubbing his hands together like a mad scientist.

"What's going on?" Garol stormed up the driveway.

"Come see this move," Whirby said waiving quickly.

"I signed up to be mayor. I am ready to go. What is this debate shit? I'm not having it."

Whirby took his eyes off the chessboard. "It isn't that easy. You have to go through the debate process."

"I thought you said no one else wanted the job?"

"No one does."

"So how are we going to have a debate?"

"What's the worry? It's impossible to lose a debate when you're the only one debating." He looked Garol over and said, "Almost impossible."

"Look, I didn't know about the debates, I'm not doing it."

"You'll be the only person in history to lose an election as the only candidate. Is that what you want?"

Garol didn't answer.

"What's the real problem?" Whirby asked.

"I don't speak in public. I don't do that."

"You didn't think a mayor would ever give speeches?"

Garol took his time. "I figured I could make laws and post them."

"You can after the election. All you have to do is show up and let people get to know who they are following. They just want to feel comfortable with you, that's all."

Garol didn't answer.

"You'll do great. Now come over here and check out this move."

"People need to start being square with me," Garol said, and walked into his apartment.

———————

"Ladies and gentlemen, thank you for coming this evening as we whittle away at the issues that will help us determine the next town mayor. We have a two-party debate this evening. On the right hand side of the stage, standing behind podium number one we have our newest member to town, Sam. On the left side, we have Podium Number Two, which has probably been in town since our first election— a good long while," the Head Beaver said.

An usher tapped the Head Beaver on the shoulder and handed him an envelope. The Head Beaver pulled out the note inside and read silently. He cleared his throat, "This is really fascinating," turned to the usher, now in the back of the hall, waved the letter, and said, "Thank you." He spoke into the microphone, "We have an update on Whirby's chess game."

The crowd oohed.

"The castle has moved into the center of the board. Jumped right into the fire. The old 'leap before you look.' Right in there with its biggest fears and on stage for all to witness."

The crowd oohed again and a woman screeched, "God bless him."

The Head Beaver looked at the screeching woman and laughed. The crowd joined along. "It's not all bad. In fact it could be very good; the castle has the king in check. Not checkmate, you understand, but check." He bounced his head back, "Well at least it's something."

"Let's move on," the Head Beaver declared. "Sam, we'll begin the questioning with you. If you were elected mayor, how would you run this town? You have three minutes."

"I'll make this a place to live," Garol said quietly.

"Live here?" The Head Beaver said, confused.

"Proudly."

"You'll live here proudly?"

"Yes...and so will everyone."

"Are you going to unite the town?"

"Yes," Garol said with volume in his voice for the first time.

The audience clapped.

Once the applause subsided the Head Beaver looked at Podium Number Two. "Podium Number Two, please tell us how you'd run this town if elected mayor. You have three minutes."

The crowd patiently waited as the three minutes ticked away.

"I'm sorry Podium Number Two, that's all the time we can offer." He reassured it, saying, "These debates can be overwhelming. Don't lose faith in yourself."

The Head Beaver turned to Garol and asked, "If elected mayor, what would you do to alleviate the major and minor issues confronting the town?"

"I'd tackle the major issues confronting the town first, but while doing that I'd think about the minor issues so they could get solved at either the same time or shortly after. Then I'd solve the minor, minor issues, if there are any."

The audience hooted and cheered.

"Podium Two, please tell us how you would alleviate the major and minor issues confronting the town." the Head Beaver asked seriously.

For a minute and a half, the only noise in the hall came from the Head Beaver's stopwatch as the crowd anxiously waited for any response from Podium Two. It was broken up by someone in the audience yelling, "He doesn't care."

Twenty seconds later, a voice shouted, "No plan, he has no plan."

At two minutes and forty seconds, a voice rang out, "Pretender!" Several people agreed with, "Got that right," until the Head Beaver waved his arm to control the crowd.

Sensing the restlessness, Garol interrupted the final seconds of Podium Two's allotted time to add, "I would just like to say that I would also institute a preparedness program to ward off any issues before they begin."

The crowd settled.

"Would you like to add anything to that Podium Two?"

Podium Two elected not to speak.

"Well I can't see any reason to continue," the Head Beaver announced.

"My opponent doesn't care," Garol said with confidence, "but I do. I care about each and every last one of you and I'm not afraid to say so." Garol sneered at Podium Two. "If…I mean *when* I'm elected," Garol raised his hand, "there won't be any problems. All problems will be removed— gotten rid of. This will be a problem-less society, with no problems," Garol slammed his cast-covered forearms down on the podium.

One person stood up and clapped and then the rest of the crowd followed, clapping and hooting for two minutes. Garol stepped from behind his podium, walked off the stage and up the center aisle shaking hands and saying, "Thanks for your support."

Podium Two didn't move.

Self Praise is No Recommendation

TOBY AND GAROL WALKED to the softball diamond, each with two equipment bags draped around their shoulders. Garol's head buzzed with excitement and he paid little concern to Toby's struggle to manage the heavy equipment bags, their long straps causing one to scrape the ground and the other to swing into his legs.

Garol waited for Toby fifteen yards ahead. When Toby caught up, Garol said, "Choices."

"Choices?" Toby questioned.

"Life is about choices," Garol said matter of factly. "Opportunities."

"Your choices are good?" Toby asked.

"My choices are excellent."

"That's great," Toby answered smiling.

"You bet it is. You're looking at the next town mayor. That's in the bag. I'll be honest, at first I was a little annoyed that we had to go through this whole political practice. The debating. Some people might say, why have a debate against no one? But nothing is worth anything unless you earn it. Remember I told you that."

"I will," Toby said stumbling as a bag hit his left leg.

"I'm serious. Remember this conversation. I'll be running this town pretty soon, but after that, who knows? My political career is just getting off the ground, and I'm not going to spend it running Dinktown. I'm an amazing speaker. You saw the way I fired people up. The thing about a great leader is it's not what you say, it's how you say it. Why would I stay here if I can fire up the whole country like that? Leaders are a dime a dozen, but great leaders come along once in a lifetime. You could be talking to a future president. That's all I'm saying."

"Wow! You did do really well in the debate." Toby hoisted a bag higher on his shoulder.

"I did. Nothing against my opponent. A great leader never down plays his opponent. Remember that. You have to do everything first class. That's the first lesson in Leadership 101. You could say, well, your opponent didn't say much. It was just a podium. But that's missing the big picture, which was my performance. I don't think it would've mattered who was up there against me. To be honest, I think the podium had the best chance because a person would've cracked. You can't crack wood. I mean, you can split it, but not emotionally crack it, you know. A person though can only take so much. That's scientific. Any person would've tumbled like a house of cards," Garol said, talking quickly.

"I agree," Toby said.

"I'll tell you what. When I make it, I'll make you Secretary of State or Secretary of the House. Well, maybe secretary of the guest house," Garol waited for Toby to catch up.

"I don't have any political experience," Toby said.

"Well you can start as Secretary to the Vice President's guest house. It doesn't really matter; a Secretary just answers phones and gets coffee. You can do that. Once you get to the top, you don't have to do anything. It's just like the corporate world. Become President and it's smooth sailing. People on the bottom busting their tails to get to the top do all of the work. Every once in a while you call them up and say, 'Is that report done,' then you go golfing."

"Sounds like you have experience as President," Toby said.

"No. I've always been one of the guys at the bottom."

"Busting your butt?"

"No. I always felt like I was preparing to be President. It takes a certain type of person."

They reached the field, where four men and six women dressed in leisurely sportswear waited for practice to begin. Garol only knew Whirby, Jimmy, Split, and the receptionist from the doctors' office, but recognized all the faces.

Garol and Toby dropped their equipment bags.

The receptionist said, "Hey handsome," while the rest of the team gathered around him.

Garol blushed and lost his train of thought. The new leader was at a sudden loss for words and a long silent moment ensued.

"Are we supposed to do something, coach?" Jimmy asked.

"Yes," Garol answered. "Let's play some catch to warm up. The mitts are in this bag," Garol unzipped the large bag.

There were twenty four different mitts in the bag, of varying sizes and to accommodate both right and left handed players. The players dug into the bag and pulled out what they wanted. Garol looked at the empty bag, then noticed every player had gloves on both hands. Split and a player Garol only recognized from town had a mitt on their heads.

Garol blinked to clear his vision. His first thought was to end the season, but instead he said, "Everyone raise the hand you throw with."

Everyone did.

"Ok, now take that mitt off and put it in the bag," Garol said.

The team followed orders.

"Those of you with a mitt on your head, please put it in the bag." Split dropped his head and looked sheepishly around to the other players.

"I'll look into helmets for you guys," Garol said. He looked at Toby and said, "Will you look into that?"

Both players took the mitts off their heads and put them in the bag.

"Ok," Garol began, a little worried, "why don't we grab a ball and form a line and play some catch to warm up."

Everyone grabbed a ball and formed a single file line stretching from third base to home plate. Garol stood in disbelief as the first person in line threw the ball into the outfield, then went to the back of the line. Then the second person came up and did the same thing, until eleven ball-less people stood in a single file line, and a scattering of balls lay around the outfield. The players looked at Garol for their next task.

Garol wondered how to proceed. He leaned toward saying, "Great job, I think we're ready" and ending practice, but he walked over to the bag, grabbed a mitt and walked over to Toby. He told Toby to stand between second and third base, then walked twenty feet into the outfield. Garol told Whirby to throw him the ball.

Toby threw the ball to Garol's left, out of reach. Garol might have been able track the ball down in his younger days without his cast, but now just let it fly past him.

Garol once again thought about ending practice, but said, "Ok, everyone pair up. Now half of you line up next to me and the other half next to Toby, facing each other," Garol motioned that he wanted his line to form to his sides. "We're going to play catch with one another. Throwing the ball back and forth."

The players made lines. Garol jogged to pick up Toby's ball and came back to the line.

"Ok, throw your balls," Garol commanded. Balls flew instantly. Anticipating a wayward throw, Garol inched to his left as Toby released then lurched after another hard throw seven feet to his left. His lunge missed and he yelled, "Duck," to the man playing catch next to him, falling helplessly to the ground. The man didn't duck. Instead, he caught and immediately tossed it seven feet to the right of the person across from him. From the ground Garol watched softballs criss-cross until all the balls ended their run in the outfield due to Garol's absence.

Again he set himself and ordered, "Throw." Garol hadn't thrown any kind of ball in ten years, and his lob arched high. He watched it travel, but missed it's drop because his peripheral vision glimpsed a ball a fraction of a second before it crashed into his chest. Garol rocked on his heels, swam his arms in short circles for balance and steadied himself in time for the next ball. Garol attempted to shout, "No," but was struck by another ball and then another. Shortly, all the softballs rested in Garol's vicinity, having bounced off some part of his body.

Garol dropped to his knees. As if in shock, his body stopped working as his mind filtered the possibilities: *Am I hurt? Don't think so. Was that ineptness or a pre-planned attack? Not sure.*

Again Garol distributed the balls. He tried to figure out the routine and watched the player across from his right. He easily caught the ball, but wasn't able to throw it before the next incoming ball pounded his chest. Garol lay on the ground with eyes closed. When he opened his eyes, the entire team was hovering over him. He began laughing hard.

He stood up and said, "What the hell was that? We've got to try that again."

This time Garol remained on his feet. A few seconds after all the balls had smacked him he let out a big laugh and said, "Again." It was the same result. Garol tried it five more times, but never caught more than three balls and couldn't get any throws off.

Garol decided to take himself and Toby out of the mix and watch the players go through their juggling routine. The sight was unbelievable. The players threw in a choreographed pattern, catching the ball and transferring to their throwing hand and tossing to someone else waiting and catching another ball, all within fractions of a second. The angles they threw reminded Garol of a backgammon board. Not one of them could throw a ball straight ahead, but they could all throw perfectly to their right or left.

Out of curiosity, Garol yelled, "Reverse," and the players instantly began throwing at the opposite angle. It was the most amazing thing Garol had ever seen.

After watching for a while, Garol felt confident he'd figured out the routine and decided to put Toby and himself back in the mix. Garol decided not to start by throwing a ball so he could be more prepared to catch. Garol yelled, "Go," and the balls began flying. Garol caught the first one, but in the effort to transfer it from his glove hand to his right hand, he was struck in the face by another ball. It jerked his head back and he dropped the ball. The rest of the balls came at Garol and each time, he was late, flinching from his last hit. Garol kept having the team start again. Garol never managed to get a throw off, but after forty tries, was able to catch every ball that came his way.

Garol was excited. He couldn't remember the last time he'd been outplayed, and he assumed that if the team could do this, they could easily play softball. He ordered the team to try the juggling act ten more times and called it a day.

GAROL FELT THE TIME was right to make a move with Sara. *Why not?* He had some stuff going on now. He was increasing his handyman skills, coaching and playing softball. He hadn't had a drink or a smoke in probably four months. Maybe longer? He was going to be mayor pretty soon. It was onward and upward from there. Although he was still in the cast, he felt like he had lost a lot of weight. *I'll get the cast off when I'm mayor. That way they can't make me go back.* Seeing that mannequin in the window made Garol reflect on his younger days. *I was a stud, if do I say so myself.* It definitely was time to grace Sara with his companionship. *But how?*

Garol thought about his options. *I never see her. I could just drop by her house.* The thought left him feeling a little wobbly. *What would I say?* The only things he could think of were too canned or forced.

Garol tried out a few lines, alone in his living room, "Hey baby. What brings you here?"

"Umm, I live here," Garol answered back for Sara.

"Come on, think," Garol said in frustration. "Hey, wanna party?" he said leaning at a casual angle, to enforce how smooth he was.

"That is so stupid," Garol smacked his hand on his cast helmet, "I'm such a tool. Think!"

The more he tried to think, the less he was able to come up with. Nothing came to mind other than what an uncomfortable fool he was.

If she got a letter in the mail, I could knock on the door and hand it to her personally. She never gets anything in the mail...Bingo. I'll send her a letter. I can't hand her a letter I've written, she'll think I'm a wimp. Write it anonymously. Girls love secret admirers.

The problem was what to write. He scribbled some things down.

Hey Hot Stuff,

Hey Hot Stuff? That's stupid. He tried again.

Sara,
That Sam guy is pretty cool. Have
you had any chance to really get to
know him? I think you should. He's
really cool. Maybe if you guys talked
you would see how cool he is. He's a
really good guy.

Garol read the note to himself. *Oh God. What a dipshit.* Garol wadded both sheets of paper into a ball and threw them in the trash. He decided to give it one more try.

Sara,
I just wanted to let you know that
you're the most beautiful woman I
have ever seen.
Anonymous

Garol looked at the letter. The line, "You're the most beautiful woman I've ever seen" wasn't true. That would still be Beth, but writing "you're the second most beautiful woman I've ever seen," didn't make sense. *Just leave it.*

Garol thought about signing it anonymously. *I could sign it, "Garol." She doesn't know that name. Then I wouldn't be lying to her. It would be our little joke.*

Garol rewrote the note and signed it Garol, then stuffed it in an envelope. He was excited about delivering the mail. He couldn't wait for the bag to show up. Garol hid the letter in the book, *Beauty and the Beast* and decided to wait until the bag showed up and deliver it with the rest of the mail.

This will be good. She'll know it's from me. It will be our little game. If it is meant to be, it will happen, and I really think she and I are meant to be. Aren't we?

In the morning, Garol hopped out of bed. He couldn't wait to deliver the mail. He started to run out onto the porch to get the mailbag, but caught himself halfway to the door. A light bulb clicked in his head. He had been issued a postal carrier's uniform shortly after he began and shoved it in the closet, believing he would look foolish. Today, though, he wanted to add that little touch of professionalism. *Women love a man in uniform.* He had this image of delivering the letter, Sara seeing him in the uniform and saying, "I know this is from you. I feel the same way. You look amazing. Take me now." The two would join together in unison in a long kiss that would last forever.

Garol put the uniform on. He flipped the postal carrier hat in the air a few times, caught it with his hands, put it on top of his cast helmet, and spun in a dance move. *I wonder if I can find a cane? That would be classy.* He popped open the front door.

Garol stepped on the porch and looked around in bewilderment, trying to find the mailbag. Then he started the search all over. He looked down, then forward, then to his left and over to his right. He stepped off the porch and looked all around.

"Lose something, officer?" Whirby said.

Garol snapped his head to Whirby, "Oh, hey. I didn't see you." There was a brief pause and Garol asked, "How is the game going?"

"I thought you didn't care about the game."

"No, that's not true. Why would you think that? That stuff I said? I was just kidding. I came out here to see if you were playing. I think it's amazing how you give them all personalities. You're so creative."

"Actually, they all have their own personalities. I just help them move around the board. I do have some influence," Whirby said, a little proud. "There's only so much I can do, though," he said, frowning.

"Awesome, really awesome. Wow! That's just awesome. So what's going on in the game today?" Garol said, still looking around for the bag.

"I don't think there are going to be any moves today. I had a feeling something might happen, but it doesn't look like it."

"I'm really sorry to hear that," Garol said, looking at the side of the porch steps.

"It's probably good. I thought the castle was going to move today and I have a bad feeling he is going to move with his heart and not his head. Hopefully, this delay will give him enough time to gather his senses. Who knows?"

"That's neat, really. That is so neat," Garol said. "It just seems like it would be so cool to talk to little plastic pieces. I wish I could do that. It would be so easy to make friends. Man, is that creative. That's really creative," Garol said, now on his hands and knees to peer through the little opening in the side of the porch steps.

"You ok?"

"Me? Yeah, I'm good."

"You look a little lost. Did you lose something?"

"That's a good question. Did I lose something?" Garol said getting to his feet. "You know, I have to think about that. That's the kind of question that makes you think." Garol walked up and opened his door, "I'm definitely going to think about that."

Five days went by and the mailbag never showed up. *Where is that damn thing? Just like everything else, it's only around when you don't want it to be.*

Garol decided to take matters into his own hands. A special delivery was in order. Being the mail representative in the town, he didn't need a bag to deliver the mail. He just needed a letter and something that resembled a destination. He started to put the postal carrier uniform on again, but walking through town with only one letter in hand wearing the uniform might cause unneeded attention. He decided to travel natural, or castural, wearing only his cast.

As he approached Sara's front door, his inner voice reminded him that he was a jackass, and he turned around abruptly and headed back toward the street. Whirby, who had been out for a walk, met Garol in front of Sara's hedges.

"Hello Sam," Whirby said jubilantly.

"Hey, what are you doing here?"

"I was just about to ask you that."

"I was out for a walk. There hasn't been any mail in a while and I wanted to get some exercise."

"Great idea. Me too. Shall we walk together?" Whirby asked.

"Actually I was just ending. You go ahead."

"What do you have in your hand?"

"Oh, I forgot to deliver a letter the last time the mail went out and thought I would drop it off on my walk."

"You taking it up to Sara's?"

"Yeah."

"Can I take a look at it?"

"No. It's personal."

"For you or her?"

"Her. I don't know what's in it."

"I won't open it; I just want to look at it."

"Why?"

"Just curious," Whirby answered.

"Sorry, I can't. As a postal carrier, I have a responsibility to both sender and receiver. I don't break that code."

"You're a good man, Sam. I was just testing you. I wouldn't want you to break that code. By the way, I was thinking about what you said the other day. It is nice to see you've taken such an interest in chess. I knew you would learn to love it. The latest move is interesting. It looks like the castle finally pushed aside the circumstances holding it back and took matters into his own hands. I hate to speculate, but I really think the Castle is going to find himself thoroughly wedged between the two opposing bishops and the female horse. You can only do so much to keep someone out of trouble. Free will, I tell you, that's what gets us in trouble, but hey, it's still a wonderful thing."

"You are entertaining. I love your enthusiasm," Garol said and patted Whirby on the back with a slight push to get him going. "Thanks for the report. I'll see you later," Garol waited for Whirby to start walking away.

Garol didn't want to head up to Sara's door with Whirby still in the vicinity, so he bent over as if he had laces on his cast feet and pretended to tie them. When he could no longer see Whirby, he walked up to Sara's door, took a deep breath and knocked.

The door swung open almost immediately and Sara stepped out onto the porch. "Sam, I didn't expect you."

Garol's mind went blank, "You didn't?"

"No. How are you?"

"Good. Good. You?"

"Good, thanks," Sara answered.

Garol struggled to remember why he was there. *Say something*, "It's nice out."

"Yes it is, very nice," Sara answered smiling.

Am I wearing my cast? This must look strange. Why am I here? Leave. "Alrighty, thanks for stopping by. I mean, I'm thankful I stopped by. No, I'm sorry I stopped by. I'm sorry I bothered you, but thanks for being here," Garol turned to move down the porch steps.

Sara read her name on the letter in Garol's hand and asked, "Is that for me?"

Garol stopped and spun around. "It says Sara." He held the letter out.

"I love getting mail," Sara said with cupped hands in front of her mouth.

"I don't believe in coincidences," Garol immediately felt he'd revealed too much.

Sara looked at him confusedly.

Before she could ask anything Garol handed her the letter and said, "Open it."

Sara jumped up and down twice. "I'm so excited." She ripped the envelope open and pulled out the letter. She read it and a smile came over her face and then her lips pushed together and out and her eyes squinted. She flipped the note around and then read it again. "Do you know anyone named Garol?"

Garol began to say, "That's me," but, "That's a ridiculous name," came out.

"I like it. It's unique," Sara beamed, "How romantic. I can't wait to meet Garol."

Again, Garol almost said, "That's me," but became flustered, tangled his feet, and fell backwards, landing at the bottom of the steps on his back.

"Oh my! Are you alright?"

Garol didn't feel any pain because of the cast and just got to his feet. Again he thought about explaining, but the moment seemed to be over. Garol said, "Well I'd better be getting back," and waved goodbye before walking away.

"I THOUGHT YOU LEFT," The Man walked out of the post office carrying a bag of trash.

Garol lay face to the sky, looking like a fat, oblong planet with thirty or more softball- moons scattered around him.

"I believe you're gonna be late," The Man placed the trash bag in the dumpster.

"I can't do it." Garol had spent the afternoon juggling balls off the wall in preparation for the evening's softball practice. He began by tossing two underhanded at the wall; bouncing them back to himself, catching, tossing and repeating. Like a Richter scale, adding a third ball multiplied the challenge by ten. At least one rebellious ball (and often two) dipped with passive aggressive intent. Garol responded like a frustrated baby sitter by blaming each ball for its inability to get with the program.

"The important thing is that you try— you'll get it," The Man offered his hand to help Garol up. Garol got up and they loaded the softballs into the equipment bag.

"Trying to do something I'll never be able to is a waste of time," Garol whined.

"Sulking and moping are wastes of time. Quitting too early is a waste of life."

When Garol showed up, the players were in their positions and Toby was hitting them grounders and fly balls. Garol watched from the bench as Toby called out, "Take one," and hit a ground ball to the third baseman, who let it go through her legs and placed her mitt in front of her face, appearing to look for a hole, but then squatted and pulled the mitt over her head in an effort to hide. Again Toby called, "Take one," and hit a ground ball a foot and a half to the shortstop's left, who waved to indicate, "out of my range."

No grounders were fielded until the first baseman, Split, scooped the ball smoothly, but then flipped it to an empty first base. After the ball rolled to the fence, Split threw his glove down and yelled, "It was right to you. Can't you do anything right?

"You call that right to me? Are you insane?" a deeper voice hollered from Split.

"Oh, brother," Garol said aloud.

"Hello, Sam," a voice from behind him said.

"Hello, Gladys," Garol said, facing the field after a long silence.

"Looks like the team could use a little help."

"I don't think a little help would do much good."

"I know a great athlete who could really help the team. He's a ringer."

Garol was intrigued, but he didn't want to encourage conversation with Gladys. He said, "I don't think it would matter too much. One person can only do so much."

"He's here with me now," Gladys said.

Gladys sat on the bleachers next to the mannequin in the clothing store dressed like a baseball player. It was uncanny how much the mannequin looked like Garol at the age of 21, a spitting image of himself at his best. They were identical other than that ski sloped nose and the mismatched eyebrows: dark brown thick hair and matching eyes, high cheek bones and dimples, fit and lean muscular bodies. With the two next to each other, Garol recognized the ski-sloped nose as Gladys's. Both of her eyebrows were thin.

"You have to admit, my baby is a good looking athlete."

Garol turned back to the field, but couldn't watch the action. He felt a dizzy spell coming on and clenched his eyes shut and then took a few deep breaths. When he felt he could speak normally he said, "He is good looking."

"He's perfect looking. You know, I never see him work out. People always tell me he should be a model. I just hope it doesn't go to his head. I don't think it will. He's such a sweet boy. Never a bad word to say. A real doll, really. Just a doll." Gladys put her left arm around her son. She reached over and grabbed his right hand with hers and said, "I just love motherhood. Such a blessing."

"A real doll. Do you have two children?"

"No, just my little Doll Baby. Well, not so little anymore."

"Wait…That's the little Doll Baby you had a month ago?"

"Yep. This is my little bundle of joy."

"He grew up pretty damn quick," Garol said.

"They really do. It seems like just yesterday he was in diapers. What's a mother to do? You have to let them grow. His life is more important than mine. It probably sounds crazy coming from me."

"Not at all…His life is more important than yours," Garol answered.

"You really seem to be getting it, Sam."

"Not even close," Garol turned toward the field.

The three sat quietly for a few minutes before Gladys asked, "So what do you say, can he play?"

"The team's set."

"Oh, come on. Let Garol Jr. play."

"That's an interesting name choice, Garol Jr. Where did you come up with that?"

"He just looks like a Garol. Don't you think?"

Yeah, that's the problem.

"Can he play?"

"I'll tell you what Gladys. If he grabs a mitt and walks onto the field, he can play. Is that fair? Now if you don't mind, I have a team to coach."

"I see how it is," Gladys said.

"That's how it is," Garol said, feeling victorious. "In fact, he can jog out right now and relieve the shortstop. Or better yet, let's have him take some fly balls in center. We need a guy out there with some range."

"I should've expected as much from you."

"Life's about opportunity. This is his—go for it."

"You'll never change."

"Nope," Garol said.

"You'd really make him go out there with a sprained ankle? Father of the year," Gladys snapped.

"Stop with that Gladys. Just knock this whole thing off. I mean it."

"It's okay baby," Gladys said to Garol Jr. "I probably shouldn't say this, but I am at my wit's end with you," she said, raising her voice. "The only reason we came is because he wants to be a part of your life. You've ruined you and me, trust me on that. But be a father, will you? You missed his childhood— when does it click in that it's time? Because we'll find a way to get your attention. You can't shut your son out. It's just like trying to shut your old self out: the harder you try the harder it comes back."

Garol faced the ball diamond. The joke was getting old and Garol felt a bubble of anger inside him. He was afraid— it was rising quickly and he wasn't sure what would happen if it exploded. He concentrated on practice to calm himself down.

"Who is this?" Said a voice Garol recognized as Sara.

"This is my baby, Garol Jr."

"Garol? Did you say Garol?" Sara answered.

"Yes, that's right."

"It's nice to meet you, finally. I got your letter the other day. What a wonderful compliment. That was very sweet," Sara said.

Garol turned around in time to see Sara kiss Garol Jr. on the cheek. Garol turned back around to face the ball diamond.

Then Garol heard a deep, flat voice say, "You look very pretty and smell like wonderful flowers in bloom."

Garol knew it was Gladys talking for Doll Baby, but it drove him crazy and he was unable to concentrate on practice.

"You certainly have a way with words that makes a woman feel desirable," Sara said.

"That's my baby," Gladys said.

Garol faced the practice field. Sara had popped his bubble of anger. Garol began to feel faint, so he closed his eyes for the next ten minutes to drown out everything around him. He tried desperately, but found it impossible to ignore the banter between Gladys and Doll Baby. *I'll be damned if I ever refer to her bundle of joy as Garol Jr.*

When Garol finally opened his eyes, everyone was lying on the ground except Toby, who stood at home plate, looking at Garol. He got up and walked over to Toby.

"What's happening here?" Garol asked Toby.

"Everyone's been hit," Toby answered.

"Hit?"

"Yeah, with a softball."

"All of them? Where?"

"In the head."

"Are they ok?"

"Yeah, it's the way we usually end practice."

Like Father, Like Son

THAT MORNING, GAROL DIDN'T just deliver the mail, he delivered attitude. He trampled flower gardens, frisbeed letters with a flick of a wrist, unconcerned if they made it to their porches or not, and either ignored hollers from anyone that disapproved of his style or answered, "Life sucks," as he walked without looking back.

When Garol reached Gladys's residence, he pulled out two letters for Garol Jr. He ducked behind the tall hedges lining her property and held the letters up to the sun to glimpse what was inside. One letter was typed print, but the other letter was hand written with a nice cursive flair. *That's a girl's handwriting. Sara? Would she write him a letter? He's a mannequin. She kissed him at practice. Open them. No. Yes. What if I get caught? Say they got lost in the mail. Don't, it's a federal offense. In this town? Do it. What if someone is watching? Blame it on the mailman. I am the mailman. Shit.*

Garol nervously shoved the unopened letters in the bag as if concealing evidence and looked at the windows of the houses facing him. He thought he saw curtains move in a house across the street. He took a deep breath and said softly, "I didn't open them," as if on trial. He straightened, walked up to the gate, and entered. He noticed a lawn sign with the word "Mayor" written on it.

FOR MAYOR
GAROL JR.
THE-MAN-WHO-CAN

Doll Baby's running for mayor? Garol stepped to the side of the house and pulled the two letters out of his bag. He tore open one and read the note.

> Garol Jr.,
> We received your application to run for Mayor. Permission to join the Mayoral race has been granted.
> Good Luck,
> The Head of the Panel that Looks Over Applications and Decides who Runs for Mayor

That little son of a bitch. Who does he think he is?
"Is there a reason you're hiding in my bushes?" Gladys said.
"A reason?" Garol said.
"Why are you hiding in my bushes?"
"I felt nauseous," Garol bent down toward his bag and stashed the opened letter at the bottom. "Thought I might get sick."
"Well that sure is a coincidence. You get to my property and get the butterflies. All those caged up emotions. Thinking about old times. The passion."
"I think it's something I ate," Garol stood up. "Here's your mail." He handed the unopened letter to Gladys and walked past her.

"Is this all the mail?" Gladys yelled.

"That's it."

"We were expecting another piece. Something addressed to Garol Jr."

"Maybe it got lost?"

"Why would you say it got lost?"

"Maybe it'll be here tomorrow. Who knows what tomorrow brings?" Garol left her property.

Garol spent time in the assembly hall bathroom, revving himself up for the night's debate. *Feel the magic. Feel the magic. Feel the magic,* he reminded himself over and over. *Road to the White House. Feel the glory.*

As soon as Garol entered the hall, four hundred people jumped to their feet to welcome their new leader. Garol jogged up the stairs, waving his arms. Once at the podium, he motioned for the crowd to quiet down and have a seat. Garol looked over to the podium to his right and saw Doll Baby standing stiffly in front of it.

The Head Beaver came on stage and issued a warning. "During the last debate, people in the audience acted immaturely toward one of the speakers. Because of your harsh remarks, Podium Two dropped out of the race and is seeking counseling. You should know that we figured out later it wasn't Podium Two's lack of concern but merely a microphone problem that kept the audience from hearing his responses. I want to be clear that if such an outburst happens again, it will not be tolerated. Either the debate will be terminated immediately, or particular trouble makers will be ejected from the building.

"Moving on," The Head Beaver said, "let's introduce our debaters. On the right is Sam, whom we all remember from last week. On the left is our newest mayoral candidate, Garol Jr. Gentlemen, this debate will be a little different. I will open a topic for discussion and the two of you will give your thoughts.

At the very end of the debate, we will open the floor to questions from the audience. Let's get started."

"Gentlemen, the town is looking for a way to develop flight. How will your mayoral term bring us closer to reach that goal?"

After a minute of silence, The Head Beaver said, "Gentlemen?"

Garol grew nervous and began talking. "I think flight is important. Very important. Yep, so we should probably model an airplane after one that already exists. Yep, we could just recreate one. No need to use blowers and stuff like that. Just, ya know, make an airplane," Garol said and smiled.

A loud aaaaawwww came from the crowd.

"Not that using blowers is a bad thing. It is ingenious, really. Just that, well, they already have planes so we could make the same thing. That way we know it'll work."

"How would we get one to model?" The Head Beaver stepped in.

"Well, we could take one."

"Steal one?" The Head Beaver asked.

The crowd let out a loud aaaaawwww again.

"No, not steal, just borrow. Yep."

"Borrow a plane? Do you mean hijack a plane? Doesn't that involve kidnapping?" The Head Beaver asked.

"Aaaaawwww," the crowd said again.

"Ummmmm," Garol stalled for a brilliant thought to enter his head. "No. Well, I don't want to cut into my opponent's time," Garol deflected the question to Doll Baby.

"Garol Jr., you don't have to comment if you don't want to," The Head Beaver said, "but if you would like to comment on the absurdity of the brilliant work members of this town put forth in the efforts of flight, or any grand ideas about kidnapping or hijacking an airplane, then please do so at this time."

Doll Baby stared straight ahead. He gave the appearance that he would neither put down the admirable effort for flight nor comment on any hideous illegal activities.

"I guess we can assume that Garol Jr., or Doll Baby as he is lovingly referred to, thinks work on the airplane is going well and he favors neither kidnapping nor stealing.

"Moving on," The Head Beaver said, "Sam, if you could add one thing to this town, what would it be?"

"People should have the right to different foods. I think maybe we could add some things to the cafeteria menu. That would be nice."

"Oh, you're not happy with the free food you receive every day?"

The crowd gave out an, "Aaaaawwww."

"Well, it's not that. I just think we can spice it up," Garol said.

"How would we do that?" The Head Beaver asked.

"We could add mayonnaise and sweets, maybe some soda. Nothing's better than an extra-cheese pepperoni pizza with some Coke. Maybe some Ho-Ho's for dessert."

"Ok," The Head Beaver said. "Once again, Doll Baby, you don't have to answer. Your physical stature makes it obvious you don't indulge in such unhealthy foods, but if you have anything to add, please do so at this time."

Doll Baby said nothing, but everyone knew what he meant. The food at the cafeteria stays.

"We're going to switch gears. This time, I'm going to ask Doll Baby the question. Doll Baby, what is your number one goal for this town?"

There was a long silence as Doll Baby gathered his thoughts.

"Actually, I'm going to answer this one," The Head Beaver interrupted. "I know I'm taking some liberties. For that I apologize," The Head Beaver said to Doll Baby, "but it's very clear that Doll Baby's number one goal would be to unite the town. I feel very confident giving that answer. Doll Baby, if I'm wrong, then please say something."

Doll Baby said nothing.

"Sam, would you like to respond with a canned answer?"

"No," Garol said feeling it was better to keep quiet.

"Doll Baby, please tell the town why you would like to be mayor."

There was a long silence while the crowd waited for Doll Baby to answer.

When the time limit came, The Head Beaver said, "Oh brother, it looks like a mechanical problem with the microphone again."

They took a slight intermission to fix the microphone, but didn't have the parts.

Garol couldn't wait to get out of there.

The following day Garol showed up to his campaign headquarters and found a copy of the *Gossip* lying on his desk.

"Debate Two"

If we learned anything last night, it's that people aren't perfect. It now appears we have two candidates with completely differently styles. One likes to ramble on about nothing and one that prefers a cooler, calculated style of communicating. One stands at the podium like stacked bean bags, and the other looks cool and composed behind the podium. One buckles under pressure, while the other shows no sign of weakness in battle. One leaves us worrying about his ethics regarding flight research, while the other appears to fly the straight and narrow. In a race that originally appeared to be a landslide, things now seem to be heating up just a bit. If there is one area in which our newcomer Sam may have to watch out, it's with the ladies' vote. Garol Jr.'s good looks are getting the ladies' attention. Good luck to both men.

GAROL LOOKED AT HIS blank lineup sheet for the day's softball game between his squad and Doll Baby's, noticing the bleachers fill with townspeople and the lawn with spectators on blankets.

He put himself in the fourth batting position as the pitcher and surveyed his team, trying to imagine any of them on the field. He scratched his head and wrote Toby in the second position, playing left center field, and Split batting sixth at first base.

"Where do you want me, coach?" Whirby sat on the bench, his feet dangling five inches above the ground.

"Right where you are. What's her name?" Garol referred to the receptionist from the doctor's office playing catch with another girl.

"That's Samantha," Whirby stood up, making him an inch shorter.

"Where does she play?"

"Shortstop. She's good too. Fast. Great range."

Samantha saw Garol looking at her. She waved and said, "Hey Hot Stuff. I'm good in any position," and swung her hips as if she had a hula-hoop.

"Uh-huh," Garol huffed without inflection and penciled her into the leadoff position.

"Who's the girl she's playing catch with?"

Garol saw Sara walking his way. He tilted his head down toward the lineup sheet, but focused on her out of the corner of his eye.

"Heather," Whirby answered.

Sara moved slowly, elegantly, and looking lost as if in search of someone to take her hand and lead her to the right spot. There were two seats in the front row on Garol's side available, and Garol watched as a couple moved toward them.

Garol intercepted the couple, "Those are reserved, but there are still seats on the other side," he pointed at the bleachers on the first base line and noticed Gladys standing and waving at Sara.

Garol started to raise his hand to wave to Sara, but stopped.

"Heather plays catcher," Whirby said.

"What do you want?" Garol asked.

"We're ready to start, I need both coaches with your lineup sheets here, now." the umpire called from home plate.

"Just a second," Garol quickly scribbled in his lineup sheet, keeping an eye on Sara.

"Let's go, coach," the umpire yelled.

Garol filled in names as he walked. When he reached the conference, he heard the umpire laugh and say to Doll Baby, "That's funny, I'll have to remember that one."

"Here you go, blue," Garol said and handed over his sheet.

"Who is 'What's her face?'" the umpire asked, perusing the sheet.

"That girl over there," Garol said, pointing behind his bench.

He heard Gladys yell, "Sara honey, we're over here."

The umpire scowled at Garol. He turned to Doll Baby and said, "Garol Jr., you have the nicest handwriting. I am sorry to hear your ankle is still bothering you." The umpire turned to Garol, "You guys caught a real break. This young stud isn't going to play today."

"What do you know?" Garol said. He looked at Doll Baby's right ankle that appeared swollen at first glance, but looked like it might have been stuffed with socks.

The umpire discussed the rules and a player on Garol Jr.'s team, named Dennis, walked up behind Doll Baby and whispered something in his ear.

"Let's play ball," the umpire called. Dennis wrapped his arms around Doll Baby's neck, cupping his right hand under Doll Baby's armpit and the two pivoted slowly back to the their bench, doing their best to keep the weight off Garol Jr.'s ankle.

Garol's team began the contest in the field. It went much smoother than expected. Samantha fielded two grounders for outs and Jimmy caught a pop fly in left field for another. The only rough spot was listening to Samantha cheer between pitches, "Come on Hot Stuff, pitch it in there."

In the bottom of the first inning, Garol came up to bat with the bases loaded and no outs. He walked to the plate glancing at Sara. *She's watching.* Garol worked the count to two balls and two strikes, letting the tension mount and glowing in the attention from Sara. The fifth pitch was perfect and Garol let everyone know by smashing it over the left field fence for a grand slam. He trotted around the bases, waving his arm high. When he reached his bench, the players lined up for high fives and Samantha smacked him on the butt and said, "Way to go stud." In the fourth inning, Garol followed that up with another grand slam and his team led 8-0.

Between innings, Doll Baby gathered his team. Through his inspiration, they scored three runs in the fifth and three more in the sixth, trailing 8-6 at the top of the final inning. Their first batter hit a ball hard to right center field, but Toby tracked it down and caught it.

"Pinch hitting for Dennis is Garol Jr.," a voice announced over the speakers.

HUH? Garol watched Doll Baby inch along in small pivots as he entered the game for the first time, accompanied by Dennis, all the way to the batters' box. There, he bent Doll Baby's legs at the knees, raised his arms in a batting stance, and placed a bat in his hands.

Garol was growing annoyed on the mound and yelled, "Blue? Is there a time limit here?"

"Let's step it up," the umpire said to Doll Baby and Dennis.

Doll Baby stood in the batters' box ready to hit, eyeing Garol unwaveringly.

Gladys stood up and yelled, "Come on sweetie—give it a ride."

Garol looked at Sara. Sara watched Doll Baby.

Garol tossed a pitch off the mark of the plate.

Doll Baby didn't swing.

"Ball one," the umpire called.

"Good eye, pumpkin," Gladys hollered.

Sara clapped.

Put it right over the plate. Let him hit it. What am I, nuts? Just throw strikes. Come on. Garol looked at Sara.

Sara looked at Doll Baby with her hands held in the prayer position in front of her face.

Garol tossed a beautiful pitch with a nine-foot arc right over the plate and breathed a sigh of relief as it landed in the catcher's mitt.

"Ball two," the umpire called.

"What?" Garol yelled. "Are you blind?"

"Deep," the umpire said.

"Bullshit it was deep."

"Watch yourself," the umpire warned.

Garol threw the softball in his mitt a couple times. He looked at Sara.

Sara prayed.

Garol released a faster pitch with little arc, headed straight for Doll Baby.

The pitch hit Doll Baby and rocked him. He swayed back and forth a few times before toppling backwards like a stubborn bowling pin.

Gladys jumped up, "Is he hurt? Call an ambulance."

The crowd gasped. Some closed their eyes and prayed. No one made a sound.

The umpire leaned over and placed his fingers on Doll Baby's wrist to check his pulse.

The crowd waited.

"He's unconscious. We need someone who knows CPR?" the umpire announced.

"I do," Sara darted onto the field. She placed an arm under Doll Baby's back, gently rubbed his chest, and kissed him a few times. She turned her ear to Garol Jr.'s mouth and then both kissed and rubbed his chest simultaneously.

"Use your tongue," a voice in the crowd roared.

Sara did. She rubbed and petted and let her tongue fly all over his face and mouth. She did everything she could to bring Garol Jr. back to life.

Garol looked for a bathroom.

Silence was the only sound.

Suddenly Garol Jr. sat up, Sara's arm around his backside. She was still applying CPR.

Gladys cried, "Thank God."

The umpire tapped Sara and said, "I think he's regained consciousness."

Sara gasped, "I'll say."

The crowd awwed.

Sara and the umpire got Garol Jr. to his feet and the umpire asked Doll Baby if he wanted to continue. "The batter will stay in the game," he announced. To Doll Baby, he said, "You're one tough son of a gun and you just earned my vote for mayor."

The umpire scolded Garol, "That's warning number two. Control your emotions, that's how people get hurt."

Garol felt like public enemy number one as the crowd glared a hole through him.

The next pitch was a strike. He followed with another and the count went to full.

One more strike. Be calm. You've got the rhythm. Just like the last two.

Doll Baby's bat fell from his grasp and dropped to the dirt.

Someone in the stands shouted, "He doesn't think he can throw a strike."

Garol looked in the stands and saw Sara blow a kiss to Doll Baby.

Samantha cheered, "Throw a strike, Hot Stuff. Move on from the past, let's go."

He started his motion. As he came through, his hand brushed his leg, and he watched it fall two feet short of the plate for a ball.

"Take your base," the umpire called. "Do you need a pinch runner?"

Stoically, Doll Baby gave no indication he needed a pinch runner, was in any pain, or had just come within seconds of losing his life. The first base coach walked in and put his arm around Doll Baby's neck. They pivoted down the baseline, discussing potential game scenarios.

Garol laughed to himself. *Let this player hit the ball and Doll Baby will have to run.*

The batter hit the ball to first base. Split fielded it cleanly and tossed the ball to the personality he thought was covering first. The ball rolled out of bounds. Split threw his mitt in the dirt and yelled, "Can't you do anything right?"

"Ball out of bounds. Dead ball, runner on first goes to third and batter goes to second," the umpire announced.

The first base coached pivoted Doll Baby to third base.

"I know what you're doing," Garol said as he followed their slow trek.

The next batter hit the ball to the third baseman, who bobbled the ball and then picked it up and held it, daring Doll Baby to run home. Then, realizing he wasn't going anywhere, he looked to first base, but the runner had already reached it.

Garol told the third baseman, "You didn't need to hold him. He can't go anywhere."

"Because of his ankle?" the third baseman asked.

Samantha said, "You can hold me Hot Stuff," and pinched Garol's cast behind.

"Do you mind?" Garol snarled.

"Not at all," Samantha did a little dance spin back to her position.

Garol threw two balls and a strike to the next batter before the hitter launched a shot down the left field line that landed an inch inside fair territory.

"Foul ball," the umpire roared.

"It's fair. It was on the line," Garol argued.

The umpire strolled out to the mound and said quietly, "Look, I realize I messed up that pitch earlier. That was a strike, and I wanted to make it up to you. I'm impressed that you made the right call on that hit. It would have obviously been a double or a triple if I'd called it fair."

"Not if the guy on third can't run. Don't do me any favors."

"Even with a bad ankle, he'd have scored on that hit. He creamed that pitch. He could've crawled home." The umpire walked back behind home plate.

Garol started his windup.

"Come on stud, let go and throw a strike," Samantha cheered.

Garol threw a ball.

Have to throw a strike. Can't walk Doll Baby home. Throw a strike. Make him run.

"Let someone in, good-looking. Throw a strike," Samantha shouted.

Garol walked the batter. The third base coach pivoted Garol Jr. home from third base and the crowd stood in unison to congratulate his strength and courage for staying in the game.

Garol's team was down 11-9 when he came up to the plate, with two outs in the bottom of the last inning and a runner on first and second base. Doll Baby entered in right field, carried on the shoulders of two outfield teammates as the crowd whooped and hollered. He stood in right field with his glove in basket position just below his stomach, daring Garol to hit the ball his way.

Garol eyed the fence, knowing a home run would end the game with a victory, but his eyes kept drifting to Doll Baby's taunt. Sara watched Doll Baby, occasionally waving.

He leaned into the next pitch and hit the ball high in the air to right field.

"Long Arm of the Law"

We certainly learned about our potential leaders yesterday. One leader rushes out scoring early then desperately tries to control his surroundings to keep the illusion of security in place. An emotional grand-standing leader who snips at teammates and argues with umpires (not to mention throws at batters) all while hidden and cast out from an inability to relax, enjoy, and just let the softball fall where it may.

The other — calm, cool and collected. A leader who puts the team first and never utters a bad word. Who rallies the troops between innings, steadfast in the belief of his minions to come back against astronomical odds. Then, selflessly, and in time, mythically, stands to answer destiny's call, ignoring the pain and a close encounter with the ever-after. Appreciating every breath as if it's his last, and capitalizing.

A classic duel, coming down to a final play with a ball smashed high in the air to right field. A routine fly ball for someone with two good ankles and a clear mind, who hadn't just escaped death's clutches. A fly ball judged perfectly as it landed in Garol Jr.'s mitt, bounced off his chest, back to his mitt and to the ground. Two runners scoring and the tying run rounding second base. A showdown to test strength and courage as Garol Jr., unaided, found a way to gather his senses and pick up the ball. As Sam turned the corner for home, he threw a perfect throw to the plate.

"You're out!" the umpire yelled. "Game over."

One leader was hoisted off the field by his teammates as fans roared. The other, a broken warrior, screamed, "Bullshit" repeatedly, becoming the only player in the town's history to be kicked out of a game after it was over.

Gladys P. Calumny

It's Easy to Find a Stick to Beat a Dog

DURING THE NIGHT, THOUGHTS of Sara, Doll Baby, the game, the election, Sara and Doll Baby flirting, Beth, and football ricocheted throughout Garol's mind, clinging and dinging like a non-stop pinball game. Visions shot into view, then dropped through the gaps or spun between the bumpers, out of hope, immediately recycling themselves until the morning turned to light.

I'm a puppet in a play. My part is the fool.

Garol felt hopeless. Only a few weeks ago he was in love and felt destined for the White House. *It is a setup; like everything else in life, the world gives only because whoever controls my strings gets such a kick out of taking it all away.* What other explanation was there for the strong chance he was going to lose his heart and the mayoral election to a mannequin? Not just any mannequin, but himself as a mannequin. *How do people know what I look like? They saw me before they put me in the cast. How did they know to name him Garol Jr.? No one comes up with that name. Was The Man lying about the damage done to my license? Who is behind this?*

Garol didn't have the energy to examine his thoughts. He walked to the closet, pulled a navy pin striped suit, a white collared shirt, and a red power tie from their hangers. He walked four steps to the couch, let his body fall backwards over the arm and within seconds dozed off, blanketed by his apparel. For the next three hours, he woke up, donned an item of clothes, then disappeared into sleep until eventually he was completely dressed and conscious.

Slowly strolling to his recently erected campaign headquarters, Garol wished he were on a treadmill. He had no desire to hear his team put a positive spin on the last debate, act fired up about the election, or enthused about some ridiculous strategy for the final debate. He had no yearning to see phony smiles and hear, "Tough break in the softball game. Great throw by Doll Baby, though." *Positive spin. Keep it light.* "You played your best, you just got beat." *Really? Is that what happened?* "You can live with that, right?" *No, I can't live with my identical twin-plastic-immaculately conceived-son stealing my life out from under me. But hey, let's keep it positive.* "That's a good looking son you have." *Let's avoid real. Avoid the obvious. Avoid the facts.*

A loud crack of thunder over Garol's shoulder startled him and he spun to see an enormous black cloud marching to town from the mountain range in the west. It looked lumpy and angry enough to hail coal through sling shots.

Out of his view, a door slammed shut, spinning his head toward town. Three-foot tornadoes emerged in the streets. He counted seven and studied them in wonder as they moved, at times appearing synchronized in a choreographed dance by Mother Nature. Simultaneously stirring, flying and descending, they looked as if they were welcoming their God. Then they separately jumped and dashed like Chicken Littles in fear of the falling sky.

The door crackled open, and a few seconds later it banged shut. Garol surveyed the town. It was dark, deserted and unearthly, with the look of an old western town ripe for a showdown. The shops doors were closed and all the shades drawn. The streets were vacant, other than the miniature tornadoes, now numbering only four. Déjà vu triggered the memory of a black and white photo he'd seen shortly after his shoulder injury of a barren gold rush town taken decades after the last miners decided to seek their fortunes elsewhere.

He'd been thumbing through a LIFE Magazine silently brooding in the waiting room of a doctor's office and pondering, *How am I going to support a wife and child without football?*

Right after his shoulder separated him from football, Garol hung around the clubhouse as the players dealt with their immediate reality: a last regular season game, bowl loss, and dipping national rankings. Garol heard his teammates worry, "Get better, we need ya." He and his doctors kept quiet that the success rate of the shoulder surgery he needed to be ready for next season was only 2%. *How is that measured? What percentage is hope?*

Garol began off-season rehabbing. Initially, teammates said, "It'll be great to have you back next year." They joked and discussed their chances for a national championship. As the rehab stalled, passing teammates patted him on the back and said, "Keep it up, we need ya," doing their best to ignore the tiny amount of weight he could lift and his tired, blood-shot eyes that never reached REM sleep. They kept conversations light and passed more quickly, accident gawking at his workouts. "You'll make it," they said and held elongated smiles that lasted just long enough to make you wonder who was fooling who. Scouts and agents kept their speech elusive and positive, "Keep working." Their eyes dipped to their wristwatches and excused themselves before they committed or threw in the towel. No one came up to Garol and said what was on his mind, "Don't worry about a thing, so what you if don't play professional football? You could be a bagger at any grocery store in the nation. Nothing to worry about."

Then the inevitable came; the 2% at the bottom of the jar dried up. All chances for a comeback gone. And finally the last goodbye from teammates, as if to a stranded astronaut; a hero on an unreachable planet. Distant and protected messages as if communicated through T.V. screens that sincerely said, "We'll miss your talent. We'll miss the chance it gave us to win games," while politely not adding, "But ultimately we'll move on. Our plans have been altered, but not dashed." Because out of necessity the team had already found a new quarterback and the school was out recruiting another talented passer and the pro teams were reevaluating their draft picks. In conclusion, maybe somewhere, someday, Garol's name would come up in a group of guys sitting around drinking beers when someone asked, "Whatever happened to Garol Schand?" Someone might answer, "He messed up his shoulder. I saw that hit. Damn!"

In that physician's waiting room, barely 22 years old, Garol studied the black and white photo with wonder, feeling a strange kinship. In one of the rooms, his fiancé was listening to her doctor explain, "Take it easy. Avoid stress. Get rest. You're responsible for two." He felt as if the picture were relaying a message, telling him something no one else would. A message he knew meant something, but his anxious mind wasn't able to decrypt.

Again the door smacked closed, and Garol looked at the vibrant colors of the buildings confidently displaying themselves under the angry skies. Everything looked so new, not even a blemish, like it had been built during the night or redrawn every day by some idealistic artist with no patience for dirt, weeds, debris, dead flies, age, or paint flakes.

Again the door smacked against its building, and Garol bridged this village with the gold mining town in the black and white photo, tying the two together. As if this was that gold mining town and he were witnessing its grand opening— that happened to coincide with the last speck of gold in the area being plucked from the ground, and he was responsible for delivering the painful message, similar to the one he'd heard from his doctor, "It's all over. No one's coming." Streams of covered wagons were turning around in the road because of a sign at the far end of the street, "All the gold's mined, go home."

Garol felt an overwhelming sense of empathy. All its youthful pride and promise would crumble and particularly because the town would never receive its intended acclaim. Like the Titanic, if the Titanic had been hit by a maverick iceberg in the harbor, never even a chance to make its own mistakes. While the future would dismantle the town, the past and broken promises would leave it in solitude, rutted in constant search for purpose.

Garol thought about what the photo was trying to say the afternoon in the waiting room before his expectant, soon-to-be wife danced into the lobby, always upbeat. Was it saying that his teammates would move forward with their lives and bleachers would no longer fill to see him play? Scouts and agents would seek their fortunes elsewhere now that the gold in his right arm had been sifted? Was it an evil message explaining that he would remain in place, rotting and decaying in solitude and self-pity? Or was there some other message he couldn't see at the time? *A visual warning of the future to avoid, perhaps?* The 2%. Hopes offering that warned, "You have to move on, too. Take a different road out of town. Focus on what you have and not what's gone."

A droplet of rain smacked off the top of Garol's cast helmet and he quick-stepped to his campaign headquarters, not wanting to ruin his suit. Any hope Garol had of being bowled over by enthusiasm was abandoned the moment he opened the doors to his campaign headquarters. He was met with the backs of heads, blank stares, a few mumbles and the scurrying of feet, like rats from the light. Garol quickly found himself alone in a room with Gladys, who reclined with her feet on his desk. She was smoking a cigarette.

"I hope you're happy," Gladys's eyes burned a hole through Garol.

"Where did you get the cigarette?"

"Always thinking about yourself," Gladys blew a puff of smoke, flicked ash onto the floor, pulled her legs down from the desk and sat up.

"Give me that," Garol said, referring to the cigarette.

"No way, pal…You dirt bag," she snarled.

"What? What the hell is your problem?"

"Don't you think this election has gotten a little out of hand?" Gladys squinted at him.

"Yeah, I do," Garol said.

"Where does it stop with you? When do you stop attacking your son's self-esteem?"

"Stop with the son shit. Gladys, you are threatening my life with that crazy shit. You need to back off with that. You don't know what I've been through."

"Oh, be a man. Take some responsibility!"

"I'm not his father and I've never done anything to him."

"I can't argue with that. You've never done anything at all. I mean, you did everything you could to keep him off the softball team, so he had to go out and form his own. Which is doing so very well, as you know. Is it so hard to give him a compliment? The only reason he wanted to play softball, which was against my will, was to try to forge a relationship with you. But you are so selfish. I shouldn't tell you this, but he cried yesterday. My little angel didn't cry once during his infancy, but yesterday the dam broke…because of your inability to be a man. Oh, I loathe you."

"He never cried in the two months he was a child? That's odd."

"Yeah it is, you smart ass," Gladys barked. "It is odd. I've had it with you, I've really had it. I'm tired of saying, 'It's okay sweetie, Daddy is just working late,' or 'Daddy loves you, but he won't be home again.' It's a little late for apologies now, buddy. You missed his whole childhood. There's no going back, now."

"Ok, I won't go back."

"Stop with the sarcasm," Gladys screamed. "Show emotion! You're so hidden in your protective coating, my god, I can't stand it. When are you going to break free once and for all?"

"Calm down. Calm down, Gladys, just relax," Garol said softly with his hands in front of his chest, palms facing Gladys. "Just calm down. Calm," he walked a little closer as she sat still.

Gladys took the cigarette out of her mouth and Garol went for it just as she let it drop into her glass of water.

"Oh God! Why did you do that?" Garol yelled.

"So close, yet so far away. You'll never learn," Gladys smirked.

"What the hell does that mean? You really need to stop with this son shit. What are you trying to do to me? What did I do to deserve this?" Garol gasped.

"Still so hung up on the past. Selfish bastard. When are you going to move on? When are you going to realize that your life is today, not ten years ago?"

"Why are you setting me up? Why is everyone going along with it? You aren't God; you can't play with lives. You have to tell me what you want!"

"You really think you can control what happens? Are you that stupid? Who cares, anyway? Life is not what happens to you, it's what you do when it happens. Life is what you do when you get lemons, but you don't have any idea what I'm talking about."

"Gladys I don't, because you're nuts. What the hell are you saying? I'm stupid? Well, you're nuts. You claimed you were pregnant because I," Garol used finger quotes, "'screwed at your house.'" He dropped his fingers and continued, "You are insane, and the rest of the people in this town are only nice to you. I just figured that out. I was actually worried about your weird ass and that plastic idiot, with the messed up eyebrows—yeah, I said it— getting in my way, but not anymore. You're a kook. A complete nut-job and nobody listens to you."

"So selfish. You only think about your needs. I never should have gotten involved with you," Gladys put her head down. "It's my fault. It's all my fault."

"Absolutely. It is. But here's the good news: you never did get involved with me. There is no you and me. Never was. You can't make a baby by changing someone's light bulb. No, the only thing you get when you change a light bulb is light."

"Don't deny what happened because you're ashamed of him," Gladys demanded.

"Nothing happened. I'm not ashamed of him. I have no reason to be."

"You're ashamed. Is it because he's different?"

"Different?" Garol laughed, "Different...Wow! Somebody hand the lady a prize. We finally have a winner. Ding, ding...Bingo. I love it. Is he different? How would that be? I guess we can't really blame him. It's not his fault. After all, he only had a week to grow up. I don't have kids, but I think it's kind of rare when one goes from being a baby doll to a grown mannequin in a week. That, to me, is different, but I don't think it's his fault."

"So you admit it?"

"I do. I do. I always have. I also admit it would be incredibly difficult to be in his position. Being a plastic baby doll can't be easy. I guess we should be glad he isn't a stuffed animal. No future in that, just the hope that a kid who doesn't stink wins you at the county fair...sad life, indeed. No, he is lucky. Very lucky, actually. He's a full-grown, healthy, popular, attractive mannequin. He's in great shape. He can eat anything and never gains a pound. No vices, wonderful willpower. Looks great in a suit. Incredible, really. If he were mine, I would be very proud. My genes are not that good. In fact, be glad I didn't raise him, because he'd probably be a bitter washed up drunk by now," Garol stopped ranting and added calmly, "Feel my skin. Do you see how we are different?"

Gladys rolled her chair, swiftly, away from Garol with her legs, "Don't you try to seduce me, you son of a bitch. Any swinging willy can make a baby, but it takes a man to be a father."

"What? I'm not seducing you."

"You pig, stay away from me. Don't touch me, I'll scream."

Garol moved to the other side of the desk, away from her.

"You always do this. You always avoid the point."

"I don't always do anything. We don't ever talk to each other. You talk all the time, but we don't converse. You need to realize we are not married, don't have a child, and you're nuts. Please understand, we don't talk because the son you claim is mine is plastic. He was made in a factory...Getting through? I'm funny, I tend to avoid women who have plastic children and claim I'm the father," Garol pointed his index finger to his temple.

"Don't make me say it," Gladys said through tears.

"Ok, I won't. I'm pretty sure I don't want to hear it."

"Your son is hollow inside. He has nothing to give. He's your inner child and you can't recognize him, you are so hidden and blocked. It's so sad. You look for the world to change you. You view everything as failing you, or a setup to fail. You never see that we change from the inside. If we let the world dictate what we are on the success continuum, then we leave our fate to the wind, just blowing around with the outcome of the day. I really hoped you'd see that, but fatherhood has done nothing to change you. The sad thing is that you would say the exact thing about your father, and you let it happen again. This was your chance and you missed it. And it's not the kind of chance that goes away with a shoulder injury. It lasts even when some of the players are gone, because it's internal, not external, see?"

"Christ Gladys, what do you want? What are you doing here?"

"Ok, ok," Gladys stood up. She straightened her skirt, adjusted her bra strap and wrapped her purse strings around her shoulder. "I didn't come down here to fight. It's just when we get back together, the passion flows and the memories flood and I can't help but wonder what could've been. Silly I know, we live separate lives now. Anyway, I wanted to tell you that your son is getting engaged. I thought you should know."

"Engaged?"

"Sara. I was shocked too. Kids these days want to run into everything so quickly."

"Sara? Has he asked her yet? She hasn't answered has she?"

"He was going to ask her after the election. After he wins," Gladys walked past Garol toward the door.

"But…"

"I just thought you should know, that's why I stopped by. I thought maybe it would create some type of feeling in you, but I should have known you were incapable. Anyway, good luck

Sam. I guess now that our boy is all grown up, there really won't be any need for us to see each other. Not that you ever cared. What a shame." Gladys opened the door and walked out.

Give a Man a Rope and He'll Hang Himself

"I'M NOT LOSING TO a mannequin," Garol calmly tossed a copy of the *Gossip* on the desk.

"Calm down," Whirby said, raising his palms toward Garol.

"Don't tell me," Garol raised his voice, "to calm down."

From Garol's seated position, he was the same height as Whirby, standing on the other side of his desk. Whirby locked a smile that made him look like a ventriloquist's dummy. The two men stared at each other until Garol eventually huffed and looked away.

"Feeling better?" Whirby asked.

Again, Garol huffed. He clenched his jaw and surveyed the room, looking at an island of five desks butted together. Each had a man or woman furiously typing on a typewriter. Surrounded by large windows, a group of seven men and women animatedly discussed something in a back room. Garol couldn't hear them, but whatever they were talking about it appeared to be extremely important. Some stood, a few paced, but they all interrupted each other. Garol watched for a minute and a man who'd just finished talking passionately looked through the window and winked at Garol. Garol turned away and then back. The man had jumped into the discussion again.

Whirby was patiently waiting for Garol's attention to return. "What are these people doing?"

"They're your election committee," Whirby said.

"What does that mean? What are those people doing?" Garol said, pointing to a group of people standing around a buffet table.

"They're making buttons and signs."

"And those people?" Garol gestured to the heated discussion in the backroom. "It looks like they're about to launch an atomic bomb." Then shifted his gaze to the typists, "What the hell are those people typing?"

"Speeches, maybe. Administrative stuff. I'm not exactly sure. You don't seem focused. I feel like I'm losing you."

Garol thought about his words. "I just lost a softball game to a team coached by a mannequin. A mannequin that looks like..." Garol caught his word before it left his mouth. *A mannequin engaged to the girl I like,* he also kept from saying. "A mannequin that's for some insane reason believed to be my son and just kicked my ass in the last debate...."

Whirby said, "You need to get that magic feeling back you had after the first debate."

Garol stood up and pointed into the back office. "What the hell are they talking about?"

"They're your strategy team."

"They're wasting their time, unless they can strategize against God. My life is a setup for failure. It's 'give a little to take away.' It's 'get his hopes up so we can crush him.' What bothers me is how obvious it is. Now there's not even any planning involved. At least when I was younger, there was thought put into my destruction. A shoulder injury, now that makes sense. But now...now it's a grab bag of whatever. Any roadblock will do. So strategize away. It won't change a thing."

"Is that what you think?"

"Look at me. I'm walking around in a body cast and I'm losing an election to a mannequin rumored to be my son. If you can sell me on another explanation, I'll buy it."

"Maybe life just doesn't always turn out the way you want it to. Maybe your path is just different. Maybe it's not the touchdown, but the drive you put together. Maybe it's the opportunity to score, not the score itself. The chance to get on the field and run. Too often, we focus on results and rush right past the pursuit. If you can't be mindful of the moment, happiness will always elude you. Unless you win, you won't enjoy an ounce of your whole life. And you know the joy in winning is fleeting anyway. So maybe you're being set up for lessons, not failure. Maybe the roadblocks are to show you that you're going the wrong way."

"Sorry, not buying it." Garol knocked on his cast helmet.

A woman walked over from her typewriter and handed Whirby a sheet of paper. Whirby looked it over, thanked the woman, and handed the sheet to Garol.

"What's this?"

"A list of potential questions to help you prepare for the debate this evening."

"Where are the answers?"

"You're supposed to have those."

Garol tossed the questions on the desk. "So I'm supposed to go through all thirty of these, and they'll probably ask three?"

"It helps to be prepared. I never would've guessed it would be this close. Kind of exciting. Like being in the fourth quarter of a tie football game. Do or die time."

"Do you want to hear my answers?" Garol snarked. "Let's see." He perused the questions. "Here's a good one, 'What would you do to improve the health care system?' Easy—shoot the doctor. 'What would you do about Medium Foot?' If he behaved, I'd get him comfortable shoes. If he were bad, I'd take them away." Garol scanned the page and began laughing, "'List the reasons why you'd make a better candidate than your opponent?' I think I'll show up tonight just on the off chance this question is asked."

"You have to show up tonight."

"Is that so?"

"You are a candidate."

"I'll be there. But I'm not going to prepare. I already know the outcome."

"Where is your fighting spirit?"

"It'll be there. I guarantee that," Garol exited his campaign headquarters.

Garol saw Doll Baby and Sara talking in front of the bakery. Doll Baby faced Sara, who leaned against the railing with her back to Garol. Her arms flailed as she explained something to Doll Baby. Garol studied Doll Baby's lips to see if they moved. Then he thought he heard Sara say, "He is," and her head whipped around toward Garol.

"Hi Sam," Sara said.

Garol turned his gaze to the left. *Pretend you didn't hear her.*

"Sam," Sara repeated.

"Oh hey," Garol bobbed his head back and raised both arms to express surprise. "You must have just come out here. I didn't see you two. Either one of you."

"A little while ago," Sara said.

"That's weird, I didn't see you."

Neither Doll Baby nor Sara said anything.

"What are you guys doing out here?"

"I'm helping Garol Jr. get ready for this evening's debate. He's not feeling well," Sara said. "Lost his voice. What a time to catch a bug."

Garol couldn't think of anything to say.

"Ok, well, we'll see you tonight," Sara said and turned around.

Hearing his name called, Garol marched onstage, ready to answer questions-his way. He heard Garol Jr. called and watched closely to see how he managed to get to the podium. For two minutes, his eyes searched the assembly. Again, the speaker announced, "Let's have Garol Jr. come up to the stage."

Garol waited and watched for a trace of his immobile competitor. As the seconds ticked by with no sight of his plastic replica, Garol thought, *You're mine now. No way to get to the stage.* As the minutes passed, excitement grew in Garol. *He's not going to show up. I win.*

"Last call for Garol Jr.," the speaker pleaded.

Garol stood at his podium, confident of victory. He faced the stunned crowd, smiling. *First law—all you idiots go to the bar. Oh God! I don't want them with me. I'll have to explain to Steve why we don't want them. He'll see.*

A man walked down the center aisle and handed a sheet of paper to the Head Beaver.

"I see," the Head Beaver said clearly enough into the microphone.

"Ladies and Gentleman," the Head Beaver began, "Unfortunately, you can't have a debate when one debater feels he has something better to do. Obviously, we aren't a priority."

The crowd moaned and booed. "Who needs him," a voice cried.

"That's right. We have our leader," another voice bellowed.

"It's Sam," a voice shouted and everyone hooted.

"Please, please…please," the Head Beaver scolded. He smiled and said, "Congratulations Sam, it looks like just by showing up, you won the debate."

Garol felt a mixed sense of relief. He liked the crowd believing in him once again and the feeling everything wasn't a road to failure. He felt a little shame for blaming God. What were his motivations? Why did he want to be mayor? Because people told him he should? Because Steve Atan needed him to? And who was Steve Atan? *Why am I so intent on moving to the desert? Because he says it's great. Why am I so unhappy here? Why do I really want to be mayor? To make myself feel liked? To screw all these people over?*

Garol's thoughts were interrupted by the opening of the large double doors at the front of the meeting hall. Gladys stood momentarily, allowing the doors to open around her. She clomped down the center aisle, shouting, "Hold everything." She rushed up to the Head Beaver and began talking in a voice Garol didn't know was possible for her—quiet. Garol strained to hear her as his eyes ping-ponged between her mouth and the

Head Beaver.

Eventually the Head Beaver centered his mouth over the microphone, looked at Garol and said, "Sam, this is completely up to you, but it appears a debate is possible if you let it go on. Garol Jr. is feeling ill and has had a very difficult afternoon, but is on his way and willing to debate. Sam, it is completely up to you. As far as the rules go, you won. It's your call."

Eyes from every seat in the room bore into Garol as he weighed his options. His decision process began with: *Doll Baby's forfeit in the debate will most likely make it impossible for him to win the election. Am I really worried about losing to a mannequin? And what am I winning? I would like to give these people a piece of my mind. I would like to win though. Why? Hell if I know.* Garol felt the fight in him emerging.

"A true leader looks for opportunities to show he can lead. I want to remove all doubt," Garol slammed his cast forearms on the podium.

"Well alright," said the Head Beaver.

The crowd jumped to their feet and clapped and hooted.

Gladys shot Garol a look of hatred and darted down the center aisle and out the doors.

While the crowd still stood, the doors swung open again. Sara and Gladys held Doll Baby up on each side and walked his sick, tired body down the aisle, past the Head Beaver, up the three steps, on the stage and rested him behind the podium. Gladys kissed Doll Baby, screeched into the microphone, "My baby. My poor sick baby. He's so strong." She hugged him tight and then pointed at him and yelled, "What a leader," and exited the stage.

Sara remained at Doll Baby's side.

"Now we can get started," The Head Beaver said.

Garol noticed her hand was resting firmly on the lower part of Doll Baby's back. He couldn't take his eyes off her hand, afraid of where it might end up…other than a couple of times to look at her calves peeking out the bottom of her skirt.

The Head Beaver said, "Thank you everyone for coming out to our third and final debate. We were originally going to go with the format of asking each candidate questions, and have them answer those pre-chosen questions, but we're going to take questions from the audience instead. Let's hear what the people are concerned about."

Garol focused on Doll Baby and Sara when the first question was awarded. "Sam, in your own words, what strengths and weaknesses would you bring to the office of mayor?"

Garol didn't hear the question. He was too focused on watching the new couple.

"Sam?" The Head Beaver asked to get Garol's attention.

"Yes," Garol said snapping his head forward.

"Please answer the question," The Head Beaver said.

"I'm sorry, the question was?" Garol said. Sara was rubbing Doll Baby's back.

"Please answer in your words the strengths and weaknesses you would bring to the office of mayor," the woman repeated.

"Ummmmm, strengths?" Garol shuffled through his notes. "Oooops, that's not it."

"Your own words are fine," The Head Beaver said.

"I'm looking for those," Garol said feeling rattled.

"Time is running out, Sam."

"Well," Garol couldn't find anything in his notes. "Well, I'm a good athlete," Garol said, still fumbling through his notes. "Ummmmm, I like dogs, and I'm ummmm, good at delivering mail, and, oh and I learned how to work with my hands. I am getting pretty good. I can now fix-fix-ummmm, fix some things around the house. Depending on how broken they are. If they're not really, really, really broken, I can kind of fix them. Maybe," Garol trailed off.

There was a long silence in the meeting hall. Finally, the Head Beaver said, "Ok, that probably answers the strengths and weaknesses so we'll stop right there." He turned to Garol Jr. "Let's direct the question to you, Doll Baby; please tell the crowd your strengths and weaknesses."

Sara spoke into the microphone, "I am sorry to announce that Doll Baby is struggling with terrible laryngitis, so he will whisper his answers to me and I will say them for him."

"Oh, ok. I want to say on behalf of everyone here that we admire his strength to come down here even though he isn't feeling up to par. That says a lot right there," the Head Beaver said, as the crowd stood up and applauded.

Once the crowd sat down, Sara said, "Obviously it isn't easy for Doll Baby to be here. I hope it's not contagious," Sara winked at the audience and grabbed Doll Baby's hand. "But seriously, I would say his first strength is obviously being able to stay strong in the face of any adversity and rising to the challenge. Facing his illness and being here tonight to lead the people is only the first sign of that. Another strength if I can say so myself is what a stud he is. Oh my God!" Sara blushed. "And well, finally, his energy level. I can say first hand that this man-he-can, go all night," Sara said and fanned herself with her hands.

The crowd let out a loud, "Awwwwwwww."

"As far as weaknesses, well just look at him he's perfect. A real model."

"His eyebrows," Garol said sharply into his microphone.

The crowd grew silent and everyone looked at Garol.

"He has one eyebrow bigger than the other," Garol said.

"Well let's not make this about physical appearances," The Head Beaver said. "Let's keep to the issues."

"Let's keep it to the issues," Garol fired back and shot a look at Sara.

"Ok. Moving on," The Head Beaver said, shaking his head at Garol's outburst.

"Why don't we drop the laryngitis shit? Have Doll Baby answer for himself, explain in his own words? I have yet to hear that," Garol said loudly.

Sara pulled a piece of paper out of her skirt pocket and leaned into the microphone. "Excuse me. Excuse me," she held the note in the air. She stopped and looked at Doll Baby and said, "I know. I'm going to sweetie." Then to the audience, "Doll Baby has a note he wrote that he would like me to read to you." Sara took a second to clear her throat. "To all of you wonderful members of the town I care so deeply about, it is not that I have chosen to be a martyr, but my maker has chosen me to play the role by stealing my voice at such a great time of need. I may not be able to speak to you today, but my heart speaks. My heart cries to be heard," Sara wiped a tear from her eye. "My heart cries," she paused again, "signed, Doll Baby."

"Can we please pass some tissue boxes around?" The Head Beaver said shielding his eyes with his hands.

Other than random sniffles from the crowd, there was complete silence in the auditorium.

"He didn't write that," Garol broke the silence.

"That's quite an accusation," The Head Beaver said.

"How could he? He's a dummy," Garol said.

"No mudslinging. This is no place for your personal assessment of his mental skills."

"Not a dumb person, a mannequin," Garol yelled.

"Which one is it? A dummy or a man-who-can?" The Head Beaver asked.

"A mannequin," Garol fired back.

"A man-who-can. Garol Jr.'s come up with such a good slogan he's even inspired his competitor to his cause. I love it! Well, we've certainly gotten off track; we must stick to the issues. We want to run a clean and fair debate," The Head Beaver raised his right hand to settle a few members of the crowd fired up about their new "Man-who-can." "Doll Baby, please explain a policy you would enforce upon becoming mayor."

Sara leaned forward with her ear in front of Doll Baby's mouth and bobbed her head up and down a few times. Then she pulled her head back and began, "Doll Baby would like to institute an Honesty Policy, so that if anyone lied about their name or an insignificant event that happened to them, they would be held responsible."

"An Honesty Policy? Interesting. I wouldn't imagine any need for that here, though. Sam? What are your feelings on an Honesty Policy?" The Head Beaver asked.

Garol's eye had caught on Sara's calves again.

"Sam?" The Head Beaver asked.

"Yes," Garol said, snapping his head forward.

"An Honesty Policy?"

"Ummmm," Garol noticed Doll Baby now had his arm around Sara. "Ummm."

There was an awkward silence.

Sara was whispering something in Doll Baby's ear. Garol forgot about the question and stared directly at Sara's left hand on Doll Baby's butt.

"Honesty Policy, Sam?" The Head Beaver said a little louder than normal.

Garol looked at The Head Beaver, but he couldn't think. Doll Baby and Sara were facing each other with their arms around each other's waists. Sara's head was tilted slightly to the right. *Are they kissing?*

"He's not real," Garol said to Sara in a very weak voice.

The two remained interlocked.

"Honesty Policy Sam?" The Head Beaver asked again.

"Get your hands off of her," Garol said more loudly.

They remained interlocked.

"Honesty Policy, Sam?" The Head Beaver asked glaring at Garol.

"GET YOUR HOLLOW HANDS OFF HER," Garol yelled into the microphone.

Sara leaned around Doll Baby and looked at Garol, stunned and wide-eyed.

"I'll give you honesty," Garol walked over and swung Doll Baby around. "I told you to get your hands off of her," he said and punched him in the eye. Garol stormed out of the Town Hall and straight to the bar.

Success Has Many Fathers, Failure Is an Orphan

"THE VOTES HAVE BEEN tallied," the Head Beaver announced behind a podium atop a stage erected in the middle of Main Street. The townspeople sat in folding chairs.

Garol slumped in an aisle seat of the front row across from Doll Baby, doing his best to keep his eyes open and not move. The slightest movement took his hangover from seven to ten.

Doll Baby sat with perfect posture and looked intently ahead, serenely awaiting the Head Beaver's news. He was dressed in the same stylish navy blue pin striped suit Garol wore...or attempted to wear. Garol had had difficulty getting dressed. After thirty minutes of struggling, he managed to get his pants on...backwards. After losing a wrestling match to get them zipped, he had cinched his belt and hoped no one would notice. Then he put his tie on and realized he wasn't wearing a shirt. While he was wondering if he could salvage the mistake, Whirby yelled through his door, "It's time to go." As quickly as he could, he'd thrown on a sweatshirt, slipped into some slippers and trudged with squinted, blood-shot eyes to Main Street.

Sara sat next to Doll Baby, holding his hand. They looked like the perfect political couple. The seat next to Garol was empty. The area around Doll Baby's left eye was black with shades of blue and touches of pink. Garol smiled at the sight. *Smug bastard, stole my girl and now the election. Pretty boy.*

"I want to thank everyone for taking part in the political process. The three debates turned out to be very informative. The culmination of events yesterday and what we witnessed last night seem to have made their way into the ballot box," The Head Beaver stated.

Last night? What happened last night?

"I'm proud to announce that for the first time in our town's history, we've all come together for a unanimous decision. Every single solitary vote has been cast in favor of our new mayor," the Head Beaver stared directly at Garol.

Garol's eyes grew wide with surprise.

"Doll Baby," the Head Beaver turned to Doll Baby and slammed his gavel.

Sara jumped to her feet and the crowd erupted in a thunderous cheer. Doll Baby displayed the stoicism and maturity of an elder statesman, calmly accepting the victory.

"Ok, ok," the Head Beaver spoke into the microphone, pushing his palms up and down to settle the commotion. Once the crowd sat down, he continued, "I guess our little Doll Baby has grown up. Now that he's mayor, it's only right we refer to him by his given name, Garol Jr. What do you say we have Garol Jr. come up and say a few words?"

The chorus to "He's a Jolly Good Fellow" rang out as the crowd mobbed Doll Baby, hoisted him on their shoulders, carried him onstage, straightened him out, and stood him behind the podium. Sara placed her left arm around his back and wrapped the other around his bicep, while tears of elation flowed down her cheeks.

The crowd moved back to their seats and someone yelled, "Speech." Immediately the entire crowd began to chant, "Speech."

Sara turned to Doll Baby and sniffled, "You did it baby, you did it." She raised his hand in the air, smiled at the crowd and yelled, "Is this guy incredible or what?"

"Speech," the crowd resumed their chant.

"We love you all and thank you for your support, but if we could quiet things down for just a moment so my honey can speak that would be great," Sara said.

The crowd hushed.

Garol looked at Doll Baby's black, blue and pink eye. *God I hate you.* He stuck his tongue out at Doll Baby.

Moments passed. Sara turned to the microphone and said, "My baby is overcome with emotion." She pressed her cheek against his. When she pulled away, tears from her face rolled down from Doll Baby's eyes.

"He's crying," yelled someone in the crowd.

"Oh my God, he never cries," Sara yelled into the microphone. She put her ear against his mouth. "Ok baby," she said and nodded a few times. "Ok baby, I'll tell them. It's fine."

Sara spoke into the microphone, "I'm sorry, but Garol Jr. told me he is just too overcome with all of your love and support and is unable to find the words at this particular time to express his emotion. He looks forward to beginning immediately as your new mayor and promises to do everything in his power to make this the best place in the world for every community member."

"He loves us beyond words," a voice hooted.

"What a leader," another yelped.

"We're saved," another voice rang out.

The Head Beaver grabbed Doll Baby's shoulders and slowly pivoted him backwards to a chair and sat him down. The Head Beaver said, "WOW! I've never witnessed that much pure emotion from a politician. I'm dumbstruck."

"Dummystruck. Dummy. Dummy-struck," Garol reacted.

"WOW!" The Head Beaver looked down at Garol reclining limply in the front row. "On another note, this was an election, and although there's no question we chose the right man for the job, there's still a loser. It's only fair to hear a few words from the person we've all made it very clear that we don't want to listen to. Get the hell up here, Sam." The Head Beaver constructed an enormous plastic smile and swung his arms exuberantly stage left toward the stairs.

Samantha, six rows behind Garol, jumped up from her seat, whistled, clapped, and yelled, "Talk to me baby."

Garol didn't move.

"Get up here you big loser," the Head Beaver circled his arms toward himself, then reacted from a note he'd been handed. "Hold everything," he said very seriously. "It seems there's been a miscount in the votes."

The crowd "Oohed."

Garol froze.

"Sam did get one vote. Hey, you were told you can't vote in the election if you're running," the Head Beaver waved his finger at Garol, slumped in his chair.

The crowd "Oohed."

"We can't prove there was foul play. So some crazy so–and-so voted for him? It happens. In the end the majority kept their sanity and that's all that matters. So Sam, get the hell up here and thank your supporter."

Samantha stood and clapped.

Garol didn't move.

"Get up here you big loser," the Head Beaver circled his arms toward himself.

Garol still didn't move.

"Hurry up, nobody's waiting for you."

Garol felt numb. Only his dizziness reminded him that he was alive. He didn't want to speak to the people. He didn't want to coach their softball team, deliver their mail, or fix their house problems. He didn't want to listen to gibberish about spoon collections, Medium Foot, or chess tactics. But he did feel like letting them know that.

Garol slowly rose. *You don't want to listen to me, but you want me to speak? Ok, I will.*

Garol observed the audience from the podium. They yawned, stretched, and filed their nails. A few nodded off. One man pulled out a briefcase, popped it open and produced a calculator, a pen, and some papers. Some talked excitedly with each other about their handsome new leader. Behind him, the

Head Beaver and Sara sat on either side of Doll Baby. The Head Beaver talked enthusiastically and flailed an arm in front of Doll Baby while the other arm nestled around the new mayor's back. Sara held onto Doll Baby's hand and listened to the impassioned Head Beaver as she gazed at two of the biggest cheeses in town.

Garol sensed an introduction was not coming, so he waited for an opening. He had no idea how to begin or what he would say, but he knew he would eventually say it.

Then a man in an aisle seat stood up and began to exit.

"Sit down," Garol said to his back. A few yawners and stretchers paused, but the man continued to walk down the aisle.

"Sit down," Garol roared through the microphone.

The man spun around. Everyone looked up.

Garol pointed to his seat.

The man scooted back to his seat.

"Thank you. I'm new to politics, but I believe the correct thing for the loser to do is pretend to sincerely congratulate his opponent. So I'd like to do that as insincerely as I can. Congratulations Mr. Mannequin," Garol said and waved his arm toward Doll Baby.

The crowd jumped to their feet.

"You bet he's a man who can."

"Yeah," Garol pumped his fist in the air.

"He's so hot. A perfect ten," A woman chirped, creating laughter from the crowd.

"I would like to take a second to thank my election committee, a really bright group that donated everything to my campaign— everything except their vote. So thanks. But I think you got exactly what you deserve. A perfect figurehead. A guy on the straight and narrow who won't rock the boat as long as someone holds him up. He obviously isn't going to escape."

"Mayor for life," a voice roared.

"Finally a leader we can trust," another shouted.

"I would like to thank everyone for voting. I believe in a democracy and a government represented by the people. That is exactly why I have held my own election. Yeah. I decided to have an election for town sheriff. Oh yeah. I did it just after I walked up to the podium. I wanted this election to be run right and fair, so I kept you people out of it. I wanted to make sure we didn't include anyone whose body parts don't allow them to move. After all, a sheriff needs to enforce, doesn't he? It takes a badass and some armor to get things done. The only way to have that election was to exclude anyone who might be nuts. I realized the only one who could both vote and run for that election in this fruity little town was me. So I voted. Guess what? I won. Yeah. So although the teenage mutant mannequin might be making the laws, it's Sheriff Sam who'll enforce them. It's funny because you guys stuck me in this cast. You guys gave me no answers to get out of it. Now you guys will have to deal with it. You wanted me in this thing, well, you better watch out, because it'll take a lot more than anything you can dish out to dent it. Keep your asses in line and out of my way," Garol walked calmly off the stage, down the aisle that ran through Main Street, and back to his apartment.

December 21st
A Road to the Future

UNDER THE AWNING IN the front of Sam's bar, Garol used his hands as a squeegee to get the excess water off his clothes and face before he entered the bar. As Garol placed his hands on the long wooden handles of the double wooden doors, he thought about driving home. He couldn't afford a night out. It was a big night though and he could stop drinking tomorrow. He decided to compromise by just going in for one drink.

The bar was empty other than a couple of older men in suits talking and sipping their cocktails at a booth. This bar didn't advertise. Its clientele didn't want it to. It was one of those bars you never notice on a busy commercial drive. It was made of cinder block, painted brown. The black top in the parking lot was uneven and full of cracks. Red lettering on the torn canvas overhang, with splotches of black moss, let you know it was Sam's bar, but it could have been called 'The Hiding Place,' or 'Hole in the Wall,' because it was a place where the customers could drink and not worry about anyone who didn't share their common outlook to walk through those doors. The outlook being that life was a pain in the ass and home was a place that you didn't want to be. There were no phonies or violence, just an occasional end of the night stumbler, after a long day, bad week, or particularly rough month. The real losers, the hard core alcoholics, drank somewhere else.

The bar's strongest draw was Sam, who tended bar and never took a day off. Sam was sixty five, with a full head of white hair, stood about 5'10" and had a pouch around his midsection. He was a gifted story teller and always knew when and how to change a subject. And he had an infectious smile. Sam gave the bar its personality. He treated everyone that walked into his bar as family. He had too much tact to ask intrusive questions, but his personal life was a children's picture book, open for display. He took a joke good-naturedly, and always let the occasional nasty remark from a moody drunk roll off his back. He knew people well, knew their scars. He had checked his personal baggage years ago and built a world insulated with kindness. He wasn't just a bartender. He was a foster father for functional drunks.

The way Sam discussed his kids, his wife, and his fishing trips, Garol wasn't sure if Sam had mastered the eighty-hour day or if he'd found a way to cram all that living in to such a short time. Garol didn't ask; he was trying to shorten his days.

The impression he'd developed of Sam was that of a great man not destined for greatness. He was too good. If he were a king, he wouldn't have the ample greed to grow his empire through war. He would have spent his time making sure everyone was happy until some other greedier king moved in and wiped him out.

Garol was the bar's youngest regular. Garol masked his frustration with the outside world by saying very little, until he was on his fifth beer, usually around seven. Then the day was over, another forgotten memory. He was fairly jovial, revealed very little about where he came from or where he was going. Sam eventually learned he came in every day to avoid thinking about something, but never learned about what.

Garol waved to Sam, then headed to the cigarette machine against the wall. He put in a $5 bill and picked up his Winstons and walked to the corner barstool.

"Looks like God is really crying today," Sam nodded to Garol's soaked clothes and the rain.

"Pissing. I think he's pissing."

"Well, be glad he only had to go number 1," Sam laughed.

"He did the other one earlier. I should be thankful he washed it off," Garol laughed a little.

"Let me guess, you aren't thankful," Sam said.

"Not really."

There was an awkward pause, and Garol, hoping to avoid any self-disclosure said, "Tell me a story. A fishing story or something."

So Sam did, and when he was finished, he moved on to his family and all the wonderful things his wife and girls had done lately. Then he told a story about building a cabin with his dad and brothers when they were young. Eventually, other people entered the bar, and talking, joking, and long silent moments flowed together as naturally as they did every night.

Garol kept to himself, only engaging in conversation when otherwise unavoidable, and drank more than usual.

Around one in the morning Sam approached him, "You look like you've had a lot on your mind all night."

"Some days certainly are better than others," Garol said and raised his beer bottle. "Mind if I smoke? I don't feel like stepping outside."

"You and I are the only one's in here, go ahead."

Garol placed a cigarette in his mouth, flipped his lighter open, lit it, took a puff, exhaled and asked, "Have I ever told you about my best day?"

"No, Garol, you are a man of few words."

"Where I grew up the sky was clouded with a thick coal and factory smoke, and it was stuck in a valley, so unless it made it over the mountains and caught the wind, it just fell right back down. It was common to see women sweeping their porches. There was one woman on my block that would be out there sweeping, three, four, five times a day. (As a child she scared me.) She never spoke or even waved as we drove by on our bikes. She was so focused, I don't think she ever looked up. If so, she would've seen the ash falling all around her. Almost as much as anything I can remember from my hometown, the image of that woman has always stuck with me, as if there's a message to it, like a painting that the artist intends for you to interpret, but you can't put your finger on what they're trying to say."

"That's your best memory?"

"I'm getting to that. Sorry, I'm a little drunk and rambly right now. I had an interesting day. On the plateau of the mountain in the west was a town called Westdale. It was made up of the pricks that owned and ran the factories. They had the money. We hated them and they pitied us. They thought we were dirty and beneath them, and we looked up to them and saw too early in our childhood all that life offered, but not for us. Not if you lived in the valley."

"And Westdale was a football institution. They'd won state 23 times. Eastdale won it once in 1957. They had a 30,000 seat stadium. We had rickety old bleachers. They had a coach with a large staff. We had Mr. Binde and he taught history. They had a state of the art weight lifting facility. We had two bench presses and some free weights."

"My junior year we played them in the third game of the season and they whipped us 42-10. We ended the season losing only one more game and just barely qualified for the playoffs. So when we met in the postseason, they didn't expect much. We got lucky, it was cold, rainy and muddy and they fumbled on the opening kickoff, and we scored. When we kicked the ball off after that, they fumbled again. We scored another touchdown. And it was the kind of day where it was hard to run your offense- just above freezing, really windy and slippery. In a game like that, fourteen free points is priceless. We hung on to win 21-17. Seven, maybe nine out of ten times they would've beaten us. I mean we were good, but they were bigger, stronger, faster, better coached. They were a machine. A football factory."

"Anyway, three weeks later we won state, and my God, the valley just erupted in an all-out street party. It was insane. Hostile. It was like every valley member was pointing their fingers into the mountain and yelling, "Stick it. We whipped you."

"After that, it was like there was a pride in the community. It wasn't quite like the town got a new paint job, but more like it had been swept. Signs hung in every diner and shop saying, "Way to go Boys," or "State Champs," or "21-17." I remember there was a breakfast special called 'The David,' and it was a Goliath sized steak with beaten eggs, and you had to know the score of the Westdale game to order it. People in the valley just seemed to have more energy. They smiled more. Everywhere I went people said, "Whip em again next year," and you could tell it really meant something."

"I was named to the first team all-conference and the second team all-state. A really pretty blonde from Westdale decided I should be her boyfriend. My life quickly changed drastically."

"Initially, I felt lucky to have been given so much, but I soon realized no gifts came for free. If wining was the cure-all, it had one big side effect: the pressure to keep winning. I felt like a visitor in my life. Suddenly I felt at risk, and the risk made me doubt. I began to wonder if it mattered to my girlfriend if I won or lost on the football field, and almost wanted to explain to the townspeople when they said, "Kill Westdale next year," that we got lucky. That the truth was Goliath had been beaten but not slain, and next year he was going to come back, bigger, stronger, faster and more determined. But I sat on those thoughts."

"And something else happened. While Lisa was escorting me into the gated communities and mansions of Westdale, I saw the difference between wealth and poverty. It's life changing when you see it closely and hear it speak. For the first time I began to notice the dust. Prior to that it was always just something I lived with. It never occurred to me there were places where you didn't have to deal with it."

"So I decided I had to be perfect. That I had to win every game for us. So I worked. I worked so hard. And every day after I was done training I had this ritual of looking up in the mountain. Like it was a stare down. I would have this great workout and feel unbeatable and then look at the mountain and feel small, surrounded, outnumbered. And it would leave the question how? So I got my teammates to train with me. And we'd be out there running hills, pushing each other. I saw those guys remodel themselves into lean machines. But still I would perform the ritual and no matter how hard we worked I always felt like there was this angry monster up there just waiting for the moment to crush us. That we could never be good enough."

"During that time, as I walked home from my workout, I began to think about the woman who was always sweeping her porch. I wondered what went through her mind as she attacked that ash. What did she know? What exactly was she trying to get rid of? Or was she trying to recreate something? Had she been somewhere else, once? And why didn't she look up?"

Garol leaned his beer bottle straight up and emptied what was left in his mouth. The bartender popped the top on another bottle of beer and placed it in front of Garol. Garol took a large swig.

"There was a girl I grew up next to, named Beth. We were born a week apart. From the beginning our moms were always plopping us in cribs together. I'd probably known her four or five years before my first memory of her. Anyway, I used to go over to her house for tutoring a couple of nights a week. The Thursday night before the third game of my senior year, I had a lot on my mind. I was feeling like I was crumbling beneath the weight of my expectations. I was scared. Scared of failing. Scared of letting everyone down. Scared of losing all that had been given to me. Scared of being stuck in the valley."

"Maybe it was because I'd bitten half my nails off, but Beth could tell something was wrong, and she started prodding me, and eventually got me to open up and lay all my fears out. Acknowlege them. See them for what they were. And then she helped me break them down. To set up some kind of foundation. Some kind of insurance to let me know that losing wasn't the end of the world. That you could live with yourself if you played your best and lost. That the townspeople would get over it. That if all I was to Lisa was a quarterback to hang on her arm, I was better off without her. That true friends are friends no matter what. That the things in life that matter don't come from a scoreboard or a stat sheet. And I'm not exactly sure why, because it wasn't a message I was anticipating, but something changed and for the first time since we'd won state, I was able to ease my mind."

"I don't know why or how things happen, or if there's some kind of grand plan. I never will. But as I was leaving her bedroom where we used to study, the strangest thing occurred. And I've wondered how my life would be if it hadn't. She had a mirror on the wall above her dresser, and as we were walking out she stopped to pop out her earrings, and as I was standing behind her, for the first time in my life, I saw us together. I'll never forget because there was a feeling attached, not quite like a jolt, it was more subtle than that, but maybe like you get when you experience Déjà vu, where you don't know exactly why, but it instantly takes your mind over. I just remember thinking that we looked right together. Like sometimes you look at a couple and they just make sense. They just seem natural. Then she looked up and smiled, and we held the smile much longer than we normally would. After that she walked me out and I went home. So strange; here's someone I'd seen almost every day since I was born and for better or worse, my life changed in that moment. That because of a four second glance in the mirror, I would fall madly in love with that girl. That she would become my foundation. I never saw it coming."

"I had a great season that fall, even better than the year before, and we went undefeated. I was playing so well that we were actually favored to beat Westdale. We didn't play Westdale in a conference game that year. We met them for the first time in the playoffs, and that is the night I was referring to as the best night of my life when I started this whole drunken, out of character diatribe. We were both undefeated teams, but we met on our field because we were reigning state champions. Our stadium was small and the people of the valley got there early and filled it. There was a long stream of headlights, winding down the mountain on Old Valley road that looked like flickering Christmas tree bulbs, between the trees. It was the closest seat to the game most of those privileged pricks could find."

"It's funny, but I had a terrible game. I was nervous and felt hurried, and my passes were off almost all night. It took me three quarters to relax. We got the opening kick-off and I fumbled the first snap. The ball just popped right out of my hands. They got the ball on the twenty two yard line and quickly scored a touchdown. We got the ball back, and after two first downs I threw a terrible pass right in the hands of their linebacker. I have no idea what I was looking at. There wasn't even a receiver around him. A few plays later they scored again."

"After their second touchdown they did a mock planting of the flag, kind of like in that Iwo Jima statue, and then taunted us by pointing to the scoreboard."

"I'll never forget that feeling. It was the lowest I'd ever felt. I wanted to hide. I wanted to quit. When I was at my best I didn't think about things, but I went into the game with so much pressure on myself and a voice in my head telling me I was going to screw up and it was now amplified."

"But it was amazing because as inept as I was my teammates played like cornered rats. On defense we kept them scoreless for the rest of the half. On offense we played conservatively, running the ball, and my lineman knocked guys fifty pounds heavier, back on their heels- just pounded them all night. Finally, midway through the third quarter I read a cornerback blitz perfectly and threw a great pass for forty yards. My focus was back. You don't notice a transformation like that while it's happening, because it's the removal of thought that allows you to just do. Do what's natural. I now know that it was my teammates keeping the game close and never losing faith in me that allowed me to get up and dust myself off. I never expected them to carry the load. I honestly never thought they had it in them."

"We eventually went ahead with about six minutes left in the fourth quarter. They had a couple opportunities with the ball, but they were beaten and did nothing. I can remember looking over at their sidelines and seeing one of their players looking out of the valley, up in the hills, like he wanted to be home, and feeling an incredible sense of pride. That we beat 'em. There was nothing lucky about it. We just beat em."

"It's funny because of all the games I've ever quarterbacked, even in college, that was my worst performance, but I think about it the most. And for some reason every time I do, I think about the woman sweeping her porch. Both of us trying to escape the valley in our own way. Both of us sick of the dust. And I wonder if she was right to keep her head down. One day at a time. One battle at a time. Don't look at the overpowering army riding into town, because you can't do anything about them but worry, until they're on your field on your porch. And all worry can do is make you crippled. But then I think it was my fear that recruited my teammates. My inability to do it alone that made them better—that made the difference. And I'm back to square one. But this is one thing I do know. The things in my life that have had the greatest impact on me. The really life changing events. Whether they be great or gut-wrenching. I never saw them coming."

The night after the game I told Beth I loved her for the first time. It's amazing how some days can be so good. We took state again that year."

"Memories are funny things. The best memories can be the hardest to swallow. You don't realize when they're happening that this is as good as it gets. You think this is the beginning. You don't think about the end. Maybe I'm just drunk. Speaking of being drunk, get me two shots of tequila."

"I'm gonna need your keys big guy," Sam said and pulled out two shot glasses and poured Tequila in them.

"That's what I really love," Garol said, watching Sam pour the tequila, "Perfection…You see to me that's security, comfort.

As long as those two glasses are there, I know life will continue. They are my future. As long as they sit there, I know I will be right here, content, even happy."

Sam pushed both shot glasses in front of Garol.

"I lost my job today," Garol toasted his shot glass in the air and slammed it.

"Was it unexpected?"

"Not really. I thought I might make it another week or two though. My boss used to be my best friend. He was one of the guys on the team that won state both those years. Oh well. Life doesn't always turn out the way we think it will."

"Does it make you mad?"

"Not right now. I feel pretty good, although shit's starting to spin on me."

"What do you mean?"

"The bar. The ground. Is it too late to cancel the order on that last shot?"

"Your future?" Sam joked.

"Yeah," Garol laughed.

"Well why don't I take your last shot and put in the fridge. That way you'll always have one shot left," Sam said, then grabbed the shot and put it in the cooler.

"One shot. I could use a shot. A break. Although it may take an unbelievable one," Garol said.

"The unbelievable only happens when you believe," Sam smiled then asked, "What ever happened to the girl?"

"That story will have to wait. What do I owe you for tonight?" Garol placed his keys on the bar and handed him his credit card.

Sam ran his credit card and placed the slip in front of him. "I'll be right back. I'm going to run these bottles in the back."

Garol watched Sam walk into the back door and picked up his keys from the bar.

PART III
All The King's Horses and All the King's Men…

Attack is the Best Form of Defense

WHEN BARNEY BEAVER SANG in the new morning, Garol awoke a changed man. The bloodshot hung-over eyes were clear. The dizzy mind was determined. Garol, Sam, his cast and the past merged together in Sheriff Sam. Sheriff Sam was the law, king of a colony of nuts in the desert.

Sheriff Sam jotted a list of rules:

- Nobody can talk or laugh when I'm around.
- Nobody can come within fifty feet of me.
- Nobody can do anything crazy in my presence.
- I can do whatever I want

On the porch, Toby and Whirby sat playing chess while Jimmy and Split watched.

"Gentlemen," Garol placed the rule sheet on the door and wrote two new rules: "No chess. No loitering on my porch." He then strode leisurely to the board, placed his right forearm in its middle, winked at Whirby, and swiftly swung his arm over the board's surface.

"We're playing a game," Whirby said, shielding himself from the carnage.

"Not anymore."

Jimmy, Toby and Split scuffled on hands and knees around the porch and lawn for the chess pieces. Whirby stared at Sheriff Sam. A flurry of complaints came from all directions, which Sheriff Sam addressed by saying, "You freaks will have to gather some place else," then posed imposingly to ensure their immediate departure.

"We can't find the white castle," Jimmy announced.

"Maybe if we leave him alone, he'll reappear," Whirby glared at Garol. He picked up the chess board, spun around and said, "Let's go."

Garol laughed with power and vengeance. Delighted, he marched downtown and posted his rules next to the cafeteria entrance. He looked across the street and noticed, through a window, Doll Baby sitting at a desk.

An office. Sheriff Sam needs an office. Garol decided the bakery was the best spot. It was right next to Doll Baby and the best thing on the menu was a whole wheat, sugar-free, tasteless brownie.

Garol strutted by Doll Baby, whose head was buried in some legal documents, flashed his middle finger, and stormed into the bakery. He slammed both forearms on the counter. "Take your bland brownies and your cruddy cupcakes and beat it. This is Sheriff Sam's office."

The three workers were motionless. He thundered his covered forearms down again and they darted out the front door.

He dragged a desk from the back office to the front window so he could monitor the townspeople. They came and went as if nothing had changed. Many walked in and out of the cafeteria, not noticing the rules. A few read the rules, laughed, and walked away as unaffected and crazy as ever. Sheriff Sam seethed, insulted by their uninhibited actions. *These people need to suffer for their insanity, and for what they've done to mine.*

Garol searched the shop for something. He found exactly what he was looking for in a large orange cone, in the closet next to a mop basket and a "wet floor" sign.

Orange cone in hand, Sheriff Sam walked into the middle of Main Street, as people shuffled around him, giving no mind to the fifty-foot rule. They disregarded the 'No talking and laughing in my presence' rule. They acted goofy and showed not the least bit of fear of the "Don't do anything crazy in my presence" rule. It was maddening.

Sheriff Sam raised the orange megaphone. "Listen up. Listen up." A few people stopped and turned in his direction. "Stop," he yelled and only a few, who must have been hard of hearing, kept on with their business. "Hey, hey," he yelled and pointed to an elderly woman browsing the clothing store window. Someone tapped her shoulder and she turned to look at Sheriff Sam. A quizzical look crossed her face and she pointed to herself.

"Yeah, you, stop moving and listen." He swept around to see if anyone else was moving. Faces crowded the windows of the cafeteria and shops.

"Thank you, my god. What is it with you people? Insane," he laughed, relieved. Blank faces stared at him. "As I said yesterday, I'm Sheriff Sam. I'm in charge now. It doesn't matter what he says or does," he pointed at Doll Baby, who was still reading. He stalled, waiting for Doll Baby to turn. Then clenched his jaw. "Anyway, I posted new rules by the cafeteria door. Read them. Learn them. If you abide by them, no one gets hurt."

The crowd began moving toward the cafeteria.

"Did I say to move?" Garol yelled through the cone.

The crowd froze.

Sheriff Sam then looked over at Doll Baby, "What you are reading is unimportant. It's my rules you need to learn."

Doll Baby didn't flinch.

"Go read the rules," he barked.

He stomped over to look in on the mayor. *The people's choice. Garol Jr. What a disgrace.* Doll Baby sat at his desk, practicing perfect posture, back straight, head tilted slightly down. He was intently studying a large binder with the heading, "Extremely Important Documents." The manual was turned to page 102 of what looked like a thousand pages.

Sheriff Sam tapped on the window.

He tapped again a little louder.

Doll Baby remained focused on the documents.

"Hot shot. You're no son of mine. You hear me? Messed with the wrong guy. Haven't flipped a page since I've been standing here. I'm under your skin. I got nothing to prove and all the time in the world to prove it. Can't beat me," he waved tauntingly and stomped to his office.

Over the next two weeks, Sheriff Sam carried the megaphone and barked commands, "Move along. No fraternizing. Erase those smiles. Let's go." In the cafeteria, he constructed a throne with a chair placed on top of a table and made demands to be quiet at the slightest sounds. He listened intently and gave helpful hints, such as, "Smaller sips and chewing with your mouth closed is less noisy." Frolicking, shopping, and aimless walking were in the past. He brainstormed new rules, amending the original list two to three times daily: No talking, sitting, standing, walking, looking, laughing, peering, jeering, crouching, bowling, batting, singing, fleeing, groaning, goofing, frying, fishing, spelunking, spanking, spinning, trotting, teetering, dodging, dancing, or a bunch of other stuff. He began to write breathing a few times, but always stopped himself.

He updated the rules several times a day and at one point someone commented in frustration, "There isn't one thing we can do."

Garol perused the list and wrote, "Complaining." "It's your lucky day. I forgot that one."

The desolate Main Street made Garol proud, but he wondered jealously what might be happening out of sight. Lately he felt he'd heard voices, laughter and even singing in the distance. He opened the window next to his desk and immediately felt sure there was a noise far off. He hung his head out the window to listen. Frustrated, he reached a finger to unclog his left ear, which clunked against the micro-density fiberboard surrounding his head. *Damn cast.* He picked up his orange cone and placed the small end near his ear. A soft, soothing song came from somewhere. Garol extended his body, switching the cone from side to side as he zeroed in on the voice. He leaned too far and suddenly lost his footing and tipped, balancing on the threshold for a second as his weight slowly carried him to the exterior walkway. Through the tumble, he held the cone firmly in place. A lawman responding to an emergency call with no address, he chased the sound, side-shuffling behind his cone-covered ear down Main Street.

Like a top-notch dick, he tracked the voice to the steeple. Garol stopped to plan and suddenly caught himself captured in the beautiful song. He grew angry at the diversion and rashly raised his megaphone and declared, "The place is surrounded. Come out with your hands up."

The voice stopped.

Garol watched the front door.

Nothing happened.

He moved cautiously to the side of the building, swiveling his head and rotating his anxious body like an over-caffeinated mall cop in the midst of a scarf robbery. He watched for an escape out the rear and worked his way up the church steps and slowly pulled the door open. Once there was enough room, he stuck his marker-covered cast helmet inside.

There was no sign of anyone. Garol opened the doors wide and surveyed the room. He raised the cone to his lips, but suddenly felt self-conscious and walked back to his office.

He sat at his desk for long, lonely hours with his megaphone at the ready, but no one walked by. He looked in Doll Baby's office, but he was never around. He tried to get a drink, but Steve and the bartender were never there and all the alcohol was gone. In the short span of three weeks, the strong arm of Sheriff Sam had transformed the town into an obedient, boring, hell hole. A ghost town with no echo. He'd created a world with no diversions, entertainment, relationships, conflict, or escape. He'd expected and hoped for an uproar by the townspeople, but even Gladys gave in without a huff. He flamed his anger any way he could, but the logs to keep it burning were becoming harder and harder to drudge to the surface with meaning. With nothing to do, he was forced to do the thing in life he hated the most: ponder his life, from beginning to now. He forgot for long periods of time why he was mad.

Garol walked the streets. Several times a day, he heard the distant singing. As he entered the church, it stopped and no one was visible.

His loneliness increased at the same rate as his dictatorial power, an endless, sobering reminder of his inability to connect as the gap between him and the townspeople widened. He spent his days in thought, hoping to hear voices, any kind of distraction to keep him from the sadness. Soon he found his only sense of peace came from the voice in the steeple and he was rarely out of earshot, hiding in the bushes, listening to the wide array of songs. The beautiful voice sang gospel, pop, rhythm and blues. He watched, but never saw anyone leave.

Sheriff Sam decided to pay a visit to the doctor in the woods. He crept up to the door. A voice came from inside the house. Garol stood silent and listened. The words were muffled. He flattened his body and hugged the door as tightly as he could. His feet angled to the right, perpendicular to his body and the door sill. Focusing, he deciphered the words, "Sheriff," "Sam," "cast," "election," and "whacko."

The door flew open. Instantaneously, Sheriff Sam spilled into the doctor's foyer, losing a battle between gravity and balance. He smashed onto the oak floor and slid three feet.

"You're out," the doctor yelled, thumb out, leaning over Garol like an umpire at home plate. "Out of your mind, that is."

Jarred, Garol rolled over and looked up at the doctor, as if he were waking up after a long slumber, blinking his eyes tightly and releasing, to try and speed the return of his concentration.

"Well, you came to the right place. I'll fix you up. I shouldn't joke. Well, there's truth in humor, so I'm obviously not completely joking, but I should be more sensitive. Boy, you came in so quickly, too. There has to be something you just can't wait to admit, or confess, or whine about, or whatever."

The doctor stood up and then extended his hand down to Garol.

Garol grabbed it and raised himself about eight inches, but the doctor made no effort to pull.

"Dr. Mitchell. How do you do?" he said as their hands locked.

Garol could no longer hold himself up, so he dropped to the ground. The doctor remained in position, clutching Garol's hand and looking into his eyes. Garol grunted and again muscled himself a foot and a half off the ground, hoping the doctor would pick up his slack by pulling him to his feet. The doctor frowned and released his hand. Sheriff Sam thudded to the ground.

"Don't want to introduce yourself? I'll just call you Heavy. Holy cow, you're a load," the doctor laughed.

"What are you still doing down there? Do you need a hand up?"

"No," Garol pulled his hand toward his chest, away from the doctor's.

"Well, when you get up, come into the living room. We'll see if we can screw in those loose lug nuts floating around in that noggin," the psychiatrist said.

Garol put his head between his legs and breathed a sigh.

"You're a mess. Get in here," he heard the doctor say from the next room. With an alien accent, the doctor giggled "insane in the membrane." "I'm kidding, come on. You have to make fun of your faults, it's endearing. So you're loony. Who cares? Get in here."

Garol got up and walked into the living room.

The living room was different. There was more furniture and there were pictures on the wall. Garol eye's caught on a picture of a golf green surrounded by trees.

"Aw, yes, La Sa Vista Hills," the doctor said, noticing Garol's attraction.

"You played?" Garol asked.

"Oh yes. Used to. Loved it."

"Is this around here?"

"No, that's in the hills of La Sa Vista."

"Looks nice," Garol said.

"Exclusive, non-members only. They don't sell memberships. You have to be a non-member to play there. I was. Still am," the psychiatrist said proudly.

"Oh," Garol said and nodded, "were you good?"

"My putter had quite a reputation. My long ball was erratic, but nobody dropped their shorts as often as I did. It drove some people insane," the doctor smiled proudly and nudged Garol with his shoulder.

Dr. Mitchell sat down on the couch. "So what's bothering you? You run in, flailing around, acting like a lunatic. Hell, I thought you were trying to pull me on top of you in the hallway. I said, 'this guy needs help.' Come on, talk to me. You know you're at least half crazy. Let's nip this insanity in the bud."

Garol couldn't remember why he was there.

"Do you like to read?"

"Not really," Garol answered.

"No? What a shame. I recently found a fascinating new line of books." The doctor walked into his office and returned with a book in his hand. "Take a look at this book," he handed it to Garol.

"Dealing With Your Problems for Dipshits?"

"Dealing With Your Problems for Dipshits, that's the name of the book? It's perfect for you," the doctor smiled even wider.

"Why would I like this?"

"Don't be offended. It's just one in a series of instructional books. I think it could help."

"Help me with what? I'm not a dipshit."

"You don't have to be. It just makes things very clear, so even a dipshit can understand."

"No thanks," Garol said and gave the book back to the doctor.

The doctor snapped his fingers, "I know what you'd like." He motioned with his index finger for Garol to follow him into his study. Garol wasn't sure why he came to see the doctor, but he knew it wasn't for this. He sighed and walked into the doctor's den.

The doctor stood in front of his bookcase and pointed to the top shelf. "The complete Asshole series for psychiatry. Huh?" he smiled widely. "Impressed?"

"The Asshole series? What?"

"Yep, there's *How to Deal with Your Life for Assholes, Managing Anger for Assholes,* and my personal favorite, *Shedding your Cast and Moving on From the Past for Assholes,"* which the doctor pulled from the shelf and began thumbing through the pages.

"I didn't come here to meet with you," Garol said.

The doctor stopped in the index section. "This section pertains to moving on from the past," he opened the book toward Garol. "See, this chapter proclaims 'seek forgiveness.' The next chapter is about overcoming addictions. Then there's grieving process for loss, time, relationships, jobs, dreams. It's really an informative, fascinating read."

"Stop this shit. Are you saying I'm an asshole?" Garol yelled.

"No, it's just the name of the book."

"What if I recommended to you a book called, "Psychiatry for Goofy-Looking Lunatic Doctors that Smile Too Much, Have Large Heads and Big Bald Spots, Fish for Imaginary Sharks and Annoy the Shit Out of People?"

"Why would that offend me?" Dr. Mitchell asked, smiling widely.

"It should."

"I see. So you think the Asshole and Dipshit series hits too close to home. Now I understand. Honestly, I thought you'd be more offended by the Dipshit series than the Asshole series, but I can see how I was wrong. I am sorry. Really, they're for anyone who wants to learn. Most people aren't assholes or dipshits. What was I thinking?"

"I'm not an asshole or a dipshit."

"That's great. Keep believing. Nothing is incurable. Never stop fighting. Please take this book with you, it's really helpful. On top of the informative chapters, it tells things not to do. Those suggestions are marked by this black poison symbol," the doctor said and pointed to a skull and crossbones. "You see here it gives the helpful hint: 'Don't get drunk before the night of an election, black out, and become belligerent with the townspeople over the public announcement system.' Wow! That's sound advice. Here's another: 'If you do that, don't be an asshole and take the town hostage when you lose the election.' See it's chock full of stuff that's nice to know."

Garol had a vision of punching Doll Baby, followed by a conversation with Steve Atan about breaking into the PA System. *Is that what happened?* His knees buckled and he grabbed the doctor's chair and sat. He placed his head in his hands and stared between his knees.

After a long pause, the doctor began, "This section talks about mending the past..."

"Stop talking. Just stop," Garol said in a deflated tone, which again was followed by a long, silent pause.

"I was just going to say..."

"Don't. You win. I quit. I can never win," Garol said softly "I used to feel like I couldn't lose."

"Defeat finds everyone, but you keep looking," the doctor said sincerely.

"It tracks me down."

"You search in holes and under rocks. You paint everything black and then curse darkness."

"How would you know?"

"Someone who wants to win finds victory even in defeat. You find defeat in victory."

"You either win or you lose."

"No such thing, only quitters. The game is never over."

"So you think I'm a quitter?"

"Didn't say that, but you are on the sidelines. Maybe injured?"

"I'm no quitter. If I hadn't gotten hurt I'd have gone pro. Now I lose elections and girls to mannequins and," Garol pressed his left index finger into his right palm, "Defend myself against guys who think their hands are telephones." He raised his left hand to his ear, "Hello, anyone home? No? He's probably out fishing for imaginary sharks, I'll call back," Garol lowered his hand and rolled his eyes.

The doctor brought his left hand close to his face, "I've got a message," then waved his right hand, "I'll check it later." He lowered his hand and said, "High school and college were a while ago. Lately, any leading has been from a bar stool."

"What do you think you know about me?"

"A lot. Remember I've studied your x-rays."

"The caricature drawing with random stuff in the head? Real professional stuff."

"Does it matter where the truth comes from?"

"The truth? You want a dose? There aren't any sharks in your pond. The only thing you're going to catch in that pond is ringworm."

"This from a guy walking around in a full body cast. You know the sole purpose of a cast is to mend bones?"

"*Bodycastjellomoldification*. Don't you listen? I can't take it off."

"I'm the one that's full of it. That cast is a shield. Used to be alcohol. 'Any place to hide,' should be your motto."

"I don't have any medical experience. I don't know these things."

"I can tell you with one hundred percent accuracy, you're not jello. You are powerless, faithless and distrustful. You are a prisoner and unfortunately, only you have the key."

"I'm Sheriff Sam. No one has the courage to *talk* in my presence. I rule this town."

"Congratulations, you're a tyrant. You made it impossible to re-enter the game, unless it's gonna be solitaire."

"With these people, who just elected a plastic doll as mayor? A plastic doll that looks like me and everyone suspects I'm the father. You're right, I don't like the life I had before Nutville, but there are some things I miss. Such as, in order to have a baby you have to have sex. Also, if a woman has a baby and it's a doll, the father isn't expected to raise the kid. That falls to the closest mental institution. Here, that doll can grow up, become a mayor and marry the most beautiful woman in town. If that's the choice, then I will play solitaire."

"You should take some credit for raising him. He sounds like a fine boy. That doesn't just happen."

"I'm not like you. I can't look into a swamp and see sharks. I certainly can't take pride in being father-of-the-year to a dummy."

"That's true. The lies you tell yourself are meant to keep you down, I forgot." The doctor put his book down. "You need to get out of your mind. That's your problem. Finally, you're alcohol-free, except for the other night," he grimaced. "You're making an effort again. Would you have spoken in public anytime in the last ten years? Learned about the trades? Would you have eaten as healthily? I bet you've lost a lot of weight. All you can focus on is what hasn't gone right. Maybe you need to start dating again."

"I tried that. I was interested in a girl, but she's dating my son. And somehow I fathered a plastic mannequin by screwing in light bulbs. Kind of makes sense. The sad truth is that's the most action my dating life has had in years. These people make it impossible to get ahead."

"So the fact that you lost your cool, punched your opponent, drank to excess, and ridiculed everyone in town over the PA System is not your fault?"

"Ugh! They deserved it. I was going to lose anyway. They made winning impossible."

"Not them. Look, it's not about winning, it's about trying, caring. But you have to take responsibility. When you were born, you learned the way things are. You adapted. People raised by wolves grown up to act like wolves. My point is, we assign what is real and what isn't. Obviously some part of you believed the mannequin was real or you wouldn't have punched him. You wouldn't have been jealous. It's interesting that you were jealous of a mannequin that looks exactly like you. You really think you can't compete? Do you really think he's more fun for this girl to be with than you are? If he's the better man then you just aren't ready. So get ready. Get the next girl. Win the next election. Either way, enjoy the process. Winning only lasts for a moment. You can win a girl's heart and look at the disappointment in her eyes for the rest of your life if you stop living. You can win the election and hear complaints for the rest of your term if you aren't ready to lead. Do what you want to do, but enjoy it along the way."

"I don't know what to do. I haven't done one thing right since Beth died. I don't have any ideas anymore. I don't even know where to begin."

"The first time you picked up a football, did you throw a touchdown pass?"

"No," Garol shook his head.

"You probably threw the ball an inch, maybe two. A week later, you threw the ball a foot, but you stuck with it. After years of practice, you led your team into the end zone. Along the way, you built confidence, even though you did nothing but fail. You focused on the goal and moved in that direction. Slowly but surely, making mistakes and learning the whole time. You were defeated most of the time, but you felt you couldn't lose. Why?"

"I was young, naïve, stupid," Garol said softly.

"No, you were moving forward, focusing on the positive to get you to your goal. Every bad outcome was a chance to improve. You believed in yourself and where you were going."

"I was wrong. I never made it."

"You got as far as you could. That's what winning is. Losing is giving up."

"When do they take responsibility for their actions?"

"You came here to talk about them?"

"I don't know why I came."

"Yeah, you do. You made the long walk through the woods to visit me. You spend so much energy controlling. First your emotions, now your surroundings. You constantly build walls to protect yourself, but don't realize you are building a solitary confinement. You'll never get any control until you give up control. You have to realize the world wasn't built to revolve around you. You may not have made the pros, but someone did. No one lost any sleep— other than you— because you didn't suit up behind some center and take snaps. Things happen and most of the time it has nothing to do with you. You can only control the way you look at things. You also can't use substances for control, whether it is beer, food, or wallowing in your own pity. When that happens, you become completely powerless to believe."

Garol, with frazzled frustration, put his hands over his eyes and grunted, "Uggh."

"It doesn't sound easy, but there's nothing easier. And you don't need to go it alone."

"You gonna help?"

"All I can do is talk. Look, everyone struggles. I've been wrestling with this great white for too long. I'm stuck. I've come this close to bringing her in, but every time, she gets away. At first, I was too proud to ask for help. I wanted to bring her in myself. But I also knew I couldn't. Not alone. I couldn't accept that, though. One day I decided to give it my all. I did. I left everything I had next to the river, my best against hers. She won. But I had to bring her in. I couldn't eat, I couldn't sleep. Still, I didn't want to ask for the help I needed. So I got a new pole. A real sturdy one. Again, I failed. I got a new net. She broke through the net. I had exhausted my efforts. I couldn't go back and I couldn't go forward. Then I realized what I needed. It came as an epiphany. The poles and nets were excuses. Do you know what I lacked?"

"An imaginary boat?"

"No. Vision. I couldn't see my next challenge. I was afraid that there would be nothing to move on to. Fishing is the thing I love the most in this world, but if I mount her on the wall, I'm done, it's over. So I got on my knees and prayed to the man upstairs for direction."

"Did you get it?"

"Not yet, but I know I will."

"How?"

"Because since I've asked, peace has entered my heart. When the time is right, I will get what I asked for. Until then, I have peace of mind. I am more than just a fisherman. I love it, but I was obsessed, overcome. Now I realize that I have to help others. Maybe by helping others I will get my vision. But now I wait with one hundred percent confidence it will happen. And my pride has been broken. That is the real gift."

The two men just stared at each other. Garol stood. There was nothing left to say as the doctor walked Garol to the door. Garol exited the porch and at the bottom of the stairs, he turned to face Dr. Mitchell. He couldn't form any words. He nodded and turned to face the woods.

GAROL LAY IN BED with a deep sense of longing. He missed the days when life worked. He missed jumping up in the morning with passion. In those days, he never saw disappointment in Beth's eyes. He never felt his teammates didn't trust him to lead them to victory. He never felt anything but friendship for Mike. Now each interaction was a puzzle. Nothing was fluid. There were no buffers, no place to stride between hurdles. Just jump, jump, jump, jump, jump. He couldn't jump anymore. He couldn't run anymore. He lay alone on a barren track, surrounded by an empty football field and empty stands. No fans, no friends, no teammates, no competitors. No one interested in getting to know him. No one to believe in him. Nothing to believe in.

What happened? He knew the fall began with his injury, but it was Beth's passing that crippled him. Initially, people said it would go away in time. But it was time and all it could carry that went away. *Time only compounds the problem.* Like the tides, it scurried away with chipped dreams and eroded hopes, then returned on schedule aboard fleets filled with troops of pain, commanded by Generals

Despair and Faithlessness. Garol slid into a beer bottle and waited for the pain to stop searching. But it knew it had found its man. It set up a base station and continuously refreshed troops. It patiently took over as Garol slid further into the bottle, the only place he knew it couldn't find him.

What could I have done? Accepted the losses, mourned them? Dealt with them?

Garol shot up from bed. Acceptance was too monstrous. Every muscle in his body stressed, squeezing sweat through his pores. *It didn't happen. None of it happened.* He tried to convince himself, but couldn't believe it. He couldn't fight it anymore. He didn't have the strength or the bottle. It had happened. His life had happened. It was all right there. He saw Beth for the first time in years, smiling, waving. He gave up.

He saw the football field grow active with teammates. He saw the stands fill. He saw himself leading his team down the field. One play, then the next. He saw Beth in the stands. It was all so clear. So real. He was transported to a place where what once was, is now. The magic of old blended with today's lessons. The place had a tremendous amount of joy and love, but an awful sense of guilt and shame. Shame for shutting her out. Guilt for trying to erase her.

Garol spent the years since Beth's death cursing change. He wondered now, *would I have played football, knowing I wouldn't make it? Would I have offered the rest of my life to Beth knowing she wouldn't be here for it? Yes. Yes to both. Absolutely.*

Again, Garol clenched his muscles to the point of popping. He cried out, "I don't know how much I can take. Please, I can't take any more." Garol hoped the pleading would manifest into a prayer. Soon he lay back on the bed. A blanket of calm covered him.

Garol thought about the strange set of circumstances that had led to this moment: the cast, the town, the work at

282

Gladys's, Doll Baby, Sara, S. Atan, the psychiatrist, the election. Coordinated events to push him to the cliff that revealed the depths his life had sunk to, compared to a time when winning was as natural as smiling. A reflex. Then, interceptions and incomplete passes were kinks to rise above. Now winning was so distant it was a bad memory. A reminder of what's been lost. He lost elections and love interests to hollow representations of himself. Years ago, the idea would have been laughable, but now it was life-threatening. Years ago, he was a gladiator. Now, a wind-blown feather. A man on the run from feeling, passion, and anyone, thing or idea that might give him a glimmer of hope.

The doctor was right. He didn't start off winning. Most of the time he never won. Wanting to win and the belief he could made it all worthwhile. Getting up after being knocked down was the trick. It was throwing five interceptions in a game and then leading your team down the field for the final victory drive—and the games with a sixth interception, falling short of that victory, but waking up the next morning a little wiser. That was winning. He used to know that. *That knowledge washed away with time.*

Garol didn't want to be lonely Sheriff Sam anymore. He didn't want to make people walk on eggshells anymore. He struggled for some meaning. He wanted to connect the dots. He used to have purpose. *Life is an accident. I came into this world by accident. My shoulder was an accident. Beth was taken by an accident.* He looked at his cast. *I must have had an accident to get here.*

"God I don't know if you're there. You may or may not remember me. I used to believe. Years ago. Now, I can't get out of my own way. I can't do anything right and I can't muster the courage to go on. I know it's been a long time since you heard from me, but I got nowhere else to go. I'm not looking for any handouts, but just give me some kind of direction. Maybe keep me from tripping over myself long enough to catch my breath. Just get me on my feet so I can…"

GAROL'S EYES SNAPPED OPEN to a tickle underneath the cast on his right forearm. He clenched his muscles. The feeling waned. *An itch?* He drew his breath at an irritation he couldn't reach. He breathed out in a long, loud gasp. *Don't think about it. Don't make it come back.*

A tingle the size of a mosquito's needle bore into the center of his right thigh. His hands scratched the cast's surface. Relief came in the reemergence of the prickle in his forearm. Before Garol could react, a much larger irritation sprung up on his belly. Seconds later Garol's body felt taken over by thousands of vacationing ants scurrying among attractions. "Help! God help!"

He looked into the open closet door and noticed a single wire hanger. He ran to the hanger and snatched it. He barely unraveled the wire neck before rational thought decided to find a more sterile environment and he darted out the front door.

Doctor. Garol chased his thought out the door of his apartment, onto Main Street and into town, finally to the doctor's office where he ran through the open door to the receptionist's desk. No one was in sight. A sign on the counter read, "Physician, Heal Thyself."

"Anyone here?" Garol yelled.

He ran down the hallway. The doors of the first three rooms were open and Garol saw no one. The final door in the hallway was closed. He opened the door.

The room had a bed in the middle and a shower in the corner. Three hangers hung from a rack on the door with a towel, a shirt, and a pair of pants. On a chair next to the shower were socks, underclothes, and two jars. Underneath the chair rested a pair of running shoes.

A stainless steel cart stood by the wall. Above it, a sign read, "Cast Removal Station."

A small circular saw Garol recognized from his initial visit lay on the cart. Garol picked it up, flipped the on switch, and watched the blade spin. He turned it off and looked at the blade. He thought about yelling again, but was stopped by the itch. He placed the saw on his thigh and ran it down the length of the section. He did the same as far as he could reach on the back side, and the piece that used cover his right thigh fell to the ground. The itch urged him to remove the rest of the cast as quickly as possible.

Garol stepped over the cast remnants and hopped in the shower. He scrubbed himself as he let the warm water wash over his body.

When he stepped out, he picked up the two jars resting on the chair and sat. One jar was aloe and he rubbed the gel generously over every area of his body, letting the itch melt away. When his body was saturated, he grabbed the note out of the other jar and read. "The pants, shirt, shoes and socks are to be used for those removing casts. Please put all cast pieces in the trash bag hanging on the hook above the door and take with you. Others don't need to pick up after your stinky mess (anymore). Thanks, your loving receptionist, Samantha"

Garol looked at the thin pair of jeans that hung from the shower door. He grabbed them and read the waist, 34." *What am I gonna do with the other leg?* Garol's last jeans were 42" and getting a little snug.

He looked down at his body for the first time. There was muscle tone. He felt his stomach, then pinched what he could between his thumb and fingers. *Huh! Not much.* He hadn't had a flat stomach since college. He looked at his arms, smiled and flexed. *Not bad.* Garol stepped into the jeans. He sucked in and zipped them up. He exhaled and realized they fit fine. He finished dressing.

Garol studied the pieces of cast strewn on the floor. It looked like brick rubble from a prison break where the inmates simply went through the wall. The cast was many colored, with only a bit of white. The base was mostly black from marker drawing, but blue, purple, red and green had been used where black was no longer an option. He saw the word, "love," written in green marker and determined the piece came from the back of his upper arm. "Love" appeared to be the only part of the message, and Garol became curious as to the rest of the message and knelt down to assemble the cast as best he could. *Is that Sara's handwriting?* He began to assemble the pieces, but got confused and grabbed the remnants, put them in one of the bags and left, cast-free.

GAROL TOOK A DEEP breath, put his head down, and walked into the cafeteria for lunch. He listened for reaction. He worried someone would yell, "Get him," which would be followed by a pouncing mob. *What is there to do though? I can't run.* He didn't really believe these people were violent. In a way, he wished they were, *Just kick my ass and get it over with.* He didn't want to be hated anymore.

The cafeteria was full, but deadly silent. Initially, Garol felt relieved that no one sprung into action. He took his issued lunch and sauntered cautiously to the table with Jimmy, Toby and Whirby. For ten minutes, he sat waiting. Finally, he asked, "How's the chess game coming?"

Jimmy shook his head sideways and looked down at his plate.

"No more chess," Whirby whispered, staring at his half eaten sandwich.

"Why?" Garol asked.

"Stop talking, he'll hear you," Jimmy said softly, behind his hands.

"Who?" Garol asked.

"The Cast Man. Sheriff Sam," Jimmy whispered, then looked behind him.

Garol surveyed the cafeteria and noticed all the heads staring directly at their plates. He wanted to tell them that Sheriff Sam's been driven away for good, but didn't feel that he could.

For the next three days, he saw people scurry through the streets. Occasionally, someone would grab his arm and say, "You shouldn't walk so confidently, he doesn't like that." The townspeople cut their food to the smallest of bites so the noise of chewing would not put them in danger. Sometimes, someone would whisper, "Please don't chew so loudly, he'll come in here. He hears everything." Businesses were abandoned. He banged on shop doors, but was met by owners saying softly, "Please don't talk, he'll squash you." He asked The Man if any mail needed to be delivered, but The Man explained, "People are afraid receiving a letter could lead to joyful feelings, which could bring punishment."

"Can I have the bag?"

"What for?" The Man asked.

"I can't tell you," Garol said.

Garol filled the bag with letters for every person in town which explained, "A major announcement after dinner in the middle of Main Street. Everyone must attend." He delivered a letter to everyone in town.

Garol walked into the public announcement room and saw Barney crying in a corner.

"What's going on?" Garol asked.

"I can't announce anymore. I don't know what to do," Barney said, sniveling.

"Announce this," Garol wrote a message on a piece of paper.

Barney got to his feet, dusted off his fur and shot Garol a helpless look.

"I promise you there's nothing to be frightened of anymore. Just read that and everything will be ok," Garol said and walked to Main Street.

"Hey everybody," Barney Beaver said, his voice cracking. There were muffled tears. "Ok, I'm ok. Oh God, don't hurt me," Barney Beaver sobbed. Then a long pause. "Ok, ummmm, this just in. Can everyone meet in Main Street? It's an order of Sheriff Sam. Oh God I don't want to go, save yourselves," he screeched and dropped the microphone.

People cautiously walked into Main Street. Garol stood in the middle, holding the mail bag around his shoulder and the orange cone in his right hand.

Garol raised the orange megaphone to his mouth. "There is nothing to be frightened of."

"He shouldn't be talking," A man roared.

"We're all going to get it now," A woman screamed.

"The Cast Man is no more. I have done away with him," Garol declared triumphantly.

"No, no, you shouldn't say that. He'll hear you."

"He's coming. He's coming now," a voice bellowed.

"No, he isn't. He's never coming back," Garol yelled.

"That's a lie"

"This is a set-up."

"Look," Garol reached into his bag and raised part of the cast head. Gasps filled the air.

"It's a trick! Stay obedient, it's a trick! He's testing us."

"It's not." Garol dumped the entire bag. He assembled the cast to form Sheriff Sam. "See, I stripped his cast. We are free to be who we are. Be happy and free," Garol announced.

"Who are you?" a woman asked.

"I'm Garol."

"We're saved."

"Who's our man?"

"Sheriff Garol."

"The man who can!"

The townspeople converged upon Garol, hoisted him above their shoulders, and paraded him up and down the street.

The Better the Day, the Better the Deed

THIRTY DAYS HAD PASSED since the position of Sheriff Garol had been thrust upon his shoulders. When he wasn't delivering mail or fixing house problems, he strolled the streets, protecting and conversing with the town's members. The townsfolk seemed to have a little extra pep in their step since the reign of their tyrant was over. They gathered in the streets, wrote letters, talked and laughed. Even Gladys relaxed her stride.

Garol walked into the post office with a letter of his own. The Man walked out from behind the counter with the mailbag and draped it around Garol's shoulder. He grabbed Garol's firm bicep with his hand, "Looks like jello isn't a worry anymore."

It was the first time anyone had acknowledged that Garol had been in the cast. He smiled shyly and his eyes fell to the floor.

"You've got a letter of your own today?"

"Yeah," Garol shook his head, "Payment for services." He turned to walk out of the post office, then stopped and turned back toward The Man.

"Something else?"

"Yeah," Garol said. Their eyes locked and Garol looked at the floor, deciding whether or not to go on. He looked back to The Man, "My name's Garol. I don't know why exactly I said it was Sam. I guess I just never liked my name and figured it was a good chance to change it."

"I appreciate the honesty."

Garol continued to look at the Man.

"Something else?"

"Yeah, thanks," Garol nodded slightly.

"What for?"

"I don't know exactly, but I just feel I owe you."

The Man smiled. "You look good."

Garol turned to the door and then turned around to face The Man again.

"Where can I get a shovel?"

"The steeple. They'll have what you need."

Carrying an empty mail bag, Garol trekked to the doctor in the woods with his final letter in his hands. On the porch, he thought about knocking or looking in the window. He decided to slip the letter he'd written through the mail slot. He tiptoed down the steps and headed home.

That evening, Garol walked to the softball field. He ran the bases for exercise. After that, he took a few footballs into the outfield and threw them as far as he could, sprinted to them and threw them back the other way. He loved the training and exerting his body, the feeling he used to get from playing.

He saw someone sitting in the bleachers. Her head hung low. As he approached, he could sense a vibration. Crying? Sara? He hadn't seen her since the election. He'd heard that Doll Baby had left to be sworn in as mayor and assumed she'd gone with him.

Garol walked up to her and stood on the bleachers near her. "You ok?"

"No," she sniffled

"Can I help?"

She shrugged.

"Did you go to the capital?"

"Yeah," she nodded.

"Is Doll Baby, sorry, I mean Garol Jr. back?"

She shook her head.

"Oh,"

"He met someone else."

"He did?"

"Yeah, everything was going great until…"

"Until?"

"We were shopping. I had to get a dress. He wanted to wait outside while I went in. At first I thought it was a little odd. Then I noticed there was a woman in the department store window. As I was explaining what I wanted to do, he kept his eyes on her. She stared directly at him. I was bothered, but I didn't think much of it. I took a little while to find the right dress. It was a special occasion. I came back an hour later, and he was gone. So was the woman in the window. The next day, I went back to the store. I described him to everyone, but no one saw him. Then I saw him and the woman from the window, dressed for a wedding. It was awful. They were gazing at each other outside the women's department. They'd gotten married. He never said anything about marrying me and he marries her after one night? What's wrong with me?"

"You're perfect. He's crazy."

"Thank you," Sara said and looked at Garol for the first time.

"I've got to go," Garol excused himself from Sara.

Garol left for the church, tossing his football in the air and running to catch it, like he travelled through the valley when he was twelve. By the time he reached the property, she'd already begun singing. He grabbed a door handle in each hand and paused as a tingle, like soft fingers, crawled down his spine. The sensation made him raise his shoulders, smile, and picture her singing. Quickly, the trickle spread throughout his body, like a shot of painkiller and Garol felt euphoric. Garol closed his eyes, relaxed into a butterfly feeling in his gut, and breathed deeply.

Slowly, Garol pulled the right door open just enough to slide through and quietly sat in the back row. He watched Samantha sing. She looked so beautiful standing alone at the pulpit. Garol wondered why he hadn't noticed her before. What was different? Was it that beautiful voice? Was it seeing the softer side of her? Was it the distant glow of her voice in his darkest hour? That thin thread of line reeled him back in. She exposed his empty heart so it could fill. She had baited the monster with sweet song and courageously illuminated his loneliness, and her gentle bravery lured the troll out from under the bridge to a new life. A new mindset.

Maybe Samantha's courage attracted him. Beth was always the courageous one. He could stand in the pocket and take a hit from a large, speedy linebacker, but Beth could handle anything life could dish out. Beth's calm confidence fueled his tank, kept his head from drifting into the mountains. He did have courage in front of Beth. He could trudge up any mountain when she was watching. But without her, he couldn't navigate through a day sober. He did not even have the strength to see he lacked it, nor the ability to discern between physical and mental strength, until he listened to Samantha sing. A soft, gentle, vulnerable strength filled his lungs.

He realized that it was perfect timing. It took courage to see courage, to admit he'd had none. Most importantly, it took courage to be vulnerable, and now he was. As she sang in the pulpit, he realized she was vulnerable too. She trusted him to reciprocate. And he would. That much he knew. He would.

Samantha ended with "Amazing Grace." When Garol approached, she was crying.

"What's wrong?" Garol asked.

"That song makes me both happy and sad," she said.

"Why?"

"To me, it's both scary and uplifting. It seems so scary that sometimes you have to tear people down to raise them up, push people away to bring them closer. That when someone is lost and won't listen to directions, you have to trust that their internal compass will eventually put them back on track...or at least get them so unbearably lost that they have to give in and accept help. I guess it scares me because it is never a guarantee that it will work out, but it's a miracle when it does."

What You See is What You Get

GAROL WANTED A REASON to go see his doctor friend in the woods, so he wrote him a letter.

> Dr. Mitchell,
> Your phone bill is overdue. Please pay immediately before we shut down your service.
> Melvin K. Buntwhistle,
> Hand-Phone Bill Manager

At the end of his route, Garol voyaged to the man who made marvelous miracles of the mind. Just as he positioned his hand to knock, he heard the doctor's raised voice inside.

"Are you insane? Did you concoct this whole story just to get my professional opinion? Because I can tell you, you are one hundred percent bonkers. Whacko. A complete nutjob."

Garol spied through the front window. Dr. Mitchell spotted him, raised his right index finger, and rolled his eyes. He moved his left hand away from his ear, winced, and put his mouth back to his hand and said, "Don't yell at me. I have to go. I have a patient and very little patience. Goodbye." He took his left hand away from his ear and folded his fingers to his palm.

He snapped open the front door, "Who the hell are you? What do you want?"

"I'm Garol."

"I don't know a Garol. What kind of name is that?"

"You know me as Sam. You gave me a book for assholes."

"Looks like it worked."

"I used to wear a body cast."

"Go see a doctor and quit whining, physical pain is nothing compared to mental and emotional pain. Nobody comes in here unless they're nuts. Oh, who the hell isn't?"

Garol couldn't think of anything to say, he'd never seen the doctor in this state.

"I'm sorry. You'll have to forgive me; I spent the last fifteen minutes on the phone with some know-it-all who claims he'll turn off my phone if I don't pay my bill. Complete garbage. I'm paid up. If I hear from that guy again I'm gonna go nuts. I won't be responsible. I won't."

"How did you find out that you owed them money?"

"The irony. They called me to threaten my phone privileges. The first thing I said was, 'Are you gonna charge me for this call?' They'd better not. Then I said, 'Well if you take my phone away, then who will you harass?' I need my phone. I run a business. When I saw you on the porch I was this close," the doctor held his index finger a quarter inch from his middle finger, "this close, to saying, 'I've got a complete nutbag on the front porch that would go zip, bing out of his gourd if it wasn't for me. If you take my phone, this spaghetti head's loose with no one to straighten him out.' Because that would happen. I almost said it, but I didn't. I kept my cool."

"Who called?"

"I don't remember, probably that new mayor. I'll tear that smug prima donna's limbs off and feed them to him."

"I don't think it's him," Garol said.

"Did you hear the little pretty boy mention anything about charging for phone service?"

"I've never heard him mention anything."

"You're probably right. He's a good man. I voted for him. I think everybody did. Not that there was a choice. That other guy? Remember him?" The doctor began laughing. "Well, God loves us all. Some more than others, obviously."

Garol joined in the laughter.

"You know that clown used to come and see me? Talk about nuts. The guy asked to sit in my bookcase. I didn't let him. I said, 'Sit in the parlor where people usually sit.' Nutbag. And boy did he whine. Whine, whine, whine," the doctor shook his head. "You seem alright. Come on in. I'm not saying you're not crazy, but harmless, I imagine. So what brings you here? Is that a letter?" The doctor motioned to the envelope in Garol's hand.

"This? No. Well yeah, but not for you. No, uh-uh. Nope, not even a letter," Garol said waving his hands in front of his chest.

"Ok. You ok? Looks like a letter."

"Nope, it's an envelope. Half of a letter. Just an envelope."

"Were you going to deliver it to me?"

"No, no, just practicing. Just keeping the delivery skills sharp." Garol raised his right hand to his mouth and spoke, "Ok, well this test run is over. Log time—four hours and seventeen minutes. Over. Roger. It's a take."

Dr. Mitchell squinted at Garol. "Good man. I have a recorder just like that one. It makes great party conversation. Lunatics say the best things. Do you mind if I look at that?"

Garol opened up his hand and the doctor swiped air away from his palm. He then put his hand up to his mouth and spoke, "Testing, testing." He pressed in middle of his palm with his free index finger, "Testing, testing," he said again. The doctor nodded and said, "Works pretty well." He held his hand out in front of him and offered the device back to Garol. "It's new."

Garol followed the doctor into his parlor and had a seat on the couch against the wall.

"You can ask if you'd like." The doctor sat with his hands cupped around his right knee.

Garol couldn't think of anything to ask.

"Where to begin?" the doctor said. "I know, I know it's huge. You want to know how I dragged it in and mounted it. You want to know when I caught it, what bait I used. I know how the mind works. All those questions at the base of the funnel, trying to cram them all through at once. Can't be done. So I'll just answer them."

Garol smiled and nodded.

The doctor pointed to the wall. "She's a monster. Have you ever seen a shark that big?"

Garol turned around and saw nothing on the wall but paint. He searched the entire wall to make sure he wasn't missing something. He wasn't. He turned back and said, "No, never."

"It's a great white, so of course it's going to be big, but holy canoly, look at that thing. Can I tell you something?"

"Sure," Garol said, then realized the question wasn't rhetorical.

"I knew when I woke up this morning today was the day. I just knew. I'd asked the man upstairs for a sign and I finally got it."

"How?" Garol asked.

"You aren't going to believe it, but it came in a letter. I got a letter in the mail and the front of the letter said right on it, 'vision.' Can you believe that?"

"Wow," Garol said smiling.

"Yeah, the letter explained that there were several sunken vessels carrying treasures from all over the world at the bottom of my pond. Can you believe that? I could spend the rest of my life and probably several other lives searching for all those treasures. Who would've known? Not me. I knew if I wanted those treasures I would have to get that silly little shark up and on the wall. No time to waste on shark expeditions now. I have treasures and sunken ships to explore. Sharks are kid's stuff. Not that she's not a beauty. So I went out this morning and pulled her in. She gave a heck of a fight, bless her heart, but I got her. Well, me and the man upstairs. He certainly does work in mysterious ways. Sends his answer in a letter. What a kook. I wonder if he works for the postal services? I hope he isn't having money problems."

"You finally pulled her in," Garol said turning around to the wall again. "Wow! Huge!"

When Garol turned back around the doctor was standing over him holding out his right arm. "Feel this."

"Wet," Garol said, feeling the damp sleeve.

"She pulled me under. Do you know, I never thought about giving up. Never even occurred to me. A real fight to the death. You could be looking at me on that wall."

"Glad I'm not," Garol said and smiled.

"Me too. Hey, sorry about the rough treatment on the porch. The phone call had me in a tizzy. I have this great morning and whamo! Super idiot calls. I had just started my exercise for the day. Hey! Do you want to exercise with me?"

Garol envisioned the two men jumping around aerobically, "I actually have an exercise routine I do in the evenings."

"Not a physical workout. Do you really think I have any energy left after dragging that thing in here? No, a mental exercise. Come on, you'd love it. It'd be great for you."

"What is it?"

"What I do is look at my life like it's a play. I picture everything that's happened. Well, not everything. Not that thing at the car wash years ago. I keep it PG, if you know what I mean. I picture the events with impact. Then I bring the curtain down. I think about where the audience is. I feel it from the audience's perspective. They're on the edge of their seats, rooting for me. Wishing for a happy ending. Then I decide the ending. The goal. The finish line."

"How's that possible? Things happen. You can't know everything that will happen."

"That's why it's an exercise and not real life. It's still an adventure, but this way I'm prepared. I control where I'm heading. Things go wrong all the time, so I simply bring the curtain down on them and start over. Sometimes I even change my goal, my ending, but always I picture the ending that I want. And I picture the crowd cheering me on. It gives me support."

"I don't understand why you would do that," Garol said.

"Ok, let's say you're a quarterback of a football team."

"Ok." Garol wondered if the doctor did know who he was.

"Wouldn't you play the game out in your mind before you got on the field? Wouldn't you run through different scenarios in your head so you were prepared when they arose?"

"Yeah," Garol said, remembering all the times he'd done so.

"Did things always happen the way you thought they would?"

"No."

"Did you feel more prepared because of your efforts?"

"I guess." He'd never thought about it. He just mentally prepared that way.

"There's no guessing. If you can see it, you can believe it. If you can believe it, you can do it. Why? Because you already did. It's that simple. It may not happen the first time, or the second or the fiftieth, but it will. It always does."

"Oh," Garol felt a little enlightened.

"So, what will be the ending of your play? What are you working on?"

"I'm not working on anything," Garol said uncomfortably.

"You have to work on something. What do you want? What makes you happy?"

"I don't know," Garol shrugged shyly.

"Do you want love? Friendship? Peace of mind? Some physical achievement? You can combine them all in one play or have several plays running."

"What's your play?" Garol asked, avoiding the question.

"Well I just finished mine when I mounted that monster. Now I search for buried treasure. I can feel the crowd pulling for me as I sink to the depths of my pond. I can see the sunken vessels, rare coins, and artifacts. The crowd going frantic. I can't wait to get started."

"I'm sure you'll make it happen," Garol said, and he was.

"I've got an idea for your play. What about a story about a transvestite cowboy who steals his neighbor's laundry?"

"That's not what I had in mind."

"Probably good. That one's been done before and I hate remakes. I love the scene where he tries to convince the horse to trade in his horse shoes for pumps and ride away with him because he realizes he'll never fit in among those townspeople. The horse doesn't budge. You're watching it and you're thinking, there's no way the horse will put on those hot pink pumps. They clash with its mane. Then the final scene where he goes into the barn and the horse is wearing them on all fours. You just know they're going to ride off together. In style, too. You could've counted the dry eyes in the theater on one hand."

Garol smiled. "Well, I'll let you get to your exercise," he said and stood up.

"Probably best. Stop by anytime you want to run through a play with me. No need to come as a patient. I only let crazy people do that."

On the porch, Garol put out his hand to shake the doctor's. The doctor engulfed Garol's hand with his large palm and squeezed, which sent a shock wave down Garol's spine. "Good to see you again," the doctor said.

"I'll be seeing you," Garol said and walked into the woods.

GAROL LEANED ON HIS shovel, staring into the deep, dark hole he'd dug. Grave-digging was tiring.

Garol watched the priest walk across the lawn in the back of the steeple carrying a cross.

"You look beat, my son," the priest said.

"I am," Garol wiped sweat from his brow. He stood the shovel straight up in the earth. He reached down and pulled out the cast pieces and began tossing them in the grave.

"When you're ready, I'll offer my blessing," the priest said.

"Do you mind if I say a few words first?"

"Take all the time you need."

Garol stared at the cast at the bottom of the ditch. "Where to begin? I feel like I'm burying the worst part of me. The handicapped part that couldn't move. But also the band aid that allowed me to heal."

The father smiled.

"Beth, I'm sorry," Garol felt his eyes welling up. "I'm ashamed. I did everything I could to ignore your death. I couldn't let myself believe it happened. I locked up all those feelings, and in doing so, disregarded your life and all

305

you meant to me. All that you gave me. But you did die, and I'm here, and it's time to acknowledge that. You were the best part of me, and a minute with you is worth a lifetime." He covered his eyes and paused for a long while.

After the father blessed the grave, Garol asked Toby to help him carry a sheet of plywood to the Last Shot Saloon. Together, they nailed the plywood sheet over the door. Garol wrote on the plywood, "CLOSED INDEFINITILY."

Toby stood back and watched Garol write. "What are you doing?"

"Keeping the people safe. I am Sheriff Garol."

"I think you spelled indefinitely wrong," Toby said.

"No, there's only one F," Garol said studying the word.

That evening, Garol sat across from Whirby at the chess table. He looked at the board and saw two pieces pulled all the way to the front middle of the board: the king and queen. The rest were mixed together in rows and split equally by an aisle that ran through center of the board.

"What's going on? Looks like a wedding," Garol said.

"The final move," Whirby said and smiled. "The perfect ending. I love it when a game turns out this way. My work here is done."

"Doesn't look like a chess game," Garol said.

"What does it look like?"

"A wedding."

Jimmy walked up and handed Garol a copy of the *Gossip.*

GAS

Anyone with a nose for romance knows what I'm talking about. You've heard it all over town: Garol and Samantha. Only a fool would miss the connection these two seem to share. A couple of fools is what this beautiful combination is. Fools in love. We know, we've heard, it's in the air. So, cut it out, and take it to the next level. We all know you will. When you see these two, give them your support with a cheer, a honk, or just a little toot. Unlike Bennifer and Brangelina, these two will last forever. There's nothing that stinks about that.

Epilogue
Marriages are Made in Heaven

"GOOD THROW?" Samantha cheered and clapped.

"It was a great throw." Garol rustled Mike's hair and jogged over and picked the small cushioned football up and walked it over to Mike's twin, Sam, standing a few feet across from Mike.

"Amazing throw," Samantha cheered and clapped.

Again Garol retrieved the ball.

Garol lofted the ball towards Mike. The soft football dropped squarely in Mike's arms, bounced against his chest and landed for a two arm basket catch. "Did you see that?" Garol said, an exuberant father.

Samantha yelled from the picnic table, "Way to go."

Mike stumbled and fell to the ground, the football remained lodged in his arms.

"Garol! What did I tell you? Samantha said.

"He held on. Diving catch," Garol said.

"That's enough football for today. Gather the twins and bring them to the table."

Garol brought Mike to his feet. "Great catch," he said and grabbed both boys hands and walked them to the table.

"Thanks honey," Samantha winked at Garol. She was putting baby Jillian in her high chair.

Samantha sat and looked at the three-year-old twins. She looked at Garol. "Little men they are," she smiled. "They look so much like you," she said as a tear rolled down her cheek.

"They look like both of us," Garol said.

"Oh stop. I like it. I have three versions now. Three good men," she said, "and a wonderful little baby," Samantha leaned over and kissed Jillian on the forehead.

"Jill will be the spitting image of her mother. Look at those beautiful blues. I like that."

As if on cue Jillian released a little spittle.

"See, spitting image," Garol joked.

Samantha smiled and pointed a finger to teasingly say, 'watch yourself'.

Garol put the picnic basket on the table. He took out two turkey sandwiches on whole wheat with mustard for the boys.

Samantha held a spoonful of baby food up to Jillian's lips, said, "Yum, yum."

Garol watched the two girls. "She's really hungry today."

"I love holidays. I think this one is my favorite," Samantha said as she wiped a smidge of sauce from Jillian's cheek.

Garol nodded.

"Tell the boys about the significance of the holiday."

"Well…" Garol paused for thought. He snuck a piece of Sam's sandwich. "Years ago, an evil ogre roamed the streets in a full body cast and kept the town under his mighty tyranny."

"He could walk?" Samantha asked.

"He could. His cast was cut around all the joints."

"He wasn't physically handicapped?" Samantha asked.

"Not physically handicapped, but mentally," Garol answered.

"So why was he in a body cast and not a brain cast?" Samantha asked and looked at the boys, who were listening attentively.

"That's a good question," Garol said. "If your mind is handicapped, it doesn't matter what your body can do, because your mind controls everything. Your body is just an instrument of your mind. He falsely blamed everyone for things that had gone wrong. He added to the problems by ignoring them and then lashed out at those that tried to help him, and eventually isolated himself from all that life had to offer."

"Is that why he was angry?"

"He was angry for many reasons, but mostly because he'd stuck himself in a horrible position. He failed to acknowledge that only he could change his situation."

"Did he like kids?" Mike asked.

"No. He was a bad dude."

"Is he still here?"Sam asked.

"No. He's never coming back," Garol said and looked at Samantha.

"How do you know, Dad?" Sam asked

"Sheriff Garol chased him out of town," Garol pointed both his thumbs at himself.

Garol looked over Sam's head. He had a sudden sense of déjà vu. His seat at the picnic table overlooked town. Every bit confidently posed with the self-assurance of beauty. Trees covered the town, rolling like small mountains, only exposing elements that accentuated their style and charm: red cobblestone roads, multi-colored Painted Lady Victorian homes, ornate street lamps, and colorful signs on store fronts along Main Street. As a whole, the town represented a complete color deck for autumn with its reds, greens, browns and yellows. A hundred years old at least, the town proposed a useful sort of senility which allowed it to forget what it did not want to remember. It never occurred to the paint to peel, or the absent-minded wood to rot. The multi-hued, daydreaming leaves disregarded the changing seasons. The flourishing greenery seemed unconcerned that it lay surrounded by miles of lifeless, barren sand. Too, it was a place where people could forget.

Garol took it all in and breathed deeply. He trusted and accepted that this was the only place he'd ever want to be.

Special Thanks.

Writing this book began as a dream, turned into a chore, and ended as a spiritual journey that continues to unfold. I thank God for delivering the strength, the circumstances and the right people to help me along. I can't say thanks enough to Terri Murphy for seeing it in her heart to always lend an ear and an idea. I called her with concern or excitement too many times to count when I needed a lift in spirit, a good mind to work things through, or just and audience. I discovered during the writing of this book that it is a very solitary process attached to a strong desire to be heard and the constant fear it will never happen. Terri listened to every write and rewrite, a few times pulling her car over on the side of the road to do so and always graced me with the impression I was doing her a favor. There is no scale for the kind of audience, enthusiasm and encouragement she gave me, other than in the question to myself, "Would I have finished the book without my muse?" And the only balancing answer, "I don't think so."

To Todd Clark for taking the time to read the book in the early stages and tell me, "I've really got something here, keep going." A message I never forgot and never will.

Donna Georgen for her continuing help, enthusiasm and friendship

To Maureen Paraventi , my writing shadow, and for the special timing in which we met.

To Tina Paraventi for her help in taking the manuscript to the next level by sacrificing her time to put it together neatly. And her praise.

To Bob and Serena Stackhouse for listening and support.

To Emily Elliott for her help, support and encouragement.

To Maria Sylvester for her encouragement and coaching.

To Rebecca Hughes for her thoughts, structure and belief.

To Dad for telling me about the coal mining towns of Pennsylvania.

To Jimmy Selleck for the conversation that inspired the thought to start the story.

To Dan Clark for his enthusiasm.

And to all those that took the time out of their days to listen to a chapter, or read the novel and give important feedback: Dianne Moeller, Shannon Trantham, Robert Murphy, Greg Bohl, Mike Shockley, David Greene, Tammy Sindlinger, Kim Jackson, Laura Baker and Christa Weber.